DUPUYTREN'S CONTRACTURE

DUPUYTREN'S CONTRACTURE

A Tale of Distortion and Deception

Colin Ball

Book Guild Publishing

Sussex, England

First published in Great Britain in 2010 by
The Book Guild Ltd
Pavilion View
19 New Road
Brighton, BN1 1UF

Typesetting in Baskerville by
SetSystems Ltd, Saffron Walden, Essex

Printed in Great Britain by
CPI Antony Rowe

A catalogue record for this book is available from
the British Library

ISBN 978 1 84624 488 9

Dupuytren's [dew-pwee-trahns] Contracture:

'A hand disorder in which fingers bend towards the palm and cannot be straightened . . . caused by a thickening of normal fibrous tissue bands which pull the fingers into the palm. The tissues under the skin on the palm of the hand thicken and shorten so that the tendons connected to the fingers cannot move freely. The affected fingers start to bend more and more . . . the ring and little fingers are those most commonly involved initially but any or all fingers can be affected. The fibrous tissue that develops is much like scar tissue: it binds the skin to the coverings of the finger tendons and then shrinks and contracts to produce the deformity.

'The cause is unknown . . . uncertain if it is work related . . . evidence is sparse. Viking ancestry may be a factor but this is unproven. More common in males and in those over 60 years of age but can affect younger people, among whom it tends to develop more rapidly. Tends to run in families . . .

'If untreated the fingers will gradually be pulled into the palm, leading to difficulty using the entire hand . . . in this condition, the hand appears to be both begging and grasping simultaneously.

'Treatment should be sought before severe contracture occurs and particularly if the deformity increases rapidly.'

Acknowledgements

I want to acknowledge and offer my thanks to the people who contributed a great deal of advice and support to me during the course of my writing *Dupuytren's Contracture*.

First and foremost, Chistopher Wallace-Crabbe of Melbourne University, who greatly encouraged me with his positive and critical comments on the very earliest draft: 'Run with it,' he said. And I did so. A later draft was most helpfully critiqued by Robin Lloyd-Jones.

Then, a number of people read the manuscript at various different stages and made many helpful comments and suggestions: Bruce McNaught; Carole Sheppeard; Julian McCarthy and Barbara Snook.

For their help on various technical matters I am indebted to Nick Maurice (medical); to Rajesh Tandon (India); to my son Tom (legal) and to my daughter Sandie (Italian language).

I am also deepy grateful to Andrew Felton and Christine Quilter for their friendship and support during the final stages of preparation of this work and the beginnings of the next.

Finally, nothing would have been possible without the love, support and encouragement of my wife, Susan.

Colin Ball
April 2010

1

The Explosion

As soon as the session got under way she had a strong sense that something was about to happen.

Watching one of the men on the stage carefully from up high, she saw the signs of what she alone in the audience knew to be anger rather than mere nervousness. She knew this because he was her husband. She knew, or at least at that time she thought she knew, everything about him and, especially, everything about his mannerisms and what they meant.

Now, he shifted his chair constantly behind the table at which he sat. He picked up his pen regularly, with what he called his 'good' hand and then put it down, unused. Then a look at his watch. He alternated between sitting forward, elbows on the table, good hand under his chin, fingers rubbing his face, and then, via the transition of a movement so sudden and jerky that it was as if he had been knocked unconscious by some invisible fist, slumping backward, his arms hanging loosely down. Both hands then went to his jacket pockets, only to come out instantly to rest momentarily across his lap. Then just as suddenly he sat upright, pulled his chair forward and once again picked up the pen.

Watching, she found that her own hands were shaking so violently that she had to clasp them together, fingers tightly interlocked. She gazed down at the people in the rows in front of her, but saw no sign that anyone else might be sharing her anxiety. All she could see was the normal body-language of conference-goers at an afternoon session: heads here and there nodding into sleep; signs of 'armed resistance' (which was his way of describing people who crossed their arms when listening) among some; others nodding vigorously; a few scribbling notes.

At the podium, the Minister droned on.

She had seen the first sign of agitation in her husband the moment the Minister had begun his speech.

'Ladies and gentleman, let me first of all apologise for being here . . .'

There was a scattered ripple of polite laughter.

'. . . as of course I am no adequate substitute for the Prime Minister himself . . .'

At this, there was one loud guffaw. It came from her husband, who at the same time made one of his sudden backward jerks in his chair. His reddening face clearly visible, the Minister paused to glare across the stage at the man for a second.

'. . . but as you will all be aware and will all understand, I am sure, today's deepening crisis in the Balkans needs his complete and urgent attention'.

As the Minister said this, the noise of his strumming fingers was clearly audible through the podium microphones. He paused and looked across at the man at the table again, this time for several seconds.

A profound silence ensued, as the two men stared fixedly at each other across the stage, while the thousand or so people in the audience all held their breath.

She felt her heart pounding.

'Let me correct that,' the Minister went on, still looking at the man, 'perhaps I should say as *most* of us would understand.'

There was applause, louder and more prolonged this

time. But she gasped as her husband, on whom the Minister's gaze was still fixed, suddenly picked up the briefcase he had beside him, as if he was going to leave. But instead, he opened it, pulled out a large envelope and laid it carefully on the table before him.

The Minister watched this, as did the thousand others present, including a dark-suited young man who had been standing in the aisle at the front of the hall near to the podium. He held up the sleeve of his jacket to his mouth and spoke into it. From up high she saw it all clearly.

The Minister shook his head at the young man and continued with his speech.

When he finished, to applause she thought was somewhat restrained, the Minister left the platform immediately and quickly walked up the aisle, followed by the young man and several others whom she took to be civil servants. As this happened, the chairman of the session, who, so the agenda had informed her earlier, was head of one of the country's largest overseas aid charities, and yet seemed to her both far too young and far too establishment-looking to be so, spoke:

'Ladies and gentlemen, colleagues, the Minister informed me earlier that he would have to leave right away due to the, er, international political situation.'

There was a prolonged buzz around the auditorium, and the rows at the front that had been occupied by journalists emptied quickly. TV cameras were rapidly dismantled. Many others were leaving, too.

Slowly, the commotion subsided. Looking around, she saw that the auditorium was now half-empty. She felt a knot in her stomach as she knew it was her husband that would be the next speaker. For her, these were always anxious moments, all the more so this time as she had never seen him act as he had done during the Minister's speech. Now, however, she saw that he seemed calm. She saw him say something to the chairman, who nodded, and then both of them stood up and walked slowly together to the podium. As they did so, the hall quietened further.

'Ladies and gentlemen,' the chairman said, rather loudly, 'ladies and gentlemen, colleagues, if we could resume now . . . thank you . . . thank you very much . . . Now, this is our last speaker of the day, and since we're running a little late, in fact very late, he has in his usual modest way, well-known to many of us, suggested that I keep my introduction to the minimum. So all I can say is, Christian, over to you.'

Only now did she notice that he was holding the envelope that he had produced from his case earlier. He laid it on the podium shelf, between the two microphones, and pointed to it with his left hand, for what seemed a long time. Because of his crooked fingers, with the two smaller ones curled up, his pointed hand looked like a gun.

Then he spoke. Even before he opened his mouth, she knew from his hands, which, most unusually for him, trembled, that he was still pent up and angry, very angry. She knew an explosion was imminent.

'I wish I could say that I've never heard so much *fucking* crap . . .'

The language stunned her. She felt it hit the audience like a shock wave, sharp intakes of breath marking its impact.

'. . . but I've heard it before and so have all of you. We've been hearing it now ever since this *fucking* government was elected . . .'

Another shock wave raced across the auditorium.

'. . . you know what's in this envelope . . . ?', he went on, again pointing his hand at it like a gun.

'. . . it's all the election manifesto promises of this government and every speech made since its election by a Minister of this government on the subject we're all concerned with today, international aid and development. It's every press release their *fucking* spin doctors have put out. So it's every promise, pledge, solemn bloody undertaking, call them what you like, that they have put out . . .'

He stopped and walked across the stage to where he had sat, picked up a glass of water and drank, holding it with both hands, trembling so violently now that the water splashed onto his face and down his tie. He looked at the young chairman, who held out both hands to him and gently lowered them in a calming motion.

'Yes, I should calm down,' he said as he resumed at the podium, 'but I'm angry, and, and . . .'

He drew in a deep breath.

'. . . and I hope that at least some of you are too.'

There was a scattering of applause. She looked around and saw that those clapping, some very vigorously, were, to her surprise, the older ones. The younger ones, the 'aid groupies' as Christian often called them, seemed mostly silent.

'And what has all the rhetoric amounted to? Regularly we have been told, we have been promised, that soon, or sometime, *when economic circumstances permit*, when Northern Ireland and the Balkans and the Middle East are sorted, when pigs have been seen not only to fly over Whitehall but fly in massed formation for several days in succession, then we'll be the leading nation in the world as far as aid to the third world is concerned. Bugger the benchmark of oh point seven per cent of GDP, we'll do far better than that! That's what we were promised. And where are we? As the speech we've just heard has told us, we're still in fairy land. Promises, promises. The same mixture of ninety nine per cent hyperbole and one per cent bullshit . . . every time . . . that's where we are. We're less than a year from the start of a new millennium but all we get is the same old crap . . .'

He hesitated, breathing out noisily into the microphones for several seconds.

'That's all I have to say.'

He walked back across the stage to a stunned silence, tearing open the envelope and then, with a flourish, scattering the papers in it high into the air.

Outside, she shivered at the bottom of the steps in the cold January air. They had arranged to meet there, but everyone had long since gone and there was still no sign of him. Big Ben started to chime loudly above the noise of the early evening traffic in Parliament Square.

Above it, she heard his voice and turned to it. He was at the main doors, beckoning her back.

He embraced her in a huge bear hug as she reached him.

'Darling, I'm so sorry. Met a few old friends.'

'No, that's fine,' she said, her head nestling into the warmth of his neck, 'I thought you probably had.'

He released her and then kissed her forehead gently.

'Let's go in. I've agreed to do a short interview for Doordarshan, Indian television. Then we'll go and have a drink.'

At the far end of the foyer a camera was being set up. A young Indian girl sat in the small armchair that had been arranged in front of it, holding a clipboard. She stood up when she saw them coming.

'Darling, this is Roopa from Doordarshan and Roopa, this is my wife Claire.'

The girl smiled brightly as they shook hands. Even though it was warm inside she wore a thick padded overcoat.

'Christian and I have met several times in Delhi,' she said, 'sorry for inconvenience, we will not keep him long.'

She watched as Christian sat in the chair while the cameraman clipped a small button microphone to the lapel of his jacket and then took his place behind the camera.

'Sound check please.'

'Christian, say something please,' the girl said from where she was squatting under the camera.

'Ah, well, yes, I'm very pleased to announce that I'm taking my wife out to dinner at our favourite place this evening, which is . . .'

'That's fine,' said the cameraman.

Standing to one side behind the camera, Claire could see that her husband was now utterly relaxed and that another version of him had replaced the one she had seen earlier. On the train into Victoria station in the morning he had been tense, as she knew he always was before a speaking engagement, but this time more so than usual, for reasons she thought she now understood. They had hardly spoken then, nor in the short taxi ride to Parliament Square, nor in the brief periods they had seen each other during the breaks between sessions during the day. That was the way he was on days like this, when he was immersed in his own world. She knew that the best way to love him at such times was to leave him be, knowing that the other person he was would come back, when he was ready to, as he seemed to be now. She mused on this while the interview proceeded, not taking in what he was saying until the very end.

'So Christian, what is essence of your view?' the girl was asking him.

'It's simply, and very brutally, this,' he said. 'We must do something, and do something soon, to lessen the enormous disparities that exist between rich and poor, between haves and have-nots. No, I'm not just talking about the gulf between rich countries – which we glorify with the name "developed" – and poorer countries. The poor are every-where. They are but a few steps from here in the heart of

London, huddled in doorways, struggling to survive. Yet our great "developed" government tells them that they must stand on their own two feet, just as it tells poorer countries to do the same. To help them do this it offers tokenistic hand-outs, each accompanied by onerous, often ludicrous, patronising conditions. So it tells beggars not to beg in the streets. So it tells governments of less-developed countries not to borrow money. None of that will do. There need to be big changes, huge changes, so that the world is, how can I put it, more equal, more even, more fair, more humane . . .'

'More socialist?' the girl interrupted.

'Sure, call it that if you like – not everything Karl Marx said was wrong, you know,' he said, chuckling a little.

'And what if we don't make these changes?'

His face turned serious now and he gazed into the camera, pausing for effect and pursing his lips.

'Then I am sure, I am one hundred per cent sure, that we will witness, within the next few years, conflict and terrorism on a vast scale, on a global scale, as desperation caused by poverty and inequality turns to anger and anger to violence, and violence to death. This will happen not in faraway remote places we barely know, but on our own doorsteps. Mark my words, it will.'

Feeling movement nearby as she listened, she turned and found one of the uniformed doormen standing beside her.

He was nodding.

The Two Chairmen was busy with the quick-one-before-the-train-home crowd, but they found a table at the back.

He got the drinks and then they held hands across the table.

'Can I ask you something?' she said.

'I knew you would.'

'Did you plan it?'

'Plan what? Taking you out to dinner you mean?'

'Oh, come on darling, yes, it would have been nice to know, but you know perfectly well what I mean.'

He took a gulp of his beer.

'You mean, what happened, back there?' He cocked his head back towards the conference centre.

'You know perfectly well that's exactly what I mean.'

'To be honest, no, I didn't . . . I . . .'

He stopped, took another gulp then smiled across the table at her.

'I . . . I'm sorry . . . I . . . I just lost my temper.'

'Don't be, don't be sorry. It was a bit crude, but it was brave. I'm proud of you. I love you. I must say it was a bit of a shock, you using language like that, I mean. Will it get you into trouble?'

'Probably, but I don't care. You see, I've been thinking that . . .'

There was huge momentary roar from among the crowd at the bar and his voice was lost in it.

'Sorry, I missed that,' she said, 'you've been thinking what?'

'That . . .'

Another roar erupted. Irritated now, he turned to see what was going on.

'Little creeps,' he said, 'barely literate, more money than sense, the lot of them. How can any country that brings up people like that call itself developed?'

'Calm down, ignore them. I want to spend the evening with the calm Christian, not the angry one. You know, you do seem to have become more, how can I put it . . . more angry lately, less tolerant . . . don't you think?'

He pursed his lips and looked into his beer.

'I guess you're right. I'm sorry, but let me tell you what I was going to say when we get to Il Vicolo will you? It's too

9

noisy here. Let's just try and enjoy our drink and take in a bit of the fine culture of these lager-louts, shall we?'

She opened her mouth to speak but as she did so one of the young men at the bar walked over, bent down and mumbled something to Christian that she could not hear.

Christian stood up, banging his still half-full glass on the table as he did so.

'I've no idea what you're talking about,' he said, loudly, and then, grabbing her hand, 'let's get out of here.'

Outside, she asked, 'What was that about?'

'Seemed to think I was someone he knew.'

'And are you?'

'Of course not.'

As usual, Flavio, dressed in his best black and white, complete with bow-tie, and hair slicked down with gel, made an enormous fuss of them from the moment they walked through the door of Il Vicolo, helping them off with their coats, and then showing them to their favourite table in the corner by the window, where they could sit close together while both being able to view the evening's action, both inside and outside. And, they were pleased to see, there was only one other table occupied, by another, younger, couple, far away in the back corner. Flavio dimmed the lights as he knew they preferred it that way, and then came over to the table, not to take the order, as he had already told his daughter to bring a bottle of prosecco and some bruschetta, but to talk. They had not been to Il Vicolo since last summer's trip to Italy, so they knew that Flavio would want a full account.

She let Christian do the talking as the effort of tuning in to Flavio's fast-spoken Italian would, she knew, be beyond her.

She watched, barely attempting to listen, as another

Christian quickly emerged. This one was the Italian version: animated, even flamboyant gestures with hands and arms, utterly unconcerned with errors of grammar, pronunciation or tense, talking at great length in response to Flavio's short questions, always punctuating his remarks with his favourite words – 'allora' 'quindi' 'però' 'adesso' 'comunque'. This Christian seemed at least ten years younger than all the various other versions she knew. When he stopped to think for a moment, to find the word he was looking for, he would run a hand – usually the good one – through his thick, long, still fair, hair, something he only ever did when speaking Italian. And the hunched tenseness in his neck and broad shoulders melted away as he spoke. She knew that if he stood up now, he would as a result seem even taller than normal, especially if tiny Flavio had stood next to him. She loved this version of her husband most of all.

'Why are you looking at me like that?' Christian asked when Flavio left them.

'I'm thinking how much I love you, especially this you.'

'What do you mean, this me?'

She put her hand in his lap.

'For what is it, more than ten years now, I've lived with at least five different men, that's what I mean. And the one I like best is the one who's taking me out to dinner this evening. Next to that I like the confident one that I saw being interviewed this evening. And I even rather like the angry one, though I must say he scares me a bit, especially lately.'

'And are there any you don't like?' he said, smiling.

'Well, there's the morose, depressed one ... and he's also become a bit more apparent lately.'

'Let's not talk about *him*, not now.'

'No, I wasn't going to.'

'And are there any others?'

She thought for a while, weighing the risk of snapping

the good mood he was now clearly in with even a single injudicious word, for she knew full well that that – just a single word – could often be enough to change him from one persona to another.

'Yes, there is another,' she said, squeezing his thigh. 'It's one that I neither like or dislike . . . on the whole I rather like him, but sometimes . . . sometimes I wonder about him.'

'Wonder?'

'Yes. Now let me tell you about him. This one is full of surprises. I definitely like this part of him. He's the one who pulls rabbits out of hats, the one who brings me flowers when there's no reason to, the one who booked a band to play outside my window one anniversary, the one who showers my daughter with love . . .'

'He sounds all right to me,' he said, laughing now.

'Mmmmm, yes, all of that's alright, but he's good at surprises because he's also good at keeping secrets. So good that I sometimes think I hardly know him.'

'Oh dear.'

'It's all right. I still love him. But sometimes . . . sometimes I wish . . . sometimes I wish he'd tell me things, that's all.'

'What kinds of things?'

He was still smiling as he said this, which gave her confidence.

'Mostly about himself. He spends hours, sometimes whole days, thinking. Yet when I ask what he's thinking about or what he feels he doesn't tell me. He just says "Oh, nothing much" . . . why?'

Now he pursed his lips again. This was a danger sign, she knew, but she went on.

'Darling, for a start, there's a whole part of your life you've never told me about. Do you realise that? Is that what you think about?'

'You mean . . . ?'

'I mean that you've told me about school, you told me being married to Jane, you told me you met her at university. You haven't told me much about your relationship with her, but I don't, to be honest, want to know about that. But there's a whole lot missing, about what you did, after university. All I know is about what you do now, what you've done since I met you. But what did you do then? And . . .'

'And what?'

'And . . . well, I just learnt, over there at the conference, more about the way . . . the way you feel about things, that you have never told me about . . . about your anger, about what is making you angry . . .'

She was relieved to see he seemed relaxed and also glad that at that moment Flavio appeared to take the order.

Afterwards, they were silent for some minutes, and then he put a hand on the one she still had on his lap.

'To answer the first part of your question, I had a bad patch,' he said, 'a patch that to be perfectly honest I prefer to forget about. A lot of bad things happened, some of them things I'm not proud of, and some of which plain hurt me. I think I let too much of myself hang out, you see, and as a result I got burned. It's not that I'm keeping this from you; it's more that I prefer to keep it even from myself. Can you understand? Perhaps one day I can tell you. But not now, not now, perhaps not ever. But I will tell you one thing'

'What's that?'

'Simply that I love you.'

'I know that.'

Although he had not responded to the second part of her question, she made a conscious decision to leave it there, lest the small advance she felt she had made turn into a retreat of major proportions. But to her surprise, he looked at his crooked fingers and continued.

13

'As for the way I am at present, you're right, I . . . I . . . I am getting more and more fed up . . . I know this sounds stupid, but I find it harder and harder to bear the state this stupid country, this stupid world is in. It's mean and selfish, hard, nasty, brutish, dog eat dog, intolerant, ignorant, greedy, grasping . . . it reduces people, it corrupts people . . .'

He paused and looked again at his bent fingers.

'. . . it corrupts all of us.'

Again he looked at his fingers.

'I can get these put right, but I can't . . . oh, enough of this . . .'

His voice tailed off.

'I understand,' she said, lightly. 'Let's leave it there . . . Now, you told me earlier on that you had a little secret to reveal?'

He looked puzzled.

'Did I?'

'Yes, when we were in the pub. You said there was something you wanted to tell me, so now's your chance. I'm all ears.'

'Oh, that, yes, well, er, hmmmmm . . .'

They both laughed and she felt a sense of relief that all was well. She leaned forward, cupped her hands under her chin and stared at him.

'Come on then, out with it!'

They both giggled.

'What, here? In front of all these people?' he spluttered, loudly, causing Flavio and the other couple momentary alarm.

They calmed themselves with sips of prosecco. Claire started hiccupping.

'Oh no,' he groaned, still smiling.

'Huc.'

Mouth firmly shut, she gestured at him to continue.

14

'Well, I haven't really finally decided, because I wanted to talk to you about it first . . .'

'Huc.'

'But I'm seriously thinking of calling it quits with the firm when the current contract ends, which'll be this coming September . . . but . . .'

'HUC!'

'. . . but maybe what I did today will hasten that . . . I don't know . . . I don't think so, because snotty little Palmer is too chicken, even though the Minister's probably already been on to him, and they, the firm, they need me more than I need them just now. But what do you think, leaving aside today?'

She nodded vigorously. 'Huc.'

'You see, sixty is not far off. I fixed my pension fund payment date for then, remember, so we'd have some income, not that we'll need much . . .'

He left it there and looked carefully at her. Now it was his turn to feel relieved because all he saw in her face was contentment. Flavio appeared and served the pasta. Christian twiddled his fork in the bright yellow fettucine, picking at it, feeling suddenly not hungry.

'I think I'm all right now,' she said, after a few minutes, 'aren't you hungry?'

'Not really, to be honest.'

'You've had a big day,' she said, 'and some big things have happened. Matter of fact, I'm not very hungry myself either . . . anyway, I think what you've said is wonderful. Does it mean we can go to Italy more?'

'Yes, it certainly does, and . . .'

He stopped.

'And what?'

'Oh, nothing.'

'Nothing my foot, what is it?'

He kept fiddling with his pasta, smiling.

15

'You were talking about my passion for surprises just now, weren't you?'

'Yes?'

'Well, you remember last year when we were in Italy on your birthday?'

She remembered the day well.

'That was fun,' she said.

'This year's birthday surprise will be even better, promise!'

While intrigued, she decided to let that particular revelation lie there and instead changed tack.

'Why do you want to pack it in now? Because of what you just said?'

He twiddled for a long time now, staring down at the plate as he did so.

'Yes. I'm simply sick and tired of the hypocrisy of it all. The aid business is just as full of the greedy and grasping as any other. Parasitical consultants like me making livings, sometimes fortunes, off the backs of the poor. And I'm one of them. I don't want to be part of it any more'

'So that's what brought today's little outburst?'

'Yes and no. Ever since my last trip to India, it's been not exactly nagging at me, but sort of creeping into my thoughts more and more. I'm not enjoying what I'm doing as much as I used to, as the reality is that I'm paid to spy on them. It's always been the reality. I'm not their adviser. I'm a spy, to make sure they behave. They're fine people, great organisations, they do good things. They don't need me on their backs. And what I said to the TV people just now is, was, genuine – I really do think bad things are going to happen. So when that fat little creep of a Minister said what he said, it was, what, the straw that broke my back. I hadn't made up my mind before, but when he came out with all the crap again it sort of forced things. Do you understand?'

16

'Yes, I do. Don't think any more about it, darling. We, and I mean we, have come to a decision.'

She picked up her glass and offered it to his.

'Here's to us,' she said as they clinked.

Startled, she sat upright suddenly on the train home. She had been stroking his hands gently, especially under the two bent fingers.

'What's up?' he asked.

'It's tomorrow, isn't it, I've just remembered.'

'My appointment, you mean?'

'Yes.'

'Ha! Usually it's me that does the forgetting and you the remembering. No, I hadn't forgotten.'

She looked at the fingers carefully now.

'I'm glad you're getting them done. They really are a mess now. What did you say it was called?'

'Dupuytren's Contracture,' he said, yawning.

2

The Reunion

***Fasciectomy** [Fash-ee-eck-tom-ee]:*

'The contracture is corrected by removal of the abnormal fascia and relaxation of the overlaying skin. A variety of different skin incisions is involved, usually in a zig-zag manner down the affected fingers and into the palm. The thickened contracted tissue is removed, releasing the joint. The operation is performed under a general anaesthetic. The incisions in the fingers are always stitched. Those in the palm are also usually closed but some surgeons may leave these wounds open to heal (open palm technique).'

I have a minor medical condition. Two of the fingers of my left hand are curled up. There are lots of consequences. One is that I can only get that hand into very loose pockets, and if I do manage to get hold of the coins there, then they fall out of my hand. I am waiting here to see a doctor about it. I don't mind waiting. In fact I never mind waiting. I spend a lot of time doing it – not often in hospital waiting rooms, mind you, but more often in airports, where like every traveller, I spend time waiting, in the check-in line, in the security check line, in the lounge, at the gate, each time waiting for the next wait. And then the final wait, on the aircraft itself, up there in the sky, passing time, waiting for it to get to wherever I'm going.

I don't mind all the waiting because it gives me time to

think, and I like to think. I'm perfectly happy thinking. Sometimes it's like talking to myself, as I am now, and sometimes it's as if I'm talking to other people. In this way, even though I'm not much of a talker in real life I actually talk to myself about a lot of things, sometimes because I choose to, and sometimes because they just pop into my head.

What I'm thinking now, for example, is that collections of people waiting don't talk much. I'll bet that while I'm here – and I was here early because I somehow had it in my mind that it was a ten-thirty appointment, when it's actually at eleven – that nobody will talk.

I'm not being critical. My own natural inclination is to keep myself to myself as much as possible. That's my nature. But if the person next to me on the aeroplane is one of those types that cannot but engage in a social and friendly manner with those around them while sitting in an elongated aluminium can seven miles up in the sky for hours on end, then I'm not averse to conversation. In such a situation, where one is in very close proximity to another person, or possibly two (if you've checked in late and only middle seats are left), then conversation can at worst simply pass the time a little more quickly, and at best be informative, even enjoyable.

But there is a 'nightmare scenario' in which the time passes interminably slowly. This happens when one's unchosen conversation partner drones on at great length to expound views which are diametrically opposed to one's own.

My rule is never to ask 'big' questions to begin with. I have found for example that asking the 'what do you do (if you don't mind my asking)' question is best avoided as a conversation starter. Definitely. It's a 'big' question, to be gone into only after the small-talk preliminaries to it – where have you been? what did you think of it? and so on – have been dealt with. These preliminaries can indicate the safety or danger inherent in asking 'big' questions. They can give you clues as to whether such questions are safe or dangerous.

Twenty to eleven. My thoughts are blank for a moment. I'm now doing what I sometimes do when I need a little kick-start: looking around to see if anyone reminds me in any way of someone I know.

Goodness! The man sitting right across from me looks exactly like John Betjeman! Surely it isn't him? No, of course, he died. And quite a lot of people do look like John Betjeman: that actor, for example, Donald somebody-or-other, the one who went blind in *The Great Escape*.

This takes me back to 'big' questions again. I'm recalling lines from one of Betjeman's poems, is this right?:

> *'You ask me what it is I do?*
> *Well, actually, you know,*
> *I'm partly dah dee dah dee dah*
> *And partly P – R – O . . .'*

Can't think of the dah-dee-dah bit.

This waiting room is crowded now. I feel guilty. Because I arrived so early, I'm taking up a seat that I feel someone else should have. There's an old man over there, with two walking sticks – I'll offer him my seat.

'Very much obliged,' he says, but as he is about to sit down a young man with a plaster cast on his arm rudely pushes him aside and tries to take the seat.

'I gave the seat to this man, not you,' I say, weakly.

'Too fucking bad,' the young man says, 'now sod off!'

'I'm sorry,' I say to the old man as I move away.

Now, I'm thinking that there is a certain logic and inevitability about me-first values smacking you in the face in a private sector environment, even here in genteel West Sussex. I know this young man's type. In his twenties, with only five middling school-leaving grades, he's paid a vast salary, plus bonuses (and these include a private healthcare fund) of course, and no doubt share options, golden hellos when he got the job and unimaginable fortunes when he's 'let go' for profound incompetence when he leaves it. All for buying and selling something he never sees and probably wouldn't know what it was if he did see it: coffee futures, currency swaps, mineral rights options, whatever. Yes, I know his type, and he appals me. He is what the Iron Lady created and Mister 'New Labour' took over as a stepson and has nurtured with lavish attention ever since.

Much obliged: I haven't heard that expression in years. My dad used to use it. As I meekly back down from confrontation with the young man I'm thinking about him, and mum.

She was a cleaner who read Austen and Dickens and revelled in Shakespeare and Mozart. She played bridge and bingo with equal enthusiasm. She polished off cryptic crosswords in no time at all. She stored away knowledge in her head like hamsters store food in their pouches.

After twenty years in the army, rising to Company Sergeant Major, dad became the head caretaker at a posh boys' public school. I was a pupil there at the time (there's another word, pupil, that's long ago disappeared). I got there out of ordinary primary school via winning the one scholarship the school offered to the local proletariat each year. The school was so posh that Dad's job was called 'School Sergeant' rather than mundane 'caretaker'.

I like to think about my parents. Memories that I have long forgotten about often come back. Sometimes they are not necessarily good ones, and when they are I shut them off, but this morning they are.

It's my turn. It's eleven already.

*

21

I was shown along to the doctor's room, where, standing up and shaking my hand quite firmly he said:

'Good morning, please have a seat. I am Mr Supramanian, and I'm going to be doing your operation, but first of all would you mind if I ask you a few questions as part of a project I'm involved in? You're under no obligation of course?'

'Happy to help,' I replied, though in truth his manner struck me as being rather cold.

'Thank you. Now first, can I ask what you *do*?'

'That's odd,' I said, 'I've just been thinking about just that.'

The doctor looked puzzled, so I went on:

'What I do involves a lot of travelling, and I was just thinking – while I was waiting just now – that's it's the kind of question that's best to avoid when you are sitting next to someone on a long journey.'

'Yes, I see,' he said, looking irritated.

'What I do,' I went on, 'is pretty useless, and as a result it is hard to describe. Useful work, work that is honourable and dignified, is, on the other hand, easy to describe.'

This produced a look of extreme irritation, and a glance at his watch. So I asked a question back:

'Why do you want to know this?'

'I'm sorry, I should have explained. There are various theories about the condition you have,' he said, 'and one of them is that it is occupation-related, work-related. An international research project is going on – one I'm involved with – to see whether such a connection could exist. So can I ask you, specifically, does your work involve a lot of gripping – you know, manual work – or does it involve using your fingers a lot, or your hands in other demanding ways?'

'Apart from using a computer – a lot of my work is desk-work – no, and besides I'm strictly a two-finger typist,' I said, 'but I did work as a builders' labourer when I was a student, many years back.'

'Desk work, word-processing then?' said Mr Supramanian, 'There's a rather vociferous group of Americans already claiming a connection with computer keyboard use: even litigation against Microsoft is being rumoured. I'm sure they'll be happy to hear of you.'

As he said this a smile came to his face: 'Those of us who were and are still sceptical about repetitive strain injury are even more unconvinced about this.'

I felt myself warming to him.

'Now what about sport – do you by any chance *row?*' he asked.

'Ah, I thought we might get to rowing,' I replied, 'as I was talking to someone in the pub the other day who said that this problem I've got with my fingers originated with the Vikings. Is that the case?'

'Like the work-related connection, or possible connection,' he said, 'this is another also as-yet entirely unproven theory being investigated by the current research. But first, can I repeat: do you row?'

'No, but I managed to tip my mother into the boating pool at Butlins holiday camp in Clacton, where we used to go for holidays when I was at school.'

He laughed. Our relationship was on the up and up.

'Fortunately,' I went on, 'the pool was only a couple of feet deep, but under it there was a thick layer of greeny-black mud, as I discovered when Mum emerged from the depths.'

'Goodness,' he said, now laughing loudly, 'let's go on to ancestry then. What can you tell me on that front?'

I decided it was now safe to reply to him more expansively:

'My father had it,' I said. 'After he retired, all four fingers, but not the thumb, curled up, over a period of two years or so, in his left hand. Dad not being the type to go anywhere near a doctor if he could possibly avoid it, it took me and my sister a long time to persuade him to have it seen to, not that we knew what it was. We thought it was some form of arthritis. Meanwhile, three fingers in his right hand started to curl up. In due course, meaning a long time, Dad had the left hand done through the National Health Service, which was as slow then as it is now, which is why I'm going to spend two thousand pounds getting it done by you. I don't know whether the operation is done any differently now, but what I do recall is that Dad was in immense pain for a long time afterwards. During that time he kept telling me that he would not have the other hand done. "So long as I can still hold a pint, and throw a good dart, I'm all right," he used to say. And that was it.'

The doctor nodded: he was scribbling notes, so I went on:

'I can't tell you anything more than that, I'm afraid, apart from the fact that Dad was a through-and-through Londoner, born right next to Highbury stadium and so a life-long Arsenal supporter, a condition I have most certainly inherited from him as well.'

Mr Supramanian smiled again.

'I know nothing more – further back in Dad's family I mean – than that,' I continued, 'Dad's father was the only grandparent I ever knew. He came to stay once, not long before he died, and all I remember about him was that he was the complete opposite of my father in every way imaginable. He was coarse (I never once heard my Dad use even the mildest of bad language), mean (Dad's generosity was enormous) and evil-tempered (to the point of hitting both my sister and me, something neither Mum or Dad ever once did, when we giggled at the dinner table once when he was staying with us). Sorry, all that's irrelevant I know.

24

What I do remember is that he never had bent fingers, granddad I mean. So there the trail goes dead.'

This was a rather over-dramatic way of putting it, I knew. Since Mr Supramanian didn't stop me – he was still scribbling furiously – I carried on.

'This Viking business is strange, you see. Because my mother almost certainly had Viking ancestry.'

Mr Supramanian stopped writing.

'Really?' he asked.

'Yes,' I said, 'Her father was a seaman, and his family roots were in the Shetland Isles. In fact, there are still relatives of my mother up there. Have you heard of the Up-Helly-Aa festival?'

'No, what is it?'

'It happens once a year in the Shetlands, around now in fact, in the depths of winter. For months beforehand the men don't shave, and then they all dress up as Vikings for the festival, you know, horned helmets and all. The main event involves them dragging a Viking boat through Lerwick, the capital, and then setting fire to it. Apparently that's how Viking chiefs were cremated. Or rather they put the body on a boat out at sea and then set fire to it.'

'Fascinating,' he said, scribbling again.

'But going back to Mum, she had perfect hands,' I went on, 'all her life, even with all the hours she spent working as a cleaner, gripping scrubbing brushes, mops and things like that. So you could roll both the theories you've mentioned into one in my Mum, the only slight trouble being that she didn't have it!'

Mr Supramanian was still scribbling away on his notepad in earnest, which was satisfying.

He opened his mouth to say something to me and then instead pushed the buzzer on his intercom. There was no reply.

'Excuse me a moment,' he said and went out of the room.

While he was out I checked out his notes and discovered only that what people say about doctors is true: they were beyond the comprehension of any normal human being.

'Do you mind if we carry on a little longer?' he said when he came back, 'You are the last on the morning list, and I'm most intrigued by this possible family connection. You're the first patient I have ever seen where such a connection has been possible and I'm most anxious to get the details.'

'No, I don't mind at all – in fact if we finished now I'd only be sitting around downstairs for half an hour as my wife's gone to the hairdresser! So yes, Vikings, gripping the oars, let's talk about it. But how come Mum didn't have it? And, by the way, my sister doesn't have it either.'

'Recessive gene, probably,' Mr Supramanian said, 'something that is in the family gene pool, but doesn't necessarily show up in every generation. Take me, for example: as you see my hair is prematurely white – yet I'm only forty. But neither of my parents, who are now in their late sixties, have so much as even one grey hair between them! And I'm also considerably taller than both of them. Mind you, we can't rule your father out – he did have it, yes, but whether *you* got it from his family genes or those on your mother's side is another matter entirely.'

'That's interesting,' I said, 'My sister and I are both tall, and yet neither Mum nor Dad were. It always fascinated the two of us even when we were kids. But when I was about fourteen, something odd happened. Mum went on a TV quiz show called Criss Cross Quiz. It was like noughts and crosses. If you answered a question correctly, you could put your X or O in that box. Mum had huge general knowledge. She went up to the studios in Manchester and in her first game, knocked off the defending champion who'd won time after time for weeks previously. In those days the shows really were live. So we all watched in amazement – we had not long had a TV in fact – when the host said, "Now, presumably you'd like to carry on, or would you like to take the money?" and Mum said, "I'll take the money please." We weren't well off, you see.'

Even though all this was, I knew, irrelevant, Mr Supramanian was listening with evident interest, so I carried on:

'In today's money it would be worth several thousand pounds, money she would have risked losing if she'd taken on a challenger. Only when she returned in triumph did Mum and Dad tell me and my sister why: Dad had seen a house for sale (we'd lived in army or rented places all our lives) and the money was what was needed as a deposit. Our own house! So we were all happy. Mum was happier still when, about a week later, she got a letter forwarded by the TV company. It was from her brother, who she hadn't seen or heard of since she was in her teens: when their parents died they were separated and sent off to live with different relatives. Mum took me with her when she later travelled up north to see the long-lost brother, where he was a miner. He was tall, very tall. The recessive gene strikes again! Sorry to bore you with all this.'

'Not at all,' he said.

We talked a while longer about family matters. I told him that while, as I'd said, the trail was dead on my father's side, I did have Mum's old address book somewhere around and could give details of the relatives in the Shetlands.

'The research would very much appreciate having that,' he said, and then went on:

'Now, you're really here so that I can look at your hands, so we'd better do that hadn't we?'

He said this with a chuckle. We had fully warmed to each other now. I held out my left hand.

'No, I need to see both of them.'

27

'But the other one is fine.'

'We'll see,' he said, and asked me to spread out both hands, palms upwards, on a sheet of paper. Then he drew around their outlines, like kids do in playschool, dotted lines only where the two fingers I can't straighten would have been.

'The good news,' he said, 'is that I can deal with these two chaps on your left hand – by carrying out what's called a fasciectomy rather than a dermofasciectomy, which is a more complicated operation involving skin graft as well as surgery. And thus more expensive! In extreme cases, amputation is needed. While you are far from that, it sounds to me, from what you said, that your father's was a fairly serious case by the time he had the operation.'

'And the bad news?' I asked.

'Your right hand is already beginning to be affected, even though there's no sign yet of the fingers bending. As you know from your left hand these lumps in your palm – here, here and here – are places where your fibrous tissue bands, known as fascia, are thickening, shortening and hardening and causing the tendons connected to your fingers not to be able to do their job properly. Now, feel around the palm of your right hand – you can feel lumps here, and let's see, here – beginning to get hard.'

He was right.

'How long have I got, doc?' I whispered, hoarsely.

He smiled again.

'Two-to-three years before they're like your left hand is now.'

'I'll start saving now, then. Or maybe that address book of my mother's is worth something?'

'Now there's a thought,' he said with another smile. 'But don't you have health insurance? You're paying for this yourself?'

'Yes, I've never believed in health insurance. Health

28

should be public, in my view, not private. Sorry to moralise, I've nothing against you personally, I hope you realise that. Really, I'm criticising myself – I buy your time and thus cause someone like my Dad to have to wait a bit longer for you, or even end up having fingers amputated.'

'I see your point, similar thoughts go through my head, I can assure you. Now, let me explain a few things.'

He took the drawings.

'What I'll be doing is making a series of incisions down the two fingers, like this . . .' – he used a different coloured pen now – '. . . here, here and here, and then across the palm like this, to get at these little fellows here and here, and then straight down the palm to here. While I'm doing all this I'll be as careful as I can to avoid severing or over-stretching any nerves. If I get it wrong, you'll have some numb spots, or even a completely numb finger or two. Afterwards I'll stitch up here, here and here, but I'll leave this part of the palm open, to heal itself. When I've done all that we'll be putting your hand, with hopefully *all* your fingers stretched out flat . . .' – he smiled – '. . . in a light cast, which I'll take off when I take out the stitches two weeks after the operation.'

'Two weeks?'

'Yes, and then you'll need to do some simple physio-therapy to ensure the little chaps don't start curling up again – I'm afraid to say that it's quite common for that to happen, and also that you should not expect things ever to go completely back to the functioning that you had before.'

'They'll never be the same, you mean?'

'No, but they'll be much better and more supple than they are now, and you'll need to keep them active with an exercise that you can't do now, for obvious reasons, but let me show you. It'll be good for both your hands, helping heal the left and also stave off the future problem with the right.'

He put his hands together, like people do in India, with elbows out, as when people say 'Namaste' to greet or to thank.

'Now you push your palms and fingers hard together, trying to push the fingers back as hard and far as you can. Like this. Then relax, separate the hands, like this, and clench the fists separately – use a stress ball if you like. Then, hands together again and push, and so on – got that? You seem distracted. Are you with me?'

I wasn't.

'Are you with me?' he said again.

'Sorry, it was your hands, they distracted me. I hope I don't sound racist, but your hands are so typically, and so beautifully, Indian, if I might say. They are so soft and supple'

'Yes,' he said, 'in fact . . .'

He held up both hands apart to show me how far he could bend his fingers backwards.

'. . . one of my passions as a child, and indeed still today, was dance, all forms of dance, but especially our Indian forms. Do I detect that you share this interest?'

'Most certainly I do,' I said, 'as my work often takes me to India, and I'm particularly interested in the Kathak form. Mind you, since I have two-left-foot syndrome as well as Dupuytren's Contracture . . .'

'So you know what it's called?'

'Yes, I wanted to ask you why, but never mind now . . . the combination of the two conditions, one of which as you know is incurable and inoperable, means that I can only pursue my interest from watching rather than participating.'

He laughed loudly. I looked at my watch.

'Time to go, I expect my wife will be waiting downstairs by now. Have we covered everything?'

'Yes, as you know you are already booked in for the operation, let's see, two weeks from today in fact. We'll keep you in overnight afterwards only if you feel you're not up to going home. So I'll see you then. I have a few things to tidy up now but if you're still downstairs and your wife hasn't arrived, maybe we can have a cup of something together?'

'Thank you, fine,' I said, 'I've enjoyed our chat.'

'So have I. Thank you very much indeed for your time.'

I knew, as I sat in the waiting-cum-café area, sipping a cup of coffee that both looked and tasted more like very weak cream of mushroom soup, and watching the comings and goings of patients and staff – this being a private hospital the latter had garish uniforms that made them look more like airline crew than medical personnel – that what I had said to the doctor was entirely untrue: my wife would most certainly not be waiting downstairs for me. So let me talk about her.

Claire has many wonderful characteristics. I love, and indeed admire, her outgoing, warm-hearted, sociable, nature. I think that maybe this stems from the fact that she was born and brought up in Australia, in a place called Toowoomba, funny name. Her parents were 'ten pound migrants' and didn't last very long there, apparently. I simply do not have Claire's outgoing nature. I'm essentially an introvert. Whenever I can, I just like to sit and think. Claire talks. She talks to me, she talks to everyone. She talks to animals. She talks to trees and flowers. She even talks to people on trains! You can't stop her. She knows everyone in the village where we live. Everyone knows her and everyone likes her. I think it's partly because of the fact that she talks so much that she has hardly a trace of an Australian accent: she talked it out of herself. Just occasionally, however, she uses words I find strange, like 'ripper' and 'beaut'. She tells me that they are Australian words.

Claire cannot keep to time. She could not keep to time even if she'd been born as a clock. I don't think this has anything to do with being Australian. If it does, I'd hate to live there, I'm sure.

Claire's time language needs to be learnt. When she says 'done', or 'sorted', as she often does when she's been doing something, it actually means 'the end is vaguely in sight'. When she says 'I'll be down in five minutes', it means that at the very best half-an-hour will pass before she is ready. Or maybe longer. Likewise, when she asks me how long it is before dinner, if I speak the truth, say, 'five minutes', then I will at that very same moment turn the oven or pasta or spuds down, so as to allow another half-an-hour. I don't mind this at all – it gives me more thinking time.

I, on the other hand, hate to be late. I don't like to rush. I like to be ready not on time, but ahead of it, if possible well ahead of it. I haven't checked this out but I'm sure that being late or pushed for time causes my blood pressure to shoot up. It also puts me into a state of nervous anxiety, in which I get flustered, disorientated even. Last year, for example, when we'd gone over to Italy to spend Easter in Alfonso's house, we flew into Rimini (usually we go to Bologna), and got a hire car there. It was on the way back that the problem arose. I have to admit, very candidly, that it wasn't Claire's fault that we left a little later than we'd planned in order to get to Rimini in good time for the return flight. The front door of the house wouldn't lock properly. I found a screwdriver and some oil in the garden shed and fixed it. So off we eventually went, still in reasonable shape as far as time was concerned. But we were a good twenty kilometres down the valley when I realised that I'd left my jacket at the house. I'd taken it off when I was fixing the door. In its pockets were our passports and tickets. Rapid u-turn, back to the house, and then back down the valley again.

When we got on to the autostrada I calculated that we would get to the airport more or less exactly at the time the plane was due to leave. So I stepped on it. Claire hates it when I drive fast – she always says that at the best of times I behave in Italy as if I was an Italian, which I take as a compliment, in fact. But this was too much for her. 'Do we have to go so fast?' she kept saying. And I just kept saying 'Yes'.

Now, here's the point about being flustered. Driving along I was anxious, yes, but not flustered, no, at least not until we left the autostrada and pulled up at the toll booths. 'What the hell?' I said – there was nobody in the booth. In fact there was no booth. In spite of having travelled and driven in Italy for countless years, I'd gone in the wrong lane, the one where you can only get out if you have an autostrada card, which I don't have.

Flustered, I reversed. Straight into the car behind. Histrionics all round. More fluster . . . I won't go on. We did, in fact, get the plane – there had been a baggage handlers' dispute at Stansted, so it only arrived two hours after we did. During that time I calmed myself down with a few beers, while contemplating what the damage to the cars would cost me.

Claire's inability to keep to time, although I repeat that the Rimini episode, from origins to outcomes, was all my fault, stems, in part, from another of her slightly trying characteristics: an inability to go from A to B directly. I don't mean this just in the geographical sense, although she has the most poorly developed sense of spatial and geographical awareness of anyone I've ever known, manifest in a supreme ability to turn left when right is required, and vice versa. When she met me at the station to take me to her home soon after we first met, she got lost. But what I'm referring to here is A to B in the sense of tasks.

Here's an example. Claire gets up – that is A. 'I'll make you a cup of tea,' (this is B) she says, 'you lie in a bit.' An hour later I get up, tea-less. What has happened is this: Claire puts kettle on, goes upstairs to dial-up for email on the computer. While waiting, she remembers she needs to iron Amy's school dress. While doing so, sees a hem needs stitching, gets the needle and thread out of the sewing box, which she finds needs a tidy up. Eventually she gets the thread out and puts it on the ironing board, only to look up and see that an email has come in from her sister in Australia, with photos attached. These she studies for a while, then types a reply and selects a few photos in her pictures file to send back . . .

An hour later I bring her her tea. 'I said I'd do that,' she says. 'Hmm,' I say, and give her a kiss. This is her nature, and it only occasionally irritates me, this being when there's an anxiety-inducing knock-on effect on me, or when an extreme case occurs. Like the time she popped out early one morning to get the paper from the shop, and at lunchtime I got a call from her which began: 'You'll never guess what happened . . . met so and so, who needed a lift to so-and-so's, who . . .' She was still in her slippers when she came back.

Now while Claire's approach to tasks and time-management is thus somewhat eclectic, I have to add that, while she can't be described as organised, she is a very meticulous person. Her – and as a result our – pending tray never has anything in it. Claire makes quick decisions and then does things quickly; she hates things being left hanging around. Perhaps this is also an Australian characteristic.

I, on the other hand, am a supreme procrastinator. My deeply held personal belief, for example, is that, like wine, bank statements must be left to mature for as long as possible before they are opened; appointments with people like accountants and dentists – yes, and doctors – are burdensome if they take place more than once in a decade; and that ironing should be done no more than once a month.

If it hadn't been for Claire, frankly, I would not be here this morning. She made that decision. Without her, I would live in chaos. And her odd timekeeping habits also produce benefits for me. Like right now. While the coffee is execrable, I'm very happy here, on my own, thinking my thinking, talking to myself in my head, while watching this little corner of the world go by. It saves me, for a little while, from going back to my desk at home and doing what I should be doing.

Ah, the wonders of procrastination!

Claire is also the kind of person who will not easily let anything get in her way. She is prepared to be forceful if it's necessary. She is clear about what she wants. She is, in a word, dogged. Once she's onto a scent, she will not give up until she's followed it to the end. I'm sure that that side of her is Australian. We British are much more timid. If a saleswoman is trying to force a particular but unwanted item on her, be it lipstick or an electric oven, Claire will stick to her guns. Once she has an idea in her head – of what she'll pay, or what she wants to do – she'll stick to it. She is very determined. She asks for – and usually gets – a discount on everything she buys. I was with her in Fortnum and Mason's once and she refused to pay the price marked on a selection of English teas she wanted to send to her sister. 'I can't justify paying that much,' she said with a beguiling smile. And they caved in! 'Ripper,' she said, as she paid the money.

And she has an eye for detail, like going through every bank statement. She always reads the fine print.

Claire goes regularly to the hairdressers. To be honest, in

the ten years that I've known her, her hair has been all of black (which it is naturally), flecked, fair, blonde, even platinum blonde; every length from half-way down her back (when I first met her) to not far short of crew-cut; and every style from frizzy-curly (like the dark haired lady in Abba) to straight blonde (like the other one). Who knows what it'll be after today's visit to the hairdresser. Could be Sinead O'Connor, Syd Vicious (no, surely not)? No, more likely, it'll be Meg Ryan. She's basically stuck with the Meg style for a couple of years now, just changing the tints, subtly as far as I can see, or rather not see. She gets mad at me, in a loving kind of way, when she says, 'Notice the difference?' and I say, 'Well, no.' 'But the highlights are much stronger, and it's shorter now. See?' 'Well, no.'

Claire is, and I think most people would agree with me on this, very attractive. She's nowhere near as tall as I am, but the top of her head gets close to my chin when she's in her highest heels. She's slim, and always dresses well. She's ten years younger than me.

Claire has a daughter, Amy – my step-daughter. She is fifteen years old and is, how can I put this, quite severely intellectually handicapped. I know it's not the done thing to use those kinds of words. The correct, politically correct, words these days are 'special needs', but I find them quite meaningless. When I first met Claire, she described Amy to me as being 'autistic', and I also find this inappropriate, as autism has become a word used at the one extreme by middle-class, nouveau-riche parents to explain away their little brat's propensity to throw chairs at his school-teacher, indicating some kind of personality defect, to, at the other extreme, true intellectual disorders like Asperger's syndrome and so-called 'profound autism'.

Amy is not 'autistic', because she isn't any of those things. She has a rare genetic condition resulting in an inability to do even the most basic things for herself, limited speech and the consequent need for constant care and attention, which she certainly gets from her mother, and, I hope, since I have known her, from me. She's a most lovely girl.

When I first met Claire, one of the things that I found (and still find) really attractive are her hands and feet. They are all small and smooth. Normally feet are rather awful things. They can be in otherwise highly attractive people and certainly are in most people. Claire's feet are lovely. Her hands even more so. I am fascinated by hands. No, nothing to do with this Dupuytren's business – I've always been attracted to small, lithe, smooth hands.

'Still here?'

It was Mr Supramanian. 'May I join you? Goodness, your coffee must be stone cold – let me get you another.'

'No thanks.'

'I quite understand – it is not among the things we do well here, I fear.'

We laughed.

'Now you never really properly told me about what you do,' he said, 'Do tell me.'

'Well, my work, as I said, takes me to a lot of places around the world, but these days mostly in Asia – India, Pakistan, Sri Lanka, Bangladesh. I go in, or rather I'm sent in, to help development organisations do their work better.'

'Management consultant, then?' he asked.

'No, I prefer not to call it that, though in reality, which I'm not good at facing, that is basically what it is. But I try not to use the term. When organisations work well, you see, it's usually simply because the relationships between people in them are good. That's all that really matters.'

He nodded.

'Never mind the organigrams, never mind all the crap you read in those ridiculous books that fill the shelves of airport bookshops with titles like *The twelve commandments for business success,* or *In search of business excellence* and certainly never mind what any so-called "management guru" says at five-hundred-quid-a-head business seminars.'

He laughed.

'This is music to my ears,' he said. 'As you know the health service has been plagued with management consultants for years now.'

'So I've heard,' I said. 'And have you noticed, by the way, how these so-called management gurus often have highly unlikely, even contradictory, pedigrees? Once . . . where was I now? . . . I forget, but the country is immaterial, a young fellow in the organisation I was working with came in one morning very excited, daily newspaper in hand. "Look," he said, "we missed it, we should have been there!" The paper reported that a very distinguished management guru had given a lecture to over two thousand people at the such-and-such convention centre the previous evening. Who was this "guru"? None other than General, or rather former general, "Fighting Frank" Schultzberg, who had recently saved the world by leading several hundred thousand troops, backed by countless billions of dollars of military hardware and technology, to victory over the hapless army of some despot in the middle east. Frank retired, resting on his laurels no doubt, soon after, and became an instant management guru, the task of an army being seen as much the same as that of a business: doing battle against evil forces of darkness, known in business circles as shareholders, customers, and, very often, those nasty little people called employees. The newspaper report of the lecture informed me that each of the two thousand had paid five hundred US dollars to listen to the lecture; that it had been greeted by "rapturous and prolonged applause"; and that Frank had ever so kindly, in his remarks, given away the secret of his "three key ingredients for winning your business victory". These were, one, "when in command, *take charge*" (ah yes, Frank, of course); two, "when in charge, *do the right thing*" (brilliant, words of genius, surely Frank, I'll never forget them); and, well, I forget the third, but it was just as penetrating an insight.'

The doctor laughed so loudly that people around started to stare at us.

'But tell me, what kinds of organisations do you work with? Not the health service I take it?' he asked.

'No, I don't work with big organisations. Other people in my firm do that. I do the smaller ones. Some are small businesses – suppliers of "fair trade" products, but they are mostly non-governmental organisations working in what you might call the aid and development business.'

'Oxfam, Christian Aid, World Vision, those kinds of organisations?'

'Oh, no – I have no time at all for them. They're just agents of neo-imperialism. The ones I work with are set up and run by people – people of the countries in which they are based, I mean – for the benefit of others. While most of the pretty pathetic amount the British government devotes to overseas aid and development goes to the big boys you've mentioned, some, just a little, mind you, just the small change so to speak, goes to the organisations I work with. You see our wonderful, generous government doesn't really trust the natives. Oops, maybe that's a bit strong! So along with the crumbs of aid thrown their way, they get me as well, to spy on them, make sure they do things properly. Patronising. To be honest I'm not very comfortable about it, I feel a sense of guilt, the same kind of guilt in a way that I feel about having this operation done privately.'

As I had been speaking he had listened very carefully, encouraging me with his facial movements and gestures.

He told me that while he had lived and worked in England since he graduated from medical school, he had

kept up what he called 'a supportive association' with a
voluntary organisation that runs preventative healthcare
programmes in his home state of Orissa.

'I understand your sense of guilt about going private,' he
went on. 'I guess it's a rather inadequate way of dealing
with my own guilt that I send them money – in reality that's
what my "supportive relationship" means.'

He tapped his teaspoon on the table.

'The main organisation I work with in India is in New
Delhi,' I replied, 'but I've been to Orissa once or twice.'

'So it's presumably from your trips to India that your
interest in our dance forms comes?'

'Yes, indeed,' I said, and as I did so, I saw Claire coming
through the entrance door.

'Is that your wife?' Mr Supramanian said, as we watched
her coming towards us. 'Goodness, I know her.'

He got out of his seat as she approached.

'Sorry, running late . . .' she said and then, looking at Mr
Supramanian, went on '. . . Krishnan – goodness me!'

The two of them looked at one another, with mutual
expressions of surprise and pleasure. I suddenly felt as if I
was intruding.

'Claire, how wonderful to see you again. It must be . . .
fifteen years?' Mr Supramanian said.

'Yes, about that, I'd guess,' Claire said, and, turning to
me, went on, 'when I was a secretary at the infirmary in
Brighton, darling, long before I met you, Krishnan was one
of the young doctors I did the typing for. What a small
world!'

'Yes, do still call me Krishnan,' he said, looking first to
Claire and then to me.

'Please, Krishnan,' I said, 'make it Christian, reciprocally.
And maybe I will have that other coffee. Let me get it while
you two catch up. Tea for you darling? Another coffee for
you, Krishnan?'

When I got back, they were clearly reminiscing, but turned their attention back to me as I set the cups down.

'Your husband was telling me all about his interest in . . .' Krishnan began.

I cut him off: 'I've been telling Krishnan all about the Viking connection – you remember me telling you about what I'd been told? Well, it turns out that it could be true, in my case at least!'

'How interesting,' Claire said, 'is that really possible, Krishnan?'

The doctor looked across the table at me, a faint look of puzzlement on his face. While we had only known each other since I had walked into his office that morning, I think he knew what my steady look into his eyes meant: don't go where you were about to go, just answer her question. Which he did, at some length.

When we left, there were smiles and handshakes all round.

'He's a very good man: I think you are in good hands, darling, if you'll excuse the expression,' Claire said on the drive home, 'I'm really happy that he's doing it. He was always such a conscientious young man. He'd only just qualified when I worked for him.'

'Good, but he told me that it won't necessarily ever be quite what it was,' I said as I looked at the hand, putting the other one on her thigh as she drove.

'So, what do you think of my hair?'

'It looks great.'

'You really think so?'

'Yes I do, it looks great.'

She changed gear and then put her hand on mine.

'You're just saying that, bet you can't really see any difference.'

41

'The blonde highlights are bigger and brighter.'
'I love you.'
'Love you too.'
'Oh, by the way, Palmer rang.'
'About yesterday?'
'Didn't say, but I expect so. Sounded very terse.'
'What did you say?'
'I said you were away taking a break, out of reach, writing a report, and that he should call back in a couple of weeks.'
'By which time I'll be in hospital.'
'Exactly. Beaut eh?'
'Good girl, as Amy would say, good girl.'

3

The Three-Peaked Mountain

The woman, the man and the child were swimming in the sea. The wind was strong; the cloud was low; the water was grey, flecked with white. The three of them rose and fell in the waves.

'We should go back now,' the woman said, 'it's not safe to be out here.'

The man laughed. 'Don't be afraid, the storm will soon pass.'

The child said: 'Swimming, good girl, kick kick kick.'

The woman was anxious, anxious for herself, anxious for the child. She looked for their boat and saw it now, a long way off. But as she watched, a wave tipped it over and it was gone.

'The boat, where is the boat?' she screamed, but the man took no notice. He and the child were playing with a ball, laughing.

'Stop, stop,' she shouted, 'the boat has gone.' But they paid her no attention.

She looked for the land, but the clouds were low, joining the sea in a bank of thick mist. Now she could not see the man or the child.

'Where are you, I can't see you!' she shouted, but all she heard was the sound of laughing far away. She sank, drowning, reaching up as air bubbled from her mouth.

A hand grabbed hers and she came again to the surface. The man was laughing.

'Look,' he said, 'there's the boat.'

But it was not their boat. It was a strange boat. Along its sides were shields and oars and it had a large rectangular sail. On the boat there were men, menacing men with beards, axes, swords and horned metal helmets, running up and down from one end to the other.

'Help us, help us,' she cried, but they sailed on, oblivious. Now the man held her.

'Trust me, there is nothing to fear, the sun will come soon,' he said.

She looked all around. 'Where is the child?'

'She is on the boat,' the man said. 'The Vikings will look after her. They are good people, my ancestors. They will bring her back soon.'

'No, they will kill her.'

She looked for the strange boat. But now it was burning. The men were shouting and screaming, throwing themselves into the water. Above the din, she heard the child's screams.

Still the man laughed.

The child bobbed up between them. 'Hallo Mummy, look, good girl.'

Now the sea was calm.

'There, I told you, the clouds are lifting, soon the sun will come,' the man said, pointing to the sky.

Now the sky was blue. She saw the land, close by. A mountain appeared, a strange mountain with three peaks.

'Let's go and climb it,' the man said.

'Good, walking, good girl,' said the child.

'No,' she said, 'no, no, no.'

But the man took one of her hands and the child the other. They pulled her to the shore and then up the beach. She fell, but they would not let go. They dragged her on and on and into the trees. She was crying with pain. The man now wore a white coat, the child a blue dress.

44

In a clearing they let her go. The man threw the ball to the child. It was a big ball, white, red and green. 'Good girl,' the child said when she caught it. She threw it up into the trees, where it floated away.

'We must go back now,' the woman said, lying down. She felt prickles on her legs and looked down to see large black scorpions crawling up them. She tried to brush them off but more and more came until they covered her whole naked body.

'No,' the man said, 'we must go on. This is too good a chance to miss. Trust me. If we don't do this now, we will wait forever.'

She watched the man and the child disappear from the clearing, but they came back and dragged her again.

'You are mad,' she said, but they took no notice.

Now the trees ended and great dark slate-grey slabs of strata angled steeply upwards. Her bare feet burned at the first touch of the rocks. The man and the child dropped her and disappeared again, but she heard their laughing. Another man, a dark-skinned Indian man with pure white hair, appeared and gave her a white coat and a blue mask.

'Why?' she said.

The man said: 'These are the mountains of the moon. Beware the scorpions.'

He held out a single red rose to her but disappeared as she reached for it. The rose fell to the ground and burned to ashes on the hot rocks. She turned and started climbing. Looking up, she saw the man and the child high above her. Among the rocks, scorpions scurried, stinging her feet and hands as she climbed upwards.

Now it was cold. The grey rocks turned to white snow. Still she heard the man and the child laughing, close by again now.

'It's beautiful,' the man said, 'come and join us!'

He was sitting with the child in a steaming pool of bright

blue bubbling water in the snow. They were throwing the ball to one another.

'But it's too cold, you will freeze to death,' she said. 'You must get out'

'No, it's hot, hotter than hell,' the man said, pulling her in.

But the water was cold, freezing cold, and the shock of it stiffened her muscles and made her gasp for breath. Now the ball floated away and the man got out and ran after it. The child laughed.

'Stop, it's too dangerous,' she shouted as the ball came down and rolled to the edge of a steep precipice, 'you must stop!'

But still the man ran after it.

She pushed and clawed to get out of the pool. She saw the man lunge for the ball but he slipped and was left hanging over the precipice, his fingers locked into the frozen snow there.

'Help me, help me,' he whispered as the woman reached him.

She reached out but as she did so, the man fell. Only two bloody-stumped fingers were left of him, staining the snow.

She looked over the precipice and saw him falling.

'I'm sorry, I'm so sorry,' he called out.

4

The Night

The Ashfield Hospital

'We look forward to welcoming you to The Ashfield Hospital. The hospital opened in 1992 and became part of the nation-wide 'Pro-Fit' health services provision group in 1995. Nevertheless we are an established part of the local community.

'The hospital is modern, purpose built and well equipped, with 45 bedrooms, all en suite, 2 high dependency rooms, 3 operating theatres, complete X-ray facilities including MRI and CT Scanners, and a physiotherapy facility.

'We appreciate that coming into hospital for an operation, however minor, can cause anxiety, especially if you are not feeling one hundred per cent. We therefore go to great lengths to make your admission and stay with us as comfortable and relaxing as possible. You will thus find that we will provide you with all the care and conveniences you would expect – this means 'five star hotel' services and facilities, including free daily newspapers, in-house hairdresser, counsellor and masseur, in-room satellite TV, and entirely open visiting policies. Visitors are also welcome to dine with you, choosing from our tempting menu and our list of fine wines. And of course you are guaranteed to have your own private room! All these are just some of the reasons why having medical treatment in the private sector has become more and more popular in recent years. At 'Pro-Fit' we provide for your good health at convenient locations, in environments having an ambiance conducive to your quickest *and fullest return to good health, while of course meeting the highest clinical care standards laid down by the National Care Standards Commission.*

'Under 'Pro-Fit's' unique fixed price guarantee, should your stay be longer for recovery purposes than we, you, or your admitting consultant anticipate, no extra charges will be applied; and in the unlikely event of there being a complication with the treatment you receive within 30 days of your leaving hospital, there will also normally be no further charges.'

She woke with a start. She was disorientated. The room was almost totally dark, lit only by a thin sliver of light coming from the edge of the not-quite-closed door. While the curtains were not drawn, it was dark outside. She was in a reclining armchair, beside a bed . . . of course, Christian's bed, in the hospital.

He was not there.

She felt anxious, more so when she switched the bedside light on and looked at her watch. It was nearly midnight. They had taken him down, belatedly, at five.

After a gentle tap at the door, a blue-uniformed male nurse came in.

'I've brought you some tea,' he said, putting a tray down on the table, 'Mr Supramanian is just coming, he won't be a moment.'

'Is everything all right? What is happening? Where . . . ?'

She stopped as Krishnan came in. He motioned to the nurse to leave and then walked across to where she was now standing, by the bed, and took her hand.

'Please, Claire, you should sit down.'

She felt faint. He guided her to the chair and then sat on the side of the bed.

She opened her mouth to speak, but he pre-empted her.

'This is not easy for me, and it will I am sure be even

harder for you, Claire, but let me say that I am sorry, I am really very sorry about this.'

'Oh . . . my . . . God,' she said slowly.

'No, it's not that, not quite that, not yet that, at least.'

'Then what? Krishnan, what is it?'

He stood up and put his hands together momentarily in front of his face, bending the fingers back.

'Claire, just as we were concluding the procedure – I was putting the cast on his hand in fact, he suffered . . .'

The doctor choked on these words and tears welled in his eyes.

'. . . he suffered a cardiac arrest – his heart stopped. While we cannot be sure, the arrest was most probably caused by massive myocardial infarction – I'm sorry, I mean a heart attack in other words. We can be reasonably certain that none of this was related to the operation, it being such a minor and marginally invasive one, although it could have been a reaction, a very rare reaction, to anaesthesia. It was certainly unexpected, and in fact if he had not been where he was when it happened, I think I can safely say that he would have died immediately. Being in the operating theatre, we were able to give him immediate resuscitation. His heart actually stopped for several minutes before we were able to get it going again.'

'I see,' she said, feeling numb but nonetheless clear and unemotional, 'did he know what was happening?'

'No, he was still under the anaesthetic, he would not have known – or felt – anything. But look, I'm not saying this very well.'

She stood up and they both turned to face outwards to the window, where the curtains were still undrawn.

'Please just tell me, Krishnan, don't feel you have to hold back anything.'

He drew in a long, deep, breath, followed by another, and they stood in silence.

'He's now on a ventilator – a life support machine. It's only that that's keeping him alive at present, though whether alive is the appropriate word is another matter. The best that can be said is that as of now, he is hanging on to life by the very slimmest of threads'.

She slowly knelt down and then rested her head on the bed, clasping her arms over it. Now great gulping sobs overcame her. The doctor moved behind her and put his hands gently on her shoulders.

'Claire, it isn't all doom and gloom,' he said. 'There is a chance, even though it's a small one, that he will recover. We can't make a proper assessment until at least a day has passed.'

A nurse, a female one this time, came in, but he gestured to her to take the teacup – which was untouched – and bring back two more.

He felt Claire's sobbing subside, but remained where he was until he felt her move a little. She moved her arms from over her head to rest on the bed itself. He moved away, took out a handkerchief and wiped his face.

She stood up and turned to him. Mascara stained her face. He held out the handkerchief but she shook her head.

'Let me use the bathroom for a second,' she said.

While she was there, he sat in the armchair. The nurse returned with the tea. He sipped his, but it was scalding hot.

Fully five minutes passed before she emerged.

'I'm ready to hear more, now,' she said. 'I have some questions and I also want you to tell me whatever you feel I need to know. Then I want to see him. I want to talk to him.'

'Claire, I don't think you understand. He is currently in a coma.'

'Yes, of course I understand that, but I want to talk to

him. Whether he can hear or not, I still want to talk to him.'

'I see. Look, since there are some signs of neurological activity, he is, legally speaking, alive. The signs are faint and I fear they are actually being caused merely by muscle relaxants we used after performing the resuscitation, to help re-start the heart. But the signs are definitely there. His body temperature is also abnormal. Only once his body is clear of the drugs and his temperature stabilises, will we be able to make a proper assessment of the brain activity.'

She pursed her lips.

'Thank you. I still want to talk to him.'

'Of course. Now, you said you have some questions?'

'Yes. Well, he went down to theatre at five. Why has it taken so long for you to tell me all this?'

He motioned her to the armchair and then sat on the bed and placed his hands in his lap.

'I wish I knew myself where all the time went . . . let me be honest. Two of my colleagues had come into assist from the moment of the cardiac arrest. They stayed throughout the time, some of which, a good deal of which, went on performing an operation known as a tracheotomy.'

'A what?'

'It's an operation to make an opening in the neck, the throat I mean, into which the breathing tube, from the ventilator, can be placed. We had to do this because the upper airway seemed to be obstructed in some way so we could not get the tube in through his mouth or nose. So when you see him, you'll see all this: don't be too alarmed. The tube goes down through his vocal cords, by the way, so even if he could speak, he would not be able to.'

'And if, I mean when, he recovers, will he be able to speak again?'

'Yes, but . . .'

'But what?'

'Claire, as I said, Christian is at present being kept alive by the ventilator. What we call "brain death" has not taken place but this may well be due to the drugs still present in his system. My view, as well as that of my colleagues, is that we must wait. We had a long discussion – that is where a lot of the time has gone – about this, and there will be more discussions over the next day or two. In fact I first came up to see you at nine o'clock, but I made a judgement. You were fast asleep. I judged that you would need all the rest, all the strength, you can get to be able to cope with what I've just told you. In fact you were so deeply asleep that we were able to bring in the bed without waking you. And besides, at that stage I wasn't sure as to what I would be saying to you, as I'd agreed with my colleagues that we would make a first reassessment of Christian's condition at midnight, which we have just done.'

'And?'

'His body temperature is still not yet quite normal, and while the muscle relaxants we gave him will still be in his system, thus almost certainly distorting the true position, to an extent, I have to say that the signs, the life signs I mean, are a little better than they were earlier.'

'What do you mean?'

'There are a number of things we do – tests – in order to determine whether brain death has taken place, or whether there is still some kind of neurological function present. Firstly, we test for what is called the oculocephalic reflex. And it was there, unmistakably. The test involves opening the eyes and moving the head from side to side. When we did this there was some motion of the eyes, very small but nonetheless there. Where brain death has occurred the eyes remain fixed and do not move.'

'So that's good then?'

'Yes, but, Claire, I have to stress that these may be "false readings". Due to the drugs still in his system. But for the moment, we feel that we should at least wait and see. The one thing we have, at least for the moment, is time.'

As he said this, he stood up and turned round to face the window, looking out to the streetlights.

'We also had a positive result from a test we do for what is called the oculovestibular reflex. What we do with this is, using a syringe, inject very cold water into the ears while holding the eyes open. If there is brain function, the eyes will twitch when this happens, out of the shock of it.'

'And they did?'

He turned to face her: 'Yes, there was a response, again small, but nonetheless there.'

The door opened suddenly and the nurse came back in.

'There's a call from a Rosie somebody. She has called twice before, earlier this evening.'

'What do you want to do, Claire?' Krishnan asked.

'Ask them to put it through here – I should speak to her. She's my best friend. She's looking after my daughter at home for me.'

'Let me leave you for a short while then.'

'No, please would you stay? I want to make sure that I say the right thing, you know, tell her what the position is. I don't want to get anything wrong. Please stay.'

'Fine. More tea? Let me go and get it and I'll be right back.'

The phone rang. She let it ring three more times while she composed herself. As she spoke, Krishnan came back in and sat down again on the bed.

'Would you hold my hand please?' she said as they left the room later.

He took it: 'Of course. I thought, by the way, that you handled the call very well.'

In fact he had marvelled at it. While it was clear that the lady, Rosie, at the other end had been distraught – he could tell this from the long silences from Claire, punctuated by the occasional soft word of encouragement – Claire herself had remained calm and collected throughout. From the call he gathered that Rosie was looking after, or baby-sitting, someone called Amy – of course, the daughter. 'Did she go to the toilet before she went to bed?' Claire had asked at one point.

As they waited for the lift he asked: 'Your daughter's name is Amy?'

'Yes,' she said, 'she's my daughter from my first marriage. It was her birth that caused me to give up my job at the infirmary, remember? She's autistic – no, Christian hates me saying that. She has special needs, she's intellectually disabled. She's lovely in fact. She loves Christian.'

'It will be hard for you to tell her about all this, I fear.'

'No, it would be impossible. I've no idea whether the word "hospital" means anything to her. I told her today that that was where Christian was going. When he's away she always asks where he is. So all I'll tell her is that that is where he is, every day until, well, I don't know. Every day for now, at least.'

They fell silent in the lift, still hand in hand, but as they stepped out of it he spoke.

'We are going to have to put a gown and mask on you, I'm afraid. Then I'll take you in. Now, Claire, it will be a shock I'm sure. You'll see tubes and wires and screens and gadgets everywhere.'

'Can I hold his hand?'

'No, I fear not. One, the one we operated on, is raised up on a sling so that the wound will drain. That's normal. The other – well, you can touch it, but we've got the drip there, so touch rather than hold. To you it will look as if he's simply breathing normally in a deep sleep. Basically that's what he is doing, except that it's the ventilator that's doing the breathing for him. It makes a funny kind of sound but you'll get used to it.'

'Noisy?'

'No, these things are really quiet these days – you'll hardly notice it.'

They passed through a door marked 'High Dependency Area', into a small room where a nurse, capped, gowned and masked herself, waited. The doctor went on through a door leading out of the room. By the time he returned, capped, gowned and masked himself, she was similarly attired.

'This way,' he said, and they passed through one door, and then another, and were in the room where Christian lay. It was less cluttered than she had expected, and quiet, apart from the muted alternate humming and hissing of what she took to be the ventilator, which was smaller than she had imagined, the size of their microwave in the cottage. Above it were screens with coloured lines running across them, all moving reassuringly, registering what she took to be his pulse, heartbeat, blood pressure, or whatever.

The nurse pointed to a chair. Only when she had sat down in it did she focus fully on the figure in the bed. Krishnan was right – the tube from his neck looked horrible. He was naked from the waist up, with wires connected to parts of his chest, and also some on his head. Plastic bags containing liquid were connected to his 'good' arm. She found it difficult to look at his face, as the tube in his throat distracted her. Instead she looked at the hand, *the* hand. It was held up, as Krishnan had warned her, as if he were a policeman signalling to her to halt and come no closer. She felt Krishnan's hand on her shoulder.

'Now . . .' he said.

The sound made her jump.

'Sorry,' he said, 'yes, with someone sleeping, all one's

inclinations are to whisper, aren't they? But you can talk normally of course. Now, is there anything more you want to know?'

She shook her head.

'Then we'll leave you. Take as long as you want. Don't be alarmed if anything beeps or flashes. Every display you see here is repeated through to the room through the glass screen in there, so the duty nurse knows everything there is that needs to be known. She or I will come right in if there's anything wrong. And whatever you say can't be heard in there, I assure you.'

She nodded. He squeezed her shoulder. She felt the tears coming again but fought them back.

Alone with Christian, she rested her hand on the bed so that the tips of her fingers were just touching those of his. She closed her eyes and tried to bring a picture of him into her head, but none would come. Instead, the last frame of her dream came vividly, frighteningly, back to her now: the fall from the cliff-edge, the bloody finger stumps, and above all, the words: 'I'm sorry. I'm so sorry'.

Her eyes opened wide now.

'Thank you my darling,' she said, and realising she was whispering, she said the words again, out louder. 'Thank you my darling. I know you're there. You told me, didn't you? I heard you. I will not let you go. Don't worry, nobody will take you from me. Nobody.'

Now she moved her hand up over his, and squeezed it once.

'I love you Christian. Amy loves you. We will bring you back, I promise you. If it hadn't been for me making you do this, then none of it would have happened. So it's my fault, and it's my job to get you back. And I will get you back. Now I know you're there.'

She even smiled.

'Now, I'll tell you what I'm going to do. I'm going to go

back to the cottage. Rosie's there, looking after Amy. She sends her love, by the way. We'll have a cup of tea. Then I'm going to go to bed. I want you to speak to me again then. Will you do that? Don't keep it to yourself, darling, not now, no secrets, eh?'

She stood up and moved forward along the side of the bed. She bent down slightly, but stopped and turned to look through the glass screen, where the nurse was watching her. She pointed to her mask-covered mouth and then at Christian. The nurse shook her head.

'No, I'm afraid not,' the nurse said when she left and went back into the room behind the glass screen.

'I understand,' she replied, 'where's the doctor?'

'He's in the ante-room. Go on in and I'll come and help you get your gown off.'

There, Krishnan was stretched out awkwardly across three chairs, apparently asleep, but he quickly sat up.

'All done?' he asked as he took off his gown.

'Yes. I'm ready to go now.'

'I'll take you.'

'No, you most certainly will not. I can easily drive myself home now. You must be exhausted, so I hope you're going home now as well?'

'Yes, in a short while I will. Now, let me give you these.'

He searched various pockets before finding what he wanted: a small plastic container.

'Take one of these when you go to bed. They'll get you quickly to sleep. And if you need to, take the others, one each night before bed, in the period ahead.'

'I'm not a pill-taker, but, all right, yes I will, but just tonight. Now, Krishnan, before I go . . .'

'Yes? What is it?'

'I know this will sound utterly mad, but I know that Christian is there.'

'There? Where?'

'Sorry, I mean I know that he's alive. He spoke to me, you see.'

'What? In there just now?'

'No. In my dream. You see I had a dream about him while I was sleeping up in his room. Before you woke me. The dream ended with him calling out to me . . . I'm sorry, I know this sounds terribly silly.'

'You're tired. Come, I think I will take you home after all.'

'No, Krishnan, hear me out. He fell off a precipice – and he called out to me, saying he was sorry. That was where the dream ended. Now that was before I knew what had happened, don't you see? How could I have known if he hadn't spoken to me?'

'Claire, I know you need to look for every straw of hope and belief, so all I'll say is that strange things happen when people are under stress or grieving in some way. They imagine things, they think and do irrational things. If such imagining helps them in any way to deal with what is happening, then I for one will not question them. So yes, if your dream helps you, then . . . then . . .'

'You're telling me politely that I'm going a bit loopy, aren't you?'

'Well, yes, I suppose I am.'

'Fine, that's OK. I'll say no more except . . .'

She hesitated.

'. . . Krishnan, I just want to say thanks for all you have said and done tonight. It must have been hard. Thank you. They wouldn't let me kiss my husband, but can I kiss you instead?'

She did so, lightly on his cheek, before he could answer.

'I'll call you,' he said, 'or come to your house tomorrow, but not before late afternoon. I'll be meeting with the others then to make an assessment. And of course I or

someone will be in touch should anything, anything signifi-
cant that is, happen. And Claire . . .'

'Yes, I know, you're going to say that I must be prepared
for the worst.'

'Not quite. Just don't let your hopes get out of control.'

'I'll do that, but I have to say that I know he will come
back. I know that and nobody will make me believe
otherwise.'

'You are a very strong and determined woman, Claire, so
I won't try to argue with you. Sleep well – are you sure you
don't want me to take you home?'

'Yes, Krishnan, quite sure. Good night.'

As she parked the car on the street outside the cottage, she
heard the church clock strike three. She felt wide awake,
merely noticing rather than in any way feeling the thick
frost that had formed. Inside, she found Rosie asleep on
the sofa. She went upstairs to Amy's room where, as usual,
she found her deeply asleep too, with the duvet and pillow
scattered across the floor. But she was warm: Rosie must
have made sure the central heating remained on. She put
the duvet back over Amy and lifted her head to put the
pillow back under it. She kissed her gently.

'Don't worry, we'll get him back, I promise you,' she
whispered.

'Claire?' came a voice from downstairs as she gently
closed the bedroom door.

She went down and embraced her friend. Rosie started
crying, her face already stained with mascara.

'Rosie, don't cry,' she said after a while. 'There's something important I need to tell you. Something's happened
since I spoke to you on the phone. Let's make some tea
and I'll tell you. It's very important.'

Once they had made the tea and sat down at the dining room table, Claire carefully recounted the story of the dream and what followed. Rosie listened with ever-growing interest. Claire knew she would, because Rosie was always talking about her own dreams – she was a regular and vivid dreamer, whilst Claire's were rare and, compared to Rosie's, rather dull. So, often when they met, usually at a coffee bar in the town, the conversation would focus on discussing interpretations of Rosie's latest dreams.

Being in her forties, single (an early marriage had ended long ago), tall, leggy, slender, blonde and attractive, men featured prominently in most of Rosie's dreams, but, disappointingly, men usually rejecting or even humiliating her in some awful way. This contrasted sharply with a frequent occurrence in the coffee-bar: an attempted pick-up, although again disappointingly, this was usually by deeply unattractive males, either well past their sell-by dates, or, at the other extreme, barely out of school uniform.

Rosie had got a date or two with some rare exceptions to these general rules, but only one had led anywhere, quite recently in fact, to a state where Rosie referred to the gentleman in question in endearing terms such as 'my man' and 'my sexy fella', although this latter came out as 'my sucksy filler', betraying Rosie's birth and childhood in New Zealand. Her accent, which, unlike Claire's, had stuck with her over the years, gave Christian constant pleasure. In fact, the image of what a 'sucksy filler' might be caused him to come close dying of laughter when Rosie first introduced the owner of the description to him.

'So what now?' Rosie asked her friend.

'I don't know,' said Claire, 'except that it tells me that he is certainly alive and that as far as I'm concerned, if anyone were to try to pull the plug, I'm not going to allow it.'

'What are the rules about that kind of thing?' Rosie asked.

'I don't know, but I'm pretty sure that as next-of-kin, or whatever it's called, I have to give my permission, don't I?'

'I would think so – better get some legal or medical advice I think. Do you know anyone?'

She paused and then pointed an arm in the air, triumphantly.

'Of course! Christian's friend Nick – he's a doctor! I'll speak to him tomorrow, today, I mean'

'And I've heard of cases,' Rosie said 'of people being on life-support machines for years. There was that case in America last year, now I think about it. A girl had been in a coma for years and years and the doctors wanted to, you know, to . . . switch the thing off. That's right, and the courts ruled in their favour, and then the President stepped in and made a new law to stop them. I'll get on the internet for you. There must be stacks of stuff about that kind of thing.'

The two friends now fell silent. Claire felt her energy draining, as if some unseen hand was turning down her own connection to life. She felt her belief in Christian's aliveness seeping away.

'It's hopeless,' she said.

'No it isn't,' said Rosie, reaching out with her hands across the table, 'hold my hands and listen.'

She did so.

'Claire, I love you and I love Christian. We'll see this through. I won't let you down. Now, I think you should go to bed and I'll go home, or I can stay here if you like, whatever.'

'Yes, I'll do that – you go. I'll be fine.'

Rosie knew better than to argue. She cleared up the cups and saucers and took them into the kitchen. Claire followed her and dried up while Rosie washed.

'I've just had a horrible thought, Rosie,' she said.

'What?'

'Money, that's what'

'What do you mean?'

'Rosie, that place, the Ashfield. We've paid two thousand for the operation. What's every extra day going to cost? Five hundred? A grand? We haven't got that kind of money, I mean . . .'

Now she cried. A saucer crashed and broke on the draining board. Rosie quickly cupped Claire's face in her foamy rubber gloved hands and spoke calmly:

'Claire, darling, stop, please. Money's the last thing to worry about now. To be honest, I thought about that before you came back. All I know is that we will deal with it. I don't know how, but we will. Now, I'm going to put you to bed. I'll come back early and get Amy up. I want you to do nothing but sleep. You're exhausted, look at you. Things always look black when you're tired. Now, come on, I'll take you up.'

She lay in the dark until she heard Rosie leave and then got up and went into Christian's study. His file, marked 'Operation' lay on the desk. She picked it up and went back to bed with it. She quickly found the hospital brochure:

> *'Under 'Pro-Fit's' unique fixed price guarantee, should your stay be longer for recovery purposes than we, you, or your admitting consultant anticipate, no extra charges will be applied; and in the unlikely event of there being a complication with the treatment you receive within 30 days of your leaving hospital, there will also normally be no further charges . . .'*

She read this several times. On first reading, she felt relieved, but then, on a second and third read, she wondered: 'for *recovery* purposes . . . '?; 'there will *normally* be . . . '?

She fingered quickly through the file, looking for the more detailed terms and conditions. Nothing. She put the file down and got up again. Downstairs, in her handbag, she found the pills. She swallowed one and went back to bed.

She woke to the sound of the screeching alarm and looked at the green display – four o'clock – as she silenced it.

Through the drawn curtains the thin light of a winter's day filtered. Strange, she thought, getting light so early, and then immediately the events of the night flooded helter-skelter through her head. She sat bolt upright and looked again at the curtains, and then at the clock. Now she saw a note beside it.

'Sorry to wake you like this, darling,' she read, *'I've set the clock for 4pm. You've been out to it all day and I thought it best to leave you. I've got Amy with me. She's fine. The doctor called and will call again at five. I'll bring Amy back this evening. Love, R.'*

At five precisely, the phone rang.

'Claire?'

'Yes, Krishnan?'

'I hope I haven't woken you?'

'No, I've had a long sleep and I feel fine now – must have been that little pill I took!'

'Good, I'm glad you did.'

As he said this it dawned on her that her sleep had been dreamless, and she felt her heart sink. The hand holding the phone dropped involuntarily to her lap.

'Are you there Claire?' she heard the thin tinny voice saying from her lap. 'Claire? Are you there, Claire?'

She raised the phone again to her ear.

'Yes, I'm here, Krishnan, sorry . . . what's the news? Tell me please. Good or bad. Tell me.'

'Claire, bearing in mind that it's still less than 24 hours since . . . since, er . . . since the event, the news is neither good nor bad. There is still brain activity, there is no doubt about that. That's all good. But to be honest, I have to say I'm not optimistic. Only time will tell. I know that's not what you would want to hear, but . . .'

She cut him off.

'Only time will tell?' she said, raising her voice, 'Is that all you can say? For God's sake!'

She slammed the phone down. It rang again straight away.

'Claire, please, I know this is terrible for you, but . . .'

'But what? But bloody what?'

'But you would want me to be honest, wouldn't you?'

She put the phone back into her lap again and drew a deep breath.

'I'm sorry Krishnan,' she said after a while, 'when will you know more?'

'I'll come round to your place tomorrow, late morning. We'll know more by then. Will that be OK?'

'Fine. Please call me when you know exactly when you'll come.'

'I'll do that.'

Later, she took another of the pills from her handbag, swallowed it, and went back to bed.

64

5

The Message

Cremation

'The casket is put into the top level of the cremator's chamber and then burnt. All ornaments and fittings are left on the casket, except the name plate. The fittings are burnt with the coffin as they are typically made of plastic. When the body is burnt, bones and calcium deposits drop through to the second level of the chamber. It takes one to one and a half hours to burn a body at a heat source of 900 degrees Celsius. About 80kg will burn each hour.'

Hallo darling. Listen to me. I'm sorry. I'm so sorry.

I can't see myself. I can sense myself but all I see is . . . I can't explain. You remember that time we stayed in Rapallo? That hotel room? The one where everything was white? Everything – bed, chairs, table, desk, curtains, everything. That's how it is here.

My hand hurts, but I can't see it. It feels is if it's pointing straight up, I don't know why. There's a lot I need to tell you, darling. There's so much I need to tell you.

Please, don't cremate me. Don't do that. I'm not really a Viking. We never talked about it. Why should we have? We didn't know this would happen. I've never liked it, cremation, I mean. When you're cremated, that's it. You haven't got much time before it happens. But if you're buried it gives you more time, because, well, it takes longer for you to go. If you cremate me, then all I've got is a few days. If you bury me, then I can talk to you like this for months. I want to talk to you, like you always wanted me to.

Something silly just came to me. You remember that Woody Allen movie, where he dies? I know you didn't like him much, and you never could understand why I liked Tommy Cooper, either, could you? What was the movie called – was it *Bananas*? No, something else, can't remember: was it *Sleeper*? Anyway, in the film he dies, and then reappears outside his girlfriend's window, with long white hair, dressed in a big white gown and holding a big scythe – you remember? His girlfriend was played by Diane Keaton, I'm sure. She opens her curtains and sees Woody, all dressed up, like I said. And she says: 'Woody . . .' (or whatever his name was in the film) '. . . it can't be you? I thought you were dead?' And Woody says, 'Yes, I am dead.' And she pauses for a moment, not sure what to say, and then asks, 'Woody, what's it like being dead?' And he then pauses, too, for a while, and says: 'Do you remember that chicken casserole we had at Kreisky's restaurant?' She looks puzzled, and then Woody adds: 'It's worse!'

Sorry I haven't told that very well, and maybe it's a bit tasteless. Like the chicken? Sorry, that's even worse.

I'm sure you will have talked to me since I went: it would be your way. I remember you sometimes used to talk to your Mum even all those years after she'd died. You used to do it a lot, for a long time, remember? But I can't hear you, darling. That means your mother wouldn't have either. Sorry.

There's so much I need to tell you. I don't know where to start. I won't try for the moment. I just want you to know that I love you. I probably didn't tell you that enough. I didn't say it often enough. I wasn't appreciative enough of all the good things about you. I was too critical. I didn't support you enough. I didn't talk to you enough. I didn't tell you what I was thinking.

Strange things keep coming into my head. You know I told you many times about what a good man my Dad was. I told the doctor he never hit me, but that isn't true. It was in the period after he was demobbed from the army, but before he got the job at the school. Like a lot of old soldiers, he got a job as a policeman, not an ordinary policeman, but what was called a 'War Department Police-man'. He had about a couple of years in the job, no, a bit more.

These 'policemen' were actually just security guards by another name. Their job was to guard this big place where secret weapons were produced, atomic weapons in fact. The police and some other people who worked in the place all lived on an estate just outside the big fence that went all around the whole area. Nobody had a car. When I got the scholarship to go to the grammar school, which was miles away, I used to have to get up very early and walk a mile to the bus stop, and the same coming back in the evening.

Dad didn't like the job. It was shift-work, 6 'til 2, 2 'til 10, 10 'til 6. There was a police social club at the side of the estate. Dad started to drink a lot. I was too young to understand this properly, but I often heard him and mum having rows, usually late at night, when he came back from the club.

A lot of the time Dad wasn't at all happy. The job must have been mindless – simply walking around a fence for eight hours at a stretch – and I guess the men had hoped for, or aspired to, better things. Dad did.

So they killed themselves. I remember at least three suicides, all on the 10 'til 6 night shift, all shooting them-selves – all the police were issued with revolvers. And those that didn't kill themselves drank a lot.

One day when I got back from school Dad shouted at me as soon as I came through the door: 'Come in here!' I was frightened as he hardly ever shouted. He told me to turn out my pockets, in one of which was a whole half-a-crown piece. 'Where did you get that? You stole it didn't you? You stole it from your mum's tin in the kitchen didn't you?'

Now I was really scared, because that is exactly what I had done, and had done many times before, too.

To cut a long story short, Dad made me take my trousers and pants off, put me over his lap, and gave me a thrashing with one of his slippers. As he administered each blow he repeated 'You – must – not – steal'. Afterwards I went up to bed and cried a lot. I used to take the money because at school everyone had money, everyone had better clothes than me, better shoes, better everything. Of course they had – they were all rich kids. Nothing was worse than going over to the tuck-shop with the others and having nothing in my pocket. But Dad never gave me the chance to say that. Nor did he ever get the chance to say how much he hated doing it, at least not to me. But I heard him say so to Mum that evening. And he wasn't drunk.

Several years later, after Dad had got the job at the school and we had moved to town and bought the house, courtesy Mum's dramatic victory on Criss Cross Quiz, and I was a Prefect and House Captain at the school, the matter came up again.

As a House Captain, one of my jobs was to mete out punishments. The ultimate punishment was the cane. So as to exert some control over what was an anarchic and often very brutal approach by some of the more thuggish prefects, the headmaster asked my Dad, as part of his duties, to witness every beating, figuring out (quite correctly) that his presence alone would be enough to deter any prefect from over-stepping the mark.

The day came when I had to administer my very first

beating. I remember it very well. First year boy, name Timothy Barrie. The canes used were very whippy things. Six firm strokes. Firm. Trousers on, but check for padding.

All ready. I was terrified, and so was young Barrie. Steeling myself to get on with it I looked at Dad, and at that instant, the memory of the beating he gave me came back to me. And I believe it came back to him as well.

'I can't do this,' I said, throwing down the cane and walking out.

'I understand,' Dad said to me later.

That's really as much as I can say now. I need to rest. I haven't got any energy left to explain this but, darling, please get the note out of my wallet and take it to Alfonso.

She woke, and without hesitating for a moment, got up and went straight to the study, where she sat at the desk, switched on the light, and wrote quickly: *mountain, thinks dead, chicken(!), Dad, Barrie(??), Alfonso, note, wallet.*

After a moment's hesitation she added: *cremation – no.*

Then she went back to her bed and lay awake for the rest of the night. Only as the curtains began to lighten did she sleep again.

'What are you smiling about?' It was Rosie, holding out a cup of tea.

'Another dream, Rosie. It is him. I'm sure of it. He's speaking to me. What's the time?'

'It's getting on for ten. Don't worry, I got Amy to the bus – I've just got back. Come on, tell me more.'

'Let me shower and get dressed, then I'll tell you. But it's good, it's very good.'

Under the shower she tried to think out what to do, but her mind was racing too fast and for some reason Woody

Allen filled her head and would not go away. She got out
and dressed quickly.

As she joined Rosie at the table, the phone rang. Rosie
pointed to herself with raised eyebrows and Claire indicated
assent. While she was gone, Claire helped herself to the
toast and coffee Rosie had made. She felt hungry. The
coffee, especially, smelled and tasted good.

She ordered her thoughts as she re-read her notes.

Rosie returned: 'Doctor, funny name, sounded like
Superman. Same one I spoke to yesterday. Says he'd like to
come round at eleven, if you're up to it. I said it was fine,
that alright?'

Her mouth full, Claire nodded. Once she had swallowed,
she said: 'Fine, that's good in fact. Now, let me tell you. But
shouldn't you be at work?'

'I'm suck – can't you see? I called in first thing.'

Claire smiled at the pronunciation.

'Thanks, you're a gem. Yes, I can vouch for the fact that
you look very sick.'

They laughed.

While Rosie ate, Claire related, as fully as she could
remember, all that Christian had told her, holding her
notes in front of her as she did so. She started at the end,
with the part about the note, and then went back from
there – the story of his own thrashing, and that of this
Timothy Barrie.

'Had you ever heard that before?' Rosie asked.

'No, not that I can remember . . . no, I haven't no, never
before. If it's true, then surely it proves that I'm having
more than strange dreams, doesn't it?'

'It would to me, not that I need convincing anyway.'

'Worth checking, don't you think?'

'How?'

'There's some old boys club – he gets a newsletter every
now and then. The Old Duntonians, that's what they are.

Maybe this Timothy Barrie is known to them. Maybe he'd remember. We could find out through the school, I'm sure. Worth a try?'

'Yes, we'll do that. But what about this note, in the wallet? Can we look?'

'We'll have to wait for the doctor to come: he'll have had it with him at the hospital, because he was paying by credit card. In fact Rosie, would you mind calling him for me and ask him to make sure he brings Christian's things?'

'Sure, let me do it now.'

It took only a minute or two. 'Done, sorted, caught him just as he was leaving,' Rosie said when she came back. 'Now tell me more.'

'Two other things,' Claire continued. 'He thinks he is dead. And he is very concerned that we don't, that I don't, have him cremated.'

'Why?'

'He thinks that it will give him more time. He thinks if we have him cremated, and I suppose you can see what he means. He'll be ashes, literally, within a few days. He thinks burial gives him longer. He says that there are things he wants to tell me.'

'So we think he's not dead, but he thinks he is. That's odd. Look Claire, there's something on that front that I want to put to you. Can I?'

'Go ahead.'

'Something's got to be said around the village. If not, you'll have people knocking on your door in no time. Everyone knows he was going into hospital. You simply won't be able to cope with telling everyone the same story over and over. Anyway, do you even know what the story you'd tell people is?'

'I guess you're right. Then there's his firm, and his ex-wife, oh, and a few friends here and there. Not many.'

'No kids?'

'No.'

'Well that's makes it reasonably easy then. But let's start here in the village. Claire, what I propose is that, when the doctor comes, I'll go out and do the rounds. I'll start at the pub. I thought about writing a short letter, but I think it's better if I tell people personally, and let the pub grapevine do the rest. Otherwise, they'll all come flocking down here. What I propose to say is more or less as it is: something happened, he's in a coma and that it doesn't look good. I know it's not what you feel, but I feel it's better to say it like that. Would that be alright? And if you like, I'll do the firm and the ex– as well, if it helps you.'

'No, I should do them. But do it as you've said. It's best that way. And without being rude, can you say that I'm not up to visitors or even sympathy right now, that I just need . . .'

'A bit of space, yes. I'll do that, of course I will. People will understand. It's going to be a huge shock to everyone. Anyway, I'll sort it.'

There was a knock at the door.

'That'll be superman. I'll get going.'

Claire introduced Rosie, who was quickly gone, to Krishnan in the doorway. He held a briefcase in one hand and a parcel roughly wrapped in brown paper in the other. They sat down together on the settee.

'Did you manage to sleep more since we spoke?' he said.

'Yes, very well in fact,' she said, and after a slight hesitation, continued, 'I know that you've got things to say to me Krishnan, but before you do, there's something I want to tell you. Is that OK?'

'Of course, go ahead.'

'I know you think this is daft, but in my sleep last night he talked to me again. I'm going to tell you this straight. One of the things he told me to do I'm going to ask you to

72

do right now for me. Presumably that's his stuff in the parcel, yes? It is? Well, will you please open it and find his wallet, which I'm sure must be there.'

'Yes it is, it's right on the top in fact.'

'Now, he said that in the wallet there is a note, which I must take to a friend of ours in Italy. Would you please take the wallet and look for the note? Let's go and sit at the table, then you can take everything out and we can see what there is.'

They ended up with several piles: one of plastic cards, another of a collection of miscellaneous foreign currency banknotes, all together in one pocket of the wallet, a small pile of credit and debit card vouchers and receipts, several old yellow post-it notes with what seemed to be telephone numbers on them, driving licence, three personal cards, including Krishnan's own, and, in the deepest recesses, a collection of two paper clips, several loose staples and one bent drawing pin.

But there was no note.

They looked at each other, and Krishnan saw her tears coming. As she cried, she banged her fists violently on the table several times and then hung her head low, the tears streaming freely.

'It can't be,' she sobbed, 'it must be here. It must be.'

Now, flailing her arms, she rendered everything on the table asunder. Pieces of paper and plastic flew into the air and dropped to the floor.

'Claire, this is hard, but you must let go. Your dreams are hopes, delusions. They are . . .'

She stopped him.

'Look,' she said, delving into the scattered banknotes, 'here it is.'

She held up a bank note. Yet it was only half a bank note, one edge cut in a zig-zag manner.

'It's part of a 10,000 lire note, from Italy,' she said. 'That is the note, I know it. I have to take it to Alfonso. It means something. What, I don't know, but it means something.'

While she said this, Krishnan sifted through the rest of the notes and papers, picking up those on the floor as he did so. There was no sign of the other half.

Against his will, he felt himself intrigued.

'You see?' she said, laughing now, half-crying at the same time.

Krishnan smiled. 'You had no idea it was there, before your dream I mean?'

'No.'

'Claire, would you mind telling me what else he said to you?'

She went through it again for him. He sat and listened attentively. This time – which she hadn't done with Rosie earlier – she included the Woody Allen part, and the chicken joke. He smiled at it, and at that moment Rosie came back. Krishnan immediately stood up until she had sat down at the table.

Claire waved the note at Rosie.

'We found the note,' she said, passing it to her friend before she continued her account of the dream to Krishnan.

When she had finished, Krishnan said:

'Well, we don't have to worry about cremation just yet. Let me bring you up to date. Claire, while the medication I mentioned to you may not have fully cleared his system by now, we are reasonably certain that it is not the cause of what is still unmistakable brain activity. While his hold on life is neither great nor strong, at this stage it would be unthinkable to ask you to, er . . .'

'Give my permission to . . . ?'

'Exactly.'

'So go on, tell me more.'

74

Krishnan took a breath.

'There's not a great deal to add. Christian is in a coma. For how long that will remain the case and with what eventual outcome . . . I simply can't say. Only . . .'

'Only time will tell?'

'I was trying to avoid saying that again, Claire, given, er, what you said yesterday.'

'I'm sorry about that.'

'No need to apologise. I quite understand. If there's one thing worse than bad news, it's what we, you, are dealing with now. Uncertainty. The unknown. All I can add is that in these kinds of situations it's best to keep your expectations down. I know I've said that before, and that it's not your nature, Claire, but . . .'

His voice tailed off and he brought his hands to his lips. Rosie put her arm around Claire's shoulders. They all fell into a silence that Krishnan eventually broke.

'This Timothy Barrie business – very intriguing. You're sure you knew nothing of it?'

'Yes, I'm quite sure.'

Silence descended on them again, and this time Rosie broke it.

'Claire, I've seen pretty well everyone in the village. Everyone is in shock but everyone understands, and Andy at the pub says he'll pass on any future news. He said if you want to come over anytime, you're welcome, but realises that you're not up to it right now.'

Krishnan stood up.

'I have to go soon, but, Claire, there's more that I need to say to you. First though, I suggest you follow up this Timothy Barrie business as soon as you can: I freely admit you have me intrigued. And the business of the note as well of course. In your situation focusing on something practical will help you, I'm sure.'

He sat down again and went on, 'I should not be doing

this, but I have to warn you that the Pro-Fit executives are already on the case, so to speak. I don't know if you're aware of the, er, contractual situation, but . . .'

'I've read the brochure stuff, but I don't have the detailed terms and conditions.'

'I have a copy of them. I'll leave them with you. But even from the brochure you'll be aware that this, Christian's situation I mean, is to say the least a grey area. Now, strictly in confidence . . .'

He hesitated, and then went on.

'. . . strictly in confidence let me tell you that Pro-Fit will make matters as difficult as possible. At present, so long as Christian's condition doesn't worsen, not that it could get much worse mind you, they won't, I feel, try to push the termination button. But I still wouldn't put it past them. What they will do is to use financial pressure.'

'Oh?' Rosie and Claire responded in unison.

'Meaning they'll push the interpretation of the terms and conditions to make you pay through the nose, and start paying soon. They'll argue, and I have to admit that they'll have a case, that while Christian's heart attack took place during what they call "recovery" it was an event in no way connected with the surgery I performed. I told you that myself, if you remember, and it is almost certainly the case. And if that's not enough, they'll argue that since he didn't leave hospital, he's not covered by the clauses in the brochure about eventualities *after* leaving hospital.'

Rosie looked perplexed. 'I'll explain after,' Claire told her. Turning to the doctor she said: 'Yes, I get the gist of it.'

Krishnan continued, 'In the first instance, they'll want Christian out of The Ashfield as soon as possible. There are only two intensive care beds there, only one of them with a ventilator. What they'll do is to suggest that he is moved to one of the centres they have that are entirely focused on, er

. . . intensive care. They'll suggest the one near Tunbridge Wells. It's only an hour or so's drive from here. If they do that, take it. I'll remain medically in charge of his case, in consultation with the intensive care specialists of course. If instead you move him into the public sector, which they will of course suggest to you as first preference, then I'll lose all involvement. It won't cost you if he's there, of course, but I would argue against it. By the way, let me add that I will not charge you a penny for my involvement. Let me make that clear.'

'That's very kind.'

'It's nothing. Now that brings me to a question. Did Christian by any chance have what they call "critical illness" insurance?'

'Yes . . . and no,' Claire replied.

'Meaning?'

'He had a very good policy, until last year. As you know, these things aren't cheap. It covered him for £50,000, I think, payable on critical illness. We decided it was far too expensive, so we cut it down. I think the lump sum payment is now £5,000.'

'Oh dear, that won't last long – maybe a week – but at least it's a start. Get onto them and make a claim. Give them my details.'

He picked up his card from among the mess on the table.

'They'll do nothing until they get confirmation from me of Christian's medical condition.'

'Did you say a week?' Rosie asked.

'Yes, maybe ten days or so at most, even without my charges. Now, what else? Yes, since as you realise my position is, shall we say, ambivalent at best, I cannot be seen as being on your side in all this. In reality, I am of course, hence this conversation, and no doubt future ones, but they must remain secret, in your interests.'

'Yes, I quite understand,' Claire said.

'So what you need, if you can find someone, is your own independent medical adviser. What's your GP like?'

'Fine, but I would prefer not to use her. But when Rosie and I were talking last night, I remembered Christian's friend Nick, who's a retired GP.'

'Then get hold of him, and, I suggest, quickly. Brief him and have him contact me. When Pro-Fit contact you about the move to Tunbridge Wells – and my bet is that will be today – say that you want Nick – was that his name? – to represent you in all medical matters relating to Christian, if Nick will agree to that of course.'

'I'll do that.'

'And finally, Claire, again not to put too fine a point on it, if you happen to have a lawyer among your friends and acquaintances, then get them involved too. No, not the family solicitor. A barrister preferably, a good one, one on whom £5,000 would go in a day!'

Looking at Rosie she said: 'That's not so easy, but, Rosie, I don't suppose your "sucksy filler" is a top lawyer by any chance?'

Rosie smiled and shook her head. Krishnan looked mystified.

'Then we'll find someone. I don't know how, but we will.'

Pausing only, at the front door, to pull the 'Pro-Fit Terms and Conditions' from his briefcase and give them to Claire, Krishnan left, remarking:

'The forecast is for snow later.'

Afterwards, Claire, dazed by all that had just happened, stretched out on the settee.

'So we found the note. Now what?' she said to Rosie.

They sat silently for several minutes.

'I'll tell you exactly now what,' Rosie eventually said. 'I've got it all sorted, well, mapped out at least.'

And she went on to tell her. As she did so, Claire closed her eyes but took it all in. It made sense.

By the time she met Amy off the school bus later that day, when it was indeed snowing, a lot of the sense had already become reality. As Krishnan had predicted, Pro-Fit, in the form of a person who introduced himself as 'Manager, Extended Services' had called. As Krishnan had also predicted, he first of all suggested a transfer to a public hospital, which she declined. He then asked for permission for the transfer to Tunbridge Wells, which she gave, although she was asked to go immediately to the Ashfield to sign a consent form.

'Out of the question,' she had said, very firmly. 'Besides having a seriously ill husband, I have a special needs daughter to care for and if you want the form signed, you must get someone here.'

A courier arrived within an hour.

Meanwhile Rosie had gone to her own house to get on with her duties, equipped with one of Claire's credit cards, and soon came back with the results: Claire to take the early BA flight from Gatwick to Bologna the next day (7 am departure, taxi booked to pick her up at the house at 5 am). Hire car booked with Hertz at Bologna. The return flight was booked for the following day, in the evening. Rosie also reported that she had spoken to the Citizen's Advice Bureau about lawyers. At the mention of the word 'barristers' however, the response was 'we don't deal with that kind of thing'.

Rosie made better progress with the Old Duntonians. Pretending to be Claire, she had explained to the head-master's assistant, who doubled as the secretary of the old boys' club, that her husband wanted to contact his old friend. Rosie was told that Timothy Barrie was indeed an old boy, but was on that part of the members list marked 'private' – meaning no contact details to be given out. But as Rosie ('Claire') elaborated a story – old school mate of her husband, now 'extremely critically' ill, anxious to speak to his old friend – the lady gave in, and supplied an email address, 'But please don't tell him I gave it to you.'

They composed an email to the man in question together, focusing on the caning, but also giving details of Christian's current condition.

On the Nick front, there was disappointment. His answering message indicated he would be away for a few days skiing. So all Claire could do was leave a brief message asking for a call back.

After that, she quickly called Krishnan, only to be told that he was 'in theatre'. But he called back almost immediately and she explained what was happening.

'In that case, Claire, please be assured that I will accompany Christian on the move. I understand that they plan to move him tomorrow morning. You'll be on your way to Italy then? Very well, that's good. Rosie will be at your home number? I'll keep her in the picture. Just know that no news is good news – is that clear? Fine – I'll speak to you when you get back . . . Claire, there's one more thing. I should have told you when I saw you. If Christian were to suffer another heart attack at any time, then that would be it. There's no way he would survive it. Any news of the mysterious Mr Barrie? . . . Good, that's good. Let's hope he replies.'

She then spoke to Palmer at the firm.

'I see,' he said, curtly, 'Please keep me in touch.'

With Jane, the conversation had been difficult, as they had only ever spoken twice in all the years. She had not known that Christian was going into hospital and was, in consequence, shocked, and quickly lapsed into prolonged tearful sobs.

When they ceased, Claire gave her the 'Rosie version' of the story and promised to let her know 'one way or the other', adding, 'Jane, the doctor's advice is that we should fear for the worst.'

The insurance company was helpful and faxed a form to sign, promising minimal fuss and delay. Claire signed and returned it.

Getting off the bus, Amy asked: 'Where's Christian?'

'He's still at the hospital,' she said.

'Good, home now,' said Amy, as she usually did, and they walked there through the snow.

Right on time the next morning she heard the taxi pull up outside as she was finishing dressing, although the snow somehow softened the sound of the clunking diesel engine. Rosie was still asleep, as was Amy. Only as she got into the car did she realise that her sleep had been dreamless.

But she did not worry. She was ready to go.

6

The Note

Le Marche *[mar-kay]:*

'Located in central Italy between the Apennines and the Adriatic, the Marche region enjoys a very varied landscape going from mountains through hills to beautiful beaches. In the hinterland there are fine, ancient medieval villages, such as Mercatauro, whereas the centres along the coast such as Pesaro are suited to summer tourism, thanks to the low waters and fine sandy beaches.

'The 'marchigiani' are hard-working, orderly people who have established a network of small industries of high quality merchandise in the textile and leather sectors, and in very special niches such as high quality paper and musical instruments. Agriculture relies mostly on vegetables, olive trees and vineyards, and there is a still-thriving charcoal industry, in inland areas such as that known as the 'Mountains of the Moon'.

'Before the Roman conquest the region was inhabited by the Piceni along the coast and the Gauls in the mountains. At the time of the barbarians' invasions, it was split in two, with the southern part under the Lombards and the northern under the rule of the Eastern Roman Empire. The name of the region comes from the establishment by the Franks of 'Marche', that is, Marquisdoms.

In the 14th century the region was divided into a number of small states including the Montefeltro and later the Della Rovere in Urbino. Then the Church gradually widened its influence in the region, until in the 17th century all the territory was ruled by *the Popes. In the Napoleonic period Marche was a republic. The region was annexed to Italy in 1860, during the 2nd War of Independence.'*

The pilot's forecast of the weather expected in Bologna proved correct. Up high, the sky had been bright and blue, but soon after she heard the flaps go to the first position for landing – Christian had explained the series of noises to her when they first flew together and saw her anxiety – the brightness quickly turned to gloom and then, near darkness.

She closed her eyes, as she usually did, fighting the anxiety. The plane seemed to hesitate slightly as the flaps went down still further and then she heard the rumbling of the undercarriage going down. At least it was smooth. She hated those landings where the plane bumped and bored its way into gusts or crosswinds, sometimes so violently she had been sick. She clenched her eyes tighter and swallowed hard yet again to clear her ears.

'Make yourself yawn,' Christian often said, 'it's the best way to make your ears pop.' Amy had learned this so well that landings had often been quite fun when they were all together, as she accompanied, or rather induced, her yawns with theatrical noises: 'yaaaaoooooooooorrrrggghhhhh.'

At last the wheels banged onto the runway and only the briefest of noisy reverse thrust (that's what he had told her it was) was needed to slow the aircraft. She realised that there must be many Italians on the plane as clapping rippled through the cabin.

'Do you know where is the car?' the young man at the Hertz office asked as she picked up the key and folder.

'Yes, I remember,' she said, although actually she was not certain. But she felt it would come back to her when she went outside.

'Buon viaggio,' he said, 'and please make attention on

the autostrada – la nebbia, how do you say, the cloud? It is bad.'

'The fog,' she said.

'Yes, the fog.'

Outside, it all immediately looked familiar and she walked purposefully across to the car park and down to the level where the hire cars were. A blue Punto, the young man had said.

As she got into the car she realised she was afraid. While she had driven sometimes when they had toured around the hills near the village, that was usually when they had their own car with them. Often, when they went up to Paglio to see the marvellous vista they never tired of, and then repair to the strange little bar, Christian had encouraged her to drive, so he could enjoy his beer. But only rarely had she driven a hire car, changing the gears with the other hand. It just didn't seem right.

At the first traffic lights her tenseness increased as she realised how thick the fog was: even the lights themselves were hard to discern. Take the right here and then right again onto the Tangenziale, she remembered, but it was hard to see.

'If you ever have to do this on your own, just get on the Tangenziale and follow Ancona.' Christian had once said, 'you'll remember the rest when you pick up your ticket at the San Lazzaro toll booths.'

All of which she did. Past San Lazzaro, the city traffic disappeared and she relaxed a little, sitting back from the edge of the seat now. The visibility seemed a little better. She drove slowly, buffeted by the big trucks that rumbled past her every now and then.

She realised she was hungry and stopped at the first Area di Servizio.

She got a ham and cheese piadina and went back to the car to eat it, even though the little bar was almost deserted.

She reached for her handbag and took out the note once more from the envelope she had put it in, as she had done several times on the plane. Half a 10,000 lire note, still as crisp and clean as it must have been when it had been cut. Yet again she turned it over and over. Not a mark on it – just the strange way that it had been cut. A small dob of melted cheese promptly dropped on it from the piadina. She quickly scratched it off and put it back in the envelope, sealing it this time.

Over an hour later, as she passed the first of the exits for Rimini and saw the sign for San Marino she started to cry. Instinctively looking across to the right, hoping that by some miracle the wonderful three-peaked mountain would appear, all that appeared in her mind instead were the clearest possible pictures of their honeymoon. The airy hotel room, the rooftop, where, what was it, what had they eventually agreed to call it . . . ?

'. . . come and have a look,' Christian had said that day soon after they arrived and he had gone off for his usual prowl around.

'What is it?' she had asked.

'Well, it's either a very big bird bath or a very small swimming pool, come, look,' he had said, thrusting out his chin, raising his eyebrows and pulling his mouth back into that distinctive purse-lipped grin of his as he did so.

He took her hand and led her through the door at the end of the short corridor. There, on the rooftop to which the door opened, was, well, what was it?

'Is it a spa bath?' she had asked.

'No – I've looked – there are no jets. It's just a big, ah, let's say, bird bath. And it's hot as hell – you feel!'

He was right. But, later, they used it after dinner in the evening, when the air had cooled. Then, the water was at a perfect temperature. They had champagne sent up. The view was stunning – they could see the entire sweep of the coast from north of Rimini right down to Fano and beyond, defined at night by the sea-front lights of white, interspersed here and there with the alternating reds, yellows and greens of traffic lights and the moving reds and whites of the traffic.

She screamed out loud as two bright red lights appeared suddenly in front. Yards, feet, in front. Behind, a horn, and then another, and then yet another, blared as each of the tail-gaters got their own frights in succession.

I can't do this, she thought. She slowed the car still more and eased forward again to the very forward edge of the seat, clenching and hunched over the wheel. She was breathing heavily.

'Uscita Pesaro–Urbino 5 km' the next sign she could read told her. Now, she was relieved to reach the toll booth, when normally she would be irritated when Christian shook her arm to wake her. This way into Pesaro seemed unfamiliar, and it was, as they always used to come into the city from the south, along the coast road from Fano. But once she got to the one-way system in the city centre, she picked up her bearings: left here, get into that lane there, watch out for the turn on the right, Viale Zara. There it was.

Even this familiar place seemed strange until she realised why: the summer's chaos of parked cars was missing. She could park where they always hoped to, and usually could not, next to the steps that led down to the beach.

She got out and stood by the railings, realising as her eyes looked up to scan the full length of the shoreline that the fog had gone, pushed inland by a gentle breeze from the sea.

'Coastal effect,' Christian had once told her.

Now bare of all but sand, she conjured up in her imagination the beach of the summer, of every summer for years past since they had found Bagno Tina at the end of Viale Zara: the lines of umbrellas, sunbeds and deck-chairs, the children, their chattering parents, the occasional amorous couple, the itinerant African hawkers. She looked out to where the now flat-calm (as indeed it usually was) grey (it always seemed so blue in the summer) water met the sand, to where it was deep enough for Amy to swim, with Christian beside her encouraging her: 'Kick Amy, kick, kick kick.'

Again the tears welled.

'Signora?'

While the sound of the voice behind her was gentle, it made her jump. She turned.

'Signola, sono Aldo, proprietario del Bagno Tina. Tutt' OK? I remember you. Where are your husband and daughter?'

She held out her arms. Now the tears flooded down her face. The man stood shock-still for a moment and then opened his arms and moved forward to embrace her in response. They remained locked together for what to her seemed a long time.

'Ch'è successo?' the man whispered, after some time, while trying gently and entirely unsuccessfully to move back from the tight grasp in which she held him. 'What is the matter?'

She opened her mouth but could not produce a sound. At that moment she simply felt a profound sense of comfort, her head on Aldo's shoulders, just where it was when Christian embraced her.

She pictured Aldo and Christian as they had been in the summer, last summer: Aldo in the old white 'Salvataggio' vest and red shorts he favoured, with his wide-brimmed battered straw hat, and Christian in his light blue swimming shorts, the ones that had once been dark blue and were now much faded by the sun. In her mind she saw the two of them in the late afternoon, under the shaded area, with all the children playing their chess contest, Amy watching one of the games, totally happy and relaxed – 'Look Christian, look, good' – Christian and Aldo moving around the tables, offering advice and, more than occasionally, adjudicating a fierce argument over the legitimacy of a move.

'Ch'è successo, signora? Dov'è il tuo marito e la tua figlia?' Aldo repeated.

She released him, stood back a little and took a deep, slow breath. She realised she had never seen him dressed in anything other than vest, shorts and hat: the thick sweater and corduroy trousers he now wore seemed peculiar.

Her hesitancy in responding – she stood as if paralysed, dumbly looking at him – had two causes. First, she did not know what to say. Second, even if she did know, saying it in Italian was going to be hard, impossible even.

'My husband is . . .' she paused for a long time, '. . . he is very ill . . .'

'I am sorry, signora. Is it serious?'

At last words came properly into her head.

'Yes it is serious, so serious that he is on a machine. It is only the machine that keeps him alive – do you understand? The doctors have told me that he is . . . to all intents and purposes' (Christian loved to learn how to say those kinds of expressions in Italian and incongruously it popped into her head at that moment) '. . . *dead* . . .'

Realising this was not accurate, she went on, 'No, that is the wrong word. He is in a coma,' hoping that the word was the same in Italian.

At this, Aldo covered his face with his hands and then pushed them back through his thin fair hair.

'In coma? Madonna . . .'

He repeated this twice as he moved forward to embrace her again. But she held up her hands, feeling suddenly calm now that she had got the words out. While it seemed strange, she even felt a momentary sense of self-satisfaction that she had managed to say what she had said.

'Aldo, I must go. It will soon be dark and I want to get to

Mercatauro this evening. I am OK now. Thank you,' she said, surprising herself at her firmness and clarity.

'Signora . . .'

'Please, Aldo, I am Claire, remember?'

'Sì, mi ricordo.'

She turned towards the car.

'Signora, please wait a moment. Listen. Please. Even before you reach Fano it will be dark. You are tired. You are unhappy. You need to rest. I beg you to stay here – my brother's hotel just along the beach is open . . .' he said, pointing towards it, '. . . and you can stay there. Then early tomorrow you can go to Mercatauro. Your husband would tell you that this is best.'

'But I have to be back in Bologna tomorrow evening to return to London. I must get to Mercatauro tonight,' she replied, although she felt, deep down, that what Aldo was saying – she had understood all of it as he had spoken slowly and clearly – made sense.

'If you sleep now, you can rise early. They say the fog inland will go during the night. And while it will be dark, there will be little traffic on the superstrada from Fano. You will be rested. If you leave at six, you can be in Mercatauro, easily, by seven-thirty. How long do you need to be there?'

She did not understand this last part.

'I don't understand,' she said.

'I am sorry – I am asking why you are going to Merca-tauro, and how long you wish to be there.'

'I need to see our friend there, Alfonso – the person we rent a villa from each year. I need to see him, to . . .'

She stopped abruptly, not sure what to say. The note would be too hard to explain.

'To . . .'

Aldo interrupted her: 'There is no need to explain . . . but will it be enough for you to see him just for a few hours and then go back to Bologna?'

89

'Yes, it will be enough, I'm sure. So long as I leave Mercatauro by three o'clock in the afternoon, I can get back to Bologna by seven ... that will be fine,' she said, realising that she had instinctively decided to take Aldo's advice. 'Could you please show me the hotel?'

She went to the car and took out her bag.

'Can I leave the car here?' she asked, and Aldo nodded.

'It will be safe, but if you wish, I will park it at the hotel later,' he said.

'Thank you Aldo, you are a kind man.'

Taking her bag, Aldo led her along the esplanade that ran behind his own beach huts.

'Signora, if you don't mind me asking, can I ask whether what happened to your husband had anything to do with his hand?' he asked as they walked.

The question surprised her. As she did not answer, Aldo went on, 'You see, when your husband helped me with the chess games for the children – you remember? – last summer, one of the children noticed that some of his fingers were not straight and asked why this was so. You know what children are like! I had noticed it myself but did not like to ask. Of course your husband made a joke of it. He said that once he had tried to cheat when he was doing something, and that as a result, his fingers had immediately become bent. The children all thought that was funny!'

Aldo said all this very clearly and she understood everything. She smiled – that was exactly the kind of thing Christian would have said.

'After that, every time there was an argument when the children were playing, they started using a gesture ...'

'A what?' she asked.

'A gesture, a sign, an expression, with the fingers.'

'Ah, I understand!' she said.

'A gesture of bending the fingers as a you-are-cheating

insult to the other person. It became a little joke with all of us,' Aldo said, as they reached the door of the hotel.

Inside, there was nobody around. Aldo disappeared through a door behind the small reception desk.

So that was why, she thought. Ever since last summer Amy had taken up gesturing with her smaller fingers every now and again, while saying a word she could only now understand. She had assumed that it was just another way of expressing her concern about Christian's fingers, because she often used to say 'Christian – hand alright?' Now she knew that the other word Amy sometimes used, along with the gesture, was the Italian for 'cheat'! She chuckled to herself.

Aldo and a person she assumed to be his brother appeared through the door, talking animatedly. Eventually, the brother spoke to her.

'I am Massimo. You are most welcome to stay. My brother has told me what has happened and I am very sorry. You will rest well here,' the man said. She could now see that they were indeed brothers: although Massimo was a good deal shorter than Aldo, the facial resemblance was striking. 'Now, would you like a coffee, or perhaps some wine? Please, as you say in English I think, it is "on the houses".'

'That would be lovely – a cappuccino, please,' she said.

Massimo left and Aldo gestured to the chairs and low table that filled most of the rest of the small lobby. They sat down. She put her hands together and raised them.

'Yes,' she said, 'it was all to do with Christian's fingers. While we were here last summer we decided that he should have the operation. He had been waiting nearly two years but the . . . the health system of the government in England is very slow.'

'It is the same in Italy,' Aldo said.

'So he went to a private hospital, where it cost two thousand pounds sterling,' she went on.

'Madonna . . . due mila sterline?' Aldo whispered.

'Yes.'

'Just for two small fingers?'

'Yes.'

'And what happened?'

Again she hesitated, realising that once again this would test her Italian. She remembered Christian advising her that if you didn't know a word, improvise – such as with words ending in '-ation', try '-azione'. So she plunged in.

'I was told that the . . . operation . . . was successful, but there was a, a . . . complication . . . something to do with his heart. He never regained consciousness – how do you say it? He went into a coma, a profound coma. The doctors say that it is unlikely that he will ever recover.'

Massimo returned with a tray. Aldo started talking to him and she listened at first, gathering that he was telling his brother what she had just told him. Massimo occasionally shook his head and glanced at her. But soon a combination of the speed of the language, her own lapsing concentration and growing tiredness, and the fact that they seemed to have moved on to some other subject, caused her to lose interest. She sipped at her coffee and closed her eyes.

After some time she felt Aldo's hand on her arm.

'Signora . . . Massimo will cook something for you, then you should sleep,' he said, gently. 'He will wake you for breakfast – is six o'clock okay?'

Looking past him she saw through the glass doors that it was already dark outside.

'Let me just sleep now,' she said. 'Six o'clock will be fine tomorrow.'

In her room, fiercely lit with horrid fluorescent brightness, she asked Massimo to open the wooden interior shutters. Within a few minutes she was asleep, her bag unopened, the door unlocked.

She awoke to the sound of tapping. Before she had realised that it came from the door, it opened a little.

'Signora,' a woman's voice said, in English. 'Please come to the first floor for your breakfast'

She felt very awake, remembering immediately where she was.

'Thank you, I will come soon,' she said.

She showered quickly. Once dressed, she opened the doors to the balcony and realised that the room overlooked the beach and the sea, although in the dull glow of the street lights she could only sense rather than see them. The air was still and very much colder than it had been the previous day. She shivered and retreated inside, and then put on a minimum of make-up before going downstairs.

Massimo awaited her in the breakfast room, but she could hear other voices through the door that led into what she presumed was the kitchen.

'Buongiorno, signora, I hope you have slept well?' Massimo asked.

It was then that she realised that Christian had once again not spoken to her in the night. Her momentarily dismayed look registered with Massimo.

'Everything is alright?' he asked.

She fumbled in her bag, and found her mobile phone. No message left. Surely everything was alright? Surely Krishnan or Rosie would have contacted her if there had been any change?

'Signora – coffee, tea, chocolate?' Massimo asked.

'I would like tea please, very strong tea, with cold milk, grazie,' she said.

'I do not understand, signora – tea *forte?* What is it? Tea with grappa perhaps?'

'No. Just tea with two bags, please, due bustine.'

'Oh, due bustine, forte, benissimo.'

He went off and her mind went back again to the honeymoon in San Marino. There, at breakfast the first morning, after the champagne and warm moonlit bath of the night before, Christian had asked for strong tea for her, in both Italian and English. The waiter, a tall, old, balding and very dignified man, had insisted on communicating with them in English, quite good English, but by no means perfect English, at dinner the previous evening. Now, he acknowledged the request with a slow, graceful, single inclination of his head.

Returning soon, and placing everything on the table with a great smile and flourish, the waiter addressed her:

'For la signora, tea . . . with two baggages!'

They both burst into laughter. The waiter flushed and looked affronted.

'Something is wrong?' he asked.

'I am so sorry, signore. We do not mean to offend you, but . . .' Christian said, going on to explain to the waiter, in a mixture of Italian and English, the difference between 'baggages' and bags, and in particular, tea bags, to such effect that the waiter himself started laughing. Every morning thereafter, the waiter not only repeated, but, by clearly making some effort to study a dictionary, indeed developed the joke.

'Tea with two suitcases' he said one morning, and even 'Tea with two old bags' another. Encouraged and emboldened by the mirth this produced, on their last morning he brought no bags.

'This morning the bags are under your eyes, signore,' he said to Christian. They all roared at the boldness of it.

She smiled now at the memory. Massimo brought the tea as she did so and looked at her quizzically.

Christian's intrusion on her morning did not end there. Now she remembered his own gaffes. Her nephew had once joined them for a few days at the villa, and Christian introduced him to Alfonso. As he did so, the faintest flicker of a smile twitched at the side of Alfonso's mouth.

Afterwards, Christian checked his dictionary, knowing from Alfonso's reaction that he must have got something very wrong.

'You know what I've done?' he said to her, later, 'I've introduced him to Alfonso not as your nephew but as your nipple!'

Then there was the time Christian was telling Alfonso how much they liked the beautiful sideboard that had appeared in the villa since their last visit. Again Alfonso's mouth had twitched, but this time he spoke.

'My dear Christian,' Alfonso had said. 'Please do not say that to my wife. She will be very upset. What you are telling me is that you like the beautiful *lover* that I have installed in the house!'

Now Claire laughed at these memories, as loud as the three of them had laughed at the time, so loud now that Aldo, Massimo and a young woman appeared at the kitchen door, all looking rather anxious. She gestured with her hand to indicate there was nothing wrong.

'A happy memory,' she said.

'That is good,' Aldo said, 'now, may we discuss something with you? We have a plan.'

They joined her at the table. At a sign from Aldo, the young woman spoke, in English.

'I am Maria,' she began, 'the daughter of Massimo. I studied English at Bournemouth – you know it? – two years ago. My father and uncle have told me what has happened to you and I am very sad for you. I hope you didn't mind that I opened your door just now, but you had not locked it.'

Claire shook her head gently to encourage the young woman. As she did so, she took in her finely drawn facial features, her jet-black, bob-cut, hair, and her smooth, light olive complexion. She wore a black polo-neck sweater and dark green, tight-fitting jeans. She went on:

'Probably you don't remember me but I saw you and your husband and daughter one day at the beach last year. I remember you. Now, allora, we have discussed things between us and we have a proposal to make to you. We all feel that while you have, how do you say – obviously? – had a good sleep in the night, we feel . . . we feel that today you should not go on your own to Mercatauro and then all the way back to Bologna. And we have heard that there may be snow on the way. It will be too much for you. When did all this happen to your husband?'

'Just three nights ago,' she replied.

'Then,' Maria went on, 'it is more necessary still for you to listen to us. You must not try to do all this on your own. We propose that I should take you to Mercatauro today. I will drive you in my car. You leave the hire car here and then when we come back you only have to go from here to Bologna. I can help you in Mercatauro with translation, perhaps. I hope it will make it easier for you, and it will be good for me, for my English. If you agree we can go now.'

Claire breathed out and looked intently at each of them in turn. Each nodded their heads vigorously as their eyes met.

'You are so kind, so very kind,' she said, in Italian, 'I will go with you, thank you.'

'Brava, brava, signora,' Aldo said, loudly.

'Can I tell you something?' she went on, now speaking in English to Maria, 'When I first came to Italy, to Rome and

Florence, many, many years ago, I hated Italy, I hated Italians. I was pushed. I was robbed. I was cheated. But when Christian brought me here again years later and showed me his love of this country, he told me that you do not see the real Italy in Rome or Florence or Milan or Naples, or even in Tuscany for that matter. He told me you see it in the people, and especially in the people of Le Marche . . .'

Maria translated.

'Grazie, signora,' Aldo now said.

'No, I must thank you,' she said, and then blushed with embarrassment.

'Andiamo. Let us go,' Maria said, abruptly, 'it is already after seven.'

Only when they had got onto the superstrada after Fano, as the sky began to lighten properly, did they speak.

'Tell me what you do, Maria,' she asked.

'In the summer, I work for my father in the hotel, with my brother and younger sister. I do the reception. That's why my father suggested that I do an English course – we have a lot of English people at the hotel in the summer. You will know my brother because he works for my uncle at Bagno Tina in the summer. He is quite a simple boy so he helps in the kitchen there and also keeps the beach clean every night and morning.'

'I must know him – what does he look like?'

'He has a big scar on the side of his face, from the accident that he had, the one that damaged his brain,' Maria replied, sadly.

'Of course, yes, I remember him – he is a very gentle boy – and he was also always watching out for Amy . . . and your sister?'

'She is only fifteen, so she is still at school. In the summer she helps with the cleaning in the hotel. She likes me to teach her English. She is very, how do you say, bright?'

'Yes, that's right.'

'. . . so my father hopes she will go to university, perhaps in Urbino, which is where our family comes from.'

'And what do you do in the winter?'

'I work part-time in the big furniture store in Fano – we passed it just now. Today is one of the days I don't work, that's why I can help you.'

'And your mother?'

'She died not long after my sister was born.'

Claire put her hand on Maria's and gently squeezed it. Her skin felt soft to the touch.

'It's getting colder,' Maria said, and within a few minutes the first flakes of snow appeared. By the time they reached the junction at Ferrano, it was snowing quite heavily.

'Take the left turn here, Maria,' Claire said.

'Yes, I know,' Maria said, 'I have a friend in Arezzo, so sometimes I come this way, over the pass after Mercatauro, when I go to see her – but not in the winter of course, when the pass is closed.'

As they travelled up the valley the snow continued, but just as they passed Villanova, it stopped and within a minute or two, dazzling bright sunlight from a clear blue sky appeared, revealing a pure white snow-covered landscape. She felt her spirits rise, as they always did when they reached this part of the journey, just a few minutes away from Mercatauro, where the valley's width increased and where the hills on either side seemed to rise more softly than they did both lower down and further up towards the pass. Here, in the summer, there were usually huge fields of sunflowers. It was the softness of the place that they loved. Under the thin covering of snow, the softness seemed greater still.

'I've never seen it so beautiful,' Claire said, 'even in the summer.'

Maria looked across at her and smiled.

Reaching Mercatauro, a lump came to Claire's throat as she directed Maria into and then through the piazza, and then across the old Roman bridge and up to Alfonso's house. She was relieved to see that his car was outside and that the door to his office was ajar, the way he always left it when he was in. Smoke curled reassuringly from the kitchen chimney.

As she reached out to knock on the door, it opened, to reveal the diminutive Alfonso, who quickly broke into a broad smile as he saw her.

'Salve,' he said with delight, 'what a marvellous surprise to see you . . .'

But even as he said this, his expression began to turn from pleasure to concern as he looked past her:

'. . . but where is Christian, where is Amy – you have left them at the villa perhaps?'

Then he saw Maria in the driving seat of the car, where she had remained. Now his expression was one of puzzlement. Claire turned and beckoned to Maria to join them. As she did so she heard Valentina's voice from inside the house: 'Alfonso, who is there?'

'Come down,' called out Alfonso, 'it is Claire! No, wait, we will come up.'

As he spoke, Maria joined them.

'This is Maria,' Claire said, 'she is helping me. She will explain to you.'

Alfonso greeted her, though somewhat warily. His usually pink face had reddened and he reached nervously to scratch his neck under the collar of the shirt (blue, as ever, Claire noted) that he wore. Strangely, beads of sweat appeared on his brow and bald head, even in the cold. He motioned them to go in.

At the top of the little metal spiral staircase, Valentina greeted her happily and warmly, kissing her on both cheeks and holding both her hands, but saying nothing. Claire introduced her to Maria.

In the kitchen they sat around the table, all silent, nervous, expectant. A small fire burned in the grate, and Claire realised why Alfonso had been perspiring: it was hot in the house, hotter still here by the fire in the kitchen. Alfonso drummed his fingers on the table and then lit a cigarette.

'Coffee?' Valentina asked.

Claire knew she had to take the initiative.

'Dear Alfonso, dear Valentina,' she began, 'I am afraid that I have some bad news. Because my Italian is not very good, I am going to ask Maria to tell you what has happened and also why she is here with me. Maria speaks very good English, so I am sure it will help us all.'

'All these years I have known you and I still cannot speak a word of English. This makes me feel bad,' Alfonso said, shaking his head and staring fixedly down at the table. Claire touched his shoulder as he spoke.

'But we are still good friends, are we not?' she said, turning her head towards him. But he still gazed down at the table. She got up from her seat, went to where Valentina sat and placed her hands on her shoulders, squeezing them gently as she did so.

'Please tell us what has happened, Maria,' Alfonso said, 'and Valentina, yes, let us have coffee please.'

As Valentina started to get up, Claire, still standing behind her, pushed her gently down.

'No,' she said, 'I will make the coffee while Maria talks to you, let me, please, please let me.'

Without giving time for anyone to disagree, Maria started to tell the story, and as she busied herself behind the kitchen counter, Claire listened. She had her back to them and felt it best to keep it that way as much as possible. Maria, she heard, began by getting straight to the point: that Claire's husband was 'on the point of death' – that was how Claire understood the expression she used – and that it was only a machine that was keeping him 'perhaps alive, perhaps not', as Maria put it.

At this point Valentina started making huge sobbing noises, like somebody winded trying to catch breath. The noises quickly got louder and louder. They forced Claire to turn to look. Valentina had slumped forward across the table, reaching out to Alfonso, who now held both her hands, still staring down at the table. Maria had put her arm across Valentina's shoulders and had stopped talking. Apart from the huge heavings of her chest that accompanied Valentina's sobbing, it was as if this was a frozen frame on a film. Claire, too, stood motionless. She felt horrified at the sight and sound of such pain, but strangely unemotional herself. She turned back to the coffee machine, placed two cups under the spouts, and pushed the button.

After some time, perhaps a minute or so, as Valentina's sobs ebbed a little, Maria continued, now telling the story of how her uncle had found Claire the previous day, and how the plan that brought them both here had evolved and been put into effect.

'That was very good of you,' she heard Alfonso say to Maria.

'You would have done exactly the same I am sure,' was what she took Maria to say in reply. She put two more cups under the spouts and took the first two to the table on a tray.

As she did so, Valentina raised herself from the table. Where her face had been, the tablecloth was soaked.

'Come, Valentina, Alfonso, you have these first two,' Claire said.

As she returned with the other two cups, Valentina turned to her, now rubbing her eyes with her hands. She seemed to have aged ten years in five minutes: her smooth complexion always made her look nearer forty than fifty. Now she looked sixty. 'Where is Amy? How is she?' she asked, hoarsely.

'Do you understand what she is asking?' Maria added.

'Yes, I understand,' Claire said, 'Please tell Valentina that while I am away, Amy is being cared for by a good friend of mine who has looked after her many times in the past. So she is safe, and, I am sure, very happy. She does not know what has happened, not yet anyway. I don't know how I could get her to understand what has happened. And Maria, please explain that we do not have much time here, that we should be away by, let's say, two o'clock at the latest.'

While Maria spoke she cleared away the coffee cups and then returned to the table. Alfonso asked a question she did not fully understand as she only properly heard the end of it.

'Claire,' Maria said, 'Alfonso is asking whether there is any reason why you have come here, other than to tell them your sad news. I think what he is really asking is whether there is anything they can do to help you, whether you need help.'

Claire realised that she had left her handbag in the car.

'Please tell them there is a reason, but first I need to telephone to Amy's carer: Valentina's question has reminded me that I have not called her since I left. Please let me get the telephone from my bag from the car, make the call, and then I will tell them why I have come.'

Maria translated. Alfonso spoke, pointing to the hall where their telephone was.

'He says you can . . .'

'Yes, I understood, but no, I will use my own phone . . . it will only take a moment, please wait here.'

In the car she first found the envelope containing the

note. Then she switched on the phone, waited while it registered – she had had the sense to bring Christian's expensive roaming phone with her – and then called Rosie.

'Everything's fine,' Rosie said, 'but as usual she keeps asking where you and Christian are. What do I say about Christian?'

'Just tell her that Christian is sick, she understands that.'

'OK. How are you coping? Where are you now? Are you in Mercatauro yet?'

'Yes, I'm here. Just got here. I'm fine. Got to rush. I'll tell you everything when I get back tonight.'

'Sure. Oh, by the way, nothing from Mr Barrie yet, and Krishnan rang to say that everything is fine and Christian's move will not take place until later today.'

She went back into the house. In the kitchen the three of them were talking. Valentina had obviously freshened herself up and looked more composed now. All three looked at her, expectantly, as she came in.

'Amy is fine,' she said as she sat down.

She took the envelope from her bag and passed it to Alfonso.

'I thought so,' he said, but simply placed it before him, unopened. 'Now,' he went on, 'Maria, I do not wish to cause any offence, but I must speak to Claire alone. Can I suggest, can I request, that my wife takes you for a short walk for a few minutes? It is a beautiful day outside now.'

'Of course, I understand,' Maria responded.

Valentina directed a knowing and encouraging smile at both Alfonso and Claire.

'Andiamo,' she said to Maria.

When he heard the door slam, Alfonso opened the envelope and took out the note.

'Yes, as I thought,' he said, as he laid it on the table. He got up and went to the sideboard and took out another envelope, which he gave silently to Claire:

'Please open.'

On the envelope, in Christian's handwriting, it simply said 'To whom it may concern'. He had used his favoured green pen, she saw.

She opened it, taking out a handwritten letter, which she started to read.

The familiar handwriting, in Christian's favoured green ink, caused her to pause a moment and breathe deeply. Its date indicated that it had been written when they were here the previous year:

> *Alfonso will show you something that now belongs to you. He will show you what you might like to use it for, or rather what it would have been for if I were alive. But if I am not, then you should do whatever you want or need to with it. It is yours.*
> *C*

Looking up, she saw that Alfonso was now standing.

'Come,' he said, and led her back down the spiral stairs to his office. There, he removed a large framed architectural drawing from the wall, which revealed an old-fashioned metal safe. He fiddled with the two dials, opened it, and took out a cardboard box, which was taped up. He put it on his desk, sliced the tape open and then tipped it up.

She gasped as large quantities of banknotes spilled out, Italian 100,000 lire ones, British 50-pound ones, and American 100-dollar bills.

'What?' was the only word that came to her.

'About five hundred thousand sterline, I think,' Alfonso said, in a calm and matter-of-fact tone. 'Maybe more.'

'But, but how?'

'Every year there was more. Sometimes a little, sometimes a lot. Sometimes sterline, sometimes Americano, sometimes lire. Sometimes it came by courier. I thought you knew. Valentina knows.'

As if on cue, Valentina's voice floated down the stairs: 'We are back! We will wait up here!'

'Now,' Alfonso went on, 'let us put all this away and go. I have to show you something else.'

He called up the stairs to Valentina, but Claire was not listening, even though he spoke loudly. Her hands trembled and her head began to fill with questions.

Alfonso scooped up the money, took the letter and the note which Claire had had in her hands all the time, and by the time Valentina and Maria came down, everything was back in the safe and the drawing back over it.

'Let us make a short trip,' Alfonso said to Valentina, winking at her. 'We need to show Claire something. We will all go. It will not take long.'

Claire guessed he was taking them to the villa, but soon realised, as he turned off the main road and onto a gravel track, not only that she was wrong, but what the real destination was. Sitting in the back with Maria, she found Alfonso's eyes looking at her from the driver's mirror, where hers met his. She blinked once, for long enough for him to know that, yes, she now knew the answer to one question.

Soon, they reached the old farm buildings and got out to take in the view of the village they offered, the terracotta-red roofs now apparent as the snow had been melting quickly under the sun. Only last summer, Claire recalled, she and Christian had spent time exactly at the spot where she now stood, as they did every summer.

'It's a beautiful view,' Maria said, taking her hand.

'Yes, this is a very special place, we have coveted it for years now. We hoped one day it might be possible to buy it, but of course we . . .'

She stopped. Reverting to Italian, and now turning to direct her words at Alfonso, she went on:

'. . . we, we never had the money and the owner did not want to sell.'

'I see,' Maria said, while Alfonso thrust his head forward, raised his eyebrows, and spread his hands wide, saying, 'and too many scorpions too! Here we are in the "mountains of the moon".'

Soon, they were back in Alfonso's house. Valentina asked to be dropped off in the piazza to buy something for lunch, and Maria went with her.

'Claire,' Alfonso said, as he put more logs on the fire in the kitchen, 'every year I have asked the owner if he will sell. Every time, he said no. But he died two months ago.'

'Yes, I remember he was very old.'

'Well, only last week his son came and told me that he was willing to sell and asked me if I was still interested. Christian and I agreed I should never reveal that it was you that wanted to buy. I always told them that I wanted it for my own family. Otherwise the price would be much higher.'

'Yes, I can see that.'

'Claire – the price is good. There will be more than enough to buy it and for me to do the restructure, the renovation. Even then, there will be plenty left. But we will have to move quickly or we may lose it. I know that this is not a good time to ask. Maybe you need the money now for other things. Maybe . . .'

Again, he spread his hands wide and raised his eyebrows. They looked at each other for a few seconds, until Alfonso spoke.

'Did Christian ever show you the plans for the renovation?'

'Plans? No.'

'I did them last year for him. Would you like to see them?'

'Yes.'

Alfonso led Claire back down the staircase to his office,

where he rummaged around in a stack of rolls of paper in a corner.

'Eccoli,' he said, rolling out the papers on his desk.

There were many sheets, which Alfonso went through one by one. The last was a map of the buildings and the surrounding land that would be included in the sale, Alfonso explained. 'Olive trees here, and vines here, for your own wine. And here, the vegetable garden.'

She noticed a small cross marked in green beside the olive tree area.

'What is that?' she asked.

Alfonso lowered his head, wiping both eyes with his hands.

'It is where he told me he wanted to be buried,' he said, choking.

Their silence was broken by Valentina's voice floating down from upstairs: 'Lunch is ready!'

'Alfonso, I need to think,' Claire said, 'There is so much to think about. I hope you understand.'

'Of course.'

'Can I ask one thing?'

'Of course – anything. What is it?'

'May I have Christian's letter, please, to take with me? I will call you with my decision as soon as I can.'

'That is fine,' Alfonso said. 'I will do everything that is necessary here. Now, please stay and have lunch with us before you go. I will get the letter for you. Do you want the plans as well?'

'No, just the letter please, and the banknote.'

7

The Questions Begin

While it was nearly midnight when Claire turned the key in the door, Rosie was awake. Very much awake.

Claire, on the other hand, was tired, very deeply tired. In the taxi, the heating had been up high, further deepening her feelings of fatigue.

Now there was Rosie to deal with, not just a very awake Rosie, but one who would no doubt have her own questions.

But no, there were none, at least not to begin with.

'There's good news,' Rosie said, 'sit down and I'll tell you.'

'Christian?' she asked as she sank into the settee.

'No, but he's fine and the move has gone fine. Superman called earlier this evening and told me. He specifically asked me to let you know that there had been no deterioration. Apparently Christian's temperature went up rather a lot on the journey, but Superman said that that was to be expected, and had already gone down more or less to normal again.'

'Fine. So what's the good news then?'

'Well, my little darling, there has been a response from Timothy Barrie. I've read it and printed it out. I hope you don't mind.'

She waved a sheet of paper.

'And?'

'And, and, and, our man is not any old ordinary Timothy Barrie, sweetie!'

At this she opened her arms wide, waving the paper vigorously.

'What we have is a reply from *Sir* Timothy Barrie, Sir Timothy Barrie *QC*, Sir Timothy Barrie *big-time barrister*! Sir Timothy Barrie *just-the-man-we-need* darling! Have a look!'

She held out the sheet of paper to Claire.

My dear Claire (if I may)

I was most distressed to receive your email. I am sorry that I can, here, only reply briefly as I am in the middle of leading the prosecution in a most difficult murder trial. Let me just give you some assurance, however, on the key points.

First, you husband did save me, if temporarily, from a beating. I still recall the incident, and in consequence, feel a debt of gratitude for his actions. We remember it together when we meet at Old Duntonians dos from time to time.

Second, while it seems to me utterly fantastic that his 'communication' transmitted this incident to you (a more rational explanation would surely be that he told you about it previously and you have 'remembered' it in your dream), I hear fantastic claims made in court very often and have to admit that they can be true. It is not for me to make a judgement on these matters.

In the meantime, please do not hesitate to contact me if and when you need any help. I have a hunch that there may be some legal matters that may arise, given Christian's current condition. My complete contact details are beneath my signature, below, and I will brief my clerk to treat any call or message from you as most urgent. I pray, however, that Christian makes a full recovery. This is no doubt a most stressful time for you. My thoughts will therefore be with you at all times.

Yours sincerely
Timothy Barrie QC KCMG

Claire read it twice and then heaved a huge sigh.

'How wonderful,' she said, 'what a sweet man he sounds!'

'There's more,' Rosie went on. 'I hope you don't mind but I've replied already. Here it is, and his reply. As you'll see, I've given him the full details and asked him he if would help with legal advice and representation, and he replied straight away. Here, look.'

Claire read them quickly: 'You're an absolute wonder!'

Rosie joined her on the settee, took the emails and read them again herself: 'We definitely have a new friend in Timothy Barrie. And a KCMG isn't just any old knighthood, you know, it's the top one!'

'Really?'

'Yes, and I've looked him up on the internet. He's done some very big trials, you know, including that awful one last year – the road rage one where the bloke got out of his car at some traffic lights and beat the two people in the car behind him to death – you remember?'

'No, Rosie, I can't say that I do, not right now. Anyway, any other news?'

'Not really, but, oh, there was something in the post today. I put it somewhere. Must be up in the study I think. I also printed out some of the stuff about our new-found knight in shining armour. I'll go and look.'

Energised and brightened by the conversation with her friend, and the warm-but-comfortable temperature in the house, Claire went to the fridge and poured two glasses of white wine, wondering at the same time if she felt like eating. No, she quickly concluded, much too late.

'Here we are,' Rosie said as she joined her in the kitchen. 'It's from India, addressed to Christian.'

'Oh? Must be to do with his work I expect.'

Now it was a rule – of her own making – that she never opened Christian's letters, but after a moment's hesitation while she looked at the hand-written envelope and realised that what was inside was a card, she reached in the drawer for a knife and slit it open. She always opened mail in this way, hating the mess that resulted from tearing envelopes apart, especially the way Amy tore them open, which resulted in a very large number of small torn fragments of paper all over the floor.

They returned to the settee in the living room, where Claire took out what indeed proved to be a card.

On its cover was a sketch of an Indian woman dancing, her arms outstretched, palms upturned and fingers curved gracefully back, her sari a deep, rich purple, her delicate feet bare, and her long black hair flowing over her shoulders.

'Beautiful,' Rosie said.

Claire opened and read the short handwritten note:

Dear Christian-Bhai
    All of us at Gharana Kathak Kendra wish you all the best for successful operation and speedy recovery.
    R

'Must be from one of the organisations Christian works with,' Rosie said.

'I guess so – Gharana Kathak Kendra – doesn't ring a bell, though.'

'What's the postmark?'

She looked carefully at the envelope. 'Looks like New Delhi doesn't it?'

Rosie took it: 'Yes, I think so. That's where he used to go a lot isn't it?'

'Yes.'

'What a nice thought of them,' Rosie said.

'Yes it is,' she said, turning the card over. On the back cover was printed:

Kathak is the most popular form of Indian classical dance. In February each year many of the most famous Kathak dancers gather in New Delhi to perform over a week-long festival.

111

Below this a rubber stamp had been roughly applied, conveying what appeared to be an address but too partial and indistinct to be legible.

'Strange,' said Claire.

'Maybe Superman, whatsisname, Krishnan, might know something. He's from India isn't he?'

They both picked up their glasses and sipped.

'Now,' Rosie said, 'are you up to telling me your news?'

'Not really, but yes, I'll tell you what I know, as far as I can.'

'Leave it 'til tomorrow if you like, darling – you look all in.'

'Yes I am, but the news from our barrister man has perked me up, I must say.'

'Let me fill us up, and then I'm all ears.'

Claire gave her account, the details and length of which surprised even the narrator. Then Rosie, who had consumed the whole of her second glass while Claire spoke, and even replenished it again at one point, put her hands to her face and blew out fiercely through them.

'Yes,' Claire said, 'quite.'

'I don't believe it. How much did you say?'

'Over five hundred thousand pounds, according to Alfonso, in different currencies.'

'Like?'

'Pounds, US dollars, lire, maybe other things. I didn't exactly look carefully, to be honest.'

They both sipped again.

'Where on earth . . . ?' Rosie began.

'Exactly, where on earth did he get the money? We've never had that kind of money,' Claire said, 'or rather, not to my knowledge. He never said anything about this to me. Not once. And, did I say, Alfonso said he's been giving him, or sometimes sending him, the money for years, now, bit by bit?'

'No, you didn't mention that,' said Rosie, 'which would appear to rule out the only idea that I've come up with.'

'What's that?'

'Well, this sounds silly, but maybe he won the lottery, or something like that?'

'Not silly, Rosie. That's about the first, or maybe I should say the only, thought that's come into my head, but then if that had happened, why would he be paying it instalments?'

'I see your point.'

'And, Rosie, can I ask you something?'

'That I shouldn't tell anyone about it?'

'Yes.'

Each took another sip, or in Claire's case, a gulp, draining the glass, which Rosie promptly refilled.

'Let's come at this from another angle,' Rosie now said. 'In a way this doesn't surprise me. Forget about the money for a moment. Christian was always one for surprises, wasn't he? Like what he did on your birthday when you were in Italy last year? Remember? You told me about it.'

'Yes, I do', she said, sighing and then yawning, 'but look, I need to go to bed now. Let's sleep on it. Alfonso gave me a note that Christian had written last year. Doesn't say much. I'll show it to you tomorrow.'

'I'll be here when you wake,' Rosie said.

She undressed, throwing her clothes on top of her unopened bag, and got under the duvet. Yes, she thought, he loved surprises.

On that day the previous summer, she remembered, she was surprised to wake in the house in Mercatauro and find that he was not there beside her. She could hear Amy, but she wasn't in her room upstairs: they were both downstairs.

Then she heard the kitchen door close and the sound of the two of them crunching the gravel as they walked up the drive. The house fell silent. Then it came to her: of course, it's my birthday. Something was afoot.

Half an hour passed before she heard them return. They came straight upstairs.

'Knock on the door Amy,' she heard Christian whisper.

As ever with Amy, the knocking was deafeningly loud. The door opened and swung back with a crash to reveal Christian and Amy both dressed in black trousers, white shirts and bow ties, Christian holding a very large silver tray. She sat up and the tray was placed before her. Christian flourished a pure white linen napkin from his arm and placed it on her.

'Happy birthday darling,' Christian said, 'Buon compleanno, signora. Siamo molto contenti.'

'Mummy happy day, si,' Amy said, or rather yelled, excitedly, 'Mummy day happy, si!'

On the tray there was a small vase containing a single rose, a bottle of prosecco, a jug of the red orange juice she loved, three glasses, a selection of pastries, and two foam-topped cups of cappuccino.

'How did you do it?' she asked.

'I planned it at the bar yesterday,' he said. 'Franco said he'd have the tray ready at nine today, which it was, on the dot, and he also lent us the black-and-white gear.'

That was just the start. Failing to resist her curiosity before they had even finished the breakfast, she asked:

'I don't want to appear greedy, but do I get a present, or two?'

'La signora should know better than to ask such questions. She should please take her bath as the transport will be ready to leave by eleven o'clock.'

'Yes, mummy, bath now, NOW!' Amy added, emphatically.

In the bathroom was a note: 'You will need to pack a bag for a night away. Ours are already in the car. Try to restrict yourself to one suitcase and no more than 10 pairs of shoes.'

She smiled.

As they left, she asked 'Where?' but he shook his head.

Three hours later they arrived at the entrance of the Hotel Subasio, Assisi's grandest hotel, to be greeted personally by the manager, which explained the brief telephone call Christian had made a few minutes before, in which he had said only two words: 'arrivo subito'.

The room, or rather the suite, was full of flowers, and clearly the best in the house, the view over the valley stunning.

Later, once they taken the short walk to the cathedral and idled at a small bar, they put Amy to bed and went down for dinner. Every single waiter gave her a red rose and they had, of course, the best table on the balcony. Only there did she get her present: two gold anklets: 'for your beautiful feet', Christian said, as he knelt down in full view of all and kissed each foot in turn . . .

Now she slept.

Hallo darling. I had a real scare earlier on. It's usually pretty calm here. Calm as in calm sea, I mean. But suddenly it started to get sort of . . . bumpy . . . like it is in turbulence in a plane.

It wasn't just that, but it also started to get hot, really hot.

You can guess what I thought. I thought, Oh God, it's cremation time. It scared the hell out of me.

Then, all of a sudden, the bumping stopped and I started to cool down, in every way. But that was scary.

*

Where was I? Scary, yes. I get scared more often than you think. I know you always thought of me as a very calm person, but to be honest, inside, I used to get scared quite a lot. Do you know I never really liked all that air travel? Not because it was boring, which it was, but because, for a start (I never told you this because I knew it would scare you if you knew) do you realise that when it takes off, on a long-distance flight, a jumbo jet weighs about 400 tons? If that isn't scary enough, do you realise that most of those 400 tons are fuel? So as you rumble along the runway, you think about all that fuel. I think about it, for sure, every time.

Then there's the turbulence. Once when I flew into Gilgit in northern Pakistan, the landing was through a huge thunderstorm. It was awful. I thought I was going to die.

Some things about work also scared me. The first day, sometimes two, in a new job at an organisation I didn't know used to scare me. I was always scared of doing the wrong thing, saying the wrong thing. Sometimes I did – like using the word 'pig' in a Muslim country or that time – and, you'll remember this, when we went to that do at the Tonga High Commission? When Mrs High Commissioner – who as you'll recall was, shall we say, of considerable girth – was trying to force another boiled potato on me and I said, 'no thank you, I'm trying to lose weight?' While putting my hand on my stomach! Remember? God, I could have died.

And the public speaking. I know you always said I was good at it and, yes, I was. But before doing a talk I always got really wound up, especially if it was a big do, like the big conference a few weeks back, when I lost my temper.

Sorry, I'm rambling away as ever. There are more import-ant things I need to tell you, darling.

There are some people I want you to tell, about what's happened. I'm sure you'll have done the locals in the village, and the firm. And you know my other friends, like

Nick – you remember him, the doctor. And . . . well, I didn't exactly have a lot of friends did I? Now, that's probably as well. If it had been you that had died I'd be in real trouble.

Darling, I'm afraid you'll need to tell Jane. Tell her I'm sorry it didn't work out all that time ago.

I guess Amy won't understand. Just give her a big kiss from me.

The firm will I am sure inform the organisations I've worked with, but there's one I want you to do yourself, once you feel able. Sorry to burden you but this is important to me. It's the one in Delhi that I used to go to every few months, doing the regular evaluation. You met the manager there, Ravindra, once when he came to England a few years back. He and I became very good friends over the years. I think you knew that. I was only there with him and his gang last November wasn't I? Look in the third drawer of my cabinet and you'll find all my work files there, in the India section. You'll find the contact stuff there. I told Ravindra about having the operation done around now. And, could you ask him to tell his friends at the gharana – that's spelt G-H-A-R-A-N-A – ah, what's happened? And I want you to . . . No . . . I'm too tired now.

She woke with a start, frightened, alarm bells ringing.

Door bells. Postman. Dressing gown.

'Sorry, Claire, 'ope I didn't wake you. I only 'eard last night, 'ow are you?'

'Fine,' she said, as she took the proffered registered envelope and pen the postman held out, along with the rest of the mail. 'Just there, the top one,' he said as he held out the pad for her to sign.

She closed the front door, but stood by it and leafed through the mail, finding another letter from India.

Different handwriting, but Delhi postmark once more.

117

She went upstairs, checked on Amy (still fast asleep and, remarkably, the duvet still on her) and then went into the study. She sat at the desk, reached for a piece of paper and on it, wrote: *hot, scared, Ravindra, third drawer, Gharana,* and then, after a moment, *what is it?*

She thought for some minutes. Her intention had been to go straight to the third drawer, but now she took out the new letter from India from the bulky pile the postman had given her, tucked as it had been between one letter telling her that she was *'Already A Winner'* and another informing her that the new spring catalogue of a mail-order firm was enclosed *'For Your Urgent Attention – Order Within Seven Days, Valuable Prize Guaranteed'.* As she did this the registered letter slid out from the bottom. She turned it over and saw that it was from the insurance company. She reached for the shiny steel letter knife and slit it. A cheque for five thousand pounds fluttered out.

'As if I didn't have enough already,' she said out loud, and then, 'Christian, what are you doing to me? Why didn't you tell me?'

She sat and sobbed, the tears falling on the letters, forming small puddles of greying liquid on them as they did so, including one on the cheque, which she quickly wiped off. After a few minutes she scooped the pile up and went downstairs, put the kettle on and stretched out on the settee.

Darling, . . . would you please . . . would you please send five hundred pounds and ask Ravindra to give it to . . . the Gharana . . . for . . .

8

The Logical Explanation

Gharana: *[ga-rah-nah]:*

'The word gharana literally means "house" and it implies the house of a teacher. It is linked to the very ancient concept of Guru-Shishya-Parampara (lineage of teacher/disciple). But the names of gharanas were almost always derived from a geographical location . . . usually the city, state or district that the founder lived in. Each gharana trains up its disciples according to its own curriculum, and it takes generations to develop a reputed house. The devoted practitioners of a gharana enrich it over the years, adding new resources to its culture. There are three types of gharana – of vocalists, instrumentalists and dancers.

'The genesis of contemporary styles of classical dances in India can be traced back to AD 1300 although the earliest archaeological evidence is a beautiful statuette of a dancing girl dated around 6000 BC.'

'Go away, go away, go AWAY!' Claire was screaming as Rosie let herself in through the front door. Rosie quickly realised that the words were not directed at her. Claire was lying on the settee, writhing as if in agony, yet at the same time evidently not fully conscious. She was sweating profusely. Her gown lay open, her naked body glistening. Amy was standing beside her, clearly very upset, as she was shaking her hands in the particular way she had that indicated great

119

anxiety. What looked like letters were littered across the floor. The room smelled rank. Seeing Rosie, Amy ran to her, crying.

'Mummy sick, no good,' she said.

'Go away, go away,' Claire screamed again, and then again.

Rosie felt at a loss, and frightened. She embraced Amy.

'It's all right, Amy, let's go up and get you in your bath.'

'Yes,' Amy said, 'bath now, mummy sick, Amy bath please.'

Upstairs, she could hear the screaming continuing as she ran the bath, and then got Amy undressed and into it. She remembered that Claire had put Krishnan's card on the door of the fridge, so she went down and got it, then returned to the study upstairs and dialled what was obviously his mobile number.

He answered right away.

'Krishnan, I'm so sorry to call you this early. It's Rosie, Claire's friend . . . yes, that's right . . . I . . . I . . . yes, I'm at her place now. It's not looking good. She's screaming away like blue murder but she's not conscious I think, at least . . . no, not fully conscious. I found Amy with her . . . no, she was downstairs on the settee. And she's very hot, sweating all over . . . No. Claire, not Amy . . . No. I don't know. She got back from Italy about midnight and we must have talked, oh, for an hour at least. So let's say two, two o'clock, around then . . . yes, maybe she stayed up, yes . . . overtired, yes . . . well, what is it now? Eight or so . . . sorry? Say that again? . . . pills, yes, I'll go and look, hold on . . .'

She put the phone down and went into the bedroom, finding the little vial of pills, as she'd hoped, on the bedside table. Downstairs, the screaming continued, if anything getting louder. She looked in the bathroom, where Amy was playing, seemingly oblivious now to the noise, with her three bright yellow plastic ducks.

'Mummy sick. Ducks happy,' she said.

'Krishnan? . . . yes, that's her, you heard it? No, that's all she says. By the way, the bed's been slept in, so she must have been there at least part of last night. I've got the pills, yes . . . alright I will.'

She put down the phone, emptied the vial onto the desk and counted eight small light blue pills and then picked up the phone again.

'Eight . . . yes I'm sure . . . yes, I think she took one that first night . . . yes, possibly two, I'm pretty sure . . . No, she didn't take them to Italy . . . yes, but how? . . . OK, I understand, yes, tea. She won't know? Quick effect? . . . yes, wash her down . . . yes, cold . . . but when can you come? . . . I see . . . all day . . . four o'clock . . . yes, I guess I'll have to . . . GP, I'll do that . . . OK . . . I understand. See you after four then. Krishnan? Can I just check this? Wake her, give her the tea with the pill in it, get her into bed, then, cold flannel, call GP if any worse, yes?'

'Right,' Rosie then said out loud to herself, 'first things first.'

She went downstairs. There, Claire's voice was quieter and hoarser now, but the message remained the same: 'Go away, go away.'

She scooped up the letters and papers from the floor, noticing as she did so the cheque from the insurance company and Claire's handwritten notes.

'Ah, I see,' she said as she read them, 'another message. Now my little darling, we're going to get you sorted.'

She pulled the sides of Claire's gown together and then stroked her hand across her friend's forehead, feeling the heat of it.

'Come on now,' she said, gently, 'let's stop this.'

A look of serenity now appeared on Claire's face. The shouting, or rather talking as it had by now become, stopped.

'Everything's all right, Claire,' Rosie said, still gently, still running her hand gently across Claire's brow, 'Everything's OK.'

'Christian?' Claire said, quietly, 'Christian?'

'No, it's me, darling, Rosie.'

At that, Claire's eyes opened, wide, and she started panting loudly.

'We've got to get to the bank, quickly, quickly, I've got to send the money to Ravindra,' she gasped.

Rosie kept stroking. 'Shush,' she said, 'whatever it is, we can do it later. Did he ask you to do that?'

'Yes, I must do it. He said it was important, for the gharana.'

The word sounded familiar, Rosie thought.

'The what?'

'The gharana, five hundred pounds, and we should send something to my mother in Toowoomba shouldn't we?'

At that, Claire closed her eyes. Rosie left her, went to the kitchen, made a cup of tea, dropped one of the little blue pills in it, then stirred it vigorously and added some cold water. When she went back to living room, Claire was sitting up. She took the tea and gulped it down greedily.

'Good girl,' said Rosie.

'Tastes funny.'

'Now,' Rosie said, 'I want you to come upstairs with me and we'll put you to bed. Will you do that for me?'

'No, the bank, we have to do the bank, cremation, hot, hot . . .' Claire mumbled.

'No, for you darling, bed, just for a nap. The banks aren't open yet, and besides, it's a foul day.'

'No?'

Rosie saw her friend's head beginning to loll. She pulled her up out of the settee and with great effort, and some rather rough handling, pushed and then pulled her up the stairs and into bed. Claire was asleep even before they reached it.

In the bathroom, where Amy was still playing happily with her ducks, Rosie half-filled a plastic bowl from the kitchen with cold soapy water that she then used to sponge her friend down from head to toe.

'Sleep well, you poor thing,' she said, as she closed the door.

'Now let's get you on your way Amy,' Rosie then said to herself.

As they were leaving the house, she heard the phone ringing, but left it.

She heaved a sigh of relief when she listened to the message when she got back. It was from Nick: 'Hallo Claire, got your message and returning your call. Something doesn't sound right. Please call me back. I'm calling at, ah, ten to nine. Bye!'

The conversation with Nick was brief. Rosie stuck to the main points: Christian's operation and subsequent condition; the situation, current and possible future, with the hospital, as per Krishnan's briefing; Claire's condition as of today; the blue pill.

'I can be with you in three hours or so,' Nick said.

He was. It was raining heavily by the time he arrived and he was unprepared for it. Rosie opened to the door to a rather bedraggled specimen. He held a battered, very old, doctor's Gladstone bag.

'I'm so glad you're here. I'm Rosie. Come in.'

She found him a towel and he rubbed it vigorously through his hair, which, like that of Krishnan, was pure white. He was a short, ruddy-faced man with a neatly trimmed full beard, this more salt-and-pepper in appearance. He fished a comb from his inside jacket pocket and ran it through his hair. As she watched him do this she remembered that he had been ski-ing, which accounted for the ruddy face, no doubt.

'There, that's better,' he said, 'Where's the daughter?'

'Amy? She's at her play school. I have to meet her off the bus at four.'

'How's she taking all this? She's special needs, isn't she, as I recall?'

'Yes, so it's hard to tell with Amy, but she was certainly upset this morning – she was in here with Claire when I arrived. Very confused, very upset.'

'I see, now, I'd better go and see Claire – has she stirred?'

Rosie shook her head: 'No, I've looked in a few times and she hasn't moved an inch.'

'I'm not surprised, if what you gave her is what I think it is. Have you been in contact with her GP?'

'No, after I'd spoken to you I felt I didn't need to.'

'Yes, that's fine. A little irregular, but no harm done I think.'

She showed him up to the bedroom door and then left him to go in on his own.

He was in there for a good half-hour. Rosie heard the floorboards creak now and then as he moved around the room, and, once, into the bathroom.

'She's basically all right,' he said when he came back down. 'Blood pressure's a little on the high side, and temperature too, but nothing to be alarmed about. She seems very, very thin – has she eaten much these past few days do you know?'

'No, I don't, but I suspect not very much. When she got back last night from Italy, we sat up talking for a bit and had a couple of glasses of wine, but she didn't eat then.'

'Italy? What on earth possessed her to go there?'

Rosie thought rapidly.

'There was some urgent business there. I think there are very close friends there that Claire must have wanted to tell herself.'

'Seems a very strange thing to do.'

'Look, Nick, there is a lot more to it ... but I think Claire, if she wants you to know, would want to tell you herself. Can we leave it at that for the moment?'

Realising that he still had it on, Nick took his stethoscope off and put it in his bag.

'I'm sorry, I shouldn't pry,' he said. 'Now, I think what I had better do is to have a word with Claire's GP, just to make sure he's in the picture. Otherwise there could be embarrassment, or worse. I have a feeling she's a little, or perhaps very, anaemic. I'll ask the GP for permission to take a sample and then we'll get it checked out.'

'I think that's a good idea. Actually, he's a she, Nick. I forget her name, but she's the only woman in the practice. It's only just up the road, on the road you would have come in on. Big old Victorian building, on the left going up the hill from here. Only 200 yards or so.'

'Yes, I saw it. Can I take one of the umbrellas?'

'Here, take the big one, you'll need it.'

He was gone for some time, which Rosie used to go through what she had found on the living room floor in the morning. First she read Claire's notes: *hot, scared, Ravindra, third drawer, Gharana, what is it?* No mention of any five hundred pounds, but *Ravindra* – yes, that was the name Claire had used this morning. And Gharana – yes, that's why she knew the word – yesterday's card – signed R, she remembered. Maybe R was Ravindra? She went and looked for the card in the living room and the study but could not find it. Must be in her bag, in the bedroom, she thought, but she decided not to pursue the matter further.

'What else?' she muttered to herself as she leafed through the letters. The cheque, payable to Claire: that was quick, she thought. She looked up at the clock, wondering if she should go to the bank when Nick got back, and pay it in. Yes, she thought, I should do that.

Then she found the new letter from India. It was unopened but from memory the handwriting looked different. She sat for a moment, which was all it took for her curiosity to get the better of her. She tiptoed all the way upstairs and quietly opened the bedroom door, as she had done when checking on Claire earlier. From the door she could see that her friend had still not moved. She tiptoed in, wincing as the floorboards creaked. There, on the bedside table she found the emails to and from Timothy Barrie, folded in two. Inside were the card and envelope from India, a sheet with Claire's handwriting on it, and another sheet with handwriting in green ink, all tucked into the folded emails.

Comparing the two Indian envelopes back downstairs she found she was right – the writing was quite different, and on the back of the new letter, there was another rubber stamp, this one clearer. And above it was written 'Ravindra Kapoor.'

She read the green handwriting sheet next, and quickly stopped herself, realising that it was the letter from Christian that Claire had referred to. She felt embarrassed at prying. The other sheet, in Claire's handwriting, she quickly guessed, was Claire's notes of the first dream-message from him that first night.

She sorted the junk mail from the rest of the letters, which left what was almost certainly an electricity bill (her own had come that morning, too), what seemed to be another card of some kind, this time with a London postmark, and, finally, another cellophane-window letter. Below the window was a logo proclaiming 'Pro-Fit'.

'All we can do is wait,' she said to herself, and then got up, went into the kitchen and made two ham sandwiches, which she wrapped on two plates with cling-film. At a loss as to what to do, she found another bottle of white wine in the fridge, opened it, and poured herself a glass.

When Nick returned, drenched again, with the umbrella blown inside out, his knock startled Rosie out of a brief wine-induced doze.

'That's fine,' he said, 'nice woman, ought to be more female GPs. She's given me permission to take the blood sample and then she'll get the test done in the fast lane. And she's given me carte-blanche with Claire. She didn't know about Christian and was, well, dumbfounded. It's horrible outside, the wind has really got up.'

Rosie struggled to take all this in.

'Sorry, missed some of that. Given you something for Claire did you say?'

'No. We've agreed that I should regard myself as Claire's doctor for the moment, and just keep her, the GP, in touch every few days, as necessary. And she's given me the number of the respite care place I gather Amy goes to from time to time. She spoke to the people there, in my presence, and the message is that Amy can go there any time from now, tonight, and stay for as long as Claire wishes. They'll also get her to school and back.'

'I know the place. That's good. Amy loves it there. There's a sandwich for us in the kitchen. Hungry?'

'Wonderful. If I hadn't given up years back, I'd have had some of that wine,' he said, taking the empty glass from Rosie's hand as he did so, 'but first, let me get this blood sample and get it up to the surgery.'

When he got back, they agreed, over the sandwiches, that the cheque should be paid in.

'I was going to ask about critical illness insurance,' Nick said. 'I'm glad at least there's something there. Look, I suggest I stay here and you go to the bank. Are you fit to drive?'

'Yes, I only had the one glass,' she replied, with a smile. 'I'll be back in time to pick up Amy from playschool. It's only round the corner from here.'

When Rosie had gone, Nick, too, tip-toed upstairs to check on Claire. From the doorway he could see her deep, regular, breathing and so went no further.

He found Rosie's neatly assembled papers and letters on the dining room table and, with nothing else to do, could not resist going through them. He read the email from Sir Timothy Barrie with interest. He knew the name. While the email to which it replied was not there, Nick felt he could guess its substance.

He glanced at the two sheets in the same hand-writing. They made no sense at all, so he left them aside. Another one in green ink he immediately recognised as being Christian's work. Like Rosie, he felt a sense of guilt, but unlike her, he read and then re-read the short letter. This was something to do with the Italy trip, he thought, but who was Alfonso?

After glancing briefly at the unopened letters (among which he particularly noted the one from Pro-Fit), and the opened one and the card from India, he re-assembled the collection on the table, and then gazed thoughtfully at it for a long time. Then he re-read the two hand-written sheets:

mountain, thinks dead, chicken(!), Dad, Barrie(??), Alfonso, note, wallet, cremation – no.
   hot, scared, Ravindra, third drawer, Gharana, what is it?

He remained mystified, but noted that Alfonso and Barrie cropped up. Then he put all the papers back in the neat pile that had been left, he presumed by Rosie, on the table.

Soon after, Rosie came back, or rather burst, through the front door, pausing only to say a breathless 'I'm late for Amy!' before rushing back out again.

A few minutes later, there was a loud knock on the door. Opening it revealed a bedraggled Indian man, holding a briefcase in one hand and struggling with a clipboard and a partly collapsed umbrella in the other.

'No, not now,' Nick said to him, 'whatever it is, no.'

'I beg your pardon?' the man said, 'who, may I ask, are you?'

'I am a doctor, someone is ill here, so would you please go away!'

As Krishnan opened his mouth to reply, several things happened, more or less simultaneously. First, the door was slammed in his face. Second, a strong gust of rain-filled wind caught hold of the partially closed umbrella, opening it and snatching it upwards from a grasp already enfeebled by having at the same time to hold his clip-board, which contained his notes of the entire day. This, too, fell from his grasp at the same moment, into a puddle in which he was standing.

Propelled powerfully and rapidly upwards, the umbrella hit and dislodged a section of the roof guttering. This quickly descended and struck him with considerable force just above his left ear, causing him to yell with pain. Within a few seconds the puddle in which he stood noticeably reddened, as did his sodden notes on the clipboard, some pages of which were becoming detached by the strong wind.

Angrily he knelt down – in the puddle – and forced open the letter box.

'Open this door! I am a doctor!' he shouted into it.

Inside, Nick also now knelt down and replied through the letter box:

'Very funny, very funny indeed. That's a good one! So you're a doctor too? Well, well, well!'

'Please help me,' Krishnan said on the other side, 'I'm badly hurt. Look.'

He put his left hand up to his ear and then pushed his blood-soaked fingers through the letter-box.

Inside, Nick observed them. Several dark red globs formed as he watched, and then dripped onto the floor below. Putting the sight of all this together with the earlier scream, which he had taken to be one of frustration rather than pain, he quickly stood up and opened the door. Krishnan was at the same time also trying to stand up, but as he did so, one of his feet caught itself awkwardly on the fallen piece of guttering. Combined with the giddiness he already felt as a result of the blow to his head, he stumbled and then fell backwards. His shoulders and head crashed heavily into the front wing of a car parked beside the pavement. The blow rendered him unconscious and created a large dinner plate-sized dent in the car, which was almost new. Nick knew this because he had bought it only just before he had left for his ski-ing holiday.

Nick's immediate, and intense, concern was, however, for the man who, he saw, was bleeding profusely from a head wound and was now slumped partly in the arch of the front wheel.

Without hesitating, he knelt down in front of him, and slapped him gently on both cheeks.

'I'm most terribly sorry,' he said, and looked up and down the narrow street for any sign of help. There was none: the weather was keeping people firmly indoors. Now Nick noticed a number of sheets of sodden white paper on the pavement and in the gutter at various points, the clipboard in the puddle, and the briefcase, which was miraculously still in the unconscious man's grip.

Krishnan moaned and opened his eyes. As his vision cleared the bearded face of the man he presumed to be his adversary, a face very close to his own, came into focus.

'Idiot,' Krishnan mumbled.

'I'm terribly sorry, most terribly sorry,' Nick repeated. 'Now, are you able to get up? Whoever you are, I need to get you inside to see to your head.'

Nick helped the man to his feet, where he wobbled uncertainly. The fact that Nick was short and the other man considerably taller enabled Nick to get Krishnan's arm around his shoulders and his own shoulder under Krishnan's armpit. By these means he got him into the house, feeling blood seeping down his own neck as he did so. As they staggered on, a trail of smeared blood was left across the living room carpet.

In the dining room, Nick grabbed hold of the tablecloth with his free hand and yanked it hard in the style of magicians showing how to do so without disturbing plates and cutlery. There were fortunately none of these on the table at this time – just the pile of notes and letters and a single candle in a glass holder. The papers and letters now fluttered, for the second time that day, to the wooden floor. The candlestick holder shattered on impact.

Nick was gratified to see that the table now revealed was a sturdy pine one. With great effort, for his new patient now seemed to have lost consciousness again, he got Krishnan up onto it and stretched him out. A quick examination revealed that the wound was just over the left ear, which had also become partly separated from the head. A profuse amount of blood was in consequence coming out, quickly forming a pool on the table.

'Oh, my goodness,' Nick said.

In the kitchen drawers he found tea towels and more tablecloths, filled and switched on the kettle and then filled the plastic washing-up bowl with hot water from the tap. Back on the dining room table, Krishnan appeared to be coming round again, but the pool of blood was now quite large. Nick bunched up a tea towel and applied it firmly to the wound, pressing hard. It quickly saturated. He applied another and then another, in the meantime using his free hand to try to mop up the pool of blood on the table with a tablecloth.

Now conscious, Krishnan said, quietly but calmly: 'How bad is it?'

'Could be worse. You have a severe laceration over the ear, which needs to be stitched. I'll need you to do your bit. Are you up to that? Otherwise I can't move.'

'Yes, I think so.'

'I'm going to put a new cloth over the wound and I want you to use your own hand to keep it pressed firmly into your head. Then I can get what I need to fix you up. Clear?'

Nick helped Krishnan to move his hand onto the required spot. He then threw the original tablecloth over the man, leaving only the head visible, and went off in search of his Gladstone bag. It was a lifetime habit of Nick's never to go anywhere by road without a good assortment of dressings, medicine and equipment in his bag. He knew he had everything he needed. He took the bag into the kitchen, opened it, and took out the necessary items.

In a casserole dish he placed the things he needed to sterilise, and then poured boiling water from the kettle over them.

It was at this moment that Rosie returned. The concern she felt at what she had found outside the still open front door – briefcase, clipboard, guttering, sodden papers, and a red tinge to the pavement she could not understand – had increased to alarm as she took in the trail of smeared blood across the living room carpet. Her feelings then quickly escalated to horror when she saw the scene in the dining room: what appeared to be a body stretched out under a blood-stained sheet on the table, with blood-soaked cloths here and there on the table and floor; broken glass crunching under her feet; and what appeared to be Claire's papers and letters scattered around.

'What on earth?' she said loudly, leaving her mouth open in stunned amazement.

'Rosie, thank goodness you're back. I need you. Quickly, come in here and help,' came Nick's voice from the kitchen.

'I need clean towels – lots of them, quickly. This man has had a rather serious accident,' he continued as she joined him.

'Shouldn't we just call for an ambulance?' Rosie asked.

'Rosie, I am a doctor, remember? Now will you please get what I need?'

Only as Nick took away the tea towel covering his patient's head did Rosie realise who it was.

'Oh my God, it's Krishnan!' she said.

'Rosie, is that you?' Krishnan said quietly, his eyes closed and squeezed tight in anticipation of what he knew would be a rather painful few minutes, even with the local anaesthetic Nick was applying.

'Yes,' said Rosie.

'So, you know this man?' Nick said, impatiently.

'He's the surgeon who operated on Christian.'

About to insert the first stitch, Nick stopped and looked up and around at Rosie. 'What?'

'Yes, I spoke to him this morning before I spoke to you. He said he'd come and see how Claire was when he'd finished his appointments and rounds today.'

'And now look where I am,' said Krishnan, quietly still, but with a nonetheless clear tone of sarcasm in his voice.

'It's all my fault, Nick,' said Rosie, 'I meant to tell you he would be coming and I clean forgot.'

Nick was at a loss for words.

'Can we please get on with it?' said Krishnan.

Half an hour later Krishnan was in Amy's bed upstairs, his ear and forehead – where other less severe abrasions had become apparent – heavily bandaged. With Nick's help he had completely undressed before he got into it, and agreed with Nick's post-operative diagnosis that, while the symptoms of shock were not serious, and there were no signs of concussion, a mild sedative was in order.

Nick drew the curtains and said; 'I know this will sound terribly inadequate, but I am most profoundly sorry for what has happened. I don't know what else to say. I feel completely wretched about the whole thing. Now we must call your wife – should we do that?'

'No, I'm not married. Let me just rest a little. Switch the light off would you, please?'

By the time Nick got downstairs, Rosie had got the washing machine going and was hard at work on the pine table with a good old-fashioned scrubbing brush. Nick went out to clear up in the street, bringing in Krishnan's briefcase and clipboard, both of which were in an extremely sorry condition. As he went up the street picking up the loose papers, he realised they were beyond salvation and threw them in a litter-bin. Then he cleared up in the kitchen before turning his attention to the dining room floor, working around Rosie. The candlestick holder had been reduced to dozens of tiny razor-sharp fragments.

'I suggest you pick up the letters and papers and then use the Hoover on the glass. Then I'll run a mop over the floor. It's parquet, but a bit of water won't hurt it.'

'Where's Amy?' Nick asked.

'When I picked her up, I made a unilateral decision that I'm now absolutely certain was the right one.'

'Oh?'

'I took her straight up to the respite place in my car. I just thought it the right thing to do, and thank God I did! Imagine the effect all this would have had on her, especially after this morning's goings-on! When we're straight, perhaps you could tell me exactly what happened.'

'Yes. Where's the Hoover?'

'Cupboard under the stairs. It wouldn't surprise me if you find a corpse in there as well. Nothing would surprise me right now.'

A little later, having finished in the dining room, they surveyed the state of the living room carpet. Rosie tried a few tentative wipes with a soapy cloth, but these seemed to worsen things. They decided simply to cover as much of the stained area as possible with a rug.

'Where are Krishnan's clothes?' Rosie asked.

'I threw them all in the basket in the bathroom. I fear I'll have to buy him a new suit and tie. Least I can do, really.'

'Get the rest of his stuff for me and we'll do another load in the machine in a while. And then you can go up to the village shop and get some more wine!'

'I am at your service, madam. Your every wish is my command.'

They laughed.

When all that could be done had been done, they sat at the dining room table and talked. Nick told Rosie the story of what had happened, and Rosie sipped her wine as he did so, unable to resist a giggle here and there. After he finished, they both eyed the pile of papers and letters on the table in front of them.

'Rosie, I have to confess that I went through those while you were out. I didn't open anything that wasn't opened of course, although I have to admit that I did read Christian's letter, the one in green. That I can add to the long list of thoughtless and unutterably stupid things I've done today.'

'I almost did the same, to be honest.'

'Now, Rosie . . . no, firstly there's something else I want to say . . .'

He explained that since he was retired and had no pressing obligations – his wife having stayed on in France to be with their son, who worked in Paris – he could stay for as long as needed:

'I've even brought a bag of clothes, enough for a few days. I know that I haven't exactly covered myself with glory so far, but I am here to help. And if I'm to help properly, without wishing to pry into Claire's or your affairs, I need to know a little more than what you told me this morning. That's not a criticism or a demand. Take it as a polite request. And I think I will have a little of that wine. I do allow myself the odd one every now and again, to be honest. I'll have some of that nice Chianti I got, if I may.'

'Good for you – let me git it.'

As she opened the bottle in the kitchen she thought about how to answer Nick, who at the same time was thinking about Rosie's curious pronunciation of 'get'.

She rejoined him at the table: 'Cheers,' she said and they clinked glasses.

After a short while, Rosie said: 'I'll tell you as much as I know, but I don't know everything there is to know. You see . . .'

She started with Claire's first dream-message, and its results – the half banknote, the trip to Italy, and the contact

136

with Sir Timothy Barrie. She also explained who Alfonso was.

'And what exactly happened in Italy?'

Now she thought for a few seconds before continuing.

She explained that Alfonso had given Claire the letter from Christian, picking it out of the pile and then reading it.

'Cold,' she murmured.

'Are you?' Nick asked.

'No, I mean the tone of the letter. Impersonal, I suppose I mean. Don't you think? Doesn't say "dear" or "love" or anything like that.'

'Let me see it again. Is it money that Alfonso had?' Nick asked, as he read.

She hesitated, remembering what her friend had asked, and thinking that Nick seemed more like a detective than a doctor.

'It's not for me to say.'

'I see. Yes, the letter does seem rather impersonal, you're right. And is it your view that Claire had no idea at all about whatever it was before she went there?'

'I'm absolutely certain.'

'And that she had never heard of Sir Timothy Barrie's existence?'

'No. I'm certain of that, too.'

'How very strange, how very, very strange. So anyway, this . . .' He picked out one of the handwritten sheets from the pile, which now had pink stains on it.

'This is her record, her notes on that first dream?'

'Yes, I think that's what it is.'

'Which means that this . . .' he picked out the other sheet, '. . . would be notes on a second dream?'

'Probably, yes, but I think she had that dream last night, the one she must have woken up from when I found her this morning. So I have no idea what all that means, I'm afraid, except that in her rantings this morning she was going on about having to send five hundred pounds to this Ravindra character to give to this Gharana, whatever or whoever it is, and something about her mother, who's been dead for donkey's years.'

'Who is Ravindra?'

'Somebody Christian knows in India, I think.'

'And Gharana?'

She fished in the pile for the card: 'No idea, except that this came while she was away, and the word comes up in it, look.'

She passed him the card and he read it again, saying, 'I wonder what it is? You say she saw the card before the most recent dream?'

'Yes.'

'So maybe the word just lodged in her consciousness and then came up in her dream.'

'I suppose that's possible, yes. But it's odd that this other letter from India is from this Ravindra character, and it arrived this morning, after the dream.'

'But did she know him, or know of him, before? Now I think about it she could have come across this Barrie character, couldn't she? I know she said she hadn't, but it's possible. And she could have come across the banknote, the half banknote, at some time, couldn't she?'

Once again she felt she was being questioned by a detective.

'I don't know. Are you saying that she's making all this up?'

'No. I'm simply saying that there could be a rational, logical explanation for all this, or at least for a lot of it.'

'Meaning?'

'Meaning that she's in a highly distraught state. She's not acting rationally. Rushing off to Italy like that was, well, not exactly rational. And I've seen many examples of what

138

happens to people when they're distraught, when they're in a state of grief, which also comes into play here. In those kinds of, ah, conditions, one result is that imaginations run riot. When that happens, the brain does funny things. Old, forgotten memories – real or false – can come back, sometimes in vivid or terrifying form. For example, Christian could have told the story of Barrie's beating to her years ago, perhaps at some dinner party, and she only took it in subconsciously. Likewise the bank note. Likewise Ravindra . . . do you see what I mean?'

'So what you're saying is that you don't believe a word of it all. You sound like a bloody policeman!'

'No, hold on, Rosie, I'm just saying that there could be other explanations. Let's face it, the notion of dead people communicating with the living, through dreams or any other means, is pretty fantastic.'

'But he's not dead.'

'That's not the point, Rosie.'

She felt irritated, and conveyed this in the manner she glared at Nick.

'Rosie, please,' he went on. 'I'm simply trying to keep an open mind about this. It's the way my mind works. I'm still absorbing it all myself. You've had a bit longer than me in that respect. Maybe this is real rather than fantasy. I just don't know, but I'll tell you what . . .'

At this point a monstrous, piercing, intense, drawn-out, high-pitched scream upstairs caused both of them to jerk their heads back in simultaneous, sudden, shock.

They raced up the stairs, Nick in the lead.

In Amy's bedroom they found Claire, completely silent now, staring in horror at Krishnan, who was partly sitting up in bed blinking, resting on his elbows.

Rosie went and took Claire in her arms: 'It's OK, it's OK darling,' she whispered in her friend's ear. At the same time, Nick sat on the side of the bed.

'Just relax,' he said quietly to Krishnan.

The silence that followed was broken by Krishnan starting to chuckle.

'I think I've worked this out,' he said, 'Claire has woken and come in to check on her daughter, and . . .'

Now Claire spoke, and she was also laughing:

'. . . and found a sick man instead!'

Looking at Krishnan's bandages, Nick joined in: 'No, a Sikh man?'

'No, I'm sick but not Sikh,' said Krishnan. Now all four of them were laughing loudly.

'Did you know?' Krishnan went on, 'that while all Sikhs are Singhs . . .'

'. . . not all Singhs are Sikhs, yes,' Nick added.

'I think this is a sick joke,' Rosie said, while releasing Claire from her embrace.

The laughter subsided.

Rosie cleared her throat. Speaking slowly and with exaggerated solemnity, she said:

'Claire, darling, here is the short version of why we are gathered here today . . .'

They all giggled.

'We are gathered here today . . . in the spirit of world harmony and peace.'

'Amen,' said Nick.

Krishnan mumbled something that sounded like 'teak'.

'Er . . . ripper,' said Claire.

'Amy is in respite care,' Rosie continued, 'I took her there today. While I was doing so, your friend Mr Krishnan Supramanian, who I believe you know, but he is the one in the bed, in case you don't recognise him, met the gentleman who is now sitting beside him, who is Mr, or rather Doctor – retired – Nick Moffat. Say hello to Claire, Nick.'

Nick got up and gave Claire a hug and then remained beside her, holding her hand gently.

'Now,' Rosie continued, 'these two doctors did not get on very well together on first acquaintance, and they ended up having a bit of a fight, during which Mr Supramanian here was struck a severe blow on the head . . .'

'Is this true?' Claire asked, turning towards Nick.

'May I continue please?' Rosie said loudly. Smiling, the others all turned their attention to her.

'He was struck on the head by a blunt, heavy metal instrument commonly known as a length of iron guttering, which you will now find outside your front door. But, the person responsible for this, Doctor Moffat, having a good side to him which makes up for his darker and more violent one, immediately ministered unto his opponent by performing a major operation on your dining room table, and the two have now shaken hands on the matter.'

'An excellent, if rather incomplete, summary if I may say so, Rosie,' said Krishnan, 'although I hate to think about what the table looks like now.'

They re-assembled a short time later around the table in question, with Krishnan dressed in some of Christian's clothes, which fitted surprisingly well. Before they went downstairs, however, Nick had insisted that he give both Krishnan and Claire an examination.

'You seem fine,' he said to her, 'how do you feel?'

'To be honest, Nick,' she replied with a bright smile, 'I feel absolutely, perfectly fine, really!'

Nick then went into the other bedroom and turned his attention to Krishnan.

'I think I should leave the dressing as it is for the moment, don't you?'

'Yes,' Krishnan said, 'it feels a little sore, but I don't get a sense of anything being badly wrong.'

The two of them remained in the bedroom and shared views on Claire's current condition. They agreed that she appeared to be in good shape.

'You know about the dream?' Krishnan said.

'Which one?'

'Why, has there been another?'

'We – Rosie and I – think so. It seems to be what set her off into the state she was in this morning. But neither of us knows that for certain yet.'

'I see. Let's go down, shall we?'

The two women were chatting together when they joined them.

'Before we go any further,' Rosie said, 'I think one thing we all need to do is eat '

Looking at Claire, she went on, 'I hate to think when some of us last ate.'

'I've got an idea,' Claire said. 'There's a bolognaise mix in the freezer – Christian made it last week.'

'Great,' said Rosie and Nick in unison.

'Sorry,' said Krishnan, 'no beef.'

'No, Krishnan, it's OK, it's lamb,' said Claire, 'Christian and I sort of went off beef – you know, the mad cow thing? Although he loves his veal in Italy, I must confess.'

'Then that's fine,' Krishnan said, slapping his hands on his knees, 'excellent in fact!'

'Good,' said Rosie, 'I'll fix it up. Now can I make two more proposals? First, I'll do the food and Nick will take responsibility for the drinks. OK Nick?'

'Of course.'

'Second, we need to plan ahead. So I propose that, once we've eaten, Nick should come back and stay at my house – don't worry, I promise not to seduce you – and Krishnan, do you need to go home? If so we can get a taxi.'

142

'No, I live on my own. In the circumstances . . .', he touched his ear gingerly, 'I would be very happy to stay exactly where I am.'

Claire said: 'That's fine with me. And I can promise you what Rosie promised Nick.'

The earlier laughter was renewed.

'Right,' said Rosie, 'Nick, to your duties, and Krishnan, you two, why don't you go in the sitting room so that Claire can tell you about her Italian adventure and our new legal friend and things like that?'

'Excellent,' Krishnan said, 'and may I ask a favour? Do you have any Scotch?'

Claire shook her head.

'The shop'll still be open,' said Rosie, 'it doesn't close 'til nine.'

'I'm already there,' said Nick, 'consider it done, sir. It's the least I can do!'

Anticipating and hoping that Claire would have something to say, they ate in silence. Then, with the dishes still strewn across the table, she told the story of her second dream, using her notes as a prompt. Everyone listened intently.

Afterwards, the first to speak was Krishnan.

'What I find fascinating is the business of the bumps and the feeling of heat. His temperature did go up during the transfer.'

Turning to Claire, Rosie said, 'but I told you about that before you went to bed.'

'Did you? I don't remember?' said Claire.

'Ah,' said Nick, raising his eyebrows and looking at Rosie, who pursed her lips and whispered:

'No, Nick, don't go into that now, please.'

'What's this?' asked Claire.

Nick opened his mouth to speak: 'I . . .' but Rosie interrupted: 'Nick, no!'

'Look, Rosie, I really think it needs to be said, so I am going to say it. When I was talking earlier on to Rosie I said that if you look at all this through the eyes of, shall we say, a sceptic . . .'

'Or those of some bloody detective,' Rosie snapped.

'Go on, Nick,' said Claire.

Nick went through all that he had said to Rosie earlier, point by point. Rosie glared at him throughout.

'You're right,' Claire said, sighing, when he finished. 'I'd also seen the card from the Gharana. Yes, perhaps you are right. I think we should all take a tough line from now on. Thanks, Nick. Now, leaving all that aside I want to know if Krishnan can enlighten us on this Gharana business. Can you, Krishnan?'

'Yes, I can, certainly, but before I do that can I say one thing? It's about the bumps.'

'Claire has a hatred of flying that simply came into the dream,' said Nick, quietly.

'Look, why don't you bloody well go back to France,' Rosie burst out, 'and beat a few people over the head with your bloody skis, or whatever else comes to hand?'

There was a tense silence. Rosie crossed her arms and pointedly turned her chair away from Nick.

'Come on, Nick's offering a logical explanation, not an accusation,' Krishnan went on, 'and without taking sides let me tell you something, something that none of you, including Claire, knows. The last mile or so of the drive, to where Christian now is, is along a very rough gravel driveway. You see, Pro-Fit doesn't exactly make the place well known. It's miles from anywhere. You don't find it, or the three other similar places they run, anywhere in their brochures. I'll be perfectly frank, since that seems to be the spirit of this discussion. Pro-Fit calls these places TCCs – terminal care centres. I'm sorry Claire, but you would find that out sooner or later. My point is that the last mile to it is very bumpy. As Claire knows, like Nick, I've been concerned, as all this has evolved, that she does not erect unrealistic expectations for herself. But that said, the bumps are a curiosity. How could Claire have known this before she dreamed about turbulence?'

'Fair enough,' said Nick.

Claire took a sharp breath and said: 'Well. Now, Krishnan, tell us about the Gharana please.'

'This in itself is to me another curiosity. Again I'll be frank. When I met Christian for his consultation what is it, nearly three weeks ago, he told me about his interest in Indian forms of dance. Kathak, by the way, is one such form. Now, never mind the card you got, never mind the dancing lady on the front, never mind that you saw the word "gharana" on the card before you went to bed. Never mind all of that. I'm pretty sure, Claire, from the way he behaved when you joined us that day, when we met at the hospital, that you did not know of this particular interest of Christian and, indeed, that he did not seem to want you to know of it. Now, before I go on, can I ask – am I right? Yes or no?'

'Yes. This is complete news to me,' said Claire, 'and I still want to know what or who a Gharana is.'

Krishnan sat back and gave them a lengthy description, concluding by saying: 'You'll appreciate that this does not throw much, if any, light at all on the matter at hand. It's the fact that Christian has this interest and that Claire did not know of it, that's, shall we say, a mystery.'

'I should open these other letters,' Claire said.

One was a card from Christian's office. The second one from India, from Ravindra Kapoor, did indeed also contain a card, with a drawing of the Taj Mahal on the front. Inside, in very neat and clear handwriting it read:

Dear Christian, I guess you must be having your operation around now. All of us here, and all your friends at GKK, join me in wishing you all the best, and we look forward to seeing you in good shape in February.
    Sincerely,
    Ravindra

She passed it around the table, saying: 'If it's of any interest, I had no idea Christian was planning to be going back there so soon. In fact to be honest I'm beginning to think I know very little about many things about him.'

When it got to her, Rosie said: 'The other card says that there's some kind of dance festival then, doesn't it? Any connection with the five hundred pounds I wonder?'

When it got back to her Claire laid it down and started to open the letter from Pro-Fit.

'I know what that one will say,' Krishnan said 'They want a meeting with you next week. Thursday to be precise. A copy was given to me. I have to be there. They want to talk, and I quote, about "the medical and financial implications of your husband's unfortunate condition".'

'By the way the five thousand is now in your account, darling,' Rosie said. 'I put it in earlier today.'

'The critical illness money? Good, that will help,' said Krishnan, 'and your new barrister friend as well, I think. You must get hold of him, Claire, quickly.'

'Time for bed I think,' said Nick.

Sombre now, they all stood. Claire beckoned them all together in a group hug, one that only Rosie was reluctant to join.

'Thank you,' she said.

9

The Meetings

After a brief stop at the respite care house, during which Nick remained outside, using the time to make a careful inspection of the dent in the car's front wing, they made the journey to Tunbridge Wells in silence. It was a day of clear sky, although the wind remained strong. Claire held the sketch map Krishnan had drawn for them, along with the letter she had typed for him that morning on her computer while he dictated. Fortunately his notepaper, like the other contents of his briefcase, had remained miraculously dry, although Krishnan had no choice but to consign the entire contents of his clipboard to the waste bin.

'I'll re-write my notes from memory when I get home,' he had said. 'By the greatest good fortune I still have one – a memory I mean.'

Krishnan had also carefully briefed the two of them on what to expect and do when they got there. And they had agreed, in response to an earnest reminder from Krishnan, that it was not on any account to be made known there, or indeed anywhere, that they knew or had had any contact with him.

As they bumped along the final gravel drive, they exchanged their first words.

'He was right, it certainly is rough,' Nick said.

'Awful,' said Claire.

They reached a gate that looked big and strong enough

147

to resist a tank. Only a small Pro-Fit logo gave a hint of what lay beyond it. Beneath it, and much more prominent, was a sign saying, in large lettering: *Private Facility: Trespassers Will Be Prosecuted.* There seemed no sign of life: the windows of the small booth beside the gate were of smoked glass. As they waited, they looked around, both taking in the high steel-mesh fence that stretched away on both sides.

Eventually a man emerged from the booth, clad in a dark green uniform with more than a hint of military menace about it: green beret, buttoned epaulettes and bright yellow flashes on the sleeves. As he approached, Nick lowered the window. He gave the man Krishnan's letter. He took it without a word, went to the front of the car, where he noted the registration number, and then returned to the booth.

The wind rocked the car gently as they waited. A long time passed, or what seemed a long time to them. The two of them took in the yellow tinge that winter gives to the green of the rolling fields around. After a short time a vehicle appeared on the other side of the gate: a dark green four-wheel drive, also with tinted windows. Another uniformed man got out of it, went into the booth and then reappeared on their side.

This time Nick left the window up. The man tapped on it.

'We need ID,' he said, stiffly.

Krishnan had warned them about this. They handed over their drivers' licences. The man gave Nick a form.

'You the medical adviser?' Nick nodded. 'Fill this in.'

Krishnan had also warned them about this: until Nick had his status officially recognised as Claire's medical adviser (who would normally be the patient's GP, Krishnan had said), he would not be permitted to enter. The man waited by the car while Nick completed the form and then gave it back to him.

The man went back to the booth. Another wait ensued, this one longer.

'Is this for real?' Claire said.

While neither had kept track of it, they later agreed that the time spent there had been at least 45 minutes. It ended with the gate being opened. In front, the four-wheel drive had turned round. The driver got out of it and came again to the window.

'You must follow me and then park exactly where I show you. I will then escort you into the building,' he said, while handing them passes to wear around their necks. 'You must wear these passes at all times and hand them in here as you leave. Is that clear?'

A further lengthy, and again bumpy, drive followed, the surrounding meadowland grazed by sheep along both sides. A fine white-painted Georgian mansion came into view. They were directed to park on a large gravelled area, where there were several other vehicles, and then to follow the man into the building.

Inside, the surroundings were light and airy: the Georgian exterior was just a façade, probably retained as a condition of listed building renovation, Nick thought. Perhaps as a result, the environment immediately became, or at least seemed to become, more friendly. The ceilings were all of glass, like a conservatory, giving natural light. A blonde-haired young nurse greeted them with a smile and offered them 'tea or coffee?' Soon, a young man in a white coat appeared.

'Hallo,' he said, 'I'm one of the duty doctors today' Looking at Nick he said, 'Now let's see, you're the medical adviser? Yes? You're his GP? No?'

The young man looked through the file of papers he

held. 'Oh, I see, yes, you are a family friend and retired GP? Yes?'

That is what Nick had put on the form, at Krishnan's suggestion.

'Fine. First I need to take you through a few basic things. With your husband only recently admitted,' he went on, looking at Claire, 'we are maintaining an absolutely sterile regime in his unit. That means for the next few days at least, no entry into the room itself. As you'll see, what we do have, however, is a visiting room right next to him with a full glass wall. And for patients who can communicate, which as you know, your husband cannot, we have a sound system so that two-way communication can take place across the glass wall, if you see what I mean.'

'We do,' Nick said, 'Now who do I speak to about medical matters?'

'If the patient's consulting surgeon is here – his name is Mr Supramanian – which he is not today, then you would deal with him. But if that's not the case, then the duty doctors on any given day will be happy to do so, as I will be today. We are all intensive care or palliative care specialists.'

'I see,' said Nick, 'when will this, what's his name, Supramanian, next be here?'

'I can't advise you on that,' the young man said. 'I suggest you speak directly to his office.'

'I have the number already, Nick,' Claire said, innocently. 'Now can I see my husband please? I want to talk to him.'

'But . . .' the young man said.

'I am well aware of that. But I always talk to him. It may not help him, but it certainly helps me'

As they stared at Christian through the glass, Nick held Claire's hand. After a short time he said: 'I'm going to talk to the young man. I'll leave you to talk to Christian. Take as long as you like.'

She sat and looked through the glass. The scene looked much as it had in The Ashfield – wires and tubes here, there and everywhere. But now, both his hands, she could see, were resting on the bed. He looked utterly at peace, but rather pale. She pushed the microphone button and a red light came on.

'I'm here, darling. I know you can't hear me. You're still there, I know. It's hard for me. I've seen Alfonso, so I know all about that. Darling, you haven't done anything wrong, have you? No, you wouldn't do that. You're not like that. But you must tell me. Even if you have done something wrong, it's fine, so long as it's not too wrong. I've found your old school-chum. I'm sure he'll help me, and you as well. And Nick has come. He's a lovely man. We've had quite a time since he came – it's a long story, and a bit silly, but he's here, and he's helping me. And Rosie. We've got Amy into respite. She's well. I saw her just now. Everyone in the village knows. Everyone sends their love . . .'

She hesitated.

'Why didn't you tell me about this dancing thing? We never danced. Well, we did sometimes, but you always said you felt awkward and clumsy. But we did dance on the balcony at Assisi last year, didn't we? The night of my birthday. I was thinking about it last night. No, it wasn't last night. Was it the night before? Anyway, you spoke to me. You said you were hot. You told me about being scared. You told me a lot I didn't know about you. I want you to keep talking to me, darling. Whatever it is, even if it's bad, I want you to tell me. I want you back with me. Come back to me. I can't manage without you, you know that. You're such a good man . . .'

151

She closed her eyes: 'Dear God, give him back to me, please.'

She pushed the button again and the red light went out.

They were allowed to drive back to the gate unescorted. There, they gave in their passes.

Just before they reached the end of the driveway, where it joined the road, a hearse appeared ahead. They stopped and gave way to it. Claire closed her eyes.

'Pub lunch, I think?' Nick said.

'Yes, let's do that.'

There was one just down the road: *The Stag*. A climbing rose that looked as if it had not been pruned for years covered most of the front. It had been partly blown free from the wall, exposing old timbers and red bricks. It was getting on for two o'clock, so they hurried in.

They sat at the bar, behind which a very large man, of the size of a darts champion, appeared. He had a prominent hunched back.

'Not too late to eat are we?' Nick asked.

'Yer just in toym,' the man said, 'berorder quicktho.'

'I'm sorry?' Nick said.

'He says we should order quickly,' Claire said.

They both chose gammon, egg and chips – 'Christian's favourite' Claire said – Nick a half of bitter and Claire a ginger beer.

'Bin op thurr, avya?' the man now said, jerking his thumb over his shoulder.

'You mean the medical place? Yes, we have,' Claire replied.

'Yugot sumun thurr?'

'What's he saying?' said Nick.

Claire ignored this and responded instead to the man: 'Yes, what you might call a distant relative.'

'Aino food ever goes op thurr, yuno,' the man said.

'Really?'

'Yes – oirekun they gets loyk them astronauts – plastic bags, yuno. Thasall they givum, oirekun. Starvum. Them erses go by mos'evryday. Wun jus now. You see it?'

'Yes, we did.'

'Oy seeum go by, regla.'

Throughout this exchange, Nick looked on bemusedly, sipping his beer.

'Let's move to a table,' he said.

They sat by a window. It was dark in the pub: the collapsed part of the rose obscured this window entirely. A plump lady with a grubby apron soon served the food with a smile.

'Thur you go maloves – any mustard, brown sauce?'

'Yes, please, both,' Claire replied, and then to Nick: 'Sussex burr. You don't hear it much these days. There's a couple of old guys in the village who speak like that. It's like west country, but it's a bit different, I'm told.'

As they ate, Nick talked:

'I have to confess I'm a bit concerned on a couple of fronts. I asked the young doctor who met us to show me round. There's a sort of central control room he took me to. I went to a room like it at a TV station once: screens all over the place, and about four or five people watching them. Very high tech. There are 20 rooms, units they call them, and each room has a screen. All the data from the patient, the ventilator and all that, is shown on it. There's also a TV camera in every room and the pictures go on another screen next to the one showing the medical information. The booth you were in also has a camera. I watched you, and, well, it picks up the sound as well. We could hear you, I'm afraid: you were talking about, er, dancing. Very intrusive. I asked them to turn the sound off but they wouldn't. There also appear to be cameras in various other

153

places: one at the main gate, and from what I could make out, more around the perimeter fence.'

'Eat your food, Nick. It'll get cold.'

He tucked in for a few minutes and then continued, not noticing a glob of brown sauce at the side of his mouth.

'Staffing levels are as far as I could see and learn, pretty minimal. There are two doctors on all the time, one senior and one more junior. The one we met said the senior was having his lunch while we were there. There are only about ten nursing staff on shift at any time, fewer at night, though, I think. Normally, in an intensive care unit in a hospital you would have one nurse per patient at the very least.'

He looked across at the man behind the bar.

'My hunch is that if a patient got into real difficulties, cardiac arrest, stroke, that kind of thing, they'd be stretched. And as we've found, it is so far from anywhere. But on the other hand . . .'

He paused to eat some more and wipe the sauce from his mouth.

'. . . on the other hand you have to say it is a state-of-the-art place. Apart from the staffing levels, in terms of equipment and technology you can't fault it. And, of course I should have said, Christian's condition is entirely unchanged. They are going to do tests on him next Thursday morning. These are standard tests for particular kinds of reflex, which indicate brain activity . . .'

Her mouth full and eyes watering, on this occasion because of the mustard, Claire croaked rather hoarsely: 'Yes, Krishnan told me about them.'

'I'll write all this up when we get home. May be useful at the meeting next week.'

'That'll be good, Nick,' Claire said. 'What about food – did you get what our friend behind the bar said about that?'

'No, what did he say?'

'He said he thinks they get fed out of plastic bags, like astronauts! Country folk-lore I think.'

'Well, to an extent a lot of them are fed from bags. If you're in a coma, then food, well you can't call it that, nourishment, let's say, comes through a tube that's put down into the stomach through the nose – from what I saw on the screens in the control room, I didn't see any patient being fed orally.'

While they were eating, the customers that had been there when they arrived, four or five of them, all dressed in sombre formal clothes, as if for a funeral, left. The man behind the bar now gently rang the bell.

'You don't hear that much these days,' Nick said.

Nick was pensive on the way back, drumming the steering wheel with his fingers and occasionally scratching his beard with his free hand.

'Something on your mind, I think?' Claire said after watching this for some time.

'Oh, nothing really.'

'That's exactly what Christian would say. No, there is. Tell me.'

'No, I don't think now's the time, really. Your friend Rosie would say that and I think she'd be right to.'

'Stop the car, Nick. I want to know.'

They soon found a place where several trucks had stopped, the drivers dozing in their cabs. The place was strewn with litter: a rubbish bin had been blown over by the wind. Cars and other lorries whooshed noisily by them. It was a bleak place, the hawthorn hedge behind it bare and spiky, awaiting its first spring buds.

'Let's take a little walk,' Nick said, pointing to a public footpath sign at a stile that led to a yellow-green field behind the hedge.

They climbed the stile and walked a few paces, just far enough to get away from the worst of the noise of the traffic.

'So?'

'To be honest, I was thinking about the staffing levels,' Nick said. 'At first I was shocked, but when you think about it they make sense, they make perfect sense . . .'

He kicked a piece of turf out of the ground.

'I don't know how to put this, in fact I probably shouldn't be saying it, not now, not here, certainly not to you, but . . .'

'But what?'

'When I was talking to that young doctor back there, when he answered my question about nursing levels, he gave me a sort of smirk, as if it was a stupid question to ask. In fact I did feel stupid. You see I never did private work at any time while I was practising. I just don't believe in it. It's a cancer. As soon as you have it in the system, it grows, consuming the very system in which it lives. I guess Christian had his op done privately because of waiting lists?'

'Yes, he told me his father waited years for precisely the same thing to be done and that it was more or less too late by the time his turn came up. I remember when Christian and I were talking about it he even mentioned you. He said, "Nick will never speak to me again", something like that, anyway. But going back to staffing, surely you'd expect the staffing to be better in the private system, wouldn't you?'

'Yes, that's what I thought, until it dawned on me when that little jerk of a doctor smirked at me back there.'

'What do you mean?'

'It's obvious, Claire, at least it's obvious to me now.'

'Go on.'

'Money. You can bet your life, if you'll forgive the expression, that every single one of those poor souls back there is costing Pro-Fit money. They're like unwanted clini-cal waste matter that can't be disposed of. So they are managed, as cheaply as possible, out of sight, not quite out of mind. Unlike public systems, you see, private systems have two demands on them: make people well and make people money. Or maybe the other way round. Get it?'

Nick's red face reddened yet more as he spoke.

'Don't take it out on me, Nick!' Claire yelled, turning away and marching further into the field.

Nick let her go. After a few minutes she turned and came back.

'I'm sorry,' Nick said as they got back to the car. 'I told you it wasn't the time or place.'

'I guess you're right,' Claire said, 'but I suppose I ought to be glad you let it out. Better that way, whatever Rosie thinks. Let's go home.'

They found a note from Rosie when they got back, beside which were Nick's small suitcase and Gladstone bag:

Message from Krishnan on yr voice-m: suggest mtg tomorrow to prep for mtg later in week. Call him: home all day and has day off tomorrow. I am out all day then have dinner with my man tonight. Call or leave message re mtg time tomorrow if want me there. I'll call in sick again 1st thing. Now K gone suggest N stays with you; here are bags. Love Rxxx PS Nick, no hard feelings, honest!

'Mind if I watch the TV?' Nick asked. 'The replays of the rugby will be on.'

'Of course,' Claire said, 'help yourself. I think I'd better go to the supermarket and get some supplies in.'

The next day, Monday, proved to be bright and clear again, but calmer, with only a light breeze. When Krishnan arrived, he went upstairs with Nick to have the dressings on his ear

157

changed. That did not take long: what both men really wanted to do was to talk medical matters.

While they were doing so, Rosie arrived, looking dejected.

'What's up? Still mad at Nick?' Claire asked.

'No. The depressing thought is slowly dawning on me that I will definitely have to go back to work tomorrow I'm afraid, darling.'

'I realise that. You've been an absolute brick. I don't know what I'd have done without you.'

While they hugged, Rosie whispered:

'But I've got some other news: I'll tell you later.'

Claire put mugs of tea and coffee on a tray, together with some pastries she'd bought the previous day.

'Give the guys a shout, can you Rosie? Tell them it's all ready.'

When Krishnan came back down he looked more like his normal self, now having just a small plaster over the top of his ear. While the scratches on his forehead were still visible, it was evident that they were minor, and already healing well.

Krishnan was the first to speak once they had all sat down: 'There's a lot I need to say, Claire, so do you mind if I begin?'

'Not at all.'

'This is all in no particular order, I'm afraid. First, Claire, it is imperative that later today or tomorrow you go to your bank and get a banker's cheque for five thousand pounds, payable to "Pro-Fit" and then take it to the Ashfield. When you arrive, ask to see the Chief Finance Officer, give it personally to him and ask for a receipt. Beforehand, prepare a covering letter to go with the cheque stating that it is an advance payment for the extended care services being provided to your husband but that . . .'

'Just a minute, I'd better make notes,' Claire interrupted.

'Don't worry, I'm doing that,' said Nick, waving his pen, and then, turning to Krishnan, asked: 'But what?'

'Your letter must make it clear that making the payment does not mean that you are letting Pro-Fit off the hook as far as their terms and conditions are concerned – you know, the ones concerning the recovery process and the 30-day period after an operation.'

'I still haven't looked at them properly, I'm afraid', said Claire. 'Maybe we should do that now?'

'No, I don't think that would help much, although it will all come up on Thursday, I'm sure. What I'm really getting at is that you must have your letter checked by a lawyer, hopefully this man Barrie. He's the one who should be going through the terms and conditions.'

'I get you, Krishnan,' said Nick. 'There's some kind of legal mumbo-jumbo we need to put in. What is it they say – "Without Prejudice?" – something like that, isn't it? The letter needs to say, in essence: "Here's some money, but the fact that I'm giving it to you doesn't mean that I won't be . . .", oh, I'm getting confused myself now.'

'I think we've all got the gist of it,' said Rosie. 'To me this means that we've got to get hold of Sir Timothy absolutely as soon as possible. We can send him an email later today or tonight with all key points in it, so he'll get it first thing. And we'll need to send him the Terms and Conditions.'

'What I've noted,' Nick said, 'is this: Claire and Nick to draft and send email to Barrie and also fax terms and conditions to him. To be done by this evening. Now let's move on can we? Krishnan?'

'Thanks, Nick. Keeping with Barrie for the moment, and I know this is a long shot, but if you could get him to be with you at the meeting, I think it would really have an impact. In short, I think it would put the fear of God into them. Let me just take you through who'll be there. Firstly, there'll be the administrators: these are desk-wallahs in Pro-Fit HQ. They wouldn't know a syringe from a stethoscope. All they know about and care about is the bottom line. They don't want Christian to make even the tiniest dent in this year's shareholder dividends and management perform-ance-related pay bonuses. Got it?'

Nick and Claire looked at each other.

'I don't know how many of them there'll be,' Krishnan went on, 'but the main one will be the one who called you, Claire, what they call the "Manager, Extended Services". He'll probably have one or two of his senior lackeys with him. So that's the admin people. Then, there will be the medics. That means me, the anaesthetist who was with me that day – she's a decent type by the way – and, possibly the person called "Manager, Medical Practices" in Pro-Fit admin. Unlike other admin staff, however, he is medically qualified, and I get on well with him. I've kept him fully in touch on this case, as indeed I'm required to. Then finally, there'll be you, which I take it means you, Claire, and Nick, and, let's hope, Sir Timothy.'

Nobody spoke, so Krishnan continued:

'Which reminds me. Tomorrow you must also call Pro-Fit, to tell them you will attend. I suggest, however, that you simply say that you may, repeat may, be accompanied by advisers. That'll make them realise you're no grief-stricken pushover. But if they know someone like Sir Timothy might be coming, they'll go into panic mode and line up their own heavy-duty legal mob. Now, there's another really important point for me to stress. I'm sorry to labour the point – Nick and I have just been talking about this, and I think you and Rosie know this, Claire, from what I've said before. The point is this: in the meeting, and indeed in all the dealings that will no doubt follow, I have no choice other than to be part of Pro-Fit. That doesn't mean to say that I won't be arguing for you internally, and it doesn't mean to say that I will share whatever judgements the administrators may come to. In fact it's very likely that I won't. But if they have even the slightest suspicion that I'm on your side, let alone meeting and briefing you, and all that, then I'll be taken out of the loop. Without wanting to sound immodest, I think it's important for your sake that I stay in it.'

'I think we all understand that, Krishnan. Nick and I gave no hint of any contact with you or even knowledge of you when we were at the TCC yesterday,' said Claire.

'So I understand,' Krishnan went on. 'Now, let me deal with the key issue. Basically – and I'm sure Barrie or whoever you get legal advice from will take you along this course – the easiest way for you to prove your case that the financial responsibility for Christian's continued care rests with Pro-Fit, rather than you personally, is to be able to show that there was fault, or negligence, or whatever, on either my part, or that of the anaesthetist, yes?'

'Yes,' said Nick.

'Now, as I've already said to Nick, and indeed as I originally indicated to you, Claire, the problem here is that there is no sign of such fault or negligence. The records of the operation – these things are all on computers now at places like the Ashfield, as they will be at the TCC – the records show no sign at all. It was just happenstance that the trigger – the heart business – happened during the operation. It could have happened anywhere. That is my view, and the records show no different. I've offered to go through them with Nick. I know this could be construed as defensive or secretive behaviour on my part, but all I can do is to assure you that that's not the case. If your barrister friend feels that you should nevertheless pursue that line, then of course it's not for me in any way to object. I'm simply saying, with all the honesty I can muster, that I believe it will be fruitless. My view is that the best line to pursue lies in the anomalies, inconsistencies and gaps in the Pro-Fit Terms and Conditions. I sincerely believe that to be the case.'

There was an awkward silence. Claire knew that it had to be her to respond.

'Krishnan, please, don't tax yourself on this any more. If you want to go through the records with Nick, fine. But as far as I'm concerned, I'm convinced that no fault rests with you, and that we should therefore follow your advice and go against it only if our lawyer man convinces me otherwise. And I think that's highly unlikely. Now let's please leave it there, can we?'

'There is one last thing, or at least nearly the last thing – it's about your dreams, Claire.'

'You're going to say that I should not on any account mention them or refer to them in any way at the meeting?'

'In short, yes.'

'I've thought about it a lot and, yes, I agree. I won't say a word, I promise.'

'I think that's very wise,' said Nick, 'and I take it you would have told us if there'd been any more? No?'

Claire shook her head.

'Good,' said Krishnan, 'there was something else, but I can't think what it was now ... oh yes, of course, most important – the meeting will not, I'm sure, go even a step along the way we can describe as "the matter of life or death", assuming, that is, that there's no marked deterioration in Christian's reactions to the next tests. There's a bit of an unknown there because I've been asked to do them again, in the presence of another consultant, on Thursday morning. I gather Nick was told that at the TCC yesterday. Now all I can suggest is that if, and only if, the results are in any way bad news, I'll call Nick once I leave the TCC. We've just exchanged numbers, so that is lined up. But I doubt, Nick and I both doubt, whether there will be any bad news there. Assuming that is the case, my guess is that at the meeting, the Pro-Fit people will be saying – even if you raise questions about whether you should now be paying or Pro-Fit should now be paying – that it would be premature at this stage to discuss, er, termination matters, and in any case the admin people should have no involvement in that whatsoever. It would be highly irregular if they did. It's strictly a medical matter. But I should warn you that another meeting to discuss it is more than likely. My guess would be that it would be in two or three weeks time. You must be ready for that when it comes, Claire.'

'Yes, I will, or rather I'll try to be,' Claire said. 'Now, on another matter while I think about it, if you're giving your services to me for free, as you've said, won't it look suspicious, on Pro-Fit's part I mean, if they know that?'

'Ah,' said Krishnan, 'I was going to raise that, so thanks for reminding me. As you know, for the operation itself, you, or rather Christian, paid me the total, and I then paid the Ashfield, or rather Pro-Fit, for their costs out of that. That's the way the system works. The TCC regime is different. Since the costs now lie largely with the TCC, they pay me out of what you pay them. My own fees, for one or two visits there per week, say, would not be great: at most five hundred a week. So what I was going to suggest, because you're right in what you say, Claire, is that I bill the TCC in my normal way, and then I give the money they give me back to you. How does that sound? The TCC will send you statements, I think it's every two weeks, showing every item of expenditure, by the way.'

'That's all fine with me,' Claire said, 'It's really very good of you.'

After they had finished, Nick walked Krishnan up the street to where he had left his car. They agreed that after Thursday's meeting, Krishnan would give Nick a complete set of the medical records.

No sooner had the two men gone, than, while the two women were washing up, Rosie said: 'I need to share something with you. Strictly between you and me right? I've taken a very strong fancy to Superman, and I think he has to me.'

Claire promptly dropped a mug, fortunately back into the foamy water rather than onto the floor. She looked her friend in the eye: 'Mmmmmmmmmmm – tell me more!'

'He called me yesterday and asked me out to dinner next weekend. And I said yes!'

Claire smiled, opened her mouth to speak, closed it, and then said:

'Good, I'm glad. But can I ask you one thing, while I think of it?'

'Yes, what?'

'You haven't told anyone else, including Krishnan, about the money in Italy?'

'No, just as you asked, but I had a problem with Nick.'

'How come?'

'He saw Christian's letter to you, the one in Italy, about it – you know – being yours. He, Nick, asked if it was money. I just said that it was your business, that's all. I didn't say anything else. Didn't feel I should. Glad I didn't now as, well, I'm not exactly his biggest fan right now. Anyway, it's your business. I didn't let you down.'

'That's fine then. And Krishnan?'

'No. Unless Nick has voiced any suspicions to him.'

'That's fine. Thanks for being discreet. Can we just keep it like that?

'Sorted, promise.'

Later, Nick returned and, when Rosie had gone, he said to Claire: 'I need to share something with you. Strictly between you and me . . .'

'I don't believe this,' Claire said, 'I've just had this conversation I think!'

'Uh? What?'

'Oh, never mind, go on, then.'

'It's about Krishnan, about this business of whether there was any fault on his part.'

'Did what I said upset him?'

'No, far from it. What you said was perfect. And I'm glad you said that it would be good if I went through the records with him.'

'So what's up?'

Glad that Rosie was not around, Nick said:

'Well, suppose, just suppose, Krishnan was at fault? If he was, and wanted to get us off the scent, so to speak, then what would he be doing? He'd be saying precisely what he is saying, and he would be trying to, how can I put it, ingratiate himself, with you in particular, perhaps with others too. Yes, he'd be saying things like: "there'll be no charge for my services", and "let me brief you on how to handle Pro-Fit", and so on and so on.'

'Are you saying you think he's up to no good, hiding something?'

'No, I'm not. I'm simply looking at this in just the same way that I looked at your dreams. I'm saying there's room for doubt, that there could be another explanation for his actions than good intentions. Personally I think he's a man of honesty and integrity. I think we all think that. All I'm saying is that it is no bad thing – in his interests too – if one of us, and I'm happy for it to be me, puts that judgement on hold, at least until we know more, through seeing the records. Krishnan told me that he's happy to do that after Thursday's meeting, by the way. I guess I can understand why he doesn't want to do so now, but the delay sort of adds to my worries, I must confess. And just to sound really

165

negative: how do we know he's not reporting on what's going on here, and in your head, to Pro-Fit?'

'Surely not? But you know what? – in the light of what Rosie's just told me, I'm going to go along with you, Nick.'

'Why? What did she tell you?'

'I don't usually break confidences, but this time I will. Krishnan has asked Rosie out to dinner with him. What do you read into that?'

'Hmmm,' said Nick.

As usual, Sir Timothy Barrie arrived at his chambers just after seven the following morning. A meticulous man in habits, he was dressed for court, where he anticipated being for the greater part of the day ahead. He hung his coat on a hanger that he then placed carefully on the coat rack, smoothing out its sleeves as he did so. Then he took the pink-tape-wrapped files from the bottom of his bag and placed them in three separate piles on his large, green, leather-topped antique desk. On each pile he placed a folded card bearing a name. He then completed his early morning routine: his computer having already been switched on for him by his clerk, he looked carefully at his email in-box, knowing that as he did so, the clerk, who would have heard him come in, would bring him a cup of coffee, which would be in the large white bone china cup that he favoured.

'No telephone messages, Sir Timothy,' the clerk said. He was a small, stooped, elderly man. As he placed the cup and saucer on the silver mat that was positioned in exactly the right spot beside the computer screen, his hand trembled a little.

'Thank you, Arthur. Please tell the others that we will leave for court at nine-thirty.'

'Very good sir.'

A man of substantial reputation, Sir Timothy was also of substantial, but not, he felt himself, excessive, girth. He was often described, by bar colleagues and adversaries alike, as a man of imposing stature. This caused his chair, the leather of which exactly matched that of the desk, and was similarly antique in its provenance, to creak. But it was another, more unusual, feature of Sir Timothy that gave him a truly imposing, indeed distinctive, presence: his hair. This was jet black, abundant, and as naturally and permanently fine and curly as that on a lamb's back.

'I'm the black sheep of the family' was, in consequence, a favourite one-liner of his at dinner-parties and receptions.

He studied the screen carefully. There were ten letters. He chose one, read it carefully, clicked on 'Forward', and then pushed the two buttons on his phone which would connect him to his current pupil, who had been under his guidance for the previous four months or so.

'Tom, would you come up right away please? Thank you. Come straight in.'

Anyone, even the closest colleague, who dared to 'come straight in' without such prior permission incurred a severe dressing-down. Sir Timothy's temper – mostly displayed only outside the court room – was legendary.

A tall, rather thin young man soon came in, also dressed for court, the white of his collarless shirt seemingly accentuated by his deep black skin. Sir Timothy beckoned him to sit at another green leather chair on the other side of his desk.

'Yes, Sir Timothy?'

'Tom, how many times do I have to tell you that within these walls you are Tom and I am Timothy? Now, I have just forwarded something to you. It refers to a fax that you should find in the clerk's office. It is largely self-explanatory, but let me give you some background. There are two previous emails that I will forward to you as soon as you leave. They will fill out the picture for you. As you will see, the central character was at school with me and I owe a debt of gratitude to him. He is now very seriously ill indeed. I want to do everything in my power to help. Let me be perfectly clear about that, Tom.'

'Yes, er, Timothy.'

'Good. Much as I would like you to be there, and much as I know how much you are preoccupied with our current case, I can manage without you in court today. I want you to give full attention to the matter I've just referred to. In the first instance I want you to review the letter she proposes to send, and if necessary redraft it, and study the documents she has faxed. Would you then please come back to me at, let me see . . .'

He glanced up at the large grandfather clock that stood beside the coat-rack.

'. . . at nine o'clock precisely. Bring any re-draft and any observations you have on any other matters, including the line or lines we might take, and how we can most productively use the time between now and Thursday. I suspect that there'll be some devilling to do, on who and what we are up against, but that will be for later today and tomorrow. No need to call the lady in question. I'll do that now and tell her what is happening. Any questions? No? Then, over to you, Tom. As you'll see, this is pro bono, by the way, but I believe it will be very useful experience – not just for you! So take that pained expression off your face. I know how much satisfaction you're getting from the current case, and indeed valuably, most valuably, contributing to it. But I'm counting on you on this matter and I know I can rely on you to do your usual first-class job. Now, ask Arthur to come in while you're on your way down, would you?'

The young man managed a thin smile and then left. The clerk soon appeared in his place.

'Arthur, you remember the lady, the wife of the old

school friend, that I told you about last week? Please call her right away and put her through to me.'

The clerk, who had served Sir Timothy for over twenty years, and was now close to retirement, turned to leave.

'No. Arthur, wait, I haven't finished yet. Can you do a note and circulate it to everyone to this effect: I want to think of a way in which we might, shall we say, obtain an adjournment this coming Thursday afternoon? And, may I say, I wonder if I could have the benefit of even your own preliminary thoughts on the matter, before I leave for court today?'

'Very good, Sir Timothy. I'll give the matter my full attention.'

At precisely nine o'clock there was a knock on Sir Timothy's door.

'Come.'

Tom appeared, the earlier thin smile now considerably wider.

'Ah, I see signs of some improvement of disposition? Or am I mistaken?'

'Certainly not, er, Timothy. I have, as you yourself sometimes say, "sunk my teeth into this and find the taste quite agreeable".'

As he said this, Tom realised he was pushing his relationship with his pupil-master in a rather adventurous way as the phrase he had used was a favourite one of his boss.

'Pray tell me,' said Sir Timothy, who was inwardly delighted to see this change in his pupil's demeanour.

'Here is the draft I think she should send – my proposed amendments are underlined.'

The barrister scanned the text. When he had finished, he continued: 'Excellent. Get it to her. Now, what else?'

The young pupil rose to his feet, as if he was in court.

'Notwithstanding what our client says, I think we should

169

keep open, and even lead, with the possibility of negligence here. Regardless of our client's apparently close relationship with the surgeon, it would be entirely wrong to do anything other than investigate the possibility. And regardless of the fact that the medical records to which she refers have been promised as a personal favour, they should be demanded, and their existence thus placed on formal record. It will not help our case if their transmission is a confidential arrangement between the surgeon and our client.'

'I entirely agree, Tom, but we'll need to convince her on that front, I fear. Now, what do you make of the terms and conditions she faxed?'

'At first sight, the way would appear clear to drive several coaches and horses through them. But I still think negligence is our first line of attack. If we can't convince her on that, then the terms and conditions . . . yes, very promising.'

'Subject to reading them myself, I can't comment, except that, as ever, I will trust your judgement, Tom. Now, I haven't got much time. Next steps, please.'

'I propose to go and see the lady today. I'll speak to her, email her the revised draft letter, so that she can get it off, and then take myself down there. I would like to talk more to this doctor friend that she has got with her, and I think it will be useful, as you always put it, to "sniff out the ground". Meaning I would like to see the hospital – the "scene of the crime" – and this new place that the man has been moved to. I haven't of course started devilling into Pro-Fit yet, but I have a certain source that I suspect may come in very handy in that respect.'

As he said this, Tom's smile widened still further. Now his white teeth seem to sparkle even more.

'Oh, and what or who may that source be?'

'My sister is, or rather was, a nurse at the place in question.'

'The hospital, you mean?'

'No, the place the man has been moved to. She's employed by Pro-Fit. I haven't spoken to her today, or even recently, but when I last saw her she was, to put it mildly, not exactly full of praise for them. She's on maternity leave at present. I have a feeling she'll be a rich source of more than background on this. Of course I'll do the usual devilling for previous cases in law and all that.'

'Tom, all I can say is, go full steam ahead – yes, including getting down there and meeting the dramatis personae and finding out whatever you can, with the usual discretion of course. Then would you please brief me first thing tomorrow? By the way, I have spoken to her . . .'

'You mean Claire, the wife?'

'Yes. I've told her that I've put you on the case and explained who you are. I have also, by the way, told her that you will be at the meeting she refers to on Thursday, or possibly, just possibly, you and I.'

'But that's not possible, at least for you – the trial will be going on for weeks more yet, surely?'

'Yes, but . . .'

Sir Timothy made a ludicrously exaggerated wink and continued:

'. . . but shall we just say I am looking at how we might secure a rather unexpected adjournment around Thursday lunch-time?'

Tom laughed: 'I see! I will of course not seek to deflect my distinguished learned counsel colleague from pursuing this matter. And I take it that I should not indicate any such likelihood to our new client, for fear of unrealistically raising her expectations?'

'Spot on, Tom. Good luck!'

The following day, at around the same time, the pupil reported back to his pupil-master.

'Getting straight to the key point, the company would appear to be likely to argue that their undertaking, in their brochure, that should a patient's stay *for recovery purposes . . .*'

He emphasised these latter words and those that followed:

'*. . . be longer than anticipated, no extra charges will be applied,* is nul and void in this particular case.'

'Because his condition is not related to "*recovery*" I presume, as what happened was unrelated to the operation?'

'Exactly, er, Timothy.'

'And our response would be?'

'That such a conclusion is conjecture. There is, I have discovered, a substantial body of legal precedence where such claims have been dismissed on the basis, essentially, of *in loco parentis*, where for example schools have attempted to disclaim responsibility for an accident. Much the same applies to the other relevant statement in the brochure, also elaborated in the Terms and Conditions. The relevant statement is: "in the unlikely event of there being a complication with *the treatment you receive* (my emphasis again, Timothy) within 30 days of leaving hospital, there will also normally be no further charges". Again, the argument we can make, based on the same precedents, is that any claim that the complication is *unrelated* to the treatment received is pure conjecture.'

'I take it you've taken the obvious step of finding out if the patient had any record of previous heart problems?'

'I went, with his wife and this retired GP friend, to see his current GP yesterday. There is no record whatsoever of any previous heart problems. Indeed, and if I might say, Timothy, this is a real, er, corker – he had a full medical for insurance purposes less than a year ago, at which he got an absolutely clean bill of health, which is on record.'

'Excellent, Tom. Which brings us to the question of whether there has been negligence. You were strong on that score yesterday. Have you turned up anything on that front?'

'No, I'm afraid not, except for, well, I'll come to that in a moment if I may. My view is that all we should do on the negligence front, tomorrow, is formally request that the records of the operation be handed over, on the basis of . . .'

'Ruling it out of our enquiries, as our friends in the police would say?'

'Exactly.'

'So be it. Now, pray tell me what you are "about to come to in a moment" as you just put it, Tom.'

'When I saw our client, Claire, and this retired GP character, Nick, we agreed there would be nothing to be learned, and probably much to be lost, by my visiting either the original hospital or the place, the TCC as it's called, where the man is now. Nick felt my presence at the hospital might set off alarms, and told me that any attempt to get into the TCC would be fruitless and indeed set off even more alarms, literally, I mean. On the latter front, what my sister told me confirmed what Nick said. It is evidently a fortress.'

'I see. And what else did you learn from your sister?'

'Starting with what I learned before I spoke to her, Pro-Fit is an extremely successful company. Shares in it have consistently risen in value over the years, and dividends paid consistently. It buys up, and is still buying up, other smaller health services providers. So far so good. But my sister told me that, while the consultants are treated by the firm like gods, the staff, nursing and auxiliary, are treated like, well . . . dirt. There's lots of hiring and firing, poor pay and conditions . . .'

'Just as in many other highly successful companies. Come on Tom, where's this going to get us?'

'Sorry, Timothy, yes, not relevant, I agree, but one thing

my sister said, if there's anything to it, may have some relevance. To put it in a nutshell . . .'

'And still leave room for the nut I hope, Tom, as time is pressing,' Sir Timothy said, consulting his pocket watch.

'She told me that she and other nursing staff have expressed concern from time to time that patients at the TCC are not being fed as well as they should be and that as a result, the death-rate there is high, or at least higher than it should be.'

'Rumour and conjecture, Tom. Sour grapes from poorly treated staff. And what do you expect in a place where all the patients are close to death? Goodness me! And in any case what happens at the TCC is irrelevant – what *happened* took place at the original hospital.'

'You're quite right. But my sister is a pretty level-headed person. And it seems to me . . .'

'That any patient in the TCC that is there at the company's expense, due to its most generous terms and conditions, is a potentially drain on its profits, yes, Tom. But whilst this may be useful to us at some point down the track, and I admit it could be if it is more than rumour and conjecture, it is not relevant right now, although some hard facts are what we need, and goodness only knows how we could get hold of them.'

Rather chastened, Tom could only reply: 'Yes, Timothy.'

'Well, it's pretty clear how we should proceed at the meeting, then – you'll have a song-sheet ready for me to look at first thing again tomorrow? Good. Now just one other thing – what do you make of this dreams business – did she tell you more about that?'

'Yes, it's all rather, weird isn't it? But she and the doctor friend told me that they feel that that side of things should not be referred to tomorrow, and I must say that I was quick to agree.'

'Very well.'

'I'll do the song-sheet now and see that she's happy with it. Any progress on the adjournment?'

'With any luck there will be an adjournment at lunch. The jury have requested a visit to the site of the crime. I cannot for the life of me think why,' the barrister replied, with a twinkle in his eye.

Still in his court wear, apart from having changed to a dress collar from his court one, Sir Timothy joined the others in the reception area of Pro-Fit's imposing head-quarters in St James's Street in the West End. Tom made the introductions. Already happy that there had been no message from Krishnan, Claire was overjoyed that Sir Timothy was there.

They were quickly shown up to a large meeting room on the first floor, overlooking the busy street, where the Pro-Fit team, including Krishnan and a lady Claire presumed was the anaesthetist, were already seated along one side of the table. As they took their places along the other side, Claire noticed a note being passed along to the man at the centre of the Pro-Fit group. As he read it his brow furrowed and he looked up briefly at Sir Timothy. He then whispered in the ear of the person next to him, who quickly left the room. Claire also noticed that Krishnan looked tense and that the small plaster remained above his ear. He sat immediately to the left of the seat that had just been vacated. Claire was surprised that it was Krishnan, rather than the man in the centre, whom she took to be the 'Manager, Extended Services', who spoke first.

'Welcome, everyone, please allow me to introduce those on this side of the table,' he said, in a voice whose tone clearly betrayed nervousness as well as tension.

Once the introductions had been made, Claire responded, very calmly and confidently, although she too felt nervous, as evidenced by having a stomach that felt as if it was being trodden on by an elephant:

'Thank you, I am joined by . . .'

She introduced Nick first, describing him as 'my medical adviser' and then went on:

'And this is my legal adviser, Sir Timothy Barrie QC, and his colleague Doctor Tom Yeboah-Afari.'

As they had agreed when discussing the song-sheet over the phone the previous day (Tom had said: 'It's important that they respond to us, not us to them'), Claire continued, still outwardly calmly and confidently, although the elephant had not yet budged:

'As you will I am sure realise, these past ten days have been extremely stressful for me. I want to begin by expressing my gratitude . . .'

(Tom had advised: 'A bit of flattery to begin with won't do any harm.')

'. . . to all of you at Pro-Fit, and especially Mr Supramanian, for all that you have done . . .'

Krishnan smiled thinly. The man in the centre held up his hand and said:

'Thank you. Now if . . .'

Claire interrupted:

'Please, allow me to finish. While my husband's life hangs in the balance it is not easy for me, in fact it is impossible for me, to manage everything. That's why I have asked Nick and Sir Timothy for assistance. Now I'm going to hand over to Sir Timothy.'

Without hesitation, and in spite of the fact that another man now entered the room, Sir Timothy began:

'My client's husband suffered a complication during his recovery from the operation which has made it necessary for him to remain in the care of your company. Whether that complication was through any negligence needs to be determined. I must inform you, however, that he underwent a full medical examination for insurance purposes within the past twelve months and was given an absolutely clean bill of health.'

He paused at this point, looked across the table, and then continued:

'My client therefore requests, firstly, that the full records of the operation and its immediate aftermath be made available to her. Secondly, while my client has made a payment to you in respect of her husband's continuing care in your hands, this payment has, as you are aware, been made without prejudice. I and my colleague have advised my client that our understanding and interpretation of your company's terms and conditions is that the responsibility, both financial and medical, for such continuing care is that of your company, and that, accordingly, we request you, thirdly, to place the sum given to you earlier this week in trust, or of course, return it to her.'

After another brief pause, he continued:

'Your assent to these three requests will be very much in your company's interests: Pro-Fit has a high reputation, in the eyes of the business world, the government, through the National Care Standards Commission, and the general public alike. It would not, I am sure, wish to jeopardise the esteem in which it is so held by taking action over the matters in question that might in any way be construed as hard-hearted or secretive, were they to be made known in public or more private arenas. Those are my client's requests.'

The response to this was action rather than words. The man who had just joined the meeting got up and gave a note to the man in the centre, who read it, his hand noticeably shaking as he did so. At the same time, the man on his left whispered in his ear. Krishnan looked down at his papers. Claire searched for eye contact with him and each of the Pro-Fit team in turn, and got only one response, from the anaesthetist, who returned her gaze stonily. At her side, Tom and Nick were both writing notes. Sir Timothy had moved his chair back, and sat with his fingers entwined on his stomach, slowly rotating one thumb around the other.

At last the man in the centre spoke:

'Sir Timothy, I need to consult with my colleagues privately on the matters you have raised. With your permission, we will retire in order to do so. In the meantime, I'll arrange for tea and coffee to be brought here to you. We will be as quick as we can, I can assure you, and rejoin you within no longer than twenty minutes.'

In response, Sir Timothy gave a long, slow and silent nod of assent.

Precisely twenty minutes later, the Manager, Extended Services returned, this time with only one colleague, who was the man who had belatedly joined the earlier meeting. He now spoke:

'Sir Timothy, I am responsible for legal affairs in the company. I am happy to inform you that . . .'

He paused to put on glasses, and then read from a sheet of paper:

'One: Pro-Fit will place the funds received earlier this week from your client, totalling five thousand pounds, in a trust account. Two: the medical records you have requested will be made available to you without delay . . .'

'Meaning?' Sir Timothy boomed.

'Meaning delivered personally either to you or your client, as you prefer, by no later than tomorrow evening.'

'To my client, please.'

The man referred again to his sheet of paper:

'Three: while this and indeed all these actions of the

company are entirely without prejudice to possible litigation instituted either by the company or your client, Pro-Fit agrees to meet all the costs of the patient's continuing care for a period of 30 days from the date of the original operation, or less in the event of the decease of the patient, provided that, firstly, your client agrees not to make any disclosure to any person other than you and her medical adviser of any information about this case either during or after the 30 days; and secondly, to meet all care costs after the expiry of the 30 days.'

Sir Timothy looked to Claire, who nodded vigorously. He said:

'My client is content with all that you propose, except in one respect. While she agrees to maintaining confidentiality during the 30-day period, she cannot at this stage possibly agree to continuing any such confidentiality thereafter. It is simply, if I may say, outrageous of you to seek this.'

As if expecting such a response, the Pro-Fit man replied immediately:

'We can agree to that, albeit reluctantly. Can I propose that the agreement between us, which we can draw up for your client's signature within an hour, binds both parties to a further meeting to be held no later than the day before the 30-day period ends, where all the terms of the current agreement are revisited?'

'That is wise, and therefore fully acceptable,' said Sir Timothy, who rose from his chair, quickly followed by the others, 'My client and my colleague will return in one hour's time.'

Out in the street, Sir Timothy was taken aback by Claire's spontaneous expression of relief and gratitude: a smacking kiss on the cheek. Flushed with embarrassment he said:

'Tom, I will return to chambers now, but will you take Claire and Nick to a pub that you will find in Crown Passage, just across the street, there.'

He stuck out an arm, nearly decapitating a passing traffic warden, before continuing:

'I think a celebration is in order, so here . . .', taking a card from his top pocket, '. . . the pub is called *The Red Lion.* It's still a real pub, and to be honest I find the company there much more sane and convivial than I do at the Athenaeum, my club. Give this card to the landlord and get a bottle of good champagne. You and Claire come back here in an hour. Check the agreement carefully. If in any doubt, Claire, you should not sign. Tom will advise.'

He now stuck his arm out again, this time to summon a taxi. As he got in, he said to Claire: 'So far so good I think,' and to Tom: 'Back to court for you tomorrow, young man!'

He was gone before she had time to express even a word of thanks.

The pub at the end of the narrow passageway was dowdy and thoroughly and agreeably, Claire thought, old-fashioned. No two chairs or even two tables were the same. Brim-full ashtrays, most spilling their contents, were on every table. An imitation fire glowed on one side. The walls, perhaps once white or cream, had long since been stained a light brown by years of cigarette smoke, their original colour apparent only where framed photographs had been taken, or conceivably fallen, from them. Of the many remaining, not a single one was straight. Large areas of the once red carpet now shone like black linoleum. The clientele wore a mixture of suits with gleaming black shoes and dungarees with filthy brown boots. The atmosphere was boisterous. Tom handed the card to the landlord. On it Sir Timothy had written: 'Fred, champ pls'.

'Take a seat – I'll bring it to you,' the landlord said.

When he did so, Tom held out a twenty-pound note.

'No, it's on his account, and anyway, that wouldn't cover it!' the landlord said, adding: 'Lovely bloke he is.'

An hour later the deed was done.

'Thank you, Tom,' Claire said, as they parted, 'it's been lovely to have met you.'

She kissed him lightly on his cheek and then Nick shook his hand.

'It's been a pleasure,' Tom said, 'and I'll be happy to stay involved, as of course will my boss. Take care of yourself. There's a long way to go yet.'

10

The Box

I've discovered that I still get depressions. You know what I was like when I got depressed. Everything seemed hopeless to me. I would sleep a lot, avoid talking with anyone, make a little world for myself to live in, a world that even you would not be allowed to enter. A world where I could indulge myself in my great ability in the art of self-loathing to my heart's discontent. You hated it, although you tried hard to understand it, I know.

I'm still the same. That's why I haven't spoken to you for a good while now. Nothing to say. What's the point? In fact it's worse here because I can't get away and shut myself off. I can't simply go to the bedroom and draw the curtains and get under the duvet. You can't do that here. You can't say 'leave me alone'. It isn't like that here.

I started off thinking that there was so much I wanted to say to you. But in reality there isn't. You know what? When you got really worried about my depressions you used to ask if it ever got as bad as wanting to kill myself. And I would say, no, and in any case, that I wouldn't have the guts to do so. Well, I do have the guts now. Forget what I said about cremation will you? Just get on with it.

I don't think I ever told you that in my personnel file at the firm, there's a note where I nominate you as the sole beneficiary of a life policy the firm pays for for everyone, not just me. Make sure they pay it out to you. It wouldn't surprise me if Palmer and those other cretins somehow 'forget' to tell you, so they can lay their sticky hands on it, devious little bastards.

I've failed at everything I have attempted in my life, including failing to love and look after you properly. I had such big ideas, and never delivered on one of them. Not a single one. I think it's rich, ha bloody ha, that I have now, for the first time ever, succeeded at something. I've successfully died.

I've also done things that I should not have done. I wanted to tell you about them but, the more I think about them the more I think they are best left with me, as fuel for the fire of my own self-disgust. Even that is a deceitful way of putting it. It'd be more honest to say that the truth, the reality, was always another of those things that scared me. I was never good at facing up to either. Delusion and fantasy were much more my kind of stuff. And obfuscation in good measure. Ah! – of course, I've got it now:

> *I am a young executive*
> *No cuffs than mine are cleaner*
> *I have a slim-line briefcase*
> *And I drive the firm's Cortina*

> *You ask me what it is I do?*
> *Well actually you know,*
> *I'm partly this and partly that*
> *And partly P-R-O*

Wasn't that it? Good old Betjeman. It's been taxing me for ages. It's all I am – a very ordinary, albeit no longer young, executive. Goodbye.

*

She got up and put on a dressing gown. A note from Nick told her that he had gone over to the TCC to 'see that all is well'. He'd put the post on the dining room table, along with her copy of the agreement they had signed at Pro-Fit, which she remembered he had put in his inside pocket at the time.

She pulled a sheet from the shopping list pad on the kitchen wall and took the pencil that was attached to it. Waiting for the kettle to boil, she wrote: 'Loose ends' and then 'Alfonso??' and, after a moment's thought, 'Ravindra £500??'

With her tea, she sat at the table and thought about what he had said. So typical of him at his worst, yes, but on the other hand, she felt relieved that at least he was still there. Never mind what others are saying: she knew he was there. Never mind what he had said or might say. Never mind about that money. And never mind what he had done: she knew that he was a good man. She wanted him back.

Upstairs she looked in the airing cupboard for a clean towel for her shower and was shocked by the sight of an overflowing basket of laundry awaiting ironing. She took it out immediately, went back downstairs, and started on it in the kitchen.

A lot of it was the fall-out from Krishnan's 'accident': tablecloths, bed-linen, towels and tea-towels. She put them on one side and did clothes first. There were a few shirts that she realised must be Nick's, and some of Amy's dresses and trousers. These made her realise that she should go up to the school during the day to see Amy. She stopped for a moment and wrote 'See Amy' on her list.

The first tea-towel she started on still had a vaguely pinkish tinge about it, and this reminded her of the carpet-cleaning she and Nick had started on the previous evening, which had concluded with spraying some foamy-type product over the affected area. The instructions said that it should be left to dry and then hoovered off after so-so-so many hours. She went into the living room to look at it and then got the vacuum-cleaner from under the stairs and set to work. The result was pleasing. She smiled, both at the result and at the memory of the events that had caused the problem.

The phone rang. The unmistakable sounds of a call-centre were there: a young man struggling to make himself audible against the background noise comprised of hundreds of other voices like his: '. . . new mobile phone offer . . . nothing to pay for . . .' She put the phone down and as she did so she remembered Christian telling her, not long ago, in fact: 'Do you realise that a lot of these calls now come from centres in India? Most of the staff are young graduates. They're trained to speak and understand slang and accents, and they don't just know what time of day it is here, but what the weather's like and all that. Every caller has a daily information sheet, with things like last night's football results and even today's news headlines on it. Incredible.'

She went back to look at her list in the kitchen: 'Ravindra £500'.

Pausing only to switch the iron off, she went upstairs to the study and dialled the number on the back of the envelope sent by Ravindra.

'People's Development Institute,' a voice answered.

'I would like to speak to Ravindra Kapoor please.'

'Certainly madam – you are calling from overseas I think?'

'Yes.'

'One moment please.'

Immediately music, strange sounding music, took over. She listened and thought of the Beatles' – what was that instrument in 'Norwegian Wood' called? Suddenly the music cut off:

'This is Ravindra Kapoor speaking.'

'Mr Kapoor, I am the wife of Christian, the consultant from England who works with you. We met once some years ago.'

There was a silence at the other end.

'Hallo Mr Kapoor, are you there?'

'Yes, madam, I'm sorry but I have forgotten your name.'

'It's Claire.'

'Ah yes, I remember now . . . Claire, I hope you are not calling with bad news? I know Christian was to have his operation around this time.'

'I am afraid I do have bad news . . .'

'The operation was not successful?'

'No, I regret to say that the, the result . . . is much worse. I'm sorry to tell you that Christian experienced some problem with his heart during the operation, and as a result he is now in a coma. He is alive, but barely so, and entirely unconscious. And I am advised by the doctors that there is little likelihood of recovery.'

Now there was a long silence. During it Claire thought she could hear the muffled sound of sobbing, but could not be sure.

'Mr Kapoor, are you still there?' she said again, but there was no response. She waited until, eventually, she heard his voice:

'Madam Claire, forgive me. I am overwhelmed by this news. Please accept my most heartfelt condolences.'

Now she could hear clear sounds of distress.

'Could I ask one thing, please?'

'Yes,' she said gently. 'What is it?'

'Would you please allow me to compose myself and then call you back? I have the number.'

'Yes, of course.'

The line went dead.

She opened the filing cabinet and in the third drawer

was a thick file labelled 'PDI/Ravindra'. She took it out and laid it on the desk. Opening it, the very first document was a printed one: *People's Development Institute – Ten years of progress'*. A few pages into it she found a photograph of the man she had been speaking to, which she found reassuring, as the memory of what he looked like had disappeared in the years since she had met him. She took the photograph out and put the file back in the cabinet where it belonged.

An hour passed, during which she completed most of the ironing, hearing the splattering sound of renewed rain on the windows. As she laboured – everything had completely dried out, so much steaming and spraying was needed – she felt a sense of contentment, realising that this was the first good amount of time she had spent on her own since the day of Christian's operation. She reviewed each event in her mind, including the morning's call to India. From this she concluded, with some satisfaction, that it was good that the conversation had not gone on longer, as she realised that she had not thought through what to say.

She finally got to the shower, which she spent a good amount of time cleaning before undressing and stepping in. There, she reached the point in her thoughts where she knew she was ready to renew the conversation, because she knew what she would say. She would 'risk it for a biscuit' as Christian used to say when he was playing crib in the pub. She felt calm and relaxed.

It was mid-afternoon before the phone rang again.

It was quickly evident to her that the man, Ravindra, was still in a state of shock. He told her that he had called a meeting of all the staff of the Institute, to give them the news.

'Christian was well-known to, and much respected by, all of us, even the cleaners and drivers,' he said, going on to

187

say that a number of staff had been reduced to tears, and that he had given his permission to any staff wishing to take the following day off in order to mourn and grieve in an appropriate way. Indeed, he said, he had actively encouraged staff to do this.

'But you did explain that Christian isn't actually dead?' she said.

'Yes, I did. All are fully aware of the situation, but I did repeat what you had said to me, about there being little hope of anything other than such outcome.'

She was now ready to take the initiative.

'Have you informed the gharana?' she asked, and there was a perceptible pause at the other end.

'Ah, good, Christian has shared his passion with you,' Ravindra replied.

'Yes, of course. But have you informed them?'

'Yes, I have. In fact I have just come from there now. I am calling from my home. The principal has come here with me. She is most upset.'

Now it was Claire's turn to hesitate. She thought quickly. This was not part of the plan.

'Please would you thank her for the card sent to Christian. Unfortunately, like yours, it did not arrive until after the . . . until a day or so ago. Please tell her that Christian would have been very pleased to have got it, and the same with yours.'

'I will tell her that.'

She paused again, breathed out slowly and then resumed, following her own plan:

'Ravindra, Christian has told me everything of course,' and then she repeated with emphasis, '*Everything . . .*'

After taking a breath, she went on:

'Now, I'm sure he would want me to get the money to you, as usual. The five hundred pounds, I mean, that is the usual amount isn't it? From what Christian has told me I'm sure that it's needed. He would have been bringing it with him when he came wouldn't he?'

She heard the muffled hiss of a hand being placed over phone and waited for the more whooshy sound of it being taken away. As this happened, she heard a woman's voice still speaking in the background.

'Claire? Yes, it would be most welcome, but we feel that you should not trouble yourself with the matter at the moment. You must have many other concerns just now. When you are ready, fine, but, please, take your time. You must care of yourself first.'

'I have thought about the matter and I have a plan,' she said, trying to keep a matter-of-fact tone still in her voice.

'Yes?'

'I know that Christian had planned his next visit to you to coincide with the kathak festival, which is quite soon isn't it?'

'Yes,' Ravindra said, 'in fact we were expecting him, let me see, early the week after next.'

'That's right,' she said. 'Well, here is my plan.'

'Yes?'

'I will come. I would like to meet you. And I would certainly like to meet the people at the gharana and see something of the festival. And of course I will bring the money.'

'But surely . . . ?'

'No, I'm quite clear about this. There's nothing I can do for Christian except go to see him for a short while every day or every other day. He is not conscious. Only doctors can help Christian now. I can come for a week or so.'

'But your daughter?'

'She's already being cared for at a special place. They will look after her while I'm away. I wouldn't dream of leaving if that were not so.'

As she said this she realised that she had forgotten to go up to the school to see Amy.

'I see.' Ravindra replied, 'Then may I say, you will be most welcome. Please allow me to make all the arrangements at this end. Normally when Christian comes he goes to Clarence Hotel for . . .'

'Yes, the same place, that would be beaut.'

'Beaut?'

'I'm sorry, it would be good, I mean. Let me make my airline bookings and then I'll send the details to you. I can write by email to you? I'm sure it must be in Christian's files, in one of your reports?'

'Yes – it should also be on the envelope of the card I sent.' She turned it over on the desk.

'Yes, it's there. I must go now to see my daughter. Ravindra, thank you. I've enjoyed speaking to you and I look forward to meeting you and all the others when I come.'

'Madam Claire, we will do everything in our power to comfort you and make your stay as happy as possible. Please be assured everything will be done. We will do the needful.'

It had long been dark when Nick returned.

'I decided to spend a whole day there,' he said, 'to get an idea of the routines, the ebb and flow of the place. Everything is fine.'

She put a glass of wine in his hand.

'. . . oh, thanks. You know being here is getting me into bad habits!'

'Some bad habits are good for you, in moderation, so drink it up,' Claire said. 'Ask any doctor.'

'Yes, anyway, Christian is fine. Now, I've been making plans.'

'Funny you should say that, Nick, but so have I. You tell me yours and I'll tell you mine.'

'OK. What I thought was – this is all subject to your wishes of course – what I thought was that I'll carry on here as normal tomorrow, meaning I'll go over to the TCC again, just for a short time, though.'

'I'd like to go with you if that's all right.'

'Fine, excellent, and while I think of it can I suggest you don't talk to Christian while you're with him? Remember, there's an audience, although not exactly of millions, listening to you in the control room.'

'Good point. Yes, I'll do that, or rather I won't, if you see what I mean,' she stammered.

'Then,' Nick went on, 'I thought it might be a good idea if we went over to your pub tomorrow evening, if of course you feel up to that. I've only been in briefly a couple of times and they seem a good lot. They know who I am and everyone asks after you. They're a great bunch. I think they want to ... how can I put this ... they want you to know they're there. Does that make sense? I gather Saturday night is always a bit of a hoot.'

'I think that's a great idea, Nick,' Claire said, 'but not for too long, right?'

'Sure, of course, good. Now, my wife gets back from France on Sunday. I thought that what I might do is to meet her at Heathrow, take her home and stay that night there and then come back here the next day. Obviously I've kept her in touch and she's perfectly happy for me to stay here as long as it takes.'

'Are you sure? That's terribly good of her.'

Nick laughed: 'She asked me to tell you that after almost forty years of my company she's more than happy for you to have it for a while! But look, it really is up to you. I want to help you, but I don't want you to feel put upon. If you want to say, now, "Thanks very much Nick, I can manage on my own", or whatever, than say it.'

She smiled, and said: 'I do feel I need you, Nick. I don't know about you, but I've found it very easy having you around the house – by the way I've done your ironing – and I think I'd be very lonely without someone around. Rosie will be here at the weekend, of course, which will be good as, well, women need other women, you know what I mean. But before I say any more I'd better tell you about my plans as they ask a lot of you, if I'm to go ahead with them.'

'Tell me,' Nick said.

When she had finished – she included most details of the afternoon's conversation with Ravindra – Nick thought for a moment before responding:

'I suppose you'll expect me to say that this sounds to me like another irrational decision by a woman that I've already warned about the effects grief and stress can have on the mind and body?'

'Yes, Nick, something like that. And I have listened. But I have thought this through carefully. How else . . . ?'

'Hold on, Claire, let me finish. I'm not, repeat not, going to say what you expect me to say. On the contrary, I think it's a good plan. I can't for the life of me explain why, but I've noticed, as the week has gone on, that you seem remarkably well, and, if I might say so, very much in control of yourself. And yes, you need to find out, and you're not going to do that without going there sooner or later. So, yes, do it, and, yes, between us, Rosie and I can look after things here. We are now rubbing along a little better than we were. But what about Amy – how long can she stay at respite?'

'I saw her there today and talked to the Warden. She said

that Amy can stay, if necessary, for as much as a month. There's no problem about that. But we agreed that she should spend some time at least, whenever possible, at home. I'd like to do that. So now I know your plans, I'll bring her home on Sunday morning. In fact, if you came back Tuesday, or even Wednesday, rather than Monday, I'll keep her with me until then. I won't even send her to school, so the two of us can have a reasonable amount of time together. That'll be good for her, and for me too.'

'When do you think you might leave for India?'

'I didn't want to do anything without speaking to you, and to Rosie of course. I'll speak to the agents Christian always used to get his tickets. I'll do that tomorrow, or maybe next Monday. Whenever. But I'll aim at going next weekend and then coming back the weekend after. Would that be OK?'

'Fine. Would it be all right if my wife came over for the period you're away, or at least for part of it?'

'But of course! Great idea!'

'Good. Now, Claire, can I, as a doctor, offer just one little piece of advice?' Nick said. 'I strongly advise you to go business class. It's what, probably a ten-hour journey. It'll take a lot out of you and while you're in pretty good shape now – by the way I called in on your GP this morning and your blood test result was fine – you must make it as easy as possible for yourself as you can. And from what I recall from years back, you'll find Delhi a tough place, just physically, let alone in terms of what you are going to have to deal with there on the emotional front. I know it'll cost you more, but my advice is to travel in comfort. Would you do that?'

'In a word, Nick, yes, I will. It's not as if I'm short of funds at the moment.'

Nick smiled. 'Good, that's settled then.'

As he said this he noticed a pensive look on Claire's face,

one that he had come, over the week, to recognise. 'There's something else you want to say, isn't there?'

Claire thought for a moment.

'Yes, there is,' she replied, 'It's just this. As you know I acknowledged what you said last week about the dreams. Yes, it could have been that I already "knew" about things I dreamt about, but there's one thing that, especially given my conversation with Ravindra, I cannot explain.'

'The five hundred pounds?' Nick asked.

'Exactly. Nick, if I had known, I would never have forgotten it. But I can assure you that I never knew. I'm not suggesting that you're wrong about other things, but on the business of the five hundred pounds, I'm convinced that the only way I could have got that information was from the dream. And for me, that's enough to tell me that he is, somewhere in that lifeless body of his, alive.'

'You know what, Claire?' Nick said, quietly, 'I was thinking just that when you described your conversation, the one with Ravindra I mean. I'm not entirely convinced, mind you, but you've got me thinking. And I'll tell you what . . .'

'What?'

'Another glass of wine and I'll be so convinced I might even write a piece in *The Lancet* about it!'

They laughed and Claire went to get the bottle. As she did so there was a knock at the door.

'Sign here please,' said a faint voice from under a motorcycle helmet. Inside the plastic envelope were the promised medical records.

As they entered the pub the following evening, it took only a few seconds for the many occupants of the public bar to fall completely silent. As usual early on a Saturday evening, everyone was there. And while it was also usual for those in the bar to look to see who was coming in every time the door opened, and, very often, for someone to offer some immediate provocative banter to the entrant, the silence was definitely not usual.

Andy, the publican, being behind the bar, was the last to see who had come in. As soon as he did see however, being ever a man to recognise and deal quickly with a difficult or strange situation, he raised his own glass and called out:

'Ladies and gentlemen, here is to the good health of Claire!'

'To Claire!' a number of voices responded, including that of Rosie, who had followed Claire in.

Claire felt flushed and strangely elated and at one point was persuaded by Andy ('only if you feel up to it') to make a brief speech, during which Andy held one hand, and Rosie the other. But she didn't need such support. She spoke without emotion of what had happened and of Christian's current condition, which she and Nick had seen earlier in the day to be unchanged.

Soon after it, Andy beckoned her over to the bar.

'Claire, a few of us would like a quiet word with you,' he said, 'if that's OK with you? We're in the saloon bar. Nobody else in there. No drama, just a little quiet time. Come through when you're ready.'

'Should I bring Nick and Rosie?' she asked.

'No, just you. It's, well, private.'

'I'll come right away then,' she said.

In the other bar, which was the original, sixteenth-century, part of the building, with low ceilings supported by ancient timbers on which horse-brasses were fixed and coins inserted in cracks, and a log fire blazing in the inglenook fireplace, there were, including Andy, five men seated around the fire: Pete-the-plumber, Ron-the-builder, Colin-the-weasel; Dick-the-digger (a gravedigger rather than an Australian), and Andy.

She felt uncomfortable. Apart from Andy, these were all village men that she had as little as possible to do with. She preferred that Christian had as little to do with them as possible as well. They represented, to her, the darker side of village life.

'What makes you say that?' Christian had asked her once, when they were walking back home from the pub.

'They all drink too much, they talk about their wives, who you never see, as if they were property rather than people, and pretty useless property at that, they use disgustingly bad language, and, well, that's enough to start with.'

'They're not so bad,' Christian had said.

'No,' she had replied, 'they're every bit that bad and a lot more. I always know when you've been with them.'

'How?'

'Because you've had too much to drink.'

Andy now spoke:

'Claire, we all want you to know how much we all care about you. I'm speaking for all of us, 'cos we've all spoken about this a lot over the past few days. Being the kind of bloke Christian was, sorry, is . . .'

He hesitated and glanced around the others.

'Look, to get straight to the point, and I'm sure I'm not telling you anything you don't know already, we all owe him.'

Claire looked Andy in the eye and blinked.

'. . . we all owe him, you, various amounts. You know, don't you?'

Claire gave no indication of the surprise she felt, and the anger that was welling up quickly inside her.

'Yes,' she said, simply and calmly, 'but I don't know the exact details.'

196

'Well, I'll sort out a list,' Andy continued, 'but all we want you to know is that . . . is that we're all going to sort it. And we want you to know that your husband is the greatest bloke we know. He's helped all of us, and never given a sign of it to anyone else in there, never been anything but the generous bloke he is. Now if you're short and need it now, Claire, we can sort it. We just want you to know that.'

'No, Andy,' Claire said, and then as she spoke looked to each of the men in turn, 'Money is the least of my problems just now. So you can all forget it, not just for the moment, but as far as I'm concerned, for good. I'm under no pressure, and none of you should feel any either. Or worry. Or guilt. Or embarrassment. Or anything. And, Andy, I don't need a list.'

She stood up and opened her mouth, but her determination to speak at least something of her mind dried up.

Back in the public bar, the atmosphere was still buoyant, and Claire happily immersed herself again in it, remembering Christian's phrase, 'put it in the car park', on what to do with the irritating or unexpected. Andy soon came back in, but not the others. She caught his gaze once, but looked away quickly.

Afterwards, she did not tell Nick or Rosie about what had happened. Nor did either of them ask.

After Nick had left the following morning, complaining bitterly of a hangover, and promising to go once again through the medical records, which had, at first read the previous day, shown no sign of any negligence during the operation, Claire set off on the course she had planned for the day as she lay in bed, awake early, that morning. She went to fetch Amy, and then sat down with her for an hour of her favourite pastime – going animatedly through old photo albums. There was one photo in particular, of Christian when he was a young boy, that always made Amy squeal with delight: 'Christian good boy,' she said, as always.

They had an unusual Sunday lunch – pizza – after which Amy chose a video – *Bedknobs and Broomsticks* – and Claire left her to watch it.

Once it was running, Claire went upstairs to the study to see what she could find there that might tell her something about this man she had lived with for over ten years.

'Who are you?' she said to herself as she started.

Two hours later, with *Bedknobs and Broomsticks* reaching its climax downstairs, she had discovered precisely nothing. She had been through each of the three drawers of the cabinet Christian used for his work files – the other being the one she used for their personal bills, statements and correspondence – all to no effect whatsoever.

She stopped and made tea for herself and Amy. Once *Free Willy* had been set in motion for Amy, she returned to the study. In turn, she went through, first, his part of *My Documents* on the desktop computer; then the files and folders on his laptop; then the various box files on the shelves; and finally, his briefcase. The latter turned out to be empty. As for the computers, all she was left with was the distinct impression that everything there had been sanitised: even the Recycle Bins were empty.

When she heard the closing credits rolling downstairs, accompanied by Amy's cries of 'Go Willy! Go go go!' she gave up. By now, it had long been dark.

'Eat now mummy?' Amy said as she re-joined her. She had stopped asking after Christian, as was usually the case when he had been gone for more than a few days.

'Yes,' she said, feeling tired, 'more pizza?'

Feeling guilty at her laziness, she reheated the remains of

the lunchtime pizza, and sat at the table with Amy as she ate.

'Bed now?' Amy asked.

'It's early, but yes, you can have a bubble bath and then go to bed. I've had enough of trying to find out who the hell your step-father really is,' she said.

'What mum?' said Amy.

She sighed.

'I'm sorry Amy, it doesn't matter. Come on, bath time now.'

'Good. Bath now,' Amy said, 'you OK mummy?'

'Yes, I'm OK. Let's get you upstairs.'

No sooner had she sat down, alone with her thoughts, and feeling oppressed both by them and the solitude itself, than Rosie arrived.

'I know you said you wanted the day on your own, but I thought I'd pop in, before my big night out,' Rosie said. 'I need a bit of Dutch courage – any wine left?'

'Yes, plenty' she said, 'in the fridge. Get one for me as well. What's the big night out then?'

'Don't you remember?' Rosie said, from the kitchen, 'it's my dinner date with Krishnan!'

Claire had completely forgotten about it.

'He rang me this morning,' Rosie went on, now sitting beside her on the settee, 'wanting to know if I was still happy to go out.'

'Why would he do that?' Claire asked.

'If he hadn't told me, I would have asked you. He told me – which you haven't – about what happened at the meeting at Pro-Fit.'

'Oh.'

'He said he felt a bit betrayed, at the time at least.'

'I'm not surprised,' Claire said, 'but Sir Timothy and Tom advised . . .'

'Who's Tom?'

'He's a sort of assistant to Sir Timothy, what they call a "pupil" in law firms. He does the donkey work.'

'I see. Anyway, go on.'

'They said, and Nick agreed, that we have to start with the negligence line, regardless of how good Krishnan has been to us, to me I mean. I was hoping he might bring the medical records himself, or call, or something. But he hasn't. In any case, Nick had a quick look through the records yesterday, and first impression was that they leave Krishnan in the clear. He's going to go through them again this weekend. But, Rosie, I think it's best if you don't tell Krishnan that, at least not for the moment.'

'I don't think I'll need to,' Rosie said. 'When we spoke on the phone this morning we agreed a shortlist of non-conversation topics for this evening. In fact, it's a one-item list – got it? In any case, Krishnan also said that now he has thought about it he realises that you had to do what you did. He bears no grudges, none at all. He asked me to tell you that. And I want to tell you, darling, that I bear none either.'

'What do you mean?'

'I mean I wish you'd told me about what happened. Apart from at the pub last night I haven't seen you or had a dickybird out of you all week!'

'You're right, I'm sorry' Claire said. 'Anyway, where's he taking you?'

'That place in Brighton that you really like, the one up high, towards the marina from the pier, with the lovely views. Where you can park right next to the place.'

'Mmmmm, very romantic! We used to . . .'

At that, Claire choked and started crying. Her friend put her arm across her shoulders and they sat in silence until the moment passed.

'Rosie, come back tomorrow morning will you? There's a lot I need to tell you, and ask you,' she said.

'It's been a lovely evening, Krishnan, thank you so much,' Rosie said as they walked to the car. He was holding her hand.

'Can we do this again?' he asked.

'Yes, I'd like that very much,' she said.

They stopped by the car and he took her gently in his arms and kissed her, lightly, on her lips. She felt utterly comfortable and happy.

'I know we agreed to keep off this, and we have, but will you please tell your friend that I am still on her side?'

'I've already done that, Krishnan, but I'll do it again, promise. She's asked me to pop round tomorrow.'

They drove in silence back into Brighton and then out towards London.

Entering the one-way system before Preston Park, the traffic suddenly seemed busy and soon they came to a complete stop. Police – or perhaps ambulance? – sirens could be heard, faintly at first, and then louder. Then, astonishingly, a police car roared past them, along the pavement itself, stopping a hundred yards or so ahead of them, where there were already other police cars, all with their blue lights flashing.

They looked at each other.

'Accident?' Rosie said.

'I fear so,' said Krishnan, 'I think I'd better go up there. If the traffic moves, take the car up to where the park begins, past the bridge and I'll join you there.'

He was gone for only a few minutes.

'Not an accident,' he said as he got back in the car, 'there's a cordon just up there. The policeman told me that they've raided a place where something was going on. He didn't say what. Suspect it might be drugs or something. He said we'll be able to move soon.'

Claire woke the following morning to a sound she recognised as being bad news: cold water running through the pipes. It was a quite different sound to that of the central heating pump pushing the hot stuff around. This was cold water, she knew, flowing freely from the mains into the tank, which was situated in the loft space more or less exactly above where she lay.

'Oh no,' she said, and got up. She parted the curtains and opened the window. While it was still dark, she could see, sure enough, that out of the overflow pipe from the tank above there was a steady and quite heavy discharge onto the street pavement below. 'Damn,' she said.

She got dressed in the clothes she had worn the previous day, knowing that what lay ahead and above would be, firstly, cold and secondly, dirty. She knew what she had to do: this had happened more than a few times over the years when Christian had been away. He had told her exactly what to do: 'Turn on the cold taps everywhere, and flush all the toilets. That'll stop the overflow. After a while turn off the taps. Then get up there. Take the lid off the tank and then pull up the ball-cock and hook it to the little device that hangs from the roof rafters that I've made. Once you got it up, lever the arm up and down while you put a bit of the acetic acid – you'll find the bottle by the tank – on the valve. It's the hard chalky water, you see. It builds up and clogs the valve. The acid will clear it, but don't let too much drop in the water. Then smear a good gob of vaseline, which is also up there by the tank, on the valve and keep moving it up and down. Then unhook the ball-cock and let the tank fill. Should be all right, but repeat the whole thing if it doesn't work. Got it? And don't forget to switch off the light up there before you come down. Then all you need to do is to take several hot showers to clean yourself up. Simple, eh?'

After she had run the taps for a while and flushed the toilet in the bathroom several times, she pulled the cord which released the hatchway and lowered the ladder – Christian had installed it when the problem was first discovered soon after they had bought the cottage.

In the loft she crawled carefully over the joists and got to work.

Once she had finished – she felt proud of the fact that everything was done as it should be – she let down the ball-cock and let the water flow. As she waited for the tank to fill she looked around. The loft space was so small they never used it for storage, and she was therefore surprised to see, even in the gloomy light of the 20-watt bulb, to which her eyes were now well-accustomed, the glint of something metallic between two of the joists near where the chimney stack went through the roof. Curious, she inched across and picked it up. Unlike everything else in the loft it was not dusty. While it had a place for a lock, there was none. She picked it up and then moved to a place directly under the light.

She opened it.

Inside, there was a slim envelope and a wad of money, with a red elastic band around them. She took out the envelope and flipped her thumb across the notes: all were of fifty pounds as far as she could see. There seemed to be a lot of them: fifty, seventy, possibly a hundred.

At that exact moment, she heard the sound of vigorous knocking at the front door. Very vigorous indeed. No friend or neighbour would ever knock at the door like that. Then, through the roof-tiles, over the sound of the water pouring into the tank, she heard, very clearly:

'Police!'

She closed the box and pushed it well into the space under the water tank.

'Just a minute please!' she called out, 'just wait a minute will you?'

As she descended the ladder, her heart began sinking: this must be the moment, she thought; there can be only one reason; why else would the police come to my door? But couldn't they be a bit more discreet? Do I have to look like this, covered in dust and grime, when I'm told my husband is dead?

Just before she reached the door, it shook at the impact of further loud knocking, so forceful, indeed, that it seemed that it was about to be broken down.

'For God's sake,' she shouted, 'I'm coming!'

She opened the door and took in the sight: two large figures in police uniforms, with peaked caps; behind them a police car with its blue lamps flashing in the well-advanced dawn light.

'You've come about my husband?' she said, panting for breath.

'We have indeed,' one of the men said, holding out a sheet of paper. 'We want to speak to him, we have a warrant here that gives us right of entry, search and arrest. Please stand aside.'

'What?' she exclaimed, as the two men pushed her roughly aside, entered the living room and then closed the door behind them.

'Sit down. Where is your husband?'

She felt faint. A tight vice seemed to clamp itself on her chest.

'What is this?' she said, 'what on earth is going on? My husband is not here.'

'I have to warn you that that and anything else you may say, will be taken down and may be used in evidence against you or your husband,' one of the men said, as the other produced a notebook from his hip pocket and began writing.

'What is this?' she said again. 'What in God's name is going on here? My husband is seriously ill in hospital. He is not expected to live. And you dare to come here and ... and you dare to come here and push your way into my house?'

The two policemen smirked, first to each other, and then, together, at her. Her rage boiled over.

'How dare you!' she screamed, 'now get out of my house!'

One of the policemen, the one with the notebook, nodded to the other, who immediately continued on into the house. The remaining one crossed his arms and looked sternly at Claire, who now flopped down into the nearest armchair, snorting with rage. There she listened to the sound of heavy footsteps upstairs, and the creak of the same feet going up the ladder into the loft. She turned her gaze to meet that of the remaining policeman, her eyes sparkling with indignation.

'Not a sign of him,' the one policeman said to the other when he returned.

She now averted her gaze and turned it instead to the ceiling. She recalled what Tom had said to her the previous week – 'it's important to take control', something like that – and she concentrated so well on it while the two policeman engaged in a conversation together that she did not hear a word of what they said.

When the drone of it ceased, she stood up and said: 'Will you come through here with me please.'

She showed them into the dining room and indicated that they should sit at the table.

'If you will excuse me for a moment,' she said, once they were seated, and went upstairs.

On return, she gave them the agreement she had signed with Pro-Fit: 'Would you kindly read that, and once you have done so, I will expect the following: one, an explanation; and two, an apology. In any order you like. And while you read I will do three things: firstly, I will see what kind of fright you've given to my daughter, who you may wish to know is severely mentally handicapped . . .'

'She's asleep,' the searching policeman said, quietly.

She raised her voice again: 'Shut up!'

Lowering it, she went on: 'And secondly, I will go up in the loft to see whether I have successfully dealt with the overflow problem in our cold water tank. Thirdly, I will make myself, I repeat, myself, and only myself, a cup of tea. And I will ask you to do one other thing. Go outside and switch those ridiculous lights on your car off, and while you are doing so, perhaps you would be good enough to confirm to me that the overflow from the roof has stopped.'

She left the room.

On her return, some time later, cup of tea in hand, she sat down. Only one of the policemen was there.

'Now' she said, 'over to you, constable, or is it sergeant? Or may I call you Bill perhaps?'

The man was impassive.

'My colleague is just checking the information you have just given us,' he said.

'Fine,' she said, 'I've got all day. In fact I've got all week.'

It was not long before the other policeman came back.

'I suppose you now want me to leave while you two agree your story?' she asked, smiling sweetly as she did so.

'No, that won't be necessary. I have been informed that the information this contains,' the returning policemen said, 'is correct. If we have caused any inconvenience, then . . .'

'Inconvenience?' she said, calmly, and then more loudly, 'incon*venience*?'

'By the way,' the man said, equally calmly, 'the overflow

has stopped, although there is a lot of water still flowing down the street. If you've got a broom, we will clear up for you.'

'Thank you, but I would much prefer to do it myself.'

'I'm instructed to ask you two questions,' the policeman went on, 'which, I am also asked to inform you, you may refuse to answer, if you wish first to take legal advice. I'm also asked to explain that our presence this morning was the result of a raid carried out last night by police officers in Brighton on the basis of information received about an illicit practice.'

'Really? What kind of practice?' she said.

'Among other things, gambling. My first question is this: is your husband, to your knowledge, involved in any form of gambling? Secondly: are you aware of your husband either being in possession of, or, alternatively, losing, large amounts of money at any time in the recent past? You may choose, as I have said, whether or not to answer either of these questions, but as you were cautioned earlier, please remember that anything you say . . .'

'I'm aware of that. I will answer both questions,' she said, a mental picture of Alfonso's box and the one upstairs clearly in her mind as she did so, 'the answers are no, and no. Now I have a question back: why are you here?'

'Your husband's name was found in a book in the possession of one of those arrested last night. I can say no more than that, except that several people there were able to evade arrest.'

'I see. And whose book, may I ask, was it?'

'I do not have that information, nor would I disclose it if I had.'

'Very helpful. So to sum up, you two have come into my life this morning, behaving as if you were trained by the Gestapo or the Stasi, merely on the basis of my husband's name happening to be in someone's book? Thank you very much. Now, assuming you have finished, would you kindly get out of my house?'

After finishing her tea, she went back to the loft and brought the metal box down. In the envelope was a small piece of paper which read: Andy £300 Ron £370 Colin £200 Pete £250 Dick £200.

That was all. She then counted the banknotes. They amounted to £4850.

She got Amy out of bed and they had a shower, and then breakfast, together. It was while they were eating that she remembered that Christian used to go up in the loft every two weeks, sometimes more often. 'Prevention is better than cure,' he used to say whenever he went up there.

Once she had got Amy settled in front of the television she went upstairs to the study, where she composed, with the aid of much scrutiny of Christian's big Italian/English dictionary, an email to Alfonso. It was brief and to the point, in fact, two points: that Christian's condition was unchanged; and that 'would you be so kind please as to continue to show interest in the purchase of the farmhouse, although I cannot at this time give you a go-ahead. I hope you understand . . .'

Annoyingly, Alfonso's email address was not on the computer's address book. She searched the shelf over it for Christian's filofax, wondering as she did so why she had not thought to see what it might tell her the previous day. There was no sign of it, although she knew where it should have been. After a moment's thought she went back up the loft ladder, which was still down, and crawled back over to where she had found the box earlier. She felt around between the rafters and, sure enough, there it was: its dull black leather cover made it almost invisible in the gloom.

Back in the study, resisting the temptation to go through it thoroughly, she found the address for Alfonso and sent the email. Several arrived as she did so: all junk.

She took a second shower, long and hot.

'Gambling?' she thought, as the jets pricked her skin. 'Surely not?'

'I just need to pop over and see Andy at the pub,' she said as Rosie arrived later that morning. 'Yet another day off sick for you?'

'But he won't be open yet, and, yes, funny how these viruses go away and then come back, isn't it' said Rosie, through a thin smile.

'I just want to ask him something. Won't be a few minutes – can you look after Amy? Then we'll have lunch. I've got a nice pasta bake for us.'

'Great, Amy and I will get going on the salad.'

'I won't be long,' she said as she went out into what seemed a mild, almost balmy day for February.

At the pub she found Andy out the back, rolling metal barrels around.

'Hallo darling, you're a bit early,' he said.

'Just wanted a quiet word, Andy, if that's all right.'

'No problem. Let me sort this out and I'll be with you in half a tick. Go on in and help yourself.'

When Andy came in she turned down the repeated offer of a drink as he joined her on the bar stools.

'You didn't know, did you?' he asked.

'Didn't know what?'

'About Christian lending us money? That's why you're here, isn't it?'

'Andy, can I just ask you this straight?' she replied,

ignoring the question, 'I know you and a few of the others here like a game of cards now and then. Is any of the money Christian lent to you connected with gambling?'

Andy's brow furrowed. In fact, it already was frowning, but this was his natural facial expression. For a man in his forties he was remarkable in this, and for a publican he had one other unusual feature: he was very thin, as well as tall. The wrinkles on his forehead became more pronounced at Claire's question.

'No – not in my case, and I'm pretty damn sure it's the same for the others. Cards in the pub is only ever for a pound or two here or there anyway. What I owe Christian was nothing to do with cards. It was . . .'

'No, Andy, I don't want to know. But what about the others – were they involved in gambling in any way? Big-money stuff I mean?'

'No,' Andy laughed, 'No, no way. What's up? – there's something on your mind, isn't there?'

She knew she could trust Andy with a confidence, so on that basis she told him about the morning's visit from the police, although she said nothing about the box in the loft. As she told the story, Andy's brow creased up still further, and while she spoke he moved to the other side of the bar and pulled himself a couple of squirts of bitter from the pump. He stayed there until she finished. She had been watching him as she spoke and so she ended with the words:

'Oh dear, I don't like the way you're looking, Andy.'

Leaning against the bar with his arms spread wide, Andy said:

'I'd forgotten about this, but about a couple of years ago, maybe more, when you, Rosie and a lot of the other girls went up to town to see something, what was it, Rod Stewart?, I forget, doesn't matter. That night I was going down to Brighton 'cos I heard there was a place just started, like, where you could have a quiet game of poker, brag, pontoon, stuff like that. Friend of mine told me about it. Christian was in early so I asked him if he wanted to tag along, just for a laugh, you know. So we went. It was a dirty, seedy little place, back of Preston Park, and I didn't much like the look of it. And the money that was goin' round was way out of my league. I played a few games. Christian just sat at the back watching. We didn't stay long. Now, they had a book there where you signed in. I've been to places like that before so I just put a false name of course. Didn't think to tell Christian. I'll bet the silly boy put his real name there, stupid, stupid idiot!'

Claire showed no reaction: 'But do you think he ever went back there?'

'I wouldn't think so. I never did, and I'm sure he didn't. He'd've told me. Any case, only real gamblers with big money go to places like that. That's not my league and it certainly isn't Christian's. Blimey, Christian used to get nervous when we played for more than a quid a go at the bar here!'

Although she knew that was right, a nagging claw of doubt scratched at her as she walked home. And she thought, too, of the box in Alfonso's safe.

11

The Diary

Once the pasta bake was in the oven, and it being such a mild day, they decided to go for a walk while it cooked. They called at Rosie's house to collect Monty, her little terrier. Amy was thrilled: she loved to walk Monty. Once they got off the road and onto the footpath that led through the woods, they let Amy and the dog go ahead. This enabled them to catch up with each other's news.

What Claire found most interesting about her friend's account, which focused almost exclusively on the evening before, was her description of the journey home and, in particular, the traffic hold-up in Brighton at Preston Park.

What Rosie would have found most interesting about her friend's account (had they been mentioned, which they were not) was what happened in the saloon bar on Saturday night, of which Claire said nothing, and the events of earlier that day, of which she mentioned only the overflow from the tank. She said nothing of either the box or the police. Instead, she talked a lot about her plans to visit India.

'You should get someone in to fix that tank.' Rosie said.

'Yes, I should do that,' Claire said. 'But what do you think about the plan, my trip I mean?'

'Fantastic,' Rosie replied, 'wish I could go with you myself, 'specially now that I have, shall we say, a personal interest in the country! I'll take some of the week off as leave, proper leave I'm talking about.'

'You shouldn't do that.'

'No, I will, not just for you and Amy. I've got other plans in mind!'

Claire linked her arm through that of her friend, causing both to stumble momentarily on the muddy track.

'Mmmmmmmmm,' she said, 'so it's "sucksy filla" versus "superman" now is it? So where's your money then? Come on – or are you going to string them both along?'

'I knew you'd ask that, you rotter,' Rosie said, suddenly serious, 'and you know what? I think Krishnan is, as well as being a hunk of the hunkiest order, really really really a sweet man. I remember the first time I went out with "sucksy" and all he did was talk about himself the whole time. And to be honest he still does that. Last night, Krishnan asked me about myself, almost the whole time. Not, you know, intrusively, but sensitively, in a kindly way, a way that made me feel really good. He's such a gentleman. Old-fashioned and new-fashioned, all in one, funny, really. To be honest, I'm getting a bit bored with "sucksy".'

'Rosie, you never cease to amaze me.'

'Nor do you. Now, you say you haven't even made your bookings yet? And you're planning to leave next weekend?'

'I'll do it later today or tomorrow.'

'You realise you'll need a visa don't you?'

'Do I? I thought India was part of the Commonwealth?'

'Yes, but you still need a visa, same as you do for Australia. The Commonwealth makes no difference. Doesn't mean a thing.'

'Hell!'

'Don't worry, the travel agents will probably sort it out, but I suggest that today you give me your passport, then I'll get it to the agents tomorrow when I'm up in town at work. It'll be OK.'

'You think so?'

'Yes, I'm sure. It'll work out.'

At that moment, a mud-caked Monty, followed quickly by an equally mud-caked Amy, appeared.

'Home now Mummy,' Amy yelled out, happy as a lark.

For the first time ever, as far as Claire could recall, long before the lunch had ended she was waiting for her friend to go. Reciprocally, her friend could sense this, and felt mildly affronted by it; they had not, after all, seen each other or been able to talk properly for quite some time.

'Time for me to go, I can see you need some space,' Rosie eventually said, after what seemed to Claire an eternity of talk, mostly about Krishnan, with Rosie doing most of the talking. 'Give me the passport, then I'll go back and give Monty a good wash. Would Amy like to come?'

'Monty, yes please,' said Amy.

'OK, if I come up for her in about an hour? I'll bring the passport then,' Claire said as they left.

Alone, she leafed through the diary pages of the filofax, not really knowing what she was looking for. The pages began from January the previous year.

The entries were sparse, but could fairly easily be followed. One sequence was typical. It began with an entry that read 'Dept LHR for DEL, 1015(>)'. Over the following two or three weeks, each day was marked with the > sign, until the day of an entry reading 'Arr LHR from DEL, 0545(<)'.

But as she continued, she found that not all the entries were like that. While the main colour used, as ever with Christian, was green, other colours and markings appeared, usually without any word of explanation. Some were in red, this time >> or <<. Others were /* or *\ in blue. Other symbols like @, &, ∧ appeared here and there. But never a $ or a £, which were what she was looking for most.

'Meetings, report deadlines?' she said aloud after giving the matter some thought.

The woman she spoke to at Amethyst Travel dealt with the requested booking briskly and helpfully.

'You're sure about business class?' she said at one point.

'Yes, and you'll get the visa form to me right away?'

'It'll be on your fax in a few minutes,' the woman replied. 'Get it back to me by lunch time and so long as your friend has brought the passport in by then, we'll have it back tomorrow, or let's say Thursday at the latest, so you'll easily have it all from us by Friday latest. So you'll be fine for the BA flight on Saturday. Christian's people meeting you there?'

'Yes.'

'That's good. It's a hard place to arrive. Middle of the night. Thousands of people. Hustle and bustle. I'll give you a bit of advice if you like.'

'Yes please, what is it?'

'Change just five pounds at one of the banks in the baggage hall, while you're waiting for your bags. Ask for plenty of 10- 20- and 50-rupee notes. If you don't spot the people meeting you, there'll be guys wanting to help you with your trolley. Put it this way, they won't give you much choice! You'll even find two or three of them fighting over you. Don't worry, they won't harm you. But you'll need to tip them, and the porters at the hotel when you get there. In fact never go out without plenty of small notes in your bag.'

'Thanks, I'll remember that. Anything else?'

'Watch what you eat and drink. Always drink bottled water.'

'I'll do that.'

Within a few minutes the promised fax arrived, together with the itinerary. Claire completed the form right away and returned it. The trip ahead suddenly seemed, for the first time, very real. She shuddered involuntarily: going to Italy on her own was one thing, and even that had taxed her. But India? She knew nothing at all about the place. She did not even know how long it took to get there, although Nick had said something about that, but what was it? She had not thought to ask. All she knew was that the currency was called rupees, that she should get lots of small-denomination notes, and that maybe people would try get hold of her trolley. What else did she know? Yes, places called gharanas existed there, and there was a man called Ravindra Kapoor for whom her husband had worked. Anything else? Nothing much. She pulled Christian's atlas from among the books and found India, and in it she found New Delhi. Why *New* Delhi?, she wondered and looked for an old one, but could not find such a place. She turned to a world map spread across two pages. India seemed to be far away, half-way to Australia, roughly.

She closed the book and put it back, deciding there and then that she would devote the rest of the day to Amy, conscious that once she put her on the school bus the next day, she would not see much of her for almost two weeks. She felt guilty.

It was still mild. Low grey cloud stretched from horizon to horizon, seemingly motionless, as if it was a layer of cement. The piece of guttering still stood by the front door. Even as they got into the car she had not a single thought in her head as to what to do.

She found herself heading for Brighton, where she parked near the pier. They ambled along it. Amy was excited: 'Christian here?' she asked. It was a little outing they did from time to time, and Amy loved to go on the dodgem cars with Christian, who would drive recklessly about bumping every car that he possibly could, with Amy letting out huge screams of delight every time they did so, Claire watching from the outside, flinching at every collision: she hated the things.

216

'Cars now?' Amy asked.

'No, no cars today,' she said, 'no cars.'

'No Christian?'

'No, no Christian, Christian's sick.'

She remembered Amy's other favourite activity here, and they went inside the big hall with all the slot machines. She changed five pounds (which made her think of rupee notes) into lots of copper coins. Then she watched as Amy rolled them down, one by one, into the machines that pushed piles of coins closer and closer to an edge, over which they fell, albeit occasionally, to be collected as winnings. As she watched, she thought briefly of Christian falling off the precipice. Amy loved the sound of the coins crashing down, and when some fell, she scooped them up eagerly: 'Look mummy, look, money!'

After a long time at this, and still with a bagful of coins in hand, they wandered among the slot machines. She put a coin in here and there and held Amy up so that she could pull the handle, but Amy did not show much interest, even when a modest fall of coins splattered into the tray at one machine.

'This one mummy, please,' Amy said as they reached the place where there were the big glass booths with the cranes that must be manoeuvred to try to pick up a soft toy from the heap and then drop it into the chute. 'Please, mummy, this one!'

After several attempts they were at last successful in grabbing and safely depositing a small toy that vaguely resembled a koala bear. Or was it a squirrel?

With Amy clutching her new-found animal friend, they went into the tawdry snack bar at the sea end of the hall. All this time, Claire had had one thought in her mind – that of Christian sitting at a card-table, gambling. Was it possible, she wondered?

They ate fish and chips, the former turning out to be more batter than flesh, and the latter indescribably greasy.

Claire squirted what she presumed would be tomato sauce onto Amy's chips from a large plastic tomato on the table. Instead, a watery liquid, its colour resembling that of pink nail-varnish, emerged. Nevertheless, Amy ate her lunch with relish, and then swallowed a glass of coca-cola in one huge and rapid gulp, leaving a brown-coloured upturned moustache on her face as a result. Claire hardly touched her own food, and managed but one sip of the vaguely brown cold liquid that might possibly once have been what she had ordered: strong tea.

'You all right mummy?' Amy asked as they left.

'Yes, I'm fine, Amy, shall we go shopping now?'

'Shopping, good mummy, good girl, come on,' Amy said, as she took Claire's hand and headed off back down the pier at speed.

They strolled along the front and turned into the Lanes, where they wandered aimlessly from shop to shop. In one, Claire bought Amy a pair of jeans with sequins down the side seams. Amy, who loved all things that sparkled, was thrilled, and insisted on keeping them on.

'Would you mind taking these?' Claire said to the shop assistant, as she deposited the bag of mostly two-pence coins on the counter.

'Bin gamblin' on the pier then 'ave we?' the young girl said, with a smile.

'Look!' Amy said, holding up what Claire now thought to be more grizzly than koala bear.

'And you won a bear as well, did you?' the girl said, stroking Amy's hair.

'Nice bear,' Amy yelled, still in the highest of spirits.

It got dark as they drove home.

At the front door, they found Krishnan.

'I hope you don't mind,' he said, looking serious, 'but I

just wanted to re-establish contact. I don't want to intrude. Would you prefer if I just went away?'

'I'm really happy to see you, Krishnan,' she said as she hugged him, 'really happy. In fact, you're just the man I need right now. Let me get Amy sorted.'

Krishnan looked at the guttering: 'I hope you're not expecting me to put it back?'

'No, I've got much bigger plans for you than that.'

They laughed as she opened the door.

She got Amy into an early bath, calling, 'Help yourself to a drink,' downstairs as she did so, 'and I'll have a white wine as well while you're there!'

Having apparently decided that the bear was in fact a rather unwashed and unusually shaped polar one, Amy took it into the bath with her.

'I've got what I think is some good news, and a teeny bit of bad news,' Krishnan said as they sat down together.

'I'll take the good news first I think,' she said, sensing from Krishnan's cheerful demeanour that the bad could not be all that bad.

'Christian has been seen today by a specialist neurologist, whom I know quite well in fact. He was of the opinion that the EEG activity that we've been seeing since the outset is really very encouraging. On top of that it has increased a little over the past 24 hours or so. Not dramatically, mind you, but noticeably. In fact so noticeably that the neurologist was of the opinion that . . .'

'That what?'

'. . . that a permanent EEG monitoring regime should be put in place.'

'Meaning?'

'A number of things, and this is where the little bit of bad news comes in.'

He smiled reassuringly as he said this.

'Well?'

'They have shaved Christian's hair off completely. They have to in order to get a full set of electrodes on his head. As you may have noticed, up to now, we have just made a few little bare patches here and there to get a few electrodes on him when we need to.'

'To be honest, I hadn't noticed, no.'

'Well, next time you see him, be prepared for an over-aged skinhead!'

'Not an over-aged executive then?' she said, feeling the wine relax her.

'What do you mean?'

'He's spoken to me again, first time for ages, the other night. So I'm not surprised to hear that his brain is still very much alive and, no, I don't want any lectures about my fantasies, Krishnan.'

'I wasn't going to give you any.'

'But he was very depressed,' she went on, 'and likening himself to being a "ordinary old executive", something like that, quoting from some poem.'

'I see. What else did he say? Anything of significance?'

'Nothing really. He was in the kind of mood that I know is really the pits for him. And for me.'

'Churchill was a depressive, you know. He used to call his depressions "black dog",' Krishnan said. 'So Christian was like that was he?'

'Yes,' she said, 'and yet when he was up, he was such a joy to be with. It was like he had two personalities in one body. Well, actually at least two, but that's another story. Fortunately the good one was the more common.'

'What did he do about it, about depression I mean?'

'He refused to do anything.'

'Counselling?'

'Are you kidding?'

'St John's Wort?'

'He tried it for a few months at one time and pronounced it useless junk. He said all it did was give him constipation.'

'Hmmm, yes. Although of course I only really met him the once, he didn't strike me as being likely counselling material or an alternative medicine user. I suspect he'd probably rank counsellors as scourges worse than self-proclaimed management gurus.'

'Oh, you spoke about that did you?' she asked.

'Yes, and I detected more than a little self-loathing there. He seems to hate what he does, yet at the same time gets some satisfaction from it: understandably, I think, given the kinds of organisations he works with and the work they do.'

'Ah,' she said, 'now, changing the subject, I want to ask you about India.'

'I thought you might – Rosie's told me about it. Are you sure you want to go?'

'No, to be honest, I'm not. Put it this way: I *have* to go. I have no choice. It's not curiosity. It's necessity.'

'So, what can I tell you?'

'Everything I need to know. Everything. But first let me get Amy fed and into bed. Or do you have to go? Sorry, I guess I'm presuming on you.'

'No,' he said, 'I have all the time in the world, or at least until seven o'clock, when I will be seeing a certain good friend of yours.'

In fact, barely had Krishnan started to answer Claire's many questions when the 'certain good friend' in question arrived, letting herself in as usual with her key. She thus discovered, much to her surprise, her old and new friends deep in conversation.

As was his habit, Krishnan leapt to his feet.

'Goodness,' Rosie said, 'I hope I'm not interrupting anything?'

'No, we're just good friends,' Claire said, with a twinkle in her eye. Rosie crossed her arms and grinned broadly.

'I barely know the man and you're after him already then?'

'I saw him first, remember, all those years ago,' said Claire.

While the two women laughed, Krishnan was flustered: 'I was just ... I was just giving Claire a bit of background about Delhi,' he said seriously.

'So I take it you're far too busy to spare me any time?' Rosie said, dwelling long on the word 'far'.

Krishnan still took all this very seriously: 'But you said seven o'clock?' he said.

'Only if you can fit me in, doctor,' Rosie said. 'I know you have far more important cases ahead of me in the queue!'

At last Krishnan saw the joke and relaxed.

The three of them sat together for a short time, most of it occupied by Krishnan giving Claire, who was writing everything he said down, various pieces of advice and information.

As the clock on the mantelpiece showed seven, Claire held up a hand.

'Time is up,' she said, 'now off you two go and enjoy yourselves.'

'I'll be at the TCC on Thursday as usual,' Krishnan said as they left. 'Will you come, and Nick? The neurologist will be there – he's planning to do a cerebral blood flow test – it's another way of determining the extent of blood flow to the brain.'

'Yes, we'll both be there – Nick will be back tomorrow', she said.

12

The Fears

It's passed. It always does. I'm sorry if I upset you. I just have no control over it. You know that.

As so often happens, I seem to have gone from one extreme to the other. I feel much more, don't take this the wrong way, alive. I know that's a stupid way of putting it, but it is the way I feel right now. My mind won't stop. I've been thinking about all kinds of things and my head is buzzing. I realise that there are, or rather there were, so many things in my head that I never shared with you properly: things that gave me pleasure; things that made me mad; things that drove me on; things that dragged me down. Beliefs, values, concerns, joys, worries: a whole big mix of them whirring round my head, as if it's a food blender.

We used to talk about some of them sometimes, but not often enough. You often said you never really knew what made me tick. That was my fault: you often used to ask me. 'What are you thinking about, right now?' you would ask. And I would answer: 'Nothing much,' and follow up quickly with 'I thought we might go down to the beach at Pesaro tomorrow,' so as to lead us back to easier conversational ground. No, now I think about it, I didn't always do that. Sometimes I'd open up a little, but not much and not often, like I did in Il Vicolo with you not long ago. But thinking about it now, it was usually when we were in Italy that we would get to talk about – or rather that I would allow us to talk about – subjects that were at a higher level than whether we would go to the beach tomorrow, or whether I should do the shopping at Tesco's or Sainsbury's, or how Amy's vocabulary was improving, or whether we should go over to the pub for a quick one.

Funny, isn't it? – I guess we had much more time together than a lot of couples have. Yes, I was away a lot, but when I wasn't I would more often work at home than go to the office, a place, as you know, that I hated. But when I was at home, when we were at home together, somehow all those thoughts in my head, most of them half-formed, incomplete, confused, work-in-progress, would find expression only through that part of myself labelled 'work' rather than that part labelled 'me' or 'us'. So when I'd finished up there in the study, I didn't want the thoughts to come downstairs with me. I'd done with them for the day, so I left them up there, or rather I tried to. You can't switch off thoughts. They lurk around in a kind of murky loft-space of the head. When you would try to switch on the light up there by saying: 'What are you thinking?' I'd reach out straight away and switch it back off: 'Nothing much, really.'

This isn't just about me and you. It's about me and everyone else, even that rare species known as a close friend. Not that I had many of them, but when any of those few that I did have would try switching on the light: 'What's your take on this Zimbabwe business then?', they would get the same kind of response from me. Instead of talking about the dangers of taking an over-simplistic stance on post-colonial legacies, I'd say something like: 'Don't really have one, really,' and follow up quickly with 'Anyway, how do you rate Arsenal's chances against Newcastle tomorrow?'

I'm rambling my way slowly round to something I want to tell you. Something I should have told you long ago.

About, no, not about, but pretty well exactly seven years

ago, the firm made me an offer. No, that's the wrong place to start. Let me go back further, to before I met you. As I know I've told you, in the early eighties, me and a couple of friends joined forces and set up a little consultancy outfit to help organisations run schemes for poor and unemployed people. We used to liken ourselves to the blokes that go along behind the Lord Mayor's show, cleaning up the horse-shit. The show was Thatcherism; the lady sitting atop her carriage lashing the horses with her whips of the free market and offering carrots back at the stables, carrots called individual self-interest. We did what we did, helping set up schemes for Thatcher's victims, clearing up the shit she and sods like Milton Friedman and his economic rationalism created, all the human misery of unemployment and poverty. Someone had to. We scared the wits out of the big management consultants, too. We beat them to contracts time and again. It was good work, what Paul Goodman called 'work that is unquestionably necessary and useful, that can be done keeping one's honour and dignity'.

Then one day, one of the big firms realised that while we had the knowledge, the creativity, the courage and the compassion, they, the big boys, had the capital. So this firm – that you and I now know as King, Palmer, Marriott, Gerrard – made us an offer: a hundred thousand to walk away, or a reasonably well-paid but, above all, secure job, to join them. The others took the money. I chose not to, and negotiated the kind of arrangement I have with the firm now – 'semi-detached' as Palmer puts it. But the deal was that I stopped doing the UK-based work and did more of the overseas stuff that was coming along. I didn't mind.

Then, seven years ago, they again offered me a package to get out: 'Your work, Christian, gives us a good image in the development world, but it's not turning in a good enough profit,' Palmer said to me, slimy little creep.

I thought about it: the original agreement I had with

225

them was cast-iron, I knew that. And I didn't fancy the insecurity of just working on my own. The money was tempting. But I said no. It just didn't seem right. I didn't feel I could be true to my overwhelming instinct to bring security to you and Amy by taking the money, which would not have lasted long. And then what? Well into my fifties, and bound by an agreement not to compete for work against them (the same kinds of strings were on the packages that the others took originally), the choice was obvious: stay put. I should have told you.

But the whole episode told me this: it's a filthy capitalist world we live in, so it's about time I started working seriously to get my share, our share. I wonder if you have found the note and taken it to Alfonso yet. I hope you have. There, darling, is our share. It's ours, or rather yours, now. It's because we have that that I decided that it's time to call it quits. I was going to tell you all about it when we got to Italy this year, but well, at least I told you some of the story at Il Vicolo.

That reminds me: I wish I had thought of it at the time I first saw the surgeon – funny, but I cannot for the life of me bring his name to mind – but I didn't. You remember I told you that he was doing this research about what causes this Dupuytren's business. I've developed my own theory about it.

I think it's actually caused by capitalism. Just as HIV/ AIDS is sexually transmitted, Dupuytren's is financially transmitted. As each hand reaches out to grasp wealth from another, or even to grasp a whole bag full of conspicuous consumption, a deadly unseen virus is transmitted. So Dupuytren's spreads rampantly through a grasping society. Eventually the fingers all close up entirely, into a wizened claw, so that the hand is unable to grasp again. Which all goes to show that the rich do indeed get their come-uppance. The condition of their hands is such that they are even unable to feed themselves and so they die long painful deaths. The reluctant graspers like me get the less painful quick termination as our reward. But I remember the surgeon warning me that even after the operation, now how did he put it? – something like 'things will never be quite the same again'. How right he was!

In fact that idea – yes of course I'm only joking, but, frankly, I like the imagery – actually first came to me on the beach at Pesaro last year when the children at the chess club I used to help Aldo with (you remember Aldo?) asked me why my fingers were curling up. I told them it was a sign of someone who cheated – or something like that, I forget exactly what I said – and all the kids thought it was a big joke. But cheating is, now I think about it, an integral part of grasping.

It's time to stop now.

It was good that Krishnan had warned her about Christian's changed appearance, as she was profoundly shocked by it. One of the things about Christian that she loved was his great mop of floppy fair hair, the fairness unpolluted by even a strand of grey. Now it was all gone.

This time, they were allowed to be in the room itself rather than behind the glass screen. Krishnan even allowed her to sit by the bed and hold Christian's hand. After a few minutes Nick and Krishnan left the room.

She felt he looked pale, apart from his bald head, which had pink blotches all over it. He seemed entirely peaceful. She had determined that rather than talk she would 'think' to him, but the noise of the ventilator and other bleeping sounds distracted her. So she thought repeatedly: 'Tell me more darling, tell me more, I want to know more.'

She found Nick and Krishnan talking in the corridor outside. 'Come,' Krishnan said, quietly, 'let's go and get a coffee, and I'll fill you in on what's been happening. It's still good news.'

They went to a small café area she had not seen before.

'I've been explaining to Nick,' Krishnan began, having satisfied himself that none of the doctors was around, 'that the EEG electrodes were taken off earlier today so that the cerebral blood flow study could be done. They will be put back soon. You probably noticed the marks on his head – that's where the electrodes had been.'

'Tell Claire about the results,' Nick said.

'First of all,' Krishnan said, 'let me tell you how it's done. What we do is inject a very small amount of a mild radioactive isotope into the blood stream. Then, we place a radioactivity counter – what people call a Geiger counter – over his head. If blood is getting to the brain, the counter will pick it up. The whole procedure only takes half an hour.'

'And the result?' asked Claire.

'The result is excellent. It confirms what the EEG has been indicating and what the reflex tests we've done previously have shown: that there is still some brain activity, which has indeed increased slightly since the beginning of this week.'

'So what does this tell me, what does it tell us?' Claire asked. 'How high should my hopes be?'

'To be brutally honest, Claire,' Krishnan said, 'all this tells us is that there is brain activity. It is still very, very limited, but it is there. During a coma, however, brain activity can go down as well as up, a bit like the stock market, so I'd caution against regarding the recent increase as permanent. And I'd remind you that I still fear another heart attack. All in all, I feel happy, but I'm still very far short of feeling optimistic.'

'I'm inclined to agree,' Nick added when she looked at him.

'I see,' said Claire, 'now can I tell you something? Don't

pull faces at me, please, but last night I had another dream, another message from Christian. He was so full of beans. He said his mind was buzzing and that he felt, well, 'very much alive' were his words. What I mean is that all this confirms what the EEG has shown: increased brain activity. Doesn't it?'

'But I told you about the EEG increase when I last saw you didn't I?' Krishnan said, frowning.

'Did you?'

'Yes, I'm sure I did.'

'Oh,' Claire said, feeling embarrassed, 'so we're back to your logical explanations, then. What do you think, Nick?'

'I think I just have to pass on this one, Claire. But I don't take back what I said last week, on the five hundred pound business, I mean.'

'What's that?' Krishnan asked, and Nick told him.

'Hmmm,' Krishnan said in response.

That evening, after they had finished dinner, Nick took her page by page through the medical records of the operation.

'If you have no objection, Claire, I'll take the file up to show to Sir Timothy tomorrow. I briefed him, or rather Tom, on the phone yesterday and we agreed that the records should now be sent back to Pro-Fit with a suitable covering letter from Sir Timothy on your behalf,' Nick concluded.

Claire had quickly lost interest in what Nick was saying. Each of the many pieces of paper he showed her seemed to mist over as she looked at them. Mechanically, she voiced the occasional 'Ah-ha' and 'I see'.

'That's fine with me,' she said to Nick in response to his conclusion, 'you do that. And by the way, I've realised the next meeting with Pro-Fit will have to take place early in the week after I get back from India, won't it? Do you think you could start looking at dates with Tom and Sir Timothy so that you can fix it while I'm away?'

'Of course I will,' said Nick, 'now, you should get to bed I think.'

To Claire, each hour and minute seemed to drag by with excruciatingly painful slowness over the following day. Spurred and buoyed by the arrival of her tickets and visa-stamped passport, she decided to start packing, but the clock only showed ten o'clock when her head cried out that it must surely be midday at least. She longed for company, for any form of distraction. She sent an email with her travel details to Ravindra Kapoor. Once again, she felt feelings of loneliness oppressing her.

She longed for Nick to get back from his meeting with Sir Timothy. Apart from a brief reassuring email from Ravindra, nothing happened, not even a single phone call. Not even from a call centre.

As the day passed, she felt a small knot of fear in her stomach which then grew. For all Krishnan had told her about the far-away country, which she had at the time found encouraging, it was still the unknown that she faced, and would face, indeed, in little more than 24 hours' time. By the time Nick got back, late in the afternoon, she felt almost sick with apprehension. She jumped up and hugged him tightly.

'I don't think I can do it, Nick,' she whispered.

'Yes, you can,' he said. 'Have faith in yourself. I have. We all have. You're about to do something that would scare the wits out of anyone. It would scare me, and you know, I'll bet in his heart of hearts it would scare even Christian.'

'Yes, I know it would. A few dreams back he told me just that. And I remember he and I talking once, it was while we were in Italy I think. He always used to be a bit more open about his thoughts while we were there. He was telling me about some theory about fear, about how shops, for example, try to help people overcome their fear of going in.'

'*Schwellangst* – the fear of crossing the threshold,' Nick said. 'Yes, I remember him telling me about it as well. He had quite a thing about it for a while, one of his little passions.'

'That's right, that was the word,' she said, now releasing Nick from her grip.

'So you're in an advanced state of *schwellangst*,' Nick said, chuckling, 'and the only way to cure it is to cross that threshold tomorrow. And do that you will, won't you?'

'Yes, I guess I will,' she said, feeling brighter already, 'mind you, we may not even get as far as the airport – did you hear the forecast? They're saying there'll be heavy snow tonight.'

'So I heard. But don't you worry. I'll get you there.'

'Thanks, Nick, you really are the most lovely man. Now I must get up to respite to see Amy. I don't think I'm up to the pub tonight, but you go if you like, and then we'll have a late dinner.'

'Well actually, your friends and I have made other plans.'

'Oh?'

'I'm not allowed to tell. Can you cope with a surprise?'

'After the past few weeks of rigorous training on that front, in a word, yes.'

'Good, you get up to Amy and then all will be revealed, in the comfort and safety of your own home. So it will be a nice, undemanding surprise,' Nick said, winking theatrically.

She regretted the decision she had made to walk to the respite house the moment she left it to walk home, by which time it was snowing. Although it was downhill all the way, she was walking into the teeth of what was quite quickly as near a blizzard as can be mustered in the south of England.

Rosie burst out laughing at the sight of her friend when she opened the front door.

'The Abominable Australian Snowman has arrived!' she shouted out to the others, who, on seeing her, both collapsed into convulsions.

'Or is it the Great White Hope?' Nick added.

'May I come in please, this is my house you know?' said a muffled voice from behind the thick mask of snow that covered her entire face. She left it there for effect for a second or two and then wiped it off.

'Something smells good in here, something smells very good!' she said as she took off the thick coat she had had the sense to wear on her expedition.

'For memsahib, only very best will do,' said Krishnan, pressing the palms of his hands together and moving his head from side to side in an Indian caricature. Claire also took in the fact that he was wearing what she took to be Indian clothes: a button-to-the-neck sleeveless black jacket from which the sleeves of an immaculate white shirt emerged, and equally immaculate white trousers.

'Actually the take-away is Bangladeshi, but we decided we wouldn't quibble over details,' said Rosie, who was exuding radiance and dressed in a brilliantly sparkling red evening dress.

'And the suit was made in Southall,' added Krishnan.

Not to be outdone, Nick was in shirt-and-tie.

'I'd better go and get changed, I think. Will you come with me Rosie?' Claire said.

Once she had changed, Claire beckoned Rosie to sit on the bed beside her.

'I know this is going to sound silly,' she began, 'But there's something I want to ask of you.'

'Anything. Try me.'

'It's about Amy. It only just dawned on me when I saw her just now. What if anything happened to me? You know how I hate flying. Suppose . . . ?'

'Stop it, you daft thing. You'll be fine, but not just to put your mind at rest, because you know that I love Amy as much as you do, you don't even need to ask . . .'

Rosie put her arm around her friend and squeezed hard.

'. . . and I would look after her until the day I died.'

The four friends enjoyed a relaxed and convivial evening. Krishnan explained in detail what each dish was, what spices were used in its preparation, and how to pick out, from a menu, the fieriest dishes to 'avoid at all costs', as he put it.

With everyone conscious of the need for Nick and Claire to make an early departure the following morning, the evening did not go on long. As he and Rosie got up to leave, Krishnan gave Claire a piece of paper.

'I have a cousin in New Delhi,' he said as he did so, 'she is also a doctor, and I've taken the liberty of speaking to her. Here are her details. If you have any problem, medical or otherwise, you must call her. She insists that you do that. I have of course told her about Christian. Please promise me that you'll contact her if you need to. Will you?'

'Of course I will. Thank you for being so thoughtful.'

It was still snowing, though not so heavily as earlier.

'They'll get the gritters out tonight, I'm sure,' Nick said as they all stood shivering in the open doorway, exchanging goodnights and goodbyes.

I haven't been greedy. I've always thought it absurd, in fact absolutely clearly and definitely plain wrong in fact, that some people, quite a lot of people indeed, get ridiculously huge amounts of money for the work they do, which is often not exactly very demanding, while at the same time there are people in every country, all over the world, who get little or nothing for what they do, which often amounts to a lot even just to survive from one day to the next. Who was it who said that 'they lead lives of quiet desperation'? I can't remember; it'll come to me.

Look, it's not right that people, even quite young people, should work in the city as brokers or traders or whatever it is they call themselves, and earn ridiculous money from, well, doing what? Usually buying and selling money itself. Money becomes a commodity. That's one of the problems about Christianity. As far as it is concerned it's acceptable to see and treat money as a commodity. Put a few bob in the collection on Sunday or buy the *Big Issue* every now and then and you're squeaky clean. I don't want to get into religion, but in Islam, true Islam, money can't be used like that. Stupid people who see Islam as an unmitigated evil ought to realise that.

Look at that gang of crooks, those traders, what were they called? The Flaming Ferraris. Lovely cherubic-faced public schoolboys with famous fathers, who no doubt got them fixed up with their nice comfy jobs. And those 'rogue traders'. For every one that was caught out I'll bet there were hundreds who weren't. Not that you have to act illegally to earn pots, mind you. Take Palmer and the other partners for example, and the thousands like them every-where in the city. Greasy little vermin, the lot of them. Two hundred grand a year (is that *all?*), plus the perks: perform-ance bonuses, share options, even non-performance mil-lion-pound (at the very least!) exit pay-outs when their peers or their shareholders decide that actually they are useless. And Palmer and co have the damn cheek to tell me that I'm not making enough for them!

Once, when I was in Orissa in India, looking with Ravindra at some of his projects, we were in a very tiny village way out in the sticks one evening. The village had got a TV, hooked up to a damn great satellite dish made out of old milk tins. And there they were, unimaginably poor people, leading their lives not of quiet desperation, but of grinding, awful, intolerable poverty, all gathered round this TV. And what were they watching? They were watching, live, the English FA Cup final! They were watching 22 blokes, most of them, like Beckham, on at least twenty thousand, some even fifty thousand, a week, kicking a ball around. Watched by a whole gang of multi-millionaire club owners from their private boxes, who see the players themselves as commodities, buying and selling them as if they were potatoes, very expensive potatoes, of course.

I've nothing personal against Beckham, mind you. He seems a decent enough young man to me. It just seems to me to be wrong that he should get all that, and even be seen by a lot of people as deserving or even needing it ('after all, professional footballers can rarely go on once they're into the thirties' What?), while, here, in the village in Orissa, I give the women 200 rupees (less than three pounds) to give the kids a treat. Probably the first and the only treat they'll ever get in their lives. They all go mad with joy and put garlands round my neck when we come and when we go. And I remember another thing. Unlike Beckham, the Flaming Ferraris and Palmer, who all no doubt have hands as soft and unblemished as a baby's bottom, those women in Orissa had hands as hard and gnarled as lumps of broken Sussex flint.

When I was young, in my twenties, I honestly thought we could make the world a better place. And a lot of people thought that too. There was a time when we could have done it. I tried. And then I got clobbered. I told you. When you try you have to expose yourself and I did and I got hurt. So I learned not to do that. I'm not happy about that, but I can live with it.

And what I've also learned to do is get my share. Our share I mean. I'm not happy about that either. It doesn't make the world a better place for anyone but us three, but, oh, this is too complicated . . .

13

The Princess and the Pea

At the top of the ramp leading up from the plane into the terminal were several young women all wearing the same bored expressions and identical dull pale green saris, with bodices under in an equally dull pale red. Each held a board with a name on it. Claire was surprised, and more than a little relieved, to see that one of the names was hers. She approached the lady, who looked at her without interest, said 'come', then turning abruptly away, walked rapidly off, leaving Claire struggling to keep up with her.

'Give me your passport please,' the lady said as they walked, almost trotted, along dingy concrete corridors.

'Mr Kapoor has sent you?' Claire asked as she handed over the passport.

'Who?'

'Mr Kapoor, from the PDI?'

'PDI? What is PDI? I am airport employee. Guide for VIPs. You are VIP yes?'

Claire did not know what to say. She settled for 'yes', but was worried that perhaps she was benefiting from a case of mistaken identity.

They reached a large hall, where there were a number of long queues stretching back from each immigration officer. It was well past midnight – the plane had been over an hour late in leaving Heathrow due to the snow there.

Here, the lady walked straight to the front of one of the

long queues. 'Come,' she said again to Claire, who had
hesitated, embarrassed. But nobody seemed to mind, least
of all the immigration officer, who beckoned her to come
up to the desk, where he scrutinised her face and the one
in the passport, in a very studied manner. He was a large
man with a beard and a turban. Eventually, with a flourish,
he stamped the passport and customs form and gave them
to the lady guide. 'Come,' she said again, and they trotted
into the baggage hall.

'Your baggage tag please,' she now said, giving Claire
back the passport and form. 'It is on your ticket. If you
need to change money, it is over there. I will wait here for
baggage to come.'

She pointed to a corner of the hall, and Claire headed
for it.

'You are only changing five pounds? Hotel rate will be
much worse,' the young man behind the counter said when
she handed over the note.

'No, only this,' she said, 'could I please have small notes
only?'

The young man moved his head from side to side, in the
way Krishnan had the previous evening, and then counted
the notes out carefully. She saw that many of them had seen
years of service. She thought of the hardened, gnarled
hands through which they had no doubt passed.

She walked back to the baggage carousel, which was still
empty and motionless. It looked indeed, incapable of functioning at all. She wondered whether the guide-lady should
be tipped.

Time passed, what seemed a long time, before the carousel jerked into motion. By this time there were many
passengers standing around it and the ones nearby.

'Moscow and Saudi flights have also come in, before
yours,' the lady said.

'I see,' Claire replied.

Her suitcase soon came out and the lady put it on a trolley for her.

'Your driver will be outside,' she said, 'have a pleasant stay. Pass through green channel, give this form to customs officer and show baggage tag to security on exit.'

She pointed to the form inside the passport, and then abruptly turned on her heels, leaving Claire holding a 50-rupee note out into empty space.

The nervousness she had felt throughout the flight immediately returned. Remembering Krishnan's advice, she put all the money and her passport into her bag and zipped it up, keeping only the customs form and the baggage tag in her hand. Forward progress proved difficult as the ancient trolley insisted on moving in directions other than her intended one. She changed to another, which proved more cooperative.

She passed through the doorway into what proved to be another, smaller hall, in which no more than ten people holding name cards stood. None of the names were hers. 'Your driver may be there,' Krishnan had said, 'but that place is for V-VIPs only, so probably not. But check carefully. Only if you are sure he is not there should you go on as you won't be allowed back in. And then make sure you look right after you go out. Drivers are usually on the right side.'

While she had been warned as to what to expect by Krishnan, she was nevertheless taken aback by the hubbub outside. There seemed to be thousands of people behind a long barrier, many of them holding up cards with names, so many that it was difficult to make out any one of them. The noise of the crowd, while not deafening, was nonetheless intimidating. As Krishnan had advised, she walked slowly a little way back from the barrier, looking carefully at every card she possibly could. At last, there it was: 'MRS CLAIR'. She pointed to it. The dark-skinned young man holding it appeared in front of her soon after. He was small, slim, and smartly dressed.

'You are most welcome, Madam, I am Lalit. Mr Kapoor has sent me.'

'Thank you so much for meeting me, Lalit.'

Again, as she spoke she saw Lalit making the same characteristic sideways motion of the head, indicating neither assent nor dissent.

Two rather scruffy bent old men in tattered khaki clothes appeared and started trying to wrestle the trolley from her grasp. Lalit pushed them away and shouted fiercely at them. They shuffled off.

'These are no good people,' Lalit said, as he took the trolley from her. 'Come, let us find driver.'

Once through the noisy crowd, Claire felt the chill of the night air, which had a smoky smell to it, the smell of wood burning somewhere. They approached what Claire took to be a policeman, or perhaps a soldier, as his uniform was a mix of khaki and blue, and he had a rifle. Lalit spoke to him.

'I will go to find driver,' Lalit said. 'Please wait here with this man. You will be quite safe.'

As Lalit left, the policeman saluted her smartly: 'Welcome madam. Most welcome.'

A white car, soon appeared. It looked like the old Holden her father used to drive when she was a child. She gave the policeman the 50-rupee note, to which he responded by placing his hands together and raising them to his forehead.

Once away from the airport she saw small fires glowing here and there along the roadside, around which groups of people squatted. Where there were street lights, she could see rough tent-like structures by the fires. While the road was quiet, the areas alongside it seemed to teem with life. She was able to take a lot of all this in as each time it stopped the car accelerated away only sluggishly. The noise of its engine seemed to her ears more like that of a tractor than a car.

After a while, Lalit turned round in the front seat and handed her a mobile phone.

'Mr Kapoor wishes to speak to you,' he said.

'But isn't it rather late?' she asked.

'He is there,' Lalit said, and she raised the receiver to her ear.

'Claire? Welcome, most welcome. Lalit will come to the hotel at three in the afternoon and bring you to my house. I hope by then you will be rested. Will you come?'

'Thank you Ravindra, that would be very nice. Of course I will come.'

'Good. Have a good rest. Hotel is expecting you. Please pass me back to Lalit.'

Later, Lalit made another call, and soon afterwards, they reached the hotel, where a welcoming party was assembled at the front door. A huge doorman, resplendent in colourful frock-coat and turban, opened the door for her, saluting at the same time.

'Hearty welcome to Clarence Hotel, madam,' he said as she stepped out. At the top of the steps were three dark-suited men and a young sari-clad lady who stepped forward to place a beautiful and fragrant garland around her neck.

One of the three men then stepped forward, holding out his hand.

'You are most welcome, madam. I am Hotel Manager. These are Duty Manager, and Customer Services Manager. We are all most pleased to greet you. Please accept condolences of entire staff for sad condition of your husband, Mr Christian.'

She shook hands with each of them in turn and instinctively brought her hands together after each handshake, as they did. It felt right to do this.

As they walked into the reception area, the manager gestured towards the lifts. The place had the feel of an old-style English country hotel, with subdued lighting, deep-red studded velvet seating, and large paintings of what seemed to be English landscapes on the walls, all illuminated by soft picture-lights. The lifts were old-fashioned ones, where the doors were sliding metal grilles.

'Registration can be done when you are rested,' the manager said, after a silent ascent. 'All I will need tonight is your passport. We have upgraded you to executive suite, compliments of the house. Please follow me.'

The room, or rather rooms, for the bedroom was separate from a large lounge area, were beautiful. A brightly patterned, but predominantly red, carpet covered almost the entire floor area, across part of which was stretched a finely carved wooden screen. There seemed to be large vases of flowers everywhere, with envelopes in front of each. A porter arrived with her suitcase.

'I thought you might like some tea,' the manager said. 'Your husband always asked for tea on arrival. He was very valued customer of the hotel.'

Soon, a man in a white uniform arrived with the tea tray, on which there was also a single pale blue orchid in a slender cut-glass vase. She thought momentarily of her birthday in Mercatauro.

'You are most kind,' she said to the manager.

'All staff have strict instructions not to disturb you until midday. But please call reception at any time if you need anything,' he said, as she gave him her passport.

'Good night and good sleep, madam,' he said as he left. 'I wish the circumstances of your visit were happier, however. But we will make your stay as enjoyable and comfortable as is possible in said circumstances.'

There were four cards by the flowers: one from 'Ravindra and family', one from 'All at PDI', one from 'All at GKK' and one from 'Rafiquah and son, Principal, GKK'. So this was the other R, she thought.

She studied the cards as she drank her tea. She felt tired. Then she opened the suitcase and unpacked. On top were the PDI file she had taken from the cabinet, her own diary, and Christian's filofax, which she had put in on an impulse at the last moment. All these she placed, along with the four cards, on the beautiful wooden desk which the screen was designed to hide.

She looked at her watch: it was nine o'clock in England. She took it off and moved the hands forward to two-thirty, and then took all her clothes off, switched off all the many lights one by one and got into the huge bed.

'So what have you done?' she said out loud as she lay in the cool dark room.

She was soon asleep.

Soon after returning from taking a late breakfast, where she had sat by a window, overlooking the lush gardens that surrounded the hotel, and been fussed over a great deal by the waiters, she heard a knock at her door. Opening it, she found the manager waiting outside.

'Good morning, madam Christian, you have woken earlier than I expected. I hope you have had a good night's sleep? May I please come in for a moment?'

She ushered him in and invited him to sit down in the small sitting room.

'Please sign the registration form – we have completed all details, so only signature is needed ... here and ... here, please.'

She did this, finding that her hand trembled a little.

'Now, would you prefer to leave your passport with us to

keep it in hotel safe, or to keep it yourself? Maybe you have other valuables you would prefer us to keep safe for you? Hotel is very secure, but often guests prefer us to keep valuables for them,' he said.

This reminded her of the money she had. It was still in her bag.

'Yes,' she said bringing Krishnan's advice back to mind once more, 'I have some cash I would like you to keep, and also the passport.'

The manager promptly picked up the telephone and spoke briefly into it.

'What is the language you are using, may I ask?' she said.

'It is Hindi. There are many languages in India, but Hindi and Urdu are most common. Your husband was quite proficient with both, in fact.'

'I didn't know that,' she said.

There was a knock at the door.

'That will be my chief cashier,' the manager said, getting up. 'May I?'

'Of course.'

A small bald man entered. He was dressed smartly, like the manager, in a dark suit and white shirt and tie, but had a much darker skin. He was carrying a long metal box and some papers.

'Very good morning to you, madam,' he said to her, in a rather faint croaky voice. 'I have safe deposit box for you here. Please place items you are wishing to deposit inside. I will give you receipt and then bring you your key, or you are wishing for me to keep it for you? You can have access any time, twenty four hours.'

Claire got up and, returning with the envelope containing the money and her passport, placed them in the box.

'You keep the key please,' she said.

'Very good, madam,' the cashier said, giving her a receipt, 'Please show receipt when access required.'

'Now, madam,' resumed the manager, 'while the chief cashier is here, there is one other matter,' there was a tone of hesitancy in his voice, 'concerning your account.'

'Yes, what is it?' she asked.

The two men looked at each other, and the manager gestured to the cashier to speak.

'We are wondering if you will require same arrangements as your husband,' the cashier said.

'I am not quite sure what you mean,' she replied. 'Do you mean as regards payment?'

'Yes,' the cashier said, 'yes, Mr Christian would always pay in cash . . .'

She nodded. At least that was one thing that fitted with what she did know.

'. . . but also regarding other matters . . .' the cashier went on, looking to his manager as he faltered.

The manager sat forward in his seat and tapped the tips of his fingers gently together:

'Mr Christian would usually stay with us,' he began, 'just for two-three days when he arrived, then perhaps another two-three days before he left, usually two-three weeks later. Sometimes a night or two in between. You will be staying whole week with us, or perhaps you wish to have same arrangement as your husband?'

'No, I will stay here for the whole week,' she said, 'but can I be clear about what you are saying? You are saying that Christian would come here for a few days, and then would go somewhere else? Where did he go?'

The two men looked at each other again, nervously, Claire thought. The manager responded:

'It was not for us to ask, but my own presumption was that he would be travelling to other places, in connection with his work.'

'Ah, I see,' she said, feeling relieved, 'yes, of course.'

'You will not be doing so?' the manager asked.

'No, I have no plans to do so, but let me confirm that once I have seen Mr Kapoor later today.'

Both men now wiggled their heads in the manner now familiar to her.

'Teak-a,' the cashier said as he did so, much as Krishnan had said it in her house that time.

'What does that mean?' she asked with a smile, 'I have heard it before and I'm afraid I don't have my husband's proficiency in languages.'

'It means "yes" or "OK", in Hindi language,' the cashier replied. 'Your husband spoke Hindi quite well.'

He scribbled on a piece of paper and showed it to her. On it was written *Thik-hai.* 'That is it,' he added. He then turned to ask the manager something in Hindi, but was quickly cut off.

'You must remember house rules – only English when with international guests,' said the manager sharply. He turnied to Claire: 'Please accept apologies, madam.'

The cashier put his hands together and bowed his head to her briefly.

The manager continued:

'Arrangement with Mr Christian was this: on arrival he would ask for room bill for entire period, usually two-three weeks. This he would pay in full in cash. Then on final departure hotel would refund to him due amount for period not spent here while giving him new final account. Always he would be informing us, most often on first arrival, periods he expected to be away. He said this arrangement was most beneficial to him as he would not have to keep much money in his possession while not in the hotel.'

Outwardly, Claire absorbed this information calmly.

'That seems to make sense,' she said, while feeling that it did not make sense at all. 'Do you wish me to pay now, in advance for the whole week?'

'That will not be necessary, madam,' the manager said, 'unless of course you wish to, or of course you can pay by credit card if you prefer?'

'That was my intention,' she said. 'Most of the money I have put in the box there is for other purposes. Perhaps I should leave the credit card with you now as well?'

The cashier nodded, but the manager glowered at him and said:

'Only if you wish to do so, madam. Usually we would take imprint of card on arrival for guarantee purposes, but, in your case, no, that is not necessary. Now, if everything is in order, we will leave you. I understand your driver will come for you around three o'clock. We will call you and inform you. If you are not returning until evening, may I advise you to take something warm to wear later? By evening time it becomes quite chilly.'

'Thank you,' she said, standing up, and remembering that Krishnan had given the same advice. 'Would you please arrange for some tea to be sent up now?'

'Certainly, madam.'

As she closed the door, she heard an animated conversation, in what she presumed to be Hindi, recede down the corridor.

The tea soon arrived. She tipped the man 20 rupees.

She sipped her tea, contemplating what she had learned. She flipped through the filofax to the entries for Christian's last trip to India, which had lasted just short of three weeks. Here the markings were only the green ones and the blue ones. Their meaning, or what she felt reasonably sure were their meaning, were now clear. The green marks denoted first arrival and final departure. The blue marks within them seemed to denote when he had not been staying at the hotel: or did they? She felt tempted to pick up the phone to ask the manager if he had copies of the two

247

accounts for the trip, but after a few minutes thought, decided not to, at least not for the moment.

'Let's see what Ravindra has to say,' she said to herself.

The journey to Ravindra's house was longer than she had anticipated, though as she thought it over, she realised that such anticipation was irrational. How was she to know how long it would take? She thoroughly enjoyed the ride nonetheless. It was a bright, cloudless day, the temperature reminding her of Mercatauro in late spring.

In response to her question, Lalit told her the car was called an 'Ambassador'. 'Formerly almost all cars were like this,' he went on, cheerily, 'but now many Japanese cars are here, as you see, and many people are affording cars. But Ambassador is still popular. They live long, long time. Very tough car. This one five hundred thousand miles plus!'

She sat for some time in the middle one of the back seats, leaning forward so as to see more clearly out of the windscreen between the driver and Lalit in front. She quickly noticed, and was amused by, what seemed to be an almost standard inscription on the back of all vehicles, from the largest diesel fume-belching lorry to the smallest small black and yellow, three-wheeled rickshaw: *'Horn OK Please – Use Dipper at night'*. And although Lalit had told her, as they left the hotel, that the traffic would not be bad, because it was Sunday, she was amazed by its frequent denseness, by how buses seemed crammed full of people, some of whom even hung precariously on the outside, by the doors, or even on the roof.

It was not just the buses that seemed overloaded. She counted six people squeezed into one of the many rickshaws at one point, and then what seemed to be a family of four on a small motorcycle. Here and there rather emaciated off-white cattle grazed in the narrow areas between the carriageways, and in piles of rather disgusting-looking rubbish that seemed to be everywhere, or padded slowly across roads. They seemed to be the only things for which vehicles were prepared to stop.

The vehicles all seemed to keep so close together, in spite of the other admonition many of them bore: *'Keep Distance'*. Several times she held her breath as she felt sure the car was entering (often at a laboriously built-up speed that the driver seemed reluctant to cut) a space that to her eye looked to be far too narrow for it. But neither Lalit nor the driver showed the faintest trace of concern, and each time she was proved wrong, even though only inches separated them from vehicles on both sides. Some contraptions – they could hardly be termed vehicles – were unlike any she had ever seen before: wooden trailers pulled by large-horned cows; and big-framed bicycles converted into tricycles, with large platforms for goods between the two rear wheels. These were often heavily laden, seemingly impossibly so, with loads of timber, bags of cement or piles of sand and roughly fashioned bricks, in front of which a usually skeletal man was straining to turn the pedals.

All around the traffic, excepting only in one grand open area of red-hued edifices that Lalit told her were government buildings, teemed humanity, humanity of every age, size and class, from the ragged beggars whom Lalit shooed crossly away when they appeared, tapping earnestly at her window at every traffic light, often holding up a baby, to the smartly dressed, evidently affluent occupants of the newer limousines that occasionally punctuated the rest of the traffic.

She felt a growing sense of fascination, wonder even, at all that she saw. Christian had told her nothing about it. Every time she asked 'How was India?' when he came home, all he would say was 'same as ever', or once, 'you love it and hate it all in one'. Only now did she begin to comprehend what he had meant.

It quickly became apparent to Claire that the broad smile Ravindra wore to greet her, and the warm and rich personality she soon realised lay behind it, were not just those a good host would adopt in order to make a guest feel welcome and at home, but deeply entrenched features of his character.

They had entered the area where he lived through a gate on which the words 'Friends Colony – Residents Only' were roughly inscribed. A person she took to be a security guard had opened it to them, and gave the driver a small piece of paper before allowing them to pass. The memory of her first entry into the TCC came back to her. Inside the area, were mostly terraced blocks of three of four three-storied houses, each with a small courtyard at the front, where, in most cases, shrubs and flowering plants grew from terracotta pots, giving an Italianate feel to the place. Here and there bare-footed women were sweeping the gutters of the streets with strange-looking, handle-less brushes, stooping low to do so. In marked contrast to the world outside, the place seemed clean, tidy and well ordered.

A beaming Ravindra greeted her: 'Most welcome, Claire, most welcome,' holding his hands together in a welcoming gesture. 'Please come in, as I feel it is already not quite warm enough for us to sit outside.'

He was a short, plumpish man, in both measures more so than she had anticipated from the picture in the report, which was just of head-and-shoulders. He was dressed much as Krishnan had been on Friday evening in a smart sleeveless jacket, from which the sleeves of an immaculately white shirt protruded. But the trousers Ravindra wore were like those of a jockey: tight from the knee down, where they were rucked up, as if they were made a foot or more too long for him. Like Krishnan, however, his hair was fine in texture, and pure white, as was his well-trimmed moustache.

Once they were inside, Ravindra called upstairs, and two children, a boy and a girl, soon clattered down. They stood together sheepishly. Both had pretty jet-black hair, the girl's braided into two long plaits that reached down to her waist. The boy wore a pair of black-rimmed spectacles, as did his father. Unlike their father, however, both children bore serious countenances.

Ravindra spoke first to the children: 'This is Claire-aunty, who is married to Christian-uncle,' and then to her: 'Claire, this is my son Saurav, who is ten, and my daughter Farida, who is six.'

As he said this, both children greeted her with the hands-together gesture and slight bow of the head, which she returned, feeling how meaningful the act seemed to be, compared to the western-style handshake.

'Saurav?' Ravindra said to his son.

The boy cleared his throat: 'Claire-aunty, my sister and I both wish to express sorrow at what has happened to Christian-uncle. We both love Christian-uncle very much and we hope he will soon be well again.'

The boy glanced nervously at his father, who gave a nod of encouragement, accompanied by a broadening of his smile.

Claire choked a little and felt the tears well up in her eyes. She wiped them away with a finger before replying.

'Saurav, what you have said has touched me very much . . .'

She choked again.

'. . . as you can see. I thank you – and your sister – for what you have said. You are . . .'

Again her throat tightened, and she stopped, now struggling also to cope with more tears. The little girl came and held her hands.

'Claire-aunty, please don't cry,' she said, sweetly. 'I can read you a story if you like. Christian-uncle always liked me to read him stories.'

'All in good time, Farida,' Ravindra said, 'you can read to Claire-aunty later.'

As he said this, Claire squeezed Farida's hands. 'Yes, that would be nice, Farida, in a little while, before I go. I would like you to read to me.'

Now, through a doorway at the far end of the room, emerged a young woman, bare-footed, carrying a tray, which she placed on the low table around which low armchairs and leather pouffes were arranged. The woman said nothing and did not look at any of them: like the women she had seen sweeping the streets, she walked in a stooped manner. She had skin darker than that of any Indian she had yet met, much darker even than that of the cashier at the hotel. Claire was puzzled – surely this could not be Ravindra's wife?

Having deposited the tray, the woman disappeared back through the door. Ravindra noticed that Claire seemed now ill at ease.

He turned to the children: 'Now you two run along and play with your friends, while Claire-aunty and I have some tea.'

At this the children's serious expressions disappeared and they bounded out through the front door.

'Who was the lady who came in?' Claire asked.

'That is our maid,' Ravindra replied, still smiling his broad smile.

'Maid?'

'Yes,' said Ravindra, 'she is from the south of India and speaks only Tamil. Most of the families here, families like ours where both husband and wife work, have maids, and many of them come from Tamil Nadu. It is good work for them and good for us and our children. We could not manage without her. Christian told me you call such people cleaners or home-helps in England, but in India we call them maids. I think the word is one of the many colonial legacies you have left us, in exchange for those we left you, like "char" for example, as in "a cup of char" – did you know that comes from the Hindi word "chai", which means tea?'

'No, I didn't know that!' she said, laughing now, as Ravindra started pouring the tea. 'But where is your wife?'

'I'm so sorry,' he said, 'I should have explained when you arrived. Mariana is helping Rafiquah with preparations for the dance festival. They are down at the Arts Centre. It is a huge event. Rafiquah has given me the programmes and brochures to give to you. Goodness, did you think the maid was my wife? That's why you were looking so perplexed just now?'

'Yes, I have to confess I did wonder!'

They both laughed and then fell silent. The sounds of the children playing in the street drifted through the still-open front door.

Ravindra resumed: 'Now we must make plans for the week. There are various events at the festival, all in the evenings, and the little folder Rafiquah has given me for you has all the tickets. Of course you do not have to use all, but, put it this way, the very best seat is reserved for you for every performance.'

'Will you and your wife be going?'

'Certainly. We will be with you. Sometimes the children will come, too. You will be leaving late on Friday night still?'

'Yes, the flight goes 2 am Saturday, I think.'

'Yes, BA flight. Lalit will get you there in good time. But I am asking because festival closes Friday night, with the most exciting activities, especially the performance of *aran-*

getram. So if you wish you can still attend and then go straight to airport. But maybe that will be too much?'

'Sounds good to me. What is *arangetram*, though?'

'When the teacher at a gharana feels that his or her pupil has reached a good standard,' Ravindra said, 'the student is presented for *arangetram*, which is an old Sanskrit word meaning "ascending the stage". So, the arangetram is a dance display that marks the end of training and the beginning of a student's professional or amateur dance life. Rather like flying solo for the first time. It is usually danced when the student is in his or her late teens. It is always exciting because it is moment when you may see a future star being born. There is a big party after, where everyone celebrates. You too are invited. We are hoping one day that Farida will do her *arangetram*, in a few years time.'

'I would love to be there. I'll certainly come, this week I mean, and I hope, for Farida's too, in years to come.'

'So, what else would you like to do during the week?' Ravindra asked. 'Perhaps you would like to go to Agra and see Taj Mahal? Also Jaipur? Visit markets in Delhi? Everything can be arranged, as you wish.'

She felt that the moment was right now to deal at least with some of the things she wanted to ask.

'Can we come back to that, Ravindra?' she said, 'I have a couple of questions first'

'Fire away, please.'

'When Christian came here, did he have to travel around a lot? You know, visiting projects, that kind of thing?' she asked.

'Why do you ask?' Ravindra said, still smiling.

'Hard to explain, really, I just want to have a better understanding of what his work involved, I suppose,' she said, not quite truthfully, but close enough to be able to sound sincere.

'Well,' Ravindra said, 'as you know he came, usually, three-four times a year. Only one of those involved travel outside Delhi, but it was extensive, to perhaps ten or a dozen projects we are responsible for, from Bangalore area down south to Rajasthan in the west, also Orissa, and in this and neighbouring states. We always went together, usually plus one of my senior staff. But other visits, no, he would be in the office here, whole time, analysing field reports, interviewing staff. April-May visit was always field work period.'

She knew what she wanted to know.

'How was Christian, I mean, on the field visits?' she went on. 'He told me about one visit where the villagers were watching TV, when . . .'

'Oh yes,' Ravindra said, now bringing up his feet under him, so as to sit on the couch yoga-style, 'I think I know what you are referring to – it was in Orissa?'

'Yes, Orissa.'

'I remember it, it was last year. We had the kind of discussion, even argument if you like, that we often used to have.'

'How was that?' she asked.

'Well, as you know, Christian was a very generous man, and in certain ways, quite an angry man, more angry these past few years, I feel.'

'Yes, I've seen that. But what did you argue about?'

'About poverty, about the fact that people, many people, live lives of extreme poverty, while others have wealth beyond measure,' Ravindra said, as the maid came silently back into to the room to clear away the tea tray.

'You argued about that? Surely you agree?'

'Yes, yes, Christian and I are of like mind on the matter. That is one of the reasons why we are friends, and why we like to work together. We are also of similar background, you know: both his parents and mine were humble people, ordinary people.'

'So what did you argue about?'

'You see, motivating factor for PDI is empowerment. We say to people: "We will help you, but at same time you must also help yourselves. If you do not, then what we do for you will be useless, worse than useless." This is not Thatcher-approach. This is not Mother Teresa charity-approach. This is empowerment approach, participation-approach, dignity-approach. We say: "We help you only if you also help yourself" and at same time we say; "but decisions and power must be yours; if not, then you will only become more poor".'

'And Christian disagreed?'

'No, no, no, far from it. He was of like mind. Each year he helped us get funding from UK government with good reports. Often he was angry because he said UK government wanted "quick-fix", nice stories, even photo-opportunities for visiting ministers or film- and pop-star friends of Prime Minister. Christian used to call them, what was it, vermin. One so-called pop-star came once, called "Honorary UK Ambassador, Third World Poor". Name meant nothing to me, but Christian-bhai said real name was "Third Rate Nobody" who had made fortune from one bad song, now living luxury-life, saw phoney concern about poor as way to even more luxury-life and perhaps place in House of Lords. Christian spoke to him in office one day, in my office in fact. When pop-star came out, nose was bleeding, very bad.'

'Christian hit him?'

'Yes. Afterwards I was very worried, very much worried, that PDI funds from UK would be cut, but Christian told me the story. He said that pop-star-wallah had asked him where to find, er . . . to find . . .'

'To find what?'

'To find a woman, what do you say, to find lady-friend, lady-of-night?'

'I understand. That was why he hit him?'

'Thik hai. Christian told me that he had told pop-star that he would inform UK press of such request. Thus, matter was closed. Funding remained intact.'

Claire smiled. While this was yet another revelation, she felt a sense of pride.

'You were talking about this empowerment approach, Ravindra?'

'Ah, yes, Christian-bhai said that they, UK government, any government, did not understand that empowerment-approach takes time, did not *want* to understand. He said they wanted Mother Teresa charity, soup-kitchen approach, which takes five minutes, not PDI-type approach, which takes decade, lifetime even. You can fill stomach in five minutes, and get nice pictures, but to build empowerment, it is like life-long learning, life-long labour.'

'But I still don't understand why you and Christian would argue.'

'Ha!' Ravindra exclaimed, laughing now, 'arguments were not serious. You see, to take Orissa example I think you are referring to, villagers there have bought TV set and satellite dish, home-made dish in fact, with profits from vegetable gardening project they have set up with our help. It has taken many years but is making good profit now, so we are happy. Villagers are happy. After we had spent some time there, as we were about to return to Bhubaneswar, Christian gave money to the women, as a gift. In fact this was not unusual. Often at projects he would give money from his own pocket. And it was about that that we would argue. I would say: "Christian, how can you do that? This is charity-approach. This is alms-for-poor approach!" And he would always say something like: "I'm sorry, I cannot help

257

it. I have much, they have nothing. How can I not give something?" Or words like that, every time. He would, to be honest, give away a lot of money.'

Ravindra paused and drew breath, and went on: 'Of course I understood, at a personal level. He was a generous man. He felt deep guilt.'

'About what? About there being poor people in a world of riches?'

'Yes, that, but he also had a strong sense of guilt about ... about history, about colonialism. This would always come up when he talked to people, whether villagers or bureaucrats. He used to say: "My country, which plundered great wealth from this one, has a debt which it has never repaid properly or even minimally, yet it sees this and many other countries, where situation is even worse, as being in debt to it! And now it has the cheek to send out people like me to make sure the few rupees it throws your way are being properly spent!" Sometimes Christian would become very angry about such matters. Sometimes he used to turn upon himself, saying things like: "What right do I have to come here? I am nothing. I know nothing. I am worth nothing." Things like that. Even last year he told me he was thinking about quitting this work but I begged him to keep with us.'

Claire pursed her lips and said: 'Yes, he told me about all those things.'

'Come, let us check on the children,' Ravindra said.

Outside, the air was noticeably colder and the light was beginning to fade. The children were playing cricket in the street. Claire shivered.

'Come in by half an hour,' Ravindra called out, and they went back inside.

'A glass of wine or beer perhaps?' he asked as they sat down again.

'That would be nice, yes, wine,' she said, 'and then let's

talk about what you asked earlier, about what I'd like to do this week.'

'Good,' Ravindra said, as he got up, 'let's do that.'

Claire put on the cardigan, and then the shawl, that she had brought with her.

When they were settled, she said: 'I would, if you feel it wouldn't be intrusive, like to visit your offices and meet the staff. Of course I know something of what you do, but I'd like to know more.'

'Wonderful!' Ravindra said immediately, 'all staff would like that very much. It would certainly not be seen as intrusive, least of all by me. Tomorrow would be a very good day to do that. Afterwards we can go straight to festival opening reception. British High Commissioner will be there, with British Council Director. Christian did not like either of them, especially High Commissioner, but both are making contribution to the festival, as is Swedish Ambassador, who will also be present.'

'That's fine,' she said, 'I'll give them some sweet talk.'

'Good,' said Ravindra, 'as Christian used to say, "every little grovel helps".'

She laughed.

'Then, I thought perhaps next day I could go to the gharana, and meet Rafiquah?'

'No,' Ravindra said, emphatically, 'all are very much pre-occupied with festival, especially Rafiquah. What Mariana and I had thought, and already suggested to Rafiquah, was that we would have dinner together on Thursday evening, when there is no performance. In fact Rafiquah has asked that we all come to her house. Would that be acceptable?'

'That would be lovely,' she said.

'So can I suggest, Claire, that perhaps on Tuesday, which is a very busy day for me, and also Mariana too, that you might like to go to Agra, stay night there, visit Taj Mahal next morning, which is the best time to visit, and then come back here in time for Wednesday evening performance? I feel you should not come to Delhi without going to Agra. It is 3-hour drive each way. Lalit will go with you of course. He will take care of everything, including hotel room and guide.'

'Agreed,' she said, 'which reminds me. Lalit works for you?'

'No, he works for the company PDI uses for all travel arrangements, for visitors, for staff, for me, for whoever. Lalit, I have found, is the most conscientious and considerate of all their staff. He is as a result, almost full-time on PDI work, since, as you might guess, my staff travel a lot. He is utterly reliable. In fact I may take him on soon, as I think it's time we had in-house staff for travel. But whatever you need, you just ask Lalit. He gave you his mobile number I take it?'

'Yes, he did, and that reminds me of something. I don't think you are aware of this, but the surgeon who operated on Christian is from India. He has been a great support for me these past weeks. He has a cousin, who is also a doctor, here in Delhi. I would like to visit her.'

'You are not well?' Ravindra asked.

'No, I'm fine, though Krishnan, the surgeon, has told her I am here and that I should contact her if I have any health problems. But no, I would just like to pay a call on her, just to say hello.'

'I see. Perhaps you could see her on Tuesday before you leave for Agra?'

'Yes, that would be good. I'll call her later today, or tomorrow.'

'I will inform Lalit – you have the address and everything?'

'Yes.'

The children burst in, in high spirits. 'Papa, Saurav hit three sixes. Ball is now lost!' Farida babbled, 'one day

Saurav will be India captain. Can I read story to Claire-aunty now?'

'Yes of course you can,' Claire answered as Ravindra looked at her, 'I would very much like a story now, and then I must go home to my hotel.'

Ravindra and his two children went upstairs, and shortly after, Farida came back with a book. She snuggled up close to Claire, who put her shawl around both of them.

As Farida began to read it soon became apparent to Claire that the story was an Indian version of the one she knew as the *Princess and the Pea*. As Farida read, slowly and with beautiful clarity, Claire felt tiredness creeping up on her.

'That was lovely, Farida,' she said, yawning hugely, as the girl finished. Ravindra, whom she suspected had been listening at the top of the stairs, came down.

'I have just spoken to Lalit,' he said, still smiling brightly. 'He will be here in a couple of moments, and then, if it is OK with you, he will collect you from the Clarence at eleven tomorrow and bring you to the office. I think you will find that you will sleep very well tonight. Usually at this time on his first day Christian would be ready to rest, because of jet-lag.'

At the Clarence, she was greeted elaborately by everyone from the doorman to the man she found in her suite turning back her bedclothes. As soon as she was alone, she checked the filofax again.

The blue marks within the India periods lay only within three of the four trips. The exception was the April/May trip, where the only two marks were the green ones at the beginning and end.

Sleep was a long time coming. It was as if she was a princess with a giant pea under her mattress.

261

14

The Encounter

Kathak

'The word Kathak comes from "Katha" which means a story. Kathakars or story-tellers are those who narrate stories by dancing. The dance has been therefore called Kathak. It became popular in North India in the 15th century and enjoyed its golden age during the 19th century when it was introduced to the court of the Moslem emperors and became a pastime of the nobility. The main characteristics of the Kathak dance are complicated feet movements and fast turns. More than one hundred small bells are fastened to the dancer's feet. The bells give a magnificent sound together with the complicated rhythms of a drum.

'In Kathak a vivid story is unfolded before the eyes of the audience by the dancers' body movements, sign language, eye and facial expressions. In addition, it is accompanied by narrators.

'The most thrilling item in Kathak is the Tatakar which is a challenge to a dancer's control over timing and rhythm. The dancer does not use the hands or the other parts of the body but uses only the feet to perform the various complicated talas (time measures) and its fractions. The end of the Tatakar portion is a challenge from the point of view of perfect manipulation of weight. The dancer tries to control the sound of the ankle bells and can restrict the sound to the jingling of only one or two bells or the entire collection of bells at the ankles.'

I wonder if you've seen Alfonso yet. I expect you have – you always got on with things quickly. As soon as you ever thought of something, you'd do it, even if you were halfway through doing something else.

I know you need to make your own decision on what to do, and that you always hated it whenever you thought I was telling you what to do, but it is giving me pleasure at the moment to imagine you in the old farmhouse up on the hill. I have clear pictures in my head of it, both as it is now, derelict and crumbling away, and as it will be after renovation. You remember those sketches we made all those years ago? What I especially like to imagine is how the outside area would look: a big patio between the main farmhouse and the outhouse, covered with vines that would grow along the timbers put up to link the buildings, stretching right up to the edge, where there would be a low wall or balustrade of some kind so that Amy would not fall over the edge. I imagine a big table out there, at which to sit with a glass of wine in the evening and look down over the valley and the village. Alfonso has drawn up some detailed plans.

But maybe the old boy still doesn't want to sell.

That reminds me. At the beginning of every financial year – in April, that is, my arrangement with the firm was that they would pay me a bulk amount in advance for my expenses during the year. As you know – did I ever tell you? – the arrangement I always had was that I did all my own travel and hotel bookings and payments, and inform them after each trip what had been spent and what balance still remained. Then at the end of the year, I'd either give them back any unused money, or they would pay me an extra amount if I'd overspent. Usually it would be the latter. I had two more trips to make this year, one to India in February and then one to Pakistan in late March, so there's money Palmer and those other slimy nasties will probably ask you to send back. Yes, I'll bet they will: they'll probably

263

use it on some expense account lunches, complete with £200 bottles of Margaux and Nuits Saint Georges, at Rules or some other flash place, in celebration of the fact that they don't have me around any more, a celebration made all the more sweet because it hasn't cost them a brass farthing to get rid of me!

So my advice to you is to put on the old weeping widow act and see if you can find a generosity in them that I sure as hell never was able to discover. Worth a try. I know begging and grovelling are simply not you, but give it a try. Would you? If you are uncomfortable about keeping it for yourself, then why don't you give it to Ravindra – that £500 I asked you to send him is pretty pathetic now I think about it. Ravindra would know exactly what to do with it: just say something like 'Christian told me you would know what to do with this.'

I know you'll think this is mad, but I used to keep the money up in the loft. It was the safest place I could think of. I always preferred to cash the cheque at the bank at the beginning of each year and then stash it away up there, taking what I needed for each trip. It's in a little metal box tucked away where the chimney stack goes through. Going from memory, I think there's getting on for five thousand quid left there now. If they really insist on having it back, then I guess you'll just have to go along with them.

By the way I lent a bit of money here and there to some of the guys in the pub. There's a list in the box, but throw it away because they've all paid up. It would be embarrassing for you and for them if you asked for it. Yes, I know I should have told you.

A still beaming Ravindra greeted her at the front door of the People's Development Institute, but his expression changed as he looked at her.

'You are not well, Claire?' he said, 'if I may say, you do not look well.'

'No, I'm fine,' she said, 'I just didn't sleep very well last night.'

'Then why not go back to hotel now and rest? Staff will not mind, they will all understand fully.'

'No, really, I'll be fine, but I will rest this afternoon, I promise you.'

Ravindra led her through what seemed a crowded reception area to the lift, in which a frail-looking old man in a crumpled khaki shirt and matching trousers sat on a stool. He was bare-footed. He had a vacant expression and did not look at her.

'He is blind,' Ravindra said, 'but he can operate lift.' He then spoke to the man in what she presumed to be Hindi. The man spoke back as they rode slowly upwards.

'Thik hai,' Ravindra answered him.

As they left the lift at the top, fifth, floor of the building, Ravindra said: 'He asked me to tell you that Christian-bhai was a very kind man.'

'What is "bhai"?' she asked, 'I meant to ask you yesterday.'

'It is term of respect,' Ravindra said, 'used only when addressing or speaking of someone you hold in high regard. For women, the term is "ben", so I would call you "Claire-ben" for example. For highly respected older people, term "ji" is sometimes used instead, as when we speak of "Gandhi-ji", father of India.'

In Ravindra's office, which she could see immediately was tidy and well-ordered, they sat down in the two large black leather armchairs that were together in one corner.

'Staff have asked if you would kindly make a short address to them. While I have told them what you told me, they would very much like, if you feel able, to have a few words from you. But seeing you as you are, I think perhaps that is not a good idea. They will understand.'

265

'No,' she said, 'I will do it. I hadn't expected it, but it's the least I can do.'

'Are you sure?'

'Yes, on one condition – that a few of them, two or three, tell me about what they do, about what PDI does,' she said.

'A short presentation has been prepared, to be made by two staff.'

'Wonderful. Well, I'm ready when you are.'

Ravindra lifted his phone and spoke briefly in Hindi. 'All will be assembled in ten minutes. You would like tea, or water perhaps?'

'Yes, water would be good.'

Ravindra went out, and soon another old man, in the same khaki uniform as the lift-operator, came in with a condensation-dripping plastic bottle and glass.

'Thank you,' she said, as the man filled the glass. Ravindra came back in.

'This man cannot speak,' Ravindra said. 'He was attacked and robbed by thugs, who cut his throat, severing vocal cords. There is another word you get from India – it comes from Hindi word "thuggee", meaning robber.'

The man stood before her and greeted her solemnly in the familiar way. She put down her glass and returned the gesture, seeing the ugly scar across his throat as she did so.

'All will be ready now,' Ravindra said. 'Shall we go? First I need to show you something, on the way.'

Next to Ravindra's office was another much smaller one, its door open. Ravindra pointed to the desk, on which a large vase of flowers had been placed.

'Staff have decided that this office will never be used again for anything other than individual contemplation, if worst comes to worst.'

As he closed the door, the name on it became apparent. A lump came to her throat.

They walked downstairs to the floor below, which was mostly comprised of a large meeting room. There, what must have been fifty or sixty people, most of them young, smartly and colourfully dressed, some older men in the khaki uniforms, including the two she had met, were gathered. As she entered with Ravindra, there was immediate and deep silence.

When it was over – while the whole presentation was lengthy, she had enjoyed it greatly and admired the highly professional way that it had been done, with short video extracts, in one of which Christian was seen briefly, and even lilting background music at times – Ravindra stood and indicated that she should leave with him. But when she reached the door, she said 'No' quietly and stood to the side. Ravindra realised her intention and stood beside her, gesturing to his staff that they should leave first.

As the first of them passed her, she placed her hands together and kept them there until the last had gone. She looked each person in the eye, nodded her head gently and said, quietly, 'thank you' to every single one. In return, she received the familiar gesture from each one of them in turn. As the last left – the dumb and blind men – she felt enriched and serene.

'Are you up to lunch now?' Ravindra asked when they were back in his office.

'To be honest, Ravindra, no. This has been a most moving experience and I'd like to rest now, and reflect on it,' she said.

'I think that is very wise, Claire. Let me show you out. Reception this evening is at the Arts Centre, which is close to Clarence Hotel. Lalit will come to collect you at five. If you do not feel up to it then, that will be fine. By the way, what you said just now was very much appreciated, as I am sure you could see.'

At the last set of traffic lights, the hotel entrance visible barely a hundred yards ahead, they found themselves behind one of the strange three-wheeled bicycle goods vehicles. It was heavily laden with what appeared to be steel rods. As the lights changed to green and the rider strained to start to force his pedals round, the whole contraption suddenly keeled over sideways, spilling the heavy load, which, with a deafening crash, had the initial effect of unseating two passing motorcyclists, as their machines were knocked over by the dangerous cascade of the metal rods. Fortunately neither motorcycle rider, nor the cyclist himself, seemed to be badly injured. But with half the road blocked, the traffic was quickly jammed. Horns blared and soon there was cacophony. Trapped immediately behind the cause of the chaos, there was no way they could move. Claire watched with increasing alarm as people shouted at the hapless cyclist. Some started pushing and shoving him, even kicking him, and he fell to the ground, where he cowered and covered his head in a pose half-beseeching and half self-protecting.

'Lalit, we must do something – they are hurting the man!' she said.

Lalit spoke to the driver and then jumped out. Claire watched him confront the attackers, standing over the man as he did so. They started pushing Lalit, too. Claire tried to open her door but the driver turned round and said the very first words he had ever spoken to her: 'No. Locked. Very bad men. Stay.'

At last, two policemen appeared. At the sight of them most of the attackers ran off or went back to their cars. A few, however, remained bent over the man, punching and kicking him viciously. The policemen waded in with their batons, bashing both the attackers and the hapless cyclist indiscriminately. Eventually, the cyclist, who was as old and frail as any she had seen, stood up, cowering as the policemen rained a few more blows on him. Claire could see that the poor man was weeping and wringing his hands in anguish. Lalit returned.

'Madam,' he said to her, 'the hotel is close by. I will escort you there and then come back. I think that is best. Otherwise we will be here long time.'

He opened the door for her and she got out. The noise of the horns was deafening. Lalit took her hand and guided her through the traffic, which, where it was not ensnarled in the jam, was moving free, fast and furious.

'Please wait a minute, Lalit,' she said when they entered the hotel lobby. She went to the cashier's counter.

'Please give me twenty pounds from my box, quickly please,' she said. The cashier disappeared and soon came back with the entire money envelope, from which she extracted the note.

She folded it in her palm and then walked over and pressed it into Lalit's.

'What is this?' Lalit said, 'please, madam, no tipping, no tipping is required.'

'No, Lalit. I want you to give this to the man, the man who caused the accident. Just tell him it is to help him repair his bicycle. Will you do that for me please?'

Lalit opened his hand and looked at the note.

'It is very much money, madam, too much,' he said, 'but yes, I will give it to him. Like your husband, you are very kind. Mr Christian always was giving much money. Man will be very happy. With this he can even buy new bicycle.'

269

'But where did it come from?' she said to herself in the lift.

Even though it was only a little after five o'clock, the reception was already in full swing when she arrived. It was in a large courtyard area, where hundreds of people, mostly formally dressed, were gathered in knots around which waiters circulated with trays of drinks. There was a small, low stage, beside which a musical group, all seated on cushions, played lilting Indian music. All around the area there were lanterns, real lanterns, which gave a soft flickering light to the scene as the sky above slowly darkened. Claire felt rested after her long afternoon nap.

Looking around, she saw Farida and Saurav standing with a woman she presumed to be their mother. Like her son and daughter, the woman had black hair, but it was cut short. She wore what seemed to be a long-sleeved shirt, which reached to below her knees, with matching trousers much like those Ravindra had worn, with the part below the knees all rucked up. She remembered that some of the female staff at the office meeting earlier in the day had been similarly dressed. Claire moved towards the group.

'Mummy, look, here is Claire-aunty!' Farida called out, tugging at her mother's arm, as she saw her approaching.

The woman turned and took both Claire's hands in her own.

'I am so glad to meet you, Claire. I am Mariana.'

'You look lovely. Mariana, absolutely lovely,' she said, now noticing that the blouse seemed to have gold thread in it, as it shimmered in the lights. 'Can I ask what this kind of dress is called?'

'It is called *salwar kameez*. The *salwar* is the bottom, the trousers, and the *kameez* is the dress, the shirt,' Mariana replied. 'They are very practical and comfortable. We must go shopping and get you some. You can get many different styles, some with tight trousers and some with loose ones.'

'I would like that very much.'

Ravindra soon joined them, and as he did so, Claire saw that Mariana was much the taller of the two, that she had a pale but very attractive face with a pert little nose. Claire could feel rings on the fingers of both hands, which still held hers. Like her husband, Mariana seemed to exude happiness.

'I'm sorry I was not able to greet you at the house yesterday, Claire,' Mariana said, 'Rafiquah asked me to help her with the preparations here and at the theatre, so it was a busy day.'

'Yes, Ravindra told me,' Claire said, 'but please don't apologise. Your wonderful husband and children made me feel very much at home. Farida read me a beautiful story. And thank you so much for the flowers you sent to the hotel. They are so lovely.'

She felt Mariana's hands squeeze hers, gently: 'We all pray that Christian recovers,' Mariana said. 'Is there really no hope?'

'The doctors are pessimistic, but, to be honest, I've not given up even though they tell me I must expect the worst.'

'Then we will hope with you,' Mariana said, releasing her hands.

'I hope I will get to meet Rafiquah this evening, and her son,' Claire said. 'I want to thank her too for the flowers she sent.'

'Yes, Rafiquah is here of course. She will no doubt be saying a few words soon. Then I'll introduce her. She wants very much to meet you. But her son is not here. He is doing his *arangetram* on Friday night, so he is practising day and night.'

Ravindra, who had drifted away during this discussion, now reappeared with two white men both wearing rather creased, European-style, pale linen suits.

'Claire, I would like you to meet British High Commissioner.'

'How do you do?' said the older of the two: a plump, balding, ruddy-faced man, in an upper-class, public school- and county set-honed drawl, holding out a flabby hand, which she took and shook lightly, finding it sticky.

'. . . and,' Ravindra continued, 'the Director of British Council in Delhi.'

'I'm very pleased to meet you, Claire,' said the other man, warmly, as they shook hands. He was pale, thin, with a droopy black moustache and rimless spectacles. About her own age, she guessed.

'Do I detect a touch of Sussex in that accent?' Claire asked.

'Yes, born and bred in deepest Haywards Heath,' he replied.

'We live not far from there,' she said.

'Yes, I know, Christian told me. By the way, we're all terribly sad about what's happened. Ravindra told me about it last week, and of course I informed the High Commissioner right away.'

'Quite so. Fine man, your husband,' the High Commissioner boomed in a rather slurred voice. 'Jolly fine man. One of the best. Top-notch. You have my sincerest good wishes, madam.'

He turned away and left before she could respond, but the British Council man remained.

'Actually, I don't think there was any love lost between those two,' he said. 'In fact Christian couldn't stand him, and to be honest, neither can I and most other people I know in the Diplomatic Corps and British community here. He's an embarrassment to the country. Drinks like a fish.

Notorious bottom-pincher, so watch out. Should've been sent home years ago. Old buddy of the PM's.'

There was a tapping sound and a brief piercing whine of feedback from the loudspeakers. The sound of many conversations quickly began to abate.

Claire moved, wanting to be as close as possible to the stage, where a group of men began to assemble. Three were white – the two she had just met, and another, in a dark suit, strikingly tall, with a rather unkempt mop of very fair hair. The other two were Asian in dark sleeveless Indian-style suits. They all exchanged handshakes and as they did so, the noise of the crowd fell to a low murmur of expectation.

At last a woman took to the stage, and immediately and confidently spoke into the microphone. Claire, transfixed by the woman's beauty, caught only snatches of what she was saying.

'. . . thanks also to the Swedish Ambassador . . .'

The woman was very short, compared to the men in front of whom she was standing.

'. . . Tata Industries, represented here by Shri . . .'

She had long, extremely long, black hair, which cascaded over her shoulders to well below the waist.

'. . . and our host this evening, the Centre for . . .'

The woman's hair seemed to glisten in the flickering light of the lanterns, and was caught here and there in the breeze. Her hands and fingers, which were small and delicate, sparkled with flashes of blue, green and red as she moved her arms and hands elegantly as she spoke. Like those of Mariana, the fingers bore many, many rings. And as she moved her arms in smooth graceful sweeps, Claire saw that her wrists and lower arms bore gold and silver bracelets in profusion, which made a tingling sound like a mild hiss of cymbals.

'. . . and call upon him to officially open the festival but first . . .'

Claire also took in her fine, pale skin, from that of her smooth face, which appeared untouched by any make-up, save for a lipstick that seemed to be almost black, but nonetheless immensely alluring, to her arms, where even above the elbows, there was no hint of wrinkle or flab.

She wore a bright pink sari and bodice. Claire was stunned by her radiant beauty.

'. . . in this very difficult time for her.'

Suddenly Claire realised that the woman was now looking straight at her, indeed holding out a hand towards her. There was a ripple of applause. She looked around from where she was standing beside the stage and realised that the applause was being directed at her.

She raised her hands together in acknowledgement and the gesture immediately caused the applause to swell considerably and then die down.

Claire felt a touch on her arm and turned to find Ravindra standing beside her.

As the man started speaking, Ravindra whispered to her.

'She was hoping you might say a few words, but I told her that I did not think you would be up to it.'

'Thank you,' she whispered back, 'I don't think I could have. Is she Rafiquah?'

'Yes, that is Rafiquah.'

There was more applause as the speech came to an end, which continued as all those on the platform moved forward, at Rafiquah's beckoning, to light candles on a small ornate brass stand that was in front of the stage. The music resumed, as did the low but quickly growing sound of dozens of conversations.

At the same time the waiters reappeared, now bearing platters of snacks as well as more trays of drinks. Claire rejoined Mariana and Farida, and as they all helped themselves to various passing platters, Mariana explained what

274

each dish was, adding whether it was 'veg' or 'non-veg'. To Claire, who had not eaten since breakfast, it all tasted delicious.

She had reached the stage of feeling quite full when she saw Ravindra and Rafiquah making their way through the crowd towards her. Conscious of her hands being oily and greasy from the food, she took a wad of paper napkins from a waiter, but was still cleaning them when Rafiquah arrived, her hands and arms spread wide to indicate a desire to embrace.

As they did so, Claire kept the spoiled napkins tight in one hand, which she held out from Rafiquah's back. Fortunately Mariana saw this and took them from her.

The two held each other for some time, during which Claire took in the sweet musk-like fragrance of Rafiquah's body, and the fact that she was even shorter than she was.

'My dear Claire,' Rafiquah whispered, 'what can I possibly say at a time like this except that we pray, we all pray, to all our different Gods, that he becomes well again.'

Onlookers, including Ravindra, Mariana and the children, as well as many others who took in the scene, could see both women shudder with emotion and after a moment, step back from each other while still holding and gently shaking both hands.

'He was always talking of you to me,' Rafiquah said, 'and of your daughter . . . Amy isn't it?'

'Yes, Amy,' she replied, trying to think of words that were at least somewhere in the region of truth, '. . . and of course, well . . . he talked to me about the dancing and the gharana, and about you . . .'

Get off the subject, she thought as she said this.

'Will there be dancing tonight?'

'No, not tonight,' Rafiquah said, 'just tomorrow, Wednesday and then Friday. You will be coming?'

'Not tomorrow, but the others, yes. And I gather you are inviting us to dinner at your house on Thursday? That will be lovely.'

'It will be my pleasure,' Rafiquah said, her tone of voice now rather terse. 'Now, if you will excuse me, I must make sure our sponsors are happy.'

'I have the money, Rafiquah, I will bring it on Thursday,' Claire said, very quietly now.

'That will be wonderful,' Rafiquah said, her tone still terse.

15

The Game

The room was small, its round green-topped table occupying almost the entire space. A low light, also green, hung over the table, illuminating it, and it alone. As she looked around, she could see only the hands of the players: two black hands, four brown hands, four pink hands. But she felt no fear. The hands all glowed, dully, with sweat, but not her own.

The room reeked of the pungent smoke of cigars and cigarettes, the ash of which overflowed from ashtrays onto the green cloth.

'I don't want the woman here,' a voice said, 'get her out.'

'No,' said another, 'the big man's out of it now. Her money's as good as his. It is his money, after all.'

'And it was ours before he took it,' another added.

And they laughed.

She put her hands on the metal box in front of her. 'No, it's mine now,' she said.

'I still say she should go,' the first voice said. 'Little bitch!'

'Let's drink before we play,' said another. 'Give me that Scotch.'

The bottle was passed to two of the white hands. They took it and poured a tumbler full.

'Give it to me,' a voice said, and the black hands poured another full glass.

Soon all the glasses were full except the woman's.

'You don't drink, then you don't play, you little cow,' the one nearest to her said. His brown hands took her glass and filled it to overflowing, 'Now drink it!' the voice said, loud and threatening.

She drank it down straight, slamming the glass back on the table.

'I'll take another,' she said calmly, even though her head was spinning. The brown hands filled it again.

'Don't any of you guys drink with a lady?' she said, and five hands immediately picked up five glasses and drank.

'I don't see no lady here,' said the voice beside her.

'Time to play,' she said, 'or does anyone want to go home to mummy?'

'You slut,' another voice said. 'Fifty pot, fifty to open, five card, straight.'

She won the first game, the second, the third. But in every game, the others all folded quickly, leaving her to take a meagre pot. The box was on her lap now and she put the two hundred in each time. Yet the men laughed, even as she won.

Now they played again. She looked stone-faced at her cards, which swam a little before her.

'I'm in for fifty,' said one, white hands, and the others all folded except her.

'Fifty and raise you fifty,' she said.

'Fifty and raise you two hundred,' the voice said.

'Two hundred and raise you a thousand,' she said, coolly, and the white hands trembled.

'A thousand and raise you two,' the voice said.

She paused, though she knew she shouldn't, remembering the man who had told her always to take control. Around the table, different hands seemed to move, cards under them, too quickly to take in.

'Two thousand and raise you two more,' she said, knowing it was all she had in the metal box.

'There's your two,' the voice said, 'and you little tart, how would you fancy me raising you five hundred grand?'

The hands pushed out piles and piles of notes. But she saw it was all he had.

'Give me a minute,' she said, and went into the room next door where Alfonso was waiting with the big box. 'I need the money now, Alfonso,' she said. He spread his hands wide and then picked it up and gave it to her.

She went back and spilled out the contents of the box onto the table.

'I'll see you then,' she said, spreading out three kings and two jacks.

The white hands spread out four aces.

'You got her, Palmer,' a voice said and then all the men laughed, long and loud.

'You got the silly bitch and that bastard husband of hers,' another voice said, and they all laughed again.

She stood up, swayed, held her hands to her mouth and then vomited through them over the table.

And then again, and again, and again.

The room was dark and she sensed she was alone. The smell was foul; she felt a damp stickiness seeping through her nightdress. She got up and pulled open the curtains. The bright light stunned her for a moment and, falling on to her knees, she vomited again, all over the beautiful red carpet.

She crawled into the lounge room and scrambled through the papers she had left on the desk there, scattering them willy-nilly until she found the one Krishnan had given her. She dialled the number.

'Hallo?' a woman's voice answered.

'Please help me,' she said, retching again.

'Who is this?'

'Claire, your cousin Krishnan's friend, please help me, I'm sick. I've lost all the money.'

'Money? What money? You are at the Clarence? Yes? I will be there, within half-hour.'

The phone clicked and went dead. Claire now crawled into the bathroom and kneeled in front of the toilet bowl, staying there as each successive wave of nausea, retch and vomit overwhelmed her.

Her strength gone, she fainted.

The doctor and the manager found her there, stretched out unconscious and cold on the tiled floor of the bathroom, a large lump over her left eye where it had hit something, probably the edge of the bath. The manager had opened the door to the suite only after several minutes of hammering on it, during which his initial refusal and then strong reluctance to enter were eventually overcome, all too slowly in the view of the doctor, whose pleading had reached screaming pitch by the time he turned the key.

Both of them gagged when the smell hit them as they took in the sight in the main room and then the bathroom, where they found her.

While the manager stood back and then went back to inspect the rest of the suite, the woman crouched over Claire.

'Bring me a blanket here, quickly,' she called to the manager, who immediately pulled one off the bed.

'Bed is soiled,' he said as he gave it to her, 'but second small bed is clean. We can put her there if you wish.'

'Thik hai,' she said, 'but not yet. Please go and get a

280

good woman staff member to help me. Then send women cleaners. For the moment, this is no place for men.'

The doctor tucked the blanket around and under Claire as best she could, and then bathed her face with a warm flannel. As she did so, Claire came round.

'Just rest a minute, Claire. Everything will be fine, but stay here for the moment will you? Until more help comes. Then we will get you cleaned up and into bed.'

Claire found her head would not obey her instruction to it to move in some form of acknowledgement.

She woke later to find a strange woman sitting in her chair beside the bed.

'How do you feel?' the woman said, 'I am Krishnan's cousin, Prittee.'

Claire's head throbbed with pain, and she felt nauseous again.

'I think I'm going to be sick,' she said.

The woman helped her to sit up and held the bowl under her. She retched again and again, but only a few drops of yellowy-green bile came up.

'I'm afraid it will be like this for a little while,' the doctor said, 'but it will pass. I've given you an injection for the nausea. Try to take in a little water if you can, as you are dehydrated. I have put some mineral salts in the water, which you also need. Here.'

She held out the glass to Claire, who sipped while the doctor held her up.

She lay back again.

'Prittee,' she said, 'that's a lovely name. I'm sorry to cause such a nuisance.'

'Don't worry,' Prittee said, 'I have to be on shift later, but your friends are coming to be with you, and then I will come back tonight.'

'Who?'

'Mariana, is that her name? She is coming soon. I will tell her what to do. All you need to do is rest and get better. You have had very bad food-poisoning by the look of it.'

The next time she woke it was Mariana who was sitting in the chair. Or it seemed to be. She could not focus her eyes properly.

'Mariana?' she said.

'Yes.'

'I have been so stupid. I should have given you the money. Now I've lost it.'

'Shush, money can wait. You must get yourself better.'

When she woke again the room was dark, except for the glow of the light on the desk in the lounge. She sensed someone was sitting by the bed.

'Mariana?'

'No, it is me, Prittee. Mariana will come back tomorrow. I am staying here with you tonight. Can you drink a little more for me, please?'

She did so and then slept again.

'Rafiquah is beside herself,' Mariana said as the car laboured away from the hotel. 'We know for sure of at least ten people who were taken ill after the reception, and we suspect there are many others we don't know about. Unfortunately the British High Commissioner is among the affected, and he is not pleased at all. Rafiquah is refusing to pay the company and there is talk of legal proceedings being instituted. Look at you – you have been in bed for almost three whole days. Others are the same. It is all highly embarrassing. You are here for less than a week and you spend half the time in bed.'

'To be honest, I wasn't that fussed about going to the Taj Mahal, but I'm sorry I've missed last night's performances. How did it go?' Claire asked.

'It was wonderful, truly wonderful. The most famous male Kathak dancer in the country performed . . . but so many empty seats. All because of Monday, I'm sure. I could wring their necks. Ravindra uses the same caterers for functions and conferences at PDI and he will never use them again.'

'It's too bad,' Claire said, 'but now I'm so hungry I could eat a horse! I haven't eaten anything since Monday, other than a nice boiled egg for my breakfast this morning.'

Mariana laughed: 'I don't think Rafiquah will serve horse this evening. By the way she is veg-only, so there will be no meat. I hope that you won't mind? She is preparing special egg-dish for you. After sickness, eggs are very good.'

'That's good of her,' Claire replied, gazing out at the passing traffic.

'Lalit told us what you did for the poor man involved in the accident on Monday,' Mariana went on, 'That was very good of you. I think even Ravindra would not have objected.'

'Which reminds me,' Claire said, peering into her bag, 'I've brought the money I need to give to Rafiquah.'

'To Rafiquah, yes,' Mariana said, deciding not to say anything about Claire's ramblings about money while she had been ill.

As Mariana had warned, it was a long drive, right to the very edge of the sprawling city. It was dark long before they turned off the main road and bumped their way along a roughly made up gravel track. At the end of it there was a small, isolated, brick-built house, brightly illuminated, inside and out. Tiny white fairy-lights were strung around and among the trees and shrubs.

283

They were warmly greeted at the door by Rafiquah, who to Claire looked just as beautiful and radiant as she had at the reception, even though she was now wearing very pale loose *salwar* trousers topped by a rich green, but equally loose *kameez*.

Once again, Rafiquah took both Claire's hands in her own: 'Claire, I am so deeply regretful of what has happened to you. I do hope you are feeling better now?'

'Yes, I'm fine, in fact very hungry! Mariana has told me all about it. I gather that others have been in the same boat,' Claire replied.

'Yes, including even our main sponsor. Allah has certainly not blessed me this week. Most unfortunate, but come, come in.'

Seeing shoes at the door, Claire took off her own and left them with the others.

'You don't need to,' said Rafiquah.

'No, this is not only more polite, but more comfortable,' she replied.

Mariana having gone ahead, leaving them alone, Claire reached in her bag for the envelope.

'Rafiquah, here is the money.'

'Thank you,' Rafiquah said, her tone suddenly cold again, as it had been when they parted at the reception.

The central part of the house was made up of a huge high-ceilinged lounge, furnished by large quantities of cushions of brightly coloured cloth and pouffes of bright leather. A large fan in the ceiling turned gently. There was not a chair in sight. In one corner Mariana stood, with Ravindra rising to his feet beside her.

'Now, what would you like to drink, Claire?' Rafiquah said. 'As a good Moslem I do not drink myself, but I am not so good a Moslem as not to have a bottle or two around for my guests. Or would you prefer something soft, or water? Or Scotch perhaps?'

'No, definitely not Scotch,' Claire said, firmly, 'but some white wine – that would be nice.'

Rafiquah turned to Ravindra.

'Scotch for you, I presume?' she said to him. He wiggled his head in response. Even now, Claire was still not sure whether the wiggle meant yes or no.

'And I think I will have wine too, like Claire,' said Mariana.

Rafiquah went off and soon returned with drinks, by which time Claire, like the others, had settled herself comfortably among the cushions.

'Normally I would have Sanjay here, just to serve,' Rafiquah said, 'but having disgraced me on Monday, the first job he has lost is this one.'

'And the second my conference next week,' added Ravindra, still, as ever, smiling broadly and benignly, now seated cross-legged, like a Buddha, atop a very large red leather pouffe.

'Your son is not here?' Claire asked.

'No, he is still preparing for tomorrow,' Rafiquah replied, stiffly. 'He is so nervous about it. *Arangetram* is a very big thing, you know. I still remember my own, almost forty years ago.'

'You cannot tell me you are in your fifties, Rafiquah?' Claire asked, 'surely not? You look so young.'

In response, Rafiquah smiled thinly.

'Like George Washington, I cannot tell a lie,' she said. 'Even fifties are nearly finished.'

They all laughed, but Claire did so more out of nervous astonishment than amusement and noticed that Rafiquah's amusement also seemed forced.

After a second drink, Rafiquah invited them into the small dining room to the side of the lounge. She brought in dish after dish, placing the last one immediately before Claire.

'Especially for you,' Rafiquah said. 'Eggs with spinach and, well, I won't tell you what else, but it is very mild and will, I can assure you, be very good for you.'

Again the tone of voice was stiff, like that of a mother instructing a rather trying daughter.

'Thank you,' Claire said, 'but everything looks and smells so wonderful. Can I try other things as well, and offer my own eggs for everyone?'

'Of course you may,' Rafiquah said, evenly, 'but at the risk of sounding motherly, can I advise you not to overtax your stomach?'

Claire smiled at her: 'Yes, my new-found doctor friend has already given me strict instructions on that front.'

'Most charming woman she was,' Mariana said. 'She told me she is related to the man who operated on Christian.'

'Yes, his cousin in fact,' Claire replied. 'I can't think what I would have done without her.'

The meal was eaten slowly and then the four of them retired back to the lounge, where Ravindra, fuelled now by what Claire had counted to be at least five Scotches, but, as far as she could discern, entirely unaffected by them, made a short speech.

'Claire,' he began, 'we all regret very much that your short time with us has been so disrupted this week. But we are all glad to see you well again and to have got to know you a little better during our short time together. Because tomorrow will pass quickly, and culminate in what for Rafiquah at least will be a very, very demanding evening, may I thank you on behalf of all of us, for taking the time and trouble, in your troubled times, to come here to be with us this week . . .'

Mariana clapped gently. Claire noticed Rafiquah's thin

smile return briefly, followed by a surreptitious glance at her watch.

'We are happy that Christian has shared with you, as you told me, everything about his life and work here. We are happy, too, to find that you share his passions and also his generosity of spirit. If I might say, and without wishing in any way to make presumption, we hope we can see more of you in future. You will always be welcome among us.'

Mariana clapped again and looked at her expectantly. Rafiquah also looked across at her, but with a blank, cold expression. Ravindra reached behind some cushions, from where he took a wrapped gift, which he gave to Claire. Taking and holding it, she felt obliged to respond:

'Rafiquah, Mariana, Ravindra,' she said, 'in spite of everything . . .'

Ravindra laughed.

'. . . in spite of everything, this evening alone, and my short time earlier this week with you, Ravindra and Mariana, and your lovely children, has been enough to create what will always be happy memories of this week in the future . . . whatever it holds for me . . .'

The room fell silent.

'. . . yes, whatever happens, and indeed whatever has happened . . .'

The silence continued.

'. . . I have something to tell you all. One of the reasons that I know that Christian is still alive is that he speaks to me. The doctors and others, possibly you too, all tell me that this is impossible, but I know that it is not only possible, but has happened. He speaks to me in my dreams. However mad you may think this, and therefore me, to be, and I don't care if you do, I want to tell you what Christian has said to me while I have been here this week. It is a request and it is this. Whatever happens, there may be a sum of money left. Christian wants it to come here for purposes you all know of, and I understand and agree with. I say "may" because, maybe it will be taken by others, not by me, but by others. But I will fight for it, and then if I succeed, you will have it. I simply want you to know that.'

She sat down and started to open the present. The others were still silent. The gift was a *salwar kameez* outfit, pink, with gold embroidery, much the same colour as the sari that Rafiquah had worn earlier in the week.

'May I wear it tomorrow?' she asked, 'Thank you all so much. It is just beautiful.'

'We would be delighted,' Rafiquah said, a faint warmth returning to her voice 'and as far as I am concerned all I can say is that I have no reason to doubt that Christian has spoken to you, no reason at all. I fully believe you. And if that makes me mad in the eyes of others too, then I care about it no more than you do!'

'Well said, well done,' said Ravindra.

As she stepped out of the lift in the hotel lobby the following evening, she saw that those assembled for her departure were even more numerous than those that had welcomed her on her arrival. She felt self-conscious, dressed as she was, even though the young lady from the hotel staff who had helped her had told her that her new attire suited perfectly.

'Madam,' said the hotel manager, handing her a large envelope 'may I say that you look most lovely?'

'Bill and receipts for your current stay are all here, also, as requested, copies of accounts concerning your husband's most recent stay. Everything is in order – your luggage has already been placed in the car.'

In return, she handed the manager a collection of small envelopes.

'I would be grateful if you would pass these to relevant staff,' she said, 'as tokens of my gratitude for all their work and kindness this week.'

Mariana and Ravindra had advised her as they left Rafiquah's house the previous evening that this was the most appropriate way to do the 'tipping' thing when she left.

'Most grateful,' the manager said.

She shook hands with each of the assembled staff in turn, and then proceeded to the door, outside which Lalit was waiting.

'You are looking most wonderful, like Bollywood film-star,' he said. 'All luggage is in boot. You wish to check?'

'No, Lalit,' she replied, 'of course not. Let's go, or we will be late.'

'Thik hai,' Lalit said, wiggling his head.

Shortly before they reached the Arts Centre, they became ensnarled in traffic. But the hooting of horns was restrained, almost artistic, as if this was expected in the vicinity of such a place.

'It is very big function,' Lalit turned to tell her. '*Arange-tram* night is always like this'

The foyer was packed and, consequently, hot. There was a strong smell of sweat intermingled with expensive perfume. From among the crowd, the British High Commissioner appeared.

'Claire! How utterly splendid you look! Would you do me the honour of joining me for a drink after the show?' he drawled, tapping her lightly on the very lowest part of her back, low enough down to make her start.

'Really!' she said, loudly, although it was absorbed and lost in the noise of the throng. 'Please! I am afraid that that is out of the question, not just in view of your manner, but also because I go straight to the airport from here.'

She was spared further embarrassment by the arrival of the man from the British Council, who, having witnessed what was going on, placed himself strategically between the two of them.

'I heard that you were one of those taken ill after last Monday,' he said, with a wink, 'so I thought I would step in to make sure you know that you have help close at hand.'

She smiled at him.

'Thanks' she said, watching the High Commissioner turn away and leave them. 'That revolting man has just . . .'

'I know, I saw. Time to go in, I think.'

Inside the auditorium, where it was as hot and steamy as it had been in the foyer, she was ushered to a seat in the front row, where she was relieved to find that she was between Mariana and Farida, who spoke excitedly when she saw her: 'Look mama, Claire-aunty looks so lovely.'

While Ravindra, who was in the seat the other side of Mariana, increased the scope of his usual beam, Mariana said: 'You look absolutely the part, Claire, perfect in fact,' as she sat down. Looking further along the row, Claire was relieved to see that the High Commissioner was seated some distance away.

'That horrid man has just pinched my bottom,' she whispered in Mariana's ear.

'I don't need to ask who,' Mariana whispered back, 'he is a disgrace.'

Music started, gently and quietly at first, slowly building in volume.

'First half will be performers from different parts of India, and one group from UK,' Mariana said, 'then second half will be *arangetram*.'

The music was now in full flow. The group was seated at

290

one side of the stage, partly obscured from Claire's view. She soon felt relaxed by the rhythm and beating of the drums, mixed with the sharp strident tones of the sitar (yes, that was what it was called, she now, at last, remembered) together with the melodious soft harmonies of an accordion-like instrument, and some reeded oboe-like ones. As the music grew in intensity, the temperature in the theatre seemed to rise with it. Her head began to swim.

After a crescendo, the music ceased abruptly, and then immediately resumed in the form of a gentle beating from the drums.

Mariana whispered to her: 'First will be Thaat dance. Only tabla – drums – will play.'

A single male dancer came on stage and stood with one hand extended in front of him, the other held high above his head. As the tabla played, Claire saw the dancer's eyes, eyebrows, face, neck, shoulders, arms, wrists, hands and fingers move intricately, in perfect time with the accompaniment. She marvelled at the control the young man seemed to have over his body. His hands, especially, transfixed her.

Rapturous applause followed this performance, and each one that followed. To Claire's eyes and ears, the pace of each seemed faster than the one preceding, the colours of clothes of the dancers brighter, the tinkling of the bells on their ankles more complex and sophisticated. As each began, Mariana whispered what she understood to be its name. She did not hear the words properly, but they sounded like *tora, tukra, parana, kavita.*

After about ten dances, there was a short pause.

'Tatakar is now coming,' Mariana said, 'to end the first half. This is very special.'

It was. In contrast to the previous dances, in this one the dancers used only their feet, moving them in different ways so that sometimes but a few of the many bells seemed to tinkle, at others all of them.

291

At its conclusion, a huge roar from the audience burst out. Claire felt exhausted and thrilled.

During the interval, unlike most of the audience, she and Farida remained in their seats. It seemed to cool down a little. After some time, Ravindra arrived with bottles of soft drinks, labelled 'Thumbs Up', for the two of them. The taste was sickly sweet, but at least it was refreshingly very cold.

As people drifted back to their seats a sense of expectancy seemed to replace the earlier one of excitement. Claire looked at her watch and was surprised to see it was already almost eleven o'clock. As a hush slowly settled, an announcement was made over the loudspeakers by an unseen male voice, in Hindi. Mariana said to her: 'There will be four arangetram. Very short, so time is OK for you, don't worry.'

The difference in skill and ability between the initiates and the experienced professionals of the first half was quickly evident, nonetheless Claire's fascination continued.

Soon the last of the four took to the stage. He was much taller than the rest had been, and Claire noticed, much clumsier in his movements.

She sat forward and studied him closely. He wore heavy make-up, so it was hard to make out his facial features. But she quickly saw how pale his hands and feet were, very pale, and how rigid and unbending they seemed to be, compared even to the other novices. And as he moved, sometimes losing his balance slightly, sweating profusely, the powder on his face began to disappear in little rivulets.

The face thus slowly revealed was unmistakably that of Christian as she knew he had looked as a young man from the albums she and Amy had been looking at so recently.

She gripped tightly on the armrest between her and Mariana, not realising that she was actually squeezing Mariana's wrist as tightly as a vice.

She felt faint and closed her eyes momentarily. Mariana's arms moved from under hers to squeeze her own wrist gently back.

As the young man left the stage, Claire sobbed quietly.

'You didn't know?' Mariana whispered.

Claire pulled her arm away, shaking her head. She stood and fled up the aisle, through the empty foyer, and out into the street, where Lalit saw her.

'We are late,' she said, gasping for breath, 'let's go please, Lalit, now.'

Lalit led her to the car, saying nothing.

As they neared the airport, Lalit's phone rang. After a brief conversation he closed it and turned to her.

'Mr Kapoor asks if you would please wait for him on check-in side. I am to wait with you. Important matter has come up. Earnest request that you wait for him, please.'

As he said this, Lalit saw her tears and turned to face forward again.

She checked in, and as she did so, made up her mind.

She rejoined Lalit and held out the small envelope she had kept. As she did this he held up his hands. 'No, madam, no tipping,' he said, 'not allowed.'

'I don't care about that, Lalit. You are a fine young man. You have been very good to me, always. I insist that you take it. Please?'

She held out the envelope again. He took it in both hands, which he then clasped together and raised to his bowed head.

'Goodbye Lalit,' she said, turning away.

'But madam, you must wait, please. Mr Kapoor will be angry with me if you do not wait!'

She turned back to face the young man, seeing his distress immediately: 'No, Lalit, he will not be angry, he is a good man and he will understand. My plane is going soon. Goodbye.'

She turned again and left him.

Once in the business-class lounge, she went immediately to wash her face. She had intended to change her clothes there, but the toilets were occupied.

She found a place to sit down. It was crowded. She closed her eyes and tried to calm the shock and anger she felt, breathing as slowly as she could through her nose.

She heard a polite cough nearby and opened her eyes. A man in a European-style suit was standing in front of her.

'Yes?' she said.

'There has been a mistake, madam,' the man said, 'I am the airport duty-manager. I was asked to arrange VIP lounge facilities for you. It is very crowded here. Please let me take you to the VIP lounge, where you will be more comfortable. Your flight is a little late tonight.'

She got up and the man insisted on carrying her bag for her.

Through a door labelled 'VIP Suite' they entered a lavishly furnished, wood-panelled room, lit only by low-level table lamps, and occupied by a single smartly-dressed waiter.

'Let us get you something to drink,' the manager said, 'a wine perhaps?'

'Thank you, just water please,' she said. 'Is there somewhere I can change my clothes here?'

'Yes, through there,' the man gestured towards a further door 'But, let me first ask my staff to check that it is all in order.'

The manager and the waiter both left.

The sound of the entrance door opening made her turn. It was Rafiquah who entered, bearing the glass of water.

The two women stood some distance apart for a few moments. Rafiquah held out the glass. Claire shook her head. Rafiquah put it on a table and then kneeled down, bowing her head to the ground as she did so. In this posture, she spoke:

'Claire. I know how you must feel . . .'

'How can you possibly know?' Claire barked, 'Just go away and leave me alone. You have humiliated me. He has humiliated me. He . . .'

'Claire, please hear me out. What happened happened a long time ago, fifteen years ago. Long before he met you. It happened only once. I swear all this to you in the name of God, the Merciful, in the name of Allah, peace be upon him. You must believe me. Yes, he always came to stay at my house when he was here, I guess you do know that, but nothing ever again passed between us after that first time. He was never unfaithful to you. I swear to you that that is the truth. He wanted to see his son grow up. In God's name, we thought that you knew, after what you had said to Ravindra-bhai. But we were wrong . . .'

Rafiquah sobbed, still prostrate on the floor.

'. . . I beg your forgiveness.'

'How did you get in here?' Claire asked, still with the sharp edge of anger in her tone of voice.

'The airport manager is my brother,' Rafiquah said. 'It was he who arranged for you to be met when you arrived. I knew I had to see you, so I asked him to do this for me. I could not let you go without saying what I have said.'

Claire said nothing. She could think of nothing to say.

Still kneeling on the floor, but raising her head now to look fixedly at the other woman, Rafiquah continued: 'There's something else I want to say, and then I will go. I don't know whether you will like this or not, but I too have had messages in my dreams. Or rather one message only. Christian asked me, if I ever met you, to tell you the truth, as I have just done, and to ask you to forgive him.'

'I'd have preferred him to ask me directly,' Claire replied, tartly, feeling even more irritated by this revelation.

'I'm sorry. I understand . . .'

No further words were spoken for a minute.

'Now that the boy is getting older,' Rafiquah eventually said, 'he does not need the financial support Christian used to provide. We have enough, so please, don't feel obliged to do what you said last night. And, by the way, the five hundred pounds was simply the donation he made to the festival each year, not for the boy. That is the truth.'

'So he gave you other money for the boy?' Claire asked.

'He gave me access to other money. Here, you must take this.'

As Rafiquah spoke, she held out a small envelope, which Claire took and stuffed in the pocket of her trousers.

'I have told you the truth, only the truth.'

Afterwards, Claire picked up the glass of water and scattered its contents over the place in the carpet where Rafiquah had knelt, and then left.

16

The Return

It's coming. I can feel it. My energy seems to be draining away. Oh, there is so much more to say, but I can't now. I love you darling. I always loved you, only you, apart from one other, briefly, a long, long time ago.

She was still in her *salwar kameez* when she emerged, shivering, into the arrivals hall.

'Goodness me,' Nick said brightly, as he put the thick overcoat he had brought with him over her shoulders. He was intending to go on with some remark along the lines of 'going native', but quickly took in Claire's strained appearance and changed tack.

'It's been hard, hasn't it?' he said instead, 'I can tell.'

'Very hard,' she said, simply. All other words escaped her. Her head was full of them, but they were all jumbled up. It was impossible to bring even two or three more of them together into something that might come out coherently.

In the car, Nick, too, struggled with his thoughts. He knew perfectly well what he had to say. His problem was when to say it. She sat in the front with him, and from the corner of his eye he tried to assess her. She was awake, he could see that, but seemed almost in a trance-like state.

'Will it help to tell me about it?' he asked.

'No.'

297

They were about to turn off the motorway before Nick spoke again.

'I'm afraid the news here isn't good.'

'I know,' she said, 'I know.'

'You know?'

'Yes, I know. He's fading isn't he?'

'How did you know? Did Krishnan call you? We agreed to wait.'

'No, Christian told me on the plane last night, in his usual way.'

'I see. What did he say?'

'That his energy was draining away. That the end was coming. That he was ready. And . . . no, that's all.'

'I see.'

'Don't worry, Nick. I'm ready for it as well now. I wasn't a week ago, but I am now.'

They relapsed into silence, one that was not broken until they reached the cottage.

'We fixed the guttering,' Nick said as they pulled up. It was light now.

Inside, she said: 'I'm going to have a shower and change. Could you make some tea?'

'I'll wait 'til I hear you come out,' Nick said. 'Here, let me get your case upstairs for you.'

'Where's your wife?' she asked as they sat down at the table.

'I took her back yesterday,' Nick said. 'I stayed at home with her last night, in fact.'

'And Amy? I should get up there and see her this morning, bring her home.'

'No. Rosie's seen her every day. She's fine. Amy's to stay at respite until Monday at least. I just spoke to Rosie. She'll be around any moment.'

'So what else is news?'

'Let's wait for the others – they're all at Rosie's. I'll pop up there now. I'll get a paper and some milk at the shop as well. Silly, I should've got the paper at Heathrow while I was waiting.'

There was a collection of mail on the table, but she did not feel in the mood to touch it. She felt light-headed and faintly nauseous. The room seemed to be moving slowly up and down, as if she was still on the plane.

The others all arrived together. She was surprised to see Tom among them. They were quiet, sombre even, especially Krishnan. Rosie sat next to her and took her hand.

'Now darling,' Rosie began, 'there are lots of things we need to tell you. You're tired. You look exhausted. But we've got to talk.'

Claire bowed her head and stared down at the table.

'Go on,' she said, slowly.

Rosie took a deep breath, loudly. 'Let's start with Amy. She is brilliant. She's had rather a rotten cold all week, so she hasn't been at school. But I've been to see her every day and she's much better now. She'd like to see you and if you're up to it, we can pop up there later today.'

'Yes, I'd like to do that.'

Krishnan, who, Claire now noticed, was holding Rosie's other hand, coughed lightly.

'Claire,' he said, 'I'm afraid that on the medical front, the news isn't good. I gather from Nick you're aware of that.'

'Yes I am,' she said, calmly.

'The situation is that in the past 48 hours, indications of brain activity have fallen off sharply, as I warned you they might. They might just as easily return again. But at the moment, I have to say that things don't look good. Although I hate to say it . . .'

He choked and started to cry. Nick took his other hand so that now four of them were linked physically. Only Tom sat back from this.

'. . . although there is still a chance . . .'

He choked again.

'. . . when the life signs go down this quickly . . . there is . . . there is usually . . . little hope . . . I'm so sorry.'

He immediately got up and went into the kitchen.

'Krishnan and I are going over to the TCC today,' Nick said, 'and we'll be staying as long as necessary.'

'I should come as well, then?' Claire asked.

'No. We feel you should stay here, with Rosie,' Nick continued, 'for the moment, anyway. There are things to do here. We'll call you if and when you're needed.'

Krishnan came back in and sat down, wiping his eyes.

'Now, phone calls,' said Rosie, 'I . . .'

'No, wait, Rosie,' Claire said, still with her gaze now cast down again on the table, 'there are some things I want to say now.'

'About what's happened this week?'

'Yes, I've . . .'

She could go no further. She clenched her hands into her hair, pulling it hard with both of them and at the same time letting out a scream born not of the physical pain she felt but of pure anguish. She lowered her head slowly onto the table, where she banged it up and down several times.

'Oh my darling girl,' Rosie said as she put her arm over her friend's shoulders, 'what has happened?'

With it still resting on the table, Claire turned her head to one side, towards the side where Rosie was.

'He . . . has . . . a child,' she said, almost in a whisper, '. . . a son . . . a fifteen year-old son.'

She sat back up, upright.

'And a mistress, *a bloody mistress!*'

She was shouting now, her eyes wide and blazing.

'The bloody five hundred pounds was for her and her bloody gharana! And he stayed with her every time he went! So you can go and switch that bloody machine off *NOW* as far as I'm concerned. The lying bastard. Let him die. Let him rot in hell.'

'Oh my God,' Rosie said. The three men bowed their heads.

'Ha!' Claire went on, 'Mister bloody nice guy. Everyone loves Christian, such a *lovely* man, such a *good bloke*, such a *generous, nice man.* Such a *caring* man. Christian-*bhai*, indeed. And what is he? A phoney, a fucking phoney, living in his own little secret world . . .'

Rosie opened her mouth: 'But . . .'

'But what? And I'll tell you more. You know what else he was doing?'

With eyes that seemed to be even more crazed by flashing darts of lightning, Claire looked around the table at the four of them, who were now all sat bolt upright, staring at her in amazement.

She lowered her voice:

'You know what he was doing? He was *fiddling his fucking expenses*. That's how he was piling up that money, or at least some of it. In Delhi most of the time he stayed with his lady, no doubt for fucking free, no doubt literally fucking free. And then giving his firm a phoney hotel bill. I found out how he did that. God knows what else he was doing.'

At that she got up and ran upstairs. Shocked and stunned, Krishnan, Tom, Nick and Rosie sat silently looking at each other, listening to the sound of Claire's footfalls in the room above.

'Money? What money?' Krishnan said, looking at Rosie, who lowered her head, and then at Nick, who said, 'I know nothing about this either,' and then at Tom, who shook his head slowly.

Claire soon clattered heavily back down the stairs.

'Look,' she said, throwing two filofaxes on the table with a theatrical gesture, 'just you look. I've been reading them, on the plane last night. And you know what? – some of the trips he claimed he was making didn't even exist! Look, my diary, this one, tells me when he left and when he came back.'

She was talking fast now, the words coming out helter-skelter, staccato, as she riffled through the two books:

'See? Here's one. Sri Lanka. Look at his diary – goes this day, here, you see, and then comes back here. Yes? But look in this one – mine. It says, ha! – it says we were in Italy, the whole fucking time. Ha! I don't know how he fiddled his money out of all that but I've got a pretty fucking good idea. I'll bet wherever he went he didn't go business class. I'll bet he claimed for that and went on the cheap. Bet he did. Bet he did. Fucking devious little bastard!'

She stopped, panting now, gulping in the several breaths she had not stopped to take as she had gabbled away.

Nick picked up the two filofaxes where she had left them open, comparing the entries. He quickly saw that Claire was right. He passed them to Tom, who started leafing through them.

'I made a little chart last night,' Claire went on, calmly now. 'There were two fake trips last year. He's probably been doing it for years. Leaving aside the fiddles on the real trips, he'd rake in, I'd guess, say, a thousand or two every phoney trip. Doesn't take much working out to see that that's where some at least of the money came from, does it?'

'Oh dear,' Krishnan said, looking at Rosie and raising his eyebrows.

Tom continued to flick through the two diaries, sighing as he did so.

'One of the calls this week was from Christian's firm, from someone called Palmer,' Rosie said. 'He thought I was

302

you and never gave me a chance to correct him. He said that according to their records, Christian had an unspent expenses float of about five thousand pounds that should be returned to them. Pompous little prat, he sounded. I asked him to put it in writing. It's probably in the pile there.'

'Yes, this'll be it,' Claire said as she shuffled through the letters, opening one and reading it quickly. 'Yes, that's it, I'll deal with it later.'

Looking at his watch Nick said, 'We should go soon? Should I . . . ?'

'Yes, Nick, you or Tom had better deal with that other matter then,' Krishnan responded, 'you know more about it than Rosie. Then, yes, we should go.'

'What now?' Claire asked.

Nick and Tom exchanged glances.

'You start,' Tom said.

'The police want to interview you, Claire,' Nick began. 'They called earlier in the week and I told them you were not back until today. I asked what it was about, but they wouldn't tell me anything, except that you knew what it would be about. They said it was urgent and that they would call you this morning so as to fix an appointment, hopefully, they said, today also. That's why Tom is here. I spoke to Sir Timothy but of course we're all in the dark.'

'Do you know what it's about?' Tom asked.

'Yes I do. I think I do.'

'If I'm to be able to help,' Tom said, 'I really need to know. What is it?'

'The money. I think he may have been up to something else, something even worse than fiddling expenses . . . He must have been. The money in Italy – it came from some-thing else as well. It must have . . .'

She hesitated, stopping herself.

'Look, there's more to say, but not now. I'd prefer, if you

303

don't mind, to talk to Tom alone about it. You two go on. Rosie, would you go up and see Amy? I need to think. Come on, let's all get going. Time's getting on.'

She stood up and the others followed suit. Nick and Krishnan soon left. Krishnan kissed Rosie lightly on the lips.

'I'll go as well then,' Rosie said, soon after they had gone.

'I'll go with you,' Tom added, 'then I'll come back, say, in half-an-hour?'

Claire nodded: 'I'll just have a lie down for a short while.'

The phone was ringing as she came downstairs and she heard Tom answer it.

He cupped his hand over the mouthpiece: 'Police.'

'I'll take it back upstairs, you listen.'

At the desk in the study she composed herself for a moment before picking up the receiver.

The conversation was brief. She agreed to see the Detective Inspector at two that afternoon.

'I'll be down in a minute, Tom,' she called out.

She opened the filing cabinet and quickly found what she was looking or: the file labelled 'Amethyst Travel'. She wondered why she had not bothered to look through it before.

It did not take her long to work out, from what she found and read, how he had done it. Long before each trip, real or not, a business class ticket was issued. Then, shortly before each real trip, an economy ticket was issued instead, sometimes for the same flights and dates, sometimes for different ones. The business class ticket, which he no doubt made a copy of before returning it to Amethyst, would be refunded, less a small cancellation charge. The economy ticket was thus the real ticket, but that used for claims would be the originally-issued business one. The difference would be substantial. For the trips that did not exist at all, it was even easier and even more lucrative.

'Simple,' she said to herself as she went downstairs, still holding the file.

'What were you doing?' Tom said.

'Just confirming what I said earlier,' Claire said. 'Look, I'll show you how he fiddled his travel.'

She took Tom through the papers, receipts and copies.

'Ingenious,' he said as Claire closed the file.

'Now,' he went on, 'what's this other business all about? Do you mind if I take notes?'

She took a deep breath and decided that she would tell the whole story, right from its beginnings in Italy, up to the unexpected early morning visit from the police. She concluded by relating what Rosie had told her about the police activity at Preston Park that night. Tom continued writing notes after she had finished.

'So all they have said thus far, in terms of evidence, is that Christian's name was in a book?' Tom asked, putting his pen down.

'That's right, but, I should have mentioned that I asked Andy about it.'

'Who's Andy?'

'The landlord at our pub. He told me that he had once taken Christian to some place in Brighton where there was gambling going on. Just once. He said that he thought that Christian must have put his name in some kind of "visitor's book". But he also said that it wasn't the kind of place that he thought Christian would ever go back to.'

Tom noted this.

'When the police came that morning, did they ask any specific questions?'

'Yes, they did, and I have to admit that I lied.'

'What did they ask?'

'They asked if I'd been aware of Christian having large amounts of money. Even though I'd only just found the box in the loft, although at that stage I hadn't counted the money in it, and even though of course I was well aware of the money in Italy, I said "no". It was a lie, I know, but I, how can I put it, I was flustered at the time. In any case since then, now that I've found out about how he fiddled his expenses . . .'

She paused.

'. . . and, by the way, he used to get his expenses in advance each year, I know that for a fact.'

'I see. Did they caution you before asking these questions, you know, "anything you may say may be taken down in evidence", that kind of thing?'

'Yes, they did.'

Tom scribbled on his notepad again.

'You sure there's nothing else you can tell me about it?' he asked.

'No, nothing.'

'Claire, I need to know how much money you found in Italy, you haven't told me the amount.'

'Five hundred thousand plus.'

Tom stopped writing and tapped his pen, blowing his cheeks out. 'What?'

She suddenly felt an immense tiredness enveloping her.

'Look, I need to rest a bit now, Tom, if you wouldn't mind. Would you mind waking me well before he comes?'

'Of course. You're quite sure there's nothing else I need to know? May I use your phone while you're resting? I think I'd better brief Sir Timothy about this, if you don't mind?'

'That's fine, and yes, you know all there is to know,' she said.

When she undressed, she found the small envelope the woman had given her in one of the pockets of the trousers. She opened it.

Inside was half of a 10,000 lire banknote, cut much as the

other had been, but this one dirty and crumpled, as if much used.

When the policeman arrived, Claire showed him in, took his raincoat, and introduced him to Tom, who gave him his card.

The policeman studied it, put it in his pocket, and held out his hand.

He was not what Claire expected. He seemed young, almost boyish in appearance. The removal of the raincoat revealed a smart, lightly checked blue suit, under which was a shirt that could only be described as garish: a yellow and blue striped one, with a tie that clashed horribly with it.

'I gather you've been overseas?' he said as they sat at the table, in a friendly manner that suggested the question was a conversation-starter rather than the first of a formal interview.

'Claire, you have no need at this point to answer any questions,' Tom said, as she opened her mouth to answer, 'or we can confer privately in the sitting room before you do so, or you can refer any question to me to answer if you prefer.'

'I understand, Tom, but I'll answer.'

She turned to face the policeman, but Tom cut in and addressed him himself:

'Are you not meant to caution my client to begin with?'

The policeman's face reddened.

'My apologies. I must inform you that anything you say may be taken down in evidence and used against you.'

'Thank you. In response to your question, yes, I have been overseas, to India. My husband had some unfinished business there,' she said.

'What kind of business?' the policeman asked, taking out a notebook and flipping through its pages.

'I strongly advise you not to answer,' Tom said. 'It is of no relevance at all to these enquiries.'

'Do you really think so?' the policeman asked, in a clipped voice, now grinning boyishly at Tom. 'Well, let me tell you something.'

He flipped through more of the pages of his notebook.

'We understand from his firm, your husband's firm I mean,' he went on, 'that your husband made frequent trips overseas, very frequent trips, often of quite long duration. We further understand that his firm paid him a considerable advance in cash each year to cover his expenses. The firm has provided us with all the relevant paperwork. This has led to certain suspicions on our part. We are particularly interested in his trips to Pakistan, as well as to India.'

'Suspicions about what, may I know?' Tom asked.

'I, too, do not have to answer *your* questions,' the policeman replied, tartly 'but on this occasion *I* will and I hope *you* will then reciprocate. Do we *understand* each other?'

At each emphasis he raised his voice slightly. Tom nodded, stone-faced. The policeman turned to face Claire.

'In a nutshell, one, we feel it is quite possible that your husband has claimed to have used his expenses funds for other purposes. Two, we have reason to believe that the establishment in Brighton with which your husband was associated . . .'

'Merely through his name being found in some book?' Tom interrupted.

'No, *sir*, we know more than that, but let me continue *if* you would be so kind. The establishment was almost certainly involved not just in gambling, but in drug-trafficking. So I come back to my point, if your husband was not spending such a large amount of money on expenses as he claimed, what was he doing with it? Possibly on purchasing drugs to bring back to sell in Brighton? Easy, no customs officer would suspect such an oh-so-respectable looking, er . . .'

He looked up at Tom.

'White man?' said Tom.

'*Exactly.*'

Claire banged her fist on the table. 'My husband would never ever do such a thing. How dare you suggest it. I know perfectly well what . . .'

Tom cut her off. 'Claire, we need to talk privately upstairs before you say anything,' he said to her, and then, turning to the policeman. 'This is utter, and may I say it, ridiculous conjecture.'

They went upstairs to the study, leaving the policeman strumming his fingers on the table.

'I know what you were about to say, Claire,' Tom said, 'and maybe you should, but not now.'

'Shush, lower your voice, he can hear you,' she whispered. 'What was I going to say then?'

'That you know about the expenses fiddling and that he brought it back here, and that he was saving it for the house, something like that.'

'Yes, but I was going to say more than that. I wanted to go back to his original question, about why I went to India, and tell him about the five hundred pounds. I also found out that he always gave lots of money away there, to poor people.'

'Or to buy drugs from poor people?' Tom said.

'Surely not?'

'Well, that could be the interpretation our friend downstairs might put on it . . . The money in Italy had built up over a number of years, right? If it had been gambling or fiddled expenses money alone I suspect that it wouldn't have amounted to half a million. I'm only guessing, but to me it just doesn't add up. It's possible there was more to it.'

'Drugs you mean?'

'Yes, look, every time I come through customs, they pull me over, because . . .'

'Because you're young . . . and black?'

'Right. But Christian, they wouldn't dream he'd have a bagful of dope, would they, just as our friend downstairs said just now?'

'I see what you mean.'

'Claire, I suggest for the moment you just tell him about the cash box in the loft. Show it to him. But say nothing about Italy, not for the moment. I think he's just fishing. And don't tell him about the five hundred pounds now either. OK? He might even conclude that *you* took it to buy drugs.'

'Can I suggest something else, Tom? Can we just try and unruffle his feathers a bit? Know what I mean?'

'I'll do my best. But Claire, I think you should realise that they are not going to go away, not now and probably not for a long time.'

'Like a cup of tea or coffee?' Claire chirped gaily as they rejoined the policeman.

'No thank you.'

They all settled again at the table.

'First of all, I hope you've seen the letter I sent you, I should have mentioned it earlier,' the policeman said.

'No, I haven't, but it's probably here, let me look.'

'That's it,' he said, pointing to one as she turned over the letters.

She started to open it.

'No, there's no need, not right now, unless you want to. I can tell you what it says.'

She put the torn envelope down and looked at him.

'It's an apology. I understand that the two constables who visited you were, shall we say, a little insensitive.'

'Yes, they were, but how do you know?'

'From reading their reports, and a little between the lines, it's clear that you were most upset. The letter is an official apology.'

'Thank you, but now let's go back to where we were. I only got off the plane early this morning, so I hope all this won't take long. I'm feeling pretty weary, to be honest. Tom and I have agreed that I will answer your question as best I can.'

'To go back,' the policemen said, looking through his notebook. 'I gather you told the officers who interviewed you that you had no knowledge, or suspicion, that your husband might in any way be involved in these activities?'

'That is the case. I did not, not at the time, but . . .'

'My client has since then found out more,' Tom added.

The policeman's pen hovered over his notebook.

'Recently,' Claire said, 'I discovered a sum of money in a cash box here in the house. It totalled over four thousand eight hundred pounds. Given what your two colleagues had asked, I have to admit that I wondered about it when I found it. But I have subsequently discovered that it, the money I mean, actually belonged to my husband's company. Here, look.'

She took the letter from Palmer out of the pile and passed it to the policeman, who read it.

'That seems pretty clear,' he said, 'a copy of this would be useful at some stage, if you have no objection.'

'No problem, you could even get one made up at the village shop if you like.'

'I'll do that, if you like,' Tom said, 'when we're finished, I mean.'

'Good. Now would you mind showing me the money?'

'Not at all.'

She went up and took the box from the drawer where she had hidden it under her clothes before she left for India.

'I have to confess I took a few hundred to take with me to India, to cover my costs,' she said as she gave him the box, but he merely peered into it and then closed the lid.

'And you have not come across any other money in the house, or other indications like money coming into your bank account, or indeed going from it?'

She looked at Tom, who nodded.

'No, not at all, we had only one account, a joint one, and I always looked after that. My husband was ... isn't, very good at that kind of thing. He never, ever, opened a bank statement!'

The policeman made some more notes.

'Now, if can we move on to other matters? I have some further questions.'

Claire again looked at Tom.

'I must ask that this interview be terminated here and now,' Tom replied, 'as my client has informed you, she is extremely tired, having just made a long journey. She is in no fit state to answer further questions and as you should well know, any evidence based on answers given in her condition would be strongly contested in court. I can assure you that when she is ready and able, my client will be prepared to help with your further enquiries. Do I make myself clear?'

In response the policeman flipped his notebook shut and stood up.

'I'll go with you,' Tom said, 'then I can copy the letter for you.'

As soon had the door closed behind them the policeman said, quietly and evenly:

'Now, you little piece of legal shit ...'

'I beg your pardon?'

'You heard what I said. I know that you know that there's a fucking lot more to this. And believe me, I'm not going to let you get in my way. You get my drift?'

It was like taking sweets from babies. They were always the same guys, young guys, twenties and thirties. Not so much more money than sense, but loadsamoney and no sense at all. They all had flash apartments overlooking the marina, flash boats on it, used about once a year as far as I could make out. All traders, brokers, making money out of nothing else than other people's money. I detested them, and yet they all thought I loved them all like brothers. Ha! I detested everything they stood for. A tiny number of undeserving swine like them rule the world while masses have nothing. They'll get their real come-uppance one day, the lot of them. When you have so few rich and so many poor, sooner or later something will happen to put it right. What I did to them was nothing really. I hated their pink, soft, pudgy, manicured, greedy hands.

That first time Andy took me, I picked them out. You could read them all like books. We used to play in the room over the Chinese place. No licence of course, but, I thought, what the hell. I never went up against the Chinese bloke. He was too hard. You couldn't read him. I'd just take him on now and again. Like the others, at first he thought he could read me, but I could see that he soon realised he couldn't. So we had our own unspoken little understanding.

He and I played the same game with the kids – lead them by the nose. Lose a small pot to one of them here and there, then, especially when they had had a few – none of them could take it – hit them for the big ones.

It wasn't just for the money. What gave me real pleasure was seeing them squirm, as I took from them what they had taken from others. Straight from their sweaty little hands. What I couldn't learn from their selfish little personalities I could learn from their hands. And I knew from what they told me that a lot of what they got was by swindling and cheating. They had fancy, nice sounding words for it, but that's what it amounted to. Because they never thought about people in their devious little jobs, none of them realised that poker is more about people than memory, about understanding how people tick, even about watching their hands twitch. About not letting others understand how you tick, about keeping your hands still, your mouth shut. Fools: all they understood was money. That's all anyone understands these days.

I know it was wrong, but it wasn't immoral of me to do what I did. So don't feel bad about it.

Tiring again now . . . I have a feeling this may be the last. I always loved you, only you, apart from that one other I told you about, a long, long time ago. Remember that when you think of me, even if you think ill of me and what I've done. Leave all those kinds of thoughts to me. I've thought badly about myself all my life, so I might as well keep responsibility for that now.

But I never lied to you.

There were just some things I never told you. That's different, isn't it?

Rosie and Tom agreed to let Claire sleep. There was no reason to wake her until the others came back. Instead, while Tom wrote up his notes, Rosie went to the kitchen and started getting some food ready. Yes, she thought, a good old-fashioned cottage pie. Easy to cook, easy to eat. She'd remembered to get lamb rather than beef mince, having cooked several times for Krishnan.

As she peeled potatoes, she thought about what had

happened that morning. She had never seen Claire so emotional, so angry. She had never heard her use language like that, either. It had shocked her, shocked her even more than learning that Claire had not even told her everything that had happened.

Most of all, she thought about Christian. Was fiddling expenses, particularly out of a big fat company, really that bad? Christian had never said much about his firm over the years, but from what she recalled, he regarded them, especially the partners, like Palmer, with contempt. Her own conversation with Palmer had not exactly endeared him to her.

'Little prat,' she said under her breath.

Claire and Christian had never lived lives characterised even by modest consumption. Their cars were always old. Their clothes, especially Christian's, were more Marks and Sparks than Dolce and Gabbana, that was for sure. Claire preferred charity shops to Miss Selfridge. And she knew that neither of them had private health insurance, and that Christian had no pension fund.

Then there was Amy. Christian loved her, she knew, as much as he would had she been his own daughter. There was no doubt about that. It would be natural to love his own son, this newly discovered one, just as much.

She set the potatoes on to boil.

What exactly did happen last week, she wondered as she set to work on the onions, squinting as her eyes watered. This 'mistress', who was she?

As she put the mince, onions and mushrooms on to fry, she heard the sound of Claire moving about up above. She added lots of mixed herbs, and then a good sprinkle of paprika, this latter for Krishnan's benefit.

She poured herself a glass of wine, saying her little mantra to herself: 'I love to cook with wine. Sometimes I even put it in the food.'

She called out to Tom to ask if he would like a glass.

'Yes, please,' came the reply.

Only then did she remember that the police had been coming. What was that about? When she gave Tom his wine, she asked.

'No, it's for Claire to tell you,' he said. 'Sorry, but it's not for me to say.'

By the time Claire came downstairs, looking pale and rather pinched, she thought, Rosie was applying the finishing touches, running a fork through the mashed potatoes.

'That looks good,' Claire said.

'I'll just keep it warm in the oven until the others come back,' Rosie said, glad to see her friend smiling.

'No, silly, I meant the wine!'

Rosie poured one for her and they went and sat down with Tom in the sitting room.

'I'll leave you two to talk,' Tom immediately said. 'I think I'll take a little stroll.'

'I need to talk to you, I need to tell you,' Claire said as soon as he had gone.

'I'm glad. I hoped you would. You need to tell someone. How do you feel now?'

'Confused. Fuzzy. Never make judgements when you're tired, people say, don't they?'

'Yes. Want to start with the police? What's that about?'

'Oh, nothing really,' Claire said, feeling well-practised in lying now. 'Christian's name was in the address book of someone arrested in Brighton. Illegal gambling. You saw it happen, in fact.'

'Saw what happen?'

'When you and Krishnan were coming back from your night out – the police raid in Brighton. Remember?'

'Yes I do. How weird!'

'Over and done with now, anyway, at least for the moment. What I want to talk to you about is the mistress.'

'Good, that's what I want to know about. I can't believe it. Are you sure about it?'

'Yes and no,' Claire began, and then went on to relate the events of the previous evening, thinking 'was it only yesterday?'.

She told the story as briefly and as accurately as she could, culminating in the meeting in the VIP lounge at the airport, and what Rafiquah had said there.

'So she didn't actually use word "mistress", then?' Rosie asked, after a short pause for thought.

'No, she didn't, but she wouldn't, would she? Neither would you or I in the same situation, I guess. In any case he stayed with her every time he went there. I remember her words exactly: *"he always came to stay at my house when he was here".*'

'But didn't you say that she also said they'd only er, done it, once, the first time, all those years ago, which if the boy is fifteen must mean long before he met you?'

'Yes, that's what she said. He must have been born about the same time as Amy was, come to think of it. But of course she would say that, wouldn't she?'

'So it's a question of whether you believe her or not.'

'Yes.'

'And do you?'

'Oh, Rosie, I just don't know. I don't know about anything any more. It's just too much to take in.'

'Other than that, before all this came out of the blue, you must have met her earlier in the week, yes? How did she strike you?'

'As being very, very beautiful, a bit cold in her manner at times, but reasonably easy to get along with, I suppose. Older than me, probably more like Christian's age.'

'Did you like her?'

'No, overall, I can't honestly say that I particularly liked her, but maybe my judgement's a bit clouded now. But even before, she was, how can I put it, distant, a bit aloof.'

'Jealous maybe?'

'What do you mean?'

'Well, that you were Christian's wife, not her,'

'I hadn't thought about it like that. Maybe you're right.'

'So would you trust her?'

'I suppose I would. She's a Moslem. When we spoke at the airport, she swore on her religion that she was telling me the truth. I don't know whether that means anything, mind you.'

'I don't know either. But from what you told me, I'd say you may be jumping to conclusions, about her relationship with Christian, I mean.'

'Yes, maybe you're right, that's why I wanted to talk to you about it.'

'Do you want to talk about the money, the fiddling I mean?'

'Yes, that as well.'

'Do you want to know what I think?' Rosie said, 'Even if you don't, I'm going to tell you. I can live with it, and I think you should too. It is wrong to take from the poor . . .'

'. . . but not from the rich?' Claire broke in.

'Yes, something like that. Especially given the kind of things Christian believed in, the work he did, not that I ever knew much about it. But what I knew is enough for me.'

'You really think so?'

'Yes, I do. I've been thinking about it,'

'But it still leaves me with one big problem. Why the hell has he kept these things from me all these years? Never mind the morality. Never mind right and wrong and all that. Why, oh why, didn't he tell me?'

She thought for a while, and then went on:

'All he said to me, not long ago in fact, was that something happened once, before he met me, that has since

318

made him keep himself to himself more . . . he said, "I let too much hang out, I got burned", something like that . . .'

She looked at Rosie. His words in her dream now suddenly came back to her: *I always loved you, only you, apart from one other, briefly, a long, long time ago.* Of course, that would be Rafiquah. Or would it?

'What's up?' Rosie said.

'Nothing.'

'Anyway, if you want to know my honest opinion,' Rosie said. 'There are two things, two reasons if you like, why he wouldn't necessarily tell you everything. One, he loved you. You knew that. I knew that. Everyone who ever met you could see that. Two, he might therefore fear that if he told you certain things he might lose you. He would sooner . . . sooner die than have that happen.'

Claire was about to speak when the men, including Tom, who had met the others in the street, came in, in what seemed to be good spirits.

'Good news,' Nick said.

'Reasonably good news, at least,' Krishnan added.

'Stop,' Claire said, holding one hand up and taking what was her first sip of wine from the glass in the other, 'I'm going to tell you what the good news is.'

'Go on then,' said Nick.

'I can't be precise, but somewhere between quarter to three and four-thirty this afternoon, let me take a guess at about three-fifteen, there was renewed, what do you call it, brain activity.'

'Uncanny,' said Krishnan. 'It was at three-twenty-one, to be precise.'

'You had another message then?' asked Nick.

'Yes,' Claire said, 'I had a little sleep this afternoon. It was quite a long message, but it tailed off quickly in the end. Did you see that too?'

'No, the EEG was still quite strong when we left, but that

was well over an hour ago,' Krishnan said, 'but I wouldn't be surprised if it did. In truth, Nick and I still wouldn't say anything other than what we said this morning. It could happen at any time. How do you feel now?'

'Rosie and I have had a talk,' Claire said, as the men sat down, while Rosie left them and went into the kitchen, 'I feel a lot better for it. I'm sorry about this morning. I'm especially sorry about my language. Yes, there is a son, and there is a woman, but maybe I was a bit over-the-top in describing her the way I did. Whatever happened, it was a long time ago, and as regards the expenses fiddles, well, people can do worse things and still not be pilloried for them. Like certain former government ministers who got found out.'

'And the police business?' Nick asked.

'Nothing of any importance, really,' she said, looking at Tom 'Rosie'll tell you about it, Krishnan. Christian's name cropped up on some petty case, but it must be wrong, because he had the perfect alibi for the day in question.'

'I don't understand, but how come?' said Krishnan.

'Because, as Sir Timothy would no doubt put it,' Tom said, ' "at the time of the alleged offence, m'lud, my client was on a ventilator in a terminal care facility. How therefore could he possibly have committed the offence in question?" '

The impersonation was perfect. They all laughed, albeit in a guilty, rather embarrassed way.

'Just one more thing,' Claire went on, 'I've put my anger away, most of it. So I want you both to know that I am ready for what's to come, whatever it is, whenever it is. I am ready. I can cope with it, and afterwards, whatever happens, there won't be any bitter after-tastes, physically or emotionally.'

'You are one hell of a tough woman,' Nick said.

Krishnan's mobile phone rang. Claire and Nick went to join Rosie in the kitchen, from which rather pleasing aromas were beginning to waft. 'Let's hope this isn't it already,' Nick remarked, nervously.

'I have a very large bone to pick with you,' Krishnan said, addressing Claire sternly when he rejoined them several minutes later. 'That was Prittee, my cousin in Delhi. She has told me all about it.'

Claire hung her head down. Turning to the others, Krishnan went on: 'It seems that our dear friend here was seriously ill with food-poisoning for the greater part of the week.'

Turning back to Claire, he said 'Now I want you to go straight upstairs.' And then to Nick: 'Nick, you will have to do the honours, as I don't have my things with me. From what Prittee has told me, she needs a very thorough check.'

'Will certainly do,' said Nick.

'There's something I want to tell you all,' Claire announced as they started eating. 'I don't know whether it's relevant or not, but I want to say it.'

The others all looked up.

'Go on,' Krishnan said.

'It's this. I know you'll all think this is another one of my crazy ideas, but I don't care. I have to say it, otherwise, if I didn't, I fear I might regret it. It's about Christian's depressions. When he got into them, and Rosie knows this because she always helped me cope, when he was down, he'd just get under the duvet for days on end. He wouldn't speak, he wouldn't eat, he wouldn't drink. Nothing would have any effect on him. He used to get up, I know, only when I left the house. I could tell when I got back. There were always little signs – like he'd been to the toilet and hadn't put the seat back down – but even then, I knew he didn't always get up. In fact, very rarely. What I'm saying is that it's as if he, with the help of whatever chemical it is that sloshes around up there in his head, was actually switching himself off. He could do that. I used to notice it when I got into bed and listened to him. His breathing was so faint, at first it used to scare me. Everything slowed down. I felt his pulse once and it hardly seemed to be there. It was frightening. Look, he did much the same even when he was at his best. Show him a bank statement and he'd switch off, ask him what he felt about something, ask him to face up to some reality of life, use even a single injudicious word, the same: switch off.'

'Why are you saying this now?' Tom asked.

'I'm saying it because it's dawned on me that what he's doing now, what he could be doing at least, is switching himself off. He doesn't want to face up to it any more. Maybe he's thinking: "I've done all this, I haven't got caught out. The lie has survived. But sooner or later I'm going to get caught, probably sooner. The bank statement, the statement of my life, is going to be opened. So I'm just going to do what I'm good at: switching myself off." He's just been coasting along for a while, you see, under the duvet, letting others deal with the realities.'

They had all stopped eating. Claire's food remained entirely untouched.

'In other words,' she went on, 'what he's been doing these past few weeks while "dead" has an eery resemblance to what he used to be like when he was alive. No. I'm not trying to find some new prop to keep myself believing that he's alive, and going to come back, just as he used to, out of his depressions. Although I feel a bit, shall we say, more positive about him than I did this morning, I haven't really reached the stage of wanting him back. I still feel angry, not so much about what he actually did, but at the fact that he kept it all from me. But I wouldn't feel right if I didn't tell you what I've said. And now I'll shut up.'

Krishnan shifted in his chair. 'You know there are Swamis and yogis in India who claim to be able to slow their functioning down to such an extent that they themselves can choose whether to live or die? I've seen EEG graphs of yogis, almost as flat as pancakes, hardly a trace of activity, who have induced the condition in themselves. And you know something else? I can't believe I'm saying this!'

Rosie spoke: 'Can I ask a question?'

'Yes,' said Claire.

'Is all this why you say that "you're ready"?'

'Yes, in part. I have love enough for him to let him go. I believe that's what he wants, and wants of me. And I have love enough to let him decide. I also know what I have to do – which reminds me, there's one thing I need to do right now.'

'What's that?' Rosie asked.

'I need to call Jane, you know, his ex? I want to go and see her tomorrow. Cambridge. I need to know more. I need to know how he got "burned", I need to know what happened. I need to know what happened a long time ago. It might not explain everything else, you see, but at least it might help me understand.'

'You can't possibly do that,' Nick said, visibly alarmed, 'you're totally exhausted, and besides, the call may come at any time.'

Claire snorted and drummed her fingers loudly on the table. She stared fiercely at Nick.

'It's my choice. It's my decision. He can bloody well wait for another day before I sign his life away. In fact I'm going to call Jane right now.'

She got up from the table and went upstairs.

'So long as one of us goes with her, she'll be alright,'

Rosie said to the others. 'I know her. There's nothing we can do to stop her.'

'You're right,' Tom said, quietly, conscious of the fact that all ears around the table were straining to catch the faint sound of Claire's voice on the telephone upstairs. 'And it should be me that goes. You're needed here, Rosie, for Amy's sake I mean. And you two guys will need to be at the TCC. So that leaves me. Agreed?'

Only the faintest of nods from each of them brought movement to their frozen tableau.

'Done,' Claire said emphatically as she rejoined them, her eyes blazing again in expectation of defiance.

'Will you allow us one condition?' Rosie asked.

'Being what?'

'That you allow Tom to go with you.'

'I can do the driving, but I'll leave you to it when we're there,' Tom added.

Claire took in a deep breath and looked around them all.

'OK,' she said, 'it's a deal.'

17

The Radical

On the policy of self-reliance in Tanzania
(The 'Arusha Declaration')

'*It is obvious that in the past we have chosen the wrong weapon for our struggle, because we chose money as our weapon. We are trying to overcome our economic weakness by using the weapons of the economically strong – weapons which in fact we do not possess. By our thoughts, words, and actions it appears as if we have come to the conclusion that without money we cannot bring about the revolution we are aiming at. It is as if we have said: "Money is the basis of development. Without money there can be no development."*

'*The policy of inviting a chain of capitalists to come and establish industries in our country . . . would prevent the establishment of socialism. The development of a country is brought about by people, not by money.*

'*What we are saying is that from now on we shall know what is the foundation and what is the fruit of development. Between money and people it is obvious that the people and their hard work are the foundation of development*' (*Julius Nyerere, 5 February 1967*).

'Here's my mobile number,' Tom said as they pulled up outside the red-bricked terrace house in Girton, on the outskirts of Cambridge.

They were the first words either had spoken during the entire three-hour journey.

'Just call when you're ready,' he went on, noticing the door of the house opening.

She took the slip of paper and got out without saying a word, still wondering, as she had throughout the journey, about what exactly she was going to do. She had no plan.

No sooner had Jane closed the door behind her, than she said: 'You haven't really come just to tell me what's happening, have you?'

Her tone of voice was sarcastic, and this took Claire aback. She took off her coat and offered it to Jane's outstretched hand.

'No, I guess I haven't, to be honest.'

'Here, take a seat in the front room. I've got a nice fire going. Such a horrid day. I'll make some tea. Or you prefer coffee?'

'Tea will be fine. Thank you.'

There were two single armchairs by the fireplace but Claire stood between them and faced the fire, holding her hands out for warmth. Along the mantelpiece were photos, but there was no sign of Christian's face among them. None of the faces meant anything to her, except those of Jane herself. Another man, presumably a current husband or partner, featured here and there. An old sepia wedding photo of a tall man in military uniform standing with his bride sat demurely beside him was at the centre of the collection. The resemblance of the bride to Jane was striking.

'Yes, my mother and father,' Jane said as she breezed in with a tray and set it down on a low table that occupied the centre of the room in front of the fire. The room was small, and seemed all the more so as the floor and large sofa were cluttered by Sunday newspapers spread out everywhere.

'Sorry about the mess,' Jane went on. 'Christian always hated my untidy habits.'

As Jane poured the tea, Claire took in her features, which she felt could most simply be described as semi-emaciated. Tall, her arms were long and thin, her hands wrinkled. Among the wrinkles the veins seemed to bulge hugely. Her face, in contrast, was remarkably smooth, topped by dark-brown hair cut boyishly short with prominent grey streaks. It all gave the impression of a young head on a much older body, a body that seemed too small to be supported by such long legs and joined with such long arms. She wore stylish navy blue slacks that were buttoned high over a white ruched cotton shirt, beneath which there seemed to be no evident sign of breasts.

'I don't even know what you do,' Claire said, as they sat down.

'I lecture in history at the university, based at Girton College,' Jane replied, curtly. 'My husband's at Trinity. I told him to clear off for the day, so I'm all yours. What is it that you want?'

'I want to know more about him,' she answered, knowing full well that such a revelation of ignorance, and thus of weakness, was the last thing she really wanted to convey, but nonetheless she compounded this by going on: 'I've realised I know nothing about him . . .'

At last, she brought herself to the necessary qualification: '. . . of his life before we met, I mean.'

'Just that?' Jane asked, again in sarcastic tone.

'What do you mean?'

'I mean, Claire, that my experience with him was that, while I knew all about his past, my problem was that as time went on, I knew less and less about, how can I put this, about what the hell he was doing and above all what the hell he was thinking while we were together. The closer you

327

tried to get, the more distant he got. Hands off. Keep out. No Trespassing. You mean to tell me he was no different with you?'

'No, we were close. I never felt . . .'

'Ha! Do you really expect me to believe that?'

Claire looked Jane in the eye: 'Yes I do. It's the past I want to know about. That's all.'

'While I don't believe you for a moment, I'll tell you what I can. You tell me if I'm telling you what you know already and I'll move on to something else. That'll save time. Is that OK with you?'

'That's good of you, thank you.'

'I'll start at the point where I first knew him,' Jane began, 'at university – you knew that we were at the same university together?'

Claire nodded.

'On a small campus like ours, while it wasn't small enough for everyone to know everyone, you could watch people. While we never exchanged so much as a word throughout that fresher year – in fact I only ever spoke to him once during the whole three years – for some reason I watched him. I guess even then I was attracted to him. When the first year started he was shy, gauche even, gave the impression of being constantly out of his depth, socially I mean. He seemed to exude a constant aura of embarrassment. His clothes were old-fashioned. He wore trousers with creases and a blazer rather than the jeans and sweaters most of us wore all the time. Like all the rest of us he gravitated to people and places where he felt most comfortable. For him, that meant what we called the "Christian Union" gang. You know what? I felt sorry for him. He was so quiet, so withdrawn, so . . . oh, unhappy-looking . . . especially during the first term, but throughout the year, really. As relationships formed, he seemed to be the only one without a girlfriend. That just made him seem all the more forlorn.'

'And then what?'

'When the new university year began the following September, there were two new students among the freshers. They were black. They put up a notice about themselves in the Students Union. They were a brother and sister, from Tanzania. Their father was a minister, a government minister, in the Nyerere government. They were the only black students in the university. It must have been that the brother was put in to share a room with Christian, because for a while the two of them – the man and Christian – seemed inseparable, and often all three of them. At first they all seemed to be part of the Christian Union group, but then I noticed, over the weeks, that that seemed to fade. You started to see the three of them, plus a few others, mostly blokes, in the bar together, having their meals together, getting on the bus to go into town on Saturday nights together. It was obvious that the blokes were all itching to get their hands on the sister. Faith, that was her name, now I think of it. She was the most striking girl, tall and very black, absolutely beautiful in every way. Like the model, not Naomi Campbell, the other black one. She exuded warmth, she laughed. She seemed so full of joy. And then, well, I was there when it happened. Every other Saturday there'd be a dance, what we used to call a "hop", in the Students Union. I went in with my boyfriend, and there were the two of them, dancing together. I'd never seen Christian at a hop before. I remember feeling happy for him, and amazed . . . he seemed transformed in every way. I'd never seen him so much as smile before and now there he was laughing, dancing like a mad dervish, totally uninhibited. And most amazing of all, dressed in jeans and sweater!'

Jane stopped, put her tea down and then stood up and opened a small box on the mantelpiece.

'I need a joint,' she said, 'Do you, or do you mind?'

329

'No,' Claire said, 'I don't. But you go ahead.'

The sweet smell of marijuana soon filled the room, mingling with that of the apple logs on the fire.

'It was a remarkable transformation,' Jane continued after taking a deep drag on the joint. 'From then on, those two were like one. You never saw them apart. He didn't tell you about this?'

'No. Go on.'

'I got the impression she changed him in other ways. When the summer term came, the campus was all agog with what was happening in Paris: the '68 revolution, do you remember?'

'I was only a kid at the time,' Claire said, not having the faintest clue as to what Jane was talking about.

'Yes, I guess you were,' Jane said, acidly, exhaling through her nostrils. 'Never heard of Daniel Cohn-Bendit I suppose, then?'

'Of course I have,' Claire lied.

'His picture appeared everywhere on the campus. Meetings started to be organised. I went to one, which was billed as the launch of a new society on the campus, called the *Alternative Socialism Society*. The place was packed out. And who was up there on the stage? The two of them. Faith spoke about the Arusha Declaration. In fact she read it out. She said capitalism was a scourge not just of countries like her own, but of the West too. I remember watching Christian as she spoke, and I saw not only love, but helpless adulation. He spoke as well, pretty naïve student politics stuff, now I think about it, but I remember being spellbound. He was such a gifted speaker, you have to give him that. So we had our very own Daniel Cohn-Bendit! I was next to him at the bar afterwards and made some fatuous remark about how much I'd enjoyed his speech. Soon after, he was leading student delegations in discussions with the university. I think the two of them even went to Paris at some point. '

She giggled in a girlish way at this point. Surprised at this, and to invite an explanation, Claire raised her eyebrows in a questioning manner.

'The university authorities made one major concession in the negotiations,' Jane said, laughing out loud.

'Which was?'

'That the Students Union was given permission to install a contraceptive vending machine in the men's loo!'

Now Claire laughed too.

'And then?' she asked.

'The summer came. As soon as I got back to start what would be the final year for us, I noticed that she was not there. Her brother was back, but not her. From what I could observe of Christian, he was always around, speaking at meetings, expostulating in the bar, often surrounded by freshers, expounding his ideas about alternative socialism, or "anarcho-syndicalist socialism" as he had come to call it. He was also the life and soul of every party, every hop, but there was a look in his eyes that had become more distant. As if he was acting a part rather than living it.'

'What had happened to the girl?'

'At the time, nobody knew. There was a lot of gossip about it. But there were only two people who knew – Christian and the brother – and as far as I'm aware, neither of them said anything about it. It was only years later that I found out more. More tea?'

'No, no thanks, do go on.'

'You poor thing,' Jane said, 'this is all complete news to you, isn't it?'

Claire realised that her body language had given it all away. She found that she was now sitting forward on the very edge of the seat of the armchair, her hands clasped tight together, her head lowered, her knuckles white.

'Yes, I have to confess that it is . . .' she murmured, adding, thinking of her dream, '. . . mostly.'

Stubbing out the fag-end of the joint, Jane coughed out wheezily and went on.

'Our final year at college passed off quietly. I got the impression that Christian was concentrating hard on his studies. He was still prominent in the union bar of an evening and he and Faith's brother seemed to become less close. Nothing much more to report really. Finals came, and of course Christian got a First. We graduated – I remember seeing him with his parents at the ceremony. They both seemed tiny compared to him, but they all looked happy as larks. You could tell a mile off how proud they were of him. That day was the last I saw of him for many years.'

'So you never really met at university? He told me that was where he met you.'

'Well, strictly speaking, yes, that was the case, if you take the brief conversation in the bar that night as "meeting". But no, we really only met years later.'

'How? Where?'

'Hang on. I'll come to that. The next I heard, or rather saw, of Christian was about three years – or was it four? – later. I was reading the *Guardian* one day when what should I find but a column by Christian. It was given some prominence and billed as the first of a regular monthly column, called "Alternate Currents". There was a picture of Christian, looking very long-haired and "alternative". And the blurb read something like "It's increasingly being admitted that professionally-dominated institutions and services in every field, blah blah blah . . . are not working. New thinkers and critics such as Illich and Chomsky, Freire and Schumacher, and political leaders such as Castro and Nyerere are pointing the way . . . blah blah blah. This new column will range over the entire field of human need and endeavour and report on a new generation of activists who are developing entirely fresh approaches to the way we educate, the way we care, the way we do business, even the way we do politics ... blah blah blah." That was the gist of it. You never saw this? I guess you were still too young as they say?'

'Yes. He told me he'd worked as a journalist for a time, but that was all.'

Again she spoke the lie with practised sincerity.

'The column quickly became a sort of must-read, must-quote thing, among *Guardian* readers, anyway. People used to say "Have you read this month's AC?" I have to admit I read it, not because I knew him, but because what he wrote was always ... was always good. From the early pieces I could put together what he'd been doing since university. He'd travelled extensively, overseas, to Cuba, to Vietnam, North Vietnam I mean, to Tanzania, of course, to the US, even exotic places in the Pacific. But there was a lot of stuff from here, and from Europe more widely, including, I remember, several pieces about cooperatives in the Basque region being inspired by some weird priest, and about new types of syndicates and cooperatives in Italy. He was always particularly fascinated by Italy and its particular brand of communism. All of his columns were about things that people were doing that challenged existing notions, existing orthodoxy. He called them "bottom-up" or "people-centred" activities.

Bells rang in Claire's head. She thought momentarily of Ravindra.

'That sounds familiar,' she said.

'Does it? Well, well, well,' Jane went on, acidly. 'Anyway, pretty quickly the column became a weekly one, and it seemed to get bigger and bigger. Within a short time, Christian seemed to be everywhere. Turn on the *Today* programme on the radio in the morning and you'd hear him commenting about something or other. He even got his own series of programmes on Radio 4 for a while, early Sunday evenings. *Panorama* did a segment on him. He was in the right place at the right time, you see, because, this was now '74, '75, '76, the unemployment rate was going through the roof, the inner cities were falling apart, companies and whole industries were collapsing. And there was Christian saying things like "old style institutional socialism won't deal with this, neither will old style capitalism, but people and communities can do it . . .".'

Jane paused and studied Claire coolly for a moment and then went on:

'Ministers in the Labour government started courting him, and he was brought on to some committee that was planning a new government scheme for unemployed people. But he didn't want to get into bed with just them. He talked to the Liberals and the Tories too. That was how I met him. He was invited to speak at the Liberal Party conference in '76. I was doing research for one of their MPs at the time, so I was there. Christian had them, us, all spellbound. He was amazing . . . he . . .'

Again, Jane paused. She stood up, threw a log on the fire and then took another roll-up out of the box on the mantelpiece.

'He chatted me up in the bar. In fact . . .'

She laughed, loudly and hoarsely.

'. . . I was watching him, surrounded by a group of mostly young women, all of them clearly itching to get their pants off, and I could see I caught his eye. He broke away from them and came over to me, some of them following in his wake. "I know this is corny as hell, but don't I know you from somewhere?" he said. Those were his exact words. And when I told him, he said, "of course," just like that. We were in bed together within an hour.'

'You've no need to go into every little smutty detail,' Claire said, looking down at her lap.

'No, I don't, and I shouldn't, but I have. Go on, tell me

how he did it with you if you like. Don't let me be the only one to be bitchy.'

'I'd prefer to use your toilet, if I may.'

'Go ahead. End of the hall.'

As soon as she returned, Jane went on.

'I moved in with him and got my first surprise. He had a really, really posh flat in the Barbican. Since his *Guardian* columns and his speaking seemed to be his only work, it didn't add up. He told me it was the *Guardian*'s flat.'

'Did you believe him?'

'No, but I didn't care. I soon realised that he kept a lot of things to himself, that only rarely would he open up about anything. This sound familiar?'

'Yes, he hasn't changed. Was he ever depressed?'

'No, but I know what you're getting at. We had a lot of fun together for most of those next three years. Well, for some of the time, time in bed I mean. Then he made what turned out to be his big mistake, or rather second big mistake if you count marrying me as the first. He decided to stand for parliament. As time went on, you see, he started getting more and more frustrated. He had the fame, he was adored and admired by many, but, and he kept saying this: "What we need is a new political force, otherwise I'm just prostituting myself". So when the '79 election was called, he stood as an independent for a constituency up in the north-east, where there were a lot of people involved in "alternative" stuff. He resigned from the *Guardian* and we moved up there. Dreadful damp-ridden flat. He threw himself into campaigning. I hardly saw him. He was manic. He was convinced he was going to win, and to be honest he wasn't the only one who thought so. He tapped a vein among a lot of people, a vein of disillusionment. He attracted huge publicity, not just locally, but nationally. And then, the whole thing collapsed.'

'Why? What happened?'

'They stitched him up.'

'They?'

'The parties. All three of them. They were all threatened by him, you see. So they stitched him up. After it happened Christian told me, in one the few conversations we had, that they had actually conspired together to get him. I felt that was a bit paranoid on his part at the time, but you know I honestly think he was right. The bastards did for him. They did for us, too.'

'How?'

'A week before polling day, it hit every paper, even the *Guardian*. Secret love-child in Africa. Faith's brother, himself a candidate for the Tories, their first-ever black one, quoted in every story: "My sister bore this man's child, and he dumped her before it was even born." You can guess the rest. It was truly, truly, horrible. It destroyed him, overnight, literally overnight. Surely you must have seen or heard of it?'

'No, I think I was in the States at the time – I worked as a nanny there. So that was what had happened with the African girl?'

'Actually, no. When it all broke, we had the press besieging us, camped outside the door. Christian was beside himself. Of course I asked him if it was true. And he said; "No it isn't, but the truth is even worse." And he told me. He said that they had gone together to Tanzania that summer of '68, knowing she was pregnant. Christian said she wanted to have an abortion. She had it done in Dar-Es-Salaam. She haemorrhaged and died.'

'Oh my God, oh my God,' said Claire, feeling strangely distant. She thought for a moment and then opened her mouth to speak, but Jane interrupted.

'I know what you're going to ask – as I said, he told me that *she* wanted the abortion. I asked him several times about it, and he swore that that was the truth of the matter. In fact he told me that he very much wanted her to have the baby. I believed him – he was always fond of children.'

'So what happened – what happened next I mean?'

'To cut a long story short, he eventually went outside and made a statement to the press people. I forget his exact words, but basically he said that the statement Faith's brother had made was incorrect; that this was a personal and private matter on which he had no further comment to make; and that he was withdrawing his candidacy from the election. He came inside and he told me that he would be leaving as soon as was practicable, and that we were finished. He then basically went to bed for several days and hardly spoke to me again until in the middle of the night someone came, a doctor friend of his . . .'

'Was his name Nick?'

'Yes, Nick, that was it, I'm pretty sure. Anyway, that was it. He dumped everything he had, which wasn't much, into a big suitcase, and off they went. I only ever heard from him again about a year later.'

'How was that?'

'I got a letter from him, from Tanzania. Well, it wasn't a letter. It was a photograph. It's there on the mantelpiece. You didn't notice it?'

Claire shook her head and got up.

'Over on the far right.'

She picked it up. It was a photo of a grave, or rather mostly of the wooden cross at its head. Its carved inscription read, simply, 'Faith. Dearly loved. 23 August 1968.'

Jane was crying. 'I think I'd like you to go now,' she sobbed.

'Can I ask just two more things?' Claire said. 'Did he ever go to India? Did he ever write about India?'

'India? No, not to my knowledge. And what else?'

'You never had children, why was that?'

Jane stood up and screamed. 'That's none of your bloody business. Now get out of my house and get out of my life.'

'What do you know about Tanzania, Tom?' she asked as soon as they drove off, in heavy rain.

'Tanzania? Not a lot, but try me.'

'Something called the Arusha Declaration. Know anything about that?'

'What on earth have you been doing in there? Anyway, since you ask, I do happen to know quite a bit about the Declaration. It was a sort of, how do you put it, beacon, rallying call, whatever, across Africa in the early years of independence. Not that I'd been born at the time of course, but no African, no educated African of any subsequent generation would not know of it. And of course Nyerere is still alive, you know. He was probably the most brilliant of all the post-independence African leaders. Mind you, going back to Arusha, the text has many flaws, I've always thought.'

'What do you mean?'

'Nyerere said in the Declaration that development is about people, not about money. So far so good: Africa needed self-reliance, not neo-colonialism through the investment of Western capital, that kind of thing. And that's still as true today as it was in the '60s. But in the Declaration Nyerere said some stupid things, like that in the rural villages the men spend too much time, ah, now I remember the words, "wasted in gossip, dancing and drinking", and in the bigger towns, women do very much the same thing. Why on earth are you asking about this?'

Claire wondered what to say. 'Apparently Christian was much influenced by it when he was at university.'

The swish-swish of the windscreen wipers soon sent her off to sleep.

Nick was alone in the house when they got back: he said that Krishnan and Rosie were over at the pub having a drink and that 'we're welcome to join them if we'd like to. Shall we?'

'No. not just yet. Look Nick, I need to have a word with you.'

She turned to Tom, who said, 'I get the hint. I'll go join them.'

'I had a feeling this might happen,' Nick said, as they sat down together.

'I suppose I should really be angry with you, and I would be if I didn't feel so tired. But I don't want to go there. Just tell me, Nick, tell me, please just tell me. Why didn't you . . . oh, never mind.'

'Where do I start?'

'Try '79. The election.'

'You mean he never told you? You never heard about it?'

'No. Anyway, I'm not much one for politics, never was, and nor was he for that matter. I knew that. Or at least I thought I knew it. Now I find out he stood, or nearly stood, for parliament. And I thought he hated everything to do with politics. He never once ever voted, you know. Yet another rabbit comes out of the hat!'

Nick put the fingers of one hand to his mouth, as if to bite his nails.

'Claire, please let me begin by saying that Christian was, is, my friend. So are you. But he was also my patient, and as you know we doctors are bound by certain rules regarding confidentiality. I've been sorely tempted many times during these past few weeks to put them aside, not least when you were talking about his depressions last night. But, well, that's all there is to say. Now, '79 . . . where on earth do I begin?'

'Try the night you went and took him away.'

'I see.'

'You see what?'

'You know the story up to that point? The African love-child? All that?'

'Yes, and about what he told Jane about the real truth of the matter. The abortion, all that. Look, while we're on this, forget the election for a minute. There's something else I want to know.'

'There is?'

'They never had children did they, Christian and Jane I mean, do you know why?'

Nick looked her in the eye.

'I do know why, but for reasons I needn't repeat, I feel, I cannot tell you. But surely you can guess?'

'That they . . . no, that she . . . could not?'

'I can't really say but as the saying goes, "Read My Lips" . . .'

He pursed his lips together, rolling them inwards as he did so, and held them still for a second or two, in an exaggerated but serious manner. Then, after some time, he spoke.

'Oh, the hell with this. Christian was my patient, not her. And I know from her, not Christian, that she was unable to have children, because . . . because, well, I don't actually know precisely why, but, yes, basically she was infertile. Now, may I ask you one back?'

'Do I need to guess what it is?'

'No, I don't think so.'

'After Amy was born and diagnosed, I was advised that there would be a strong chance of any other children being born with the same condition. I told Christian this not long

340

after we met and started living together and I had the operation done. He was perfectly relaxed about it, and I have to say that from day one he treated Amy as his own . . . he always loved her as if she was his own . . . And he knew what I knew.'

'Knew what?'

'That her life expectancy would be limited.'

'I didn't know that.'

'They said twenty years, at the most. She's probably on borrowed time already.'

She felt the sting of tears in her eyes as she said this and reached up to wipe them away.

'Claire, I don't want to judge or moralise, but I think you need to keep that knowledge, that Christian loved Amy, very much at the front of your mind.'

'I will, yes I will, and I have done all the time, but it's hard,' she said, sniffing, 'and in any case . . . I'm trying to do what I think he would want me to do. I mean that sincerely, honestly . . .'

Again the tears welled and a full minute passed before she went on.

'. . . now, let's move on. Tell me about what happened.'

Nick now felt free of the hesitation that had afflicted him earlier.

'I could tell,' he began, 'even on the long journey home that awful night, that he was acutely, even clinically, depressed. He alternated between the highly coherent and the rambling nonsensical, with lots of brooding silence in between. He stayed the next day with us, and during it I suggested that I get him admitted to a psychiatric unit. I was surprised when he agreed, without any argument, as he, like me, knew full well what such places were like, although I guess only I knew what effect anti-depressants would have on him. So he was admitted. And then came the big surprise.'

'Surprise?'

'Election night. I was glued to the telly as I particularly wanted to hear the result in his constituency. When it came, it was astonishing. You really don't know this?'

'No, come on, go on.'

'It was a protest vote. Or rather a protest non-vote. The turn-out was the lowest in the whole country, the lowest turn-out in a single constituency that's ever been recorded in any general election in history, before or for that matter, since.'

'So what?'

'Those who would have voted for him simply stayed away. It was immediately obvious that had he not stood down, he would have won. You didn't need to be much of a psephologist to see that.'

'A what?'

'A psephologist, someone who analyses elections and voting. On the TV that night they were all agog with it, and so were the papers for days, weeks even, afterwards. There was a sort of manhunt for him, everybody wanted to find him. But Jane, you have to hand it to her, didn't even give them my name. I was the only person who knew where he was.'

'How did he react?'

'I drove over to see him early that morning. I'd been up all night, but I could hardly wait to get to him. I bought all the papers on the way. The staff told me he'd also sat up most of the night and that he knew what had happened. But apparently he just went to bed soon after "his" result was announced, without saying a word. He was still asleep when I got to him. We had a coffee together and I couldn't get through to him. It was like he was in another world, either zapped out by the drugs, or just, as you put it, hiding in his own private world. I showed him pieces in some of the papers, all concluding that the low turn-out was a protest, and that he would have got in, easily in fact. But all he kept saying was "That bastard woman has got in, God help us now", something like that. When I said that he need only wait for a by-election to come up and stand again he just laughed, manically. He was just on another planet, basically. Then he picked up all the papers, flung them all over the place and told me to piss off. That was that.'

'And then?'

'I kept in touch with his psychiatrist, and as the next couple of weeks passed, he not only got better, but by the time I next went to see him, he was more like one of the staff than one of the patients. Apparently he would spend hours with some of the really difficult ones. When I saw him, oh, it would be less than a month after he was admitted, he was perfectly OK, back to his old self. But he wouldn't talk about the election. He simply said it was in the past and that he would never do anything like it again. Then, a few days after I saw him he apparently discharged himself and, I learnt subsequently from him, went to Italy. He told me where he'd been when he came back. That would be late summer, October maybe. He was full of beans and told me about his plans.'

'Which were?'

'He'd been talking to people he knew of through his old *Guardian* pieces. A couple of them had agreed to join him in setting up some kind of consultancy, to help organisations set up "people-centred" projects, as he called them. They started by helping set up some massive project with unemployed shipyard workers up in the north-east. From there, the whole thing took off. Interestingly, I noticed that whenever there was any press coverage of what they were doing, he kept well out of it. He left all that to his partners. We kept in touch from time to time. They took on more and more projects and very quickly got into international work, which became his patch, so to speak. From about '81 or '82 onwards he started spending a lot of time on work in India and other countries in Asia as well. That's when his connection there began, as far as I know.'

'And apart from the spell in the psychiatric place, was he well?'

'To be honest, no, I wouldn't say so. Often, when we met, or when he called, he was down, even though everything was going well, as far as I could gather, on the work front. I became his counsellor. Sometimes, for no reason at all, he'd become morose and bitter.'

'About what had happened?'

'No, far from it. He never dwelled on the past. He never talked about it, except for one thing . . .'

'The African girl?'

'Yes.'

'He loved her, didn't he?'

'Yes.'

Nick pursed his lips again, and looked away, embarrassed.

'It's all right, Nick,' Claire said, 'you may not understand this, but what you have told me helps me, helps me a great deal. Now go on – the depressions . . . ?'

Nick relaxed, visibly, and turned his face back to Claire.

'It was what was happening around him, very much in the present, that got him down from time to time. He especially detested Thatcher and everything she stood for, but at the same time he recognised that her policies were bringing him business: the more unemployed there were, the better it was for him – he turned that in on himself, felt guilty about it. But what angered and depressed him the most was that she colonised and completely distorted his working credo – that people have the *right* to control their own destiny – into it being their *duty* to do so. I think that's why he started working overseas more and more, plus the fact that he pretty quickly discovered that he had a big reputation outside the country – he was flattered by that. It made him feel good about himself. What's that saying – a prophet is not without honour except . . .'

'. . . except in his own country,' Claire said, 'yes, he used to say that from time to time and I never really understood why.'

'There's not much more to say, really. When he met you, our contact became more sporadic. I got the impression he was really happy on the odd occasions we spoke or met. He certainly talked a lot about you, and Amy.'

'Really? You're not just saying that?'

'Scout's honour,' Nick replied, raising his hand and smiling.

'And he never said anything to you about India, and about the woman and the child there?'

Nick repeated the gesture.

'No, never, I absolutely swear to you.'

'Then you go and join them at the pub, I need to have some time to myself.'

18

The Forgiveness

Examining for brain death

'The examination for brain death concludes as follows:
The patient has no gag reflex: *the movement of the breathing tube (in or out) will cause a gagging reflex in a comatose patient, but will elicit no such response in the brain-dead patient.*
The patient has no spontaneous respiration: *The patient is removed from the ventilator. With the cessation of breathing by the machine, the body will immediately start to build up metabolic wastes of carbon dioxide in the blood. When the CO2 level reaches a level of 55mm Hg, the active brain will cause the patient to breathe spontaneously. The dead brain will give no response.'*

Rosie stroked her friend's face gently and watched it slowly come to life from a deep sleep.

Claire opened her eyes and looked at her questioningly.

'It's time to go,' Rosie said, 'The boys are ready. Take your time. Tom's staying here with me, but I gather Sir T is going down there.'

As they drove through the dark, deeply frosty night, Krishnan explained to Claire the tests that would be performed to determine whether Christian was alive or not.

'Given that the EEG monitors are now close to showing

what we call "electro-cerebral silence",' Krishnan said, 'the various tests we perform, including those I've told you about, are not expected to show anything positive. The last, for spontaneous respiration, will be conclusive. If it is, the ventilator support will not be resumed if you agree.'

'I understand,' she said, numbly.

'When we get there, there will be a form to be signed, for which Nick will act as witness. Sir Timothy wants to talk to you before you do anything. You must understand that signing the form gives your permission for ventilator support to be discontinued if there is no spontaneous respiration once the carbon dioxide level in the blood reaches the specified level after its disconnection.'

'I understand,' she said again.

'There will be a second doctor, the neurological specialist I have told you about, present. He and I must both agree that the tests all indicate brain-death.'

'I understand.'

'Claire, you will want to see Christian. What I suggest is that we leave you alone with him for as long as you wish, but that you don't remain for the tests. I say this because it will be distressing for you, I'm sure.'

'I agree. I won't need long.'

Claire found it difficult be sure that the Sir Timothy who greeted her in the reception area was the same person she had met at Pro-Fit's offices. He was still taking off a huge padded winter coat, to reveal that this version was dressed in jeans and a red polo-necked woollen sweater. The thick curly hair was concealed by a garish yellow woolly pom-pom hat, which he left on.

'Now, Claire,' he said, 'let us find somewhere to talk quietly, Tom has briefed me fully, and I have also talked to Nick about the medical side of things.'

A nurse showed them to a small room that was empty, save for two chairs and an unused desk.

'Is your mind absolutely made up?' Sir Timothy asked.

'Yes, it is. I am quite clear what I need to do now.'

'But are you sure it is what you really want to do? And are you sure that you would take the same course of action, say, in a week's time?'

'What do you mean?'

'I mean that from what I have heard, the last couple of days have been most stressful and difficult for you. The business with the police, I mean. That came on top of a week that I also understand was also very demanding on you, physically and mentally. And that in turn came on top of a period during which you have been under enormous emotional pressure. Of all kinds. What I'm saying, Claire is . . .'

'That I'm not acting rationally?'

'More or less. I was going to say that at moments like this you need to act with your head, not your heart. Let me put it another way. If this was a case being heard before a judge in court, he would retire, for days, possibly weeks, before reaching a verdict. I urge you, I urge you most strongly, to do the same. You will be perfectly within your rights to say that you want that infernal machine kept on, for at least a month. I have examined precedents before coming down here. There are many. Pro-Fit know that. Whatever the medics say now, and however flat that EEG trace looks, it is still possible for him to come out of the coma. There are well-documented instances.'

Claire found herself smiling at him.

'But what I'm doing is no more and no less than Christian would want. It's not to do with what I want. It's not to do with how I feel. I know that. I'm certain of it.'

'From dreams in which he talks to you? Please, Claire, spare me that.'

She stood up and spoke fiercely now.

'No! Don't talk to me like that! I'm telling you that I know what I need to do. I am very clear about it. It's based on what I know, what I now know, not on my dreams. And I don't give a damn about precedents, legal or medical. This is about Christian and what he wants. And those wants happen to coincide with what I want.'

'Very well, then, do as you wish. Speaking with my own heart, which I suppose people like me do all too rarely, I think I do understand. But my head, no, not my conscience, just my head, demanded of me to say what I have said.'

The small room where Christian lay was crowded, but all those present quickly left when she arrived.

She moved to the bed and knelt on the floor beside it, taking his good hand in hers. It felt strangely warm, moist, alive even.

'I forgive you my darling,' she said, 'I forgive you everything, even your secrecy. I think I understand now why you were the way you were. It's up to you now. Whatever you choose – to come back or to go – then what was it Krishnan said, things will never be what they were? You were a good man. Your goodness was diminished not by you but by the times in which you lived. For all that's happened, that is how I will think of you.'

When she had said this, while she was not praying, she remained kneeling by the bed, with her hands now clasped together, crying, the tears dropping freely onto his hand beneath.

Outside, Krishnan held the form out to her. For the first time in her life, she signed something without reading it, and then walked away.

349

At the reception desk she asked the woman if she could go outside.

'It's not usually allowed, but if it helps you, then of course. Do you want your coat? It's freezing out there.'

'No, I won't be long.'

The woman opened the door for her: 'If you go a little way out from the door then the light will switch itself off.'

She walked quickly away from the building, upwards, the crunching of the loose gravel, and then of the frozen tufts of grass, diminished by the heavy frost. She climbed the small hill.

As her eyes grew accustomed to the dark, the stars appeared. When she reached the summit of the hill she stopped and turned to look at the building behind her, where the bright light had now gone off. She then rotated slowly, again and again, so that she could take in the clear, sparkling, night sky in all its beauty. On each rotation new stars seemed to appear.

She breathed calmly and deeply. Reaching into her hand-bag she found the small plastic container that Krishnan had given her that first night. She cupped one hand and tipped the remaining blue pills into it.

'I hope it will be enough,' she whispered.

With the other hand she took one pill and swallowed it. And then, quickly, another, and another, and another. Finally she took the two cut banknotes from her pocket, the one crumpled and soiled, the other clean, and clenched them into the palms of her hands.

Through a mist that began to descend, she saw the light at the door come on. Nick and Krishnan came out, running at first and then stopping as the bright light in their faces blinded them. She felt her knees give way. She sank to the ground.

And then she saw others coming out: a group of Indian dancers and musicians; Aldo from the beach in his Salvataggio vest with his straw hat on; Rosie and Amy; Tom and Sir Timothy, both wearing their court dress and wigs; an old Indian man riding a tricycle; Andy the publican, with the other hunch-backed one from down the road; Alfonso, Maria and Valentina; Lalit; Ravindra, Mariana and their children; Jane; two policemen; many men in suits.

Then came the Vikings, banging their axes and swords thunderously on their shields, and as they appeared flames began to engulf the building behind them.

And finally, she saw him walking slowly up the hill, coming closer and closer. He was smiling and holding out his hands to her, one straight and clean, the other bent and bloodied.